# Cormorant Crag

## A Tale of the Smuggling Days

*by*

George Manville Fenn

# Cormorant Crag
## A Tale of the Smuggling Days
## by George Manville Fenn

ISBN: 978-93-69077-56-4

Published by

# DOUBLE 9 BOOKS

2/13-B, Ansari Road
Daryaganj, New Delhi – 110002
info@double9books.com
www.double9books.com
Tel. 011-40042856

# ABOUT THE AUTHOR

George Manville Fenn was a very productive author of novels, a writer, an editor, and an educator from England. He was born on January 3, 1831, in Pimlico, London. He mostly learned on his own; he taught himself Italian, French, and German. During the years 1851–1854, he went to Battersea Training College for Teachers and then became the head of a state school in Alford, Lincolnshire. In the early 1850s, Fenn started to write short stories and pieces for newspapers and magazines. The Old Forest Ranger, his first book, came out in 1856. Afterward, he wrote more than 100 books, many of them for teenagers and young adults. He was one of the most famous writers of his time, and his books were well-liked and read by many people. He also worked as a reporter and writer for Fenn. Among the newspapers and magazines, he worked for was The Boy's Own Paper, which he ran from 1866 to 1874. He worked hard to make children's books better and was a strong supporter of education and reading. The Englishman Fenn passed away on August 26, 1909, in Isleworth.

# CONTENTS

# Chapter One
# A Home at Sea

"Here, you, Vince!" cried Doctor Burnet, pausing in his surgery with a bottle in each hand—one large and the other small, the latter about to be filled for the benefit of a patient who believed himself to be very ill and felt aggrieved when his medical adviser told him that he would be quite well if he did not eat so much.

"Yes, father."

The boy walked up to the surgery door at the end of the long, low granite house.

"Upon my word!" cried the Doctor; "it's lucky we have nobody here to see you. No one would ever take you for a gentleman's son."

"Why not, father?"

"Why not, sir! Look at your trousers and your boots."

Vincent Burnet looked down, and then up in his father's face.

"Trousers a bit tight across the knee," he said deprecatingly. "The cloth gave way."

"And were your boots too tight at the toes, sir? Look at them."

"They always wear out there," said Vincent; and he once more looked down, beyond the great tear across the right knee of his trousers, to his boots, whose toes seemed each to have developed a wide mouth, within which appeared something which looked like a great grey tongue.

"I don't think this pair were very good leather, father," he said apologetically.

"Good leather, sir! You'd wear them out it they were cast iron.—Ah, my dear!"

A pleasant, soft face appeared at the door, and looked anxiously from father to son.

"Is anything the matter, Robert?"

"Matter? Look at this fellow's clothes and boots!"

"Oh, Vince, my dear, how you have torn your trousers again!"

"Torn them again!—the boy's a regular scarecrow!" cried the Doctor. "I will not pay for good things for him to go cliff-climbing and wading and burrowing in caves.—Here: what are you going to do?"

"Take him indoors to sew up that slit."

"No!" cried the Doctor, filling up the bottle; and then, making a small cork squeak as he screwed it in, "Take your scissors and cut the legs off four inches above the knees."

"Robert!" cried Mrs Burnet, in a tone of protest.

"And look here, Vince: you can give up wearing shoes and stockings; they are for civilised beings, not for young savages."

"My dear Robert, you are not in earnest?"

"Ah, but I am. Let him chip and tear his skin: that will grow up again: clothes will not."

"All right, father; I shan't mind," said the boy, smiling. "Save taking shoes and stockings off for wading."

"Vincent, my dear!" cried his mother, "how absurd! You would look nice the next time Michael Ladelle came for you."

"He'd do the same, mother. He always imitates me."

"Yes; you're a nice pair," said the Doctor. "I never saw such young savages."

"You're too hard upon them, Robert," said Mrs Burnet, laying her arm on her son's shoulder. "It does not matter out in this wild place, where there is no one to see him but the fishing people; and see what a healthy, natural life it is for them."

"Healthy! natural!" cried the Doctor sharply. "So you want to see him grow up into a sort of Peter the Wild Boy, madam?"

"No," said Mrs Burnet, exchanging an affectionate glance with her sun-tanned son. "Peter the Wild Boy did not have a college tutor to teach him the classics, did he, Vince?"

"No, mother; he must have been a lucky fellow," said the boy, laughing.

"For shame, Vincent!" cried Mrs Burnet, shaking her head at the boy reprovingly. "You do not mean that."

"I believe he does," said the Doctor angrily. "I won't have any more of it. He neglects his studies shamefully."

"No, no, indeed, dear," cried Mrs Burnet. "You don't know how hard he works."

"Oh yes, I do: at egging, climbing, fishing, and swimming. I'll have no more of it; he shall go over to some big school in Germany, where they'll bring him to his senses."

"I do everything Mr Deane sets me to do, father," said the boy; "and I do try hard."

"Yes—to break your neck or drown yourself. Look here, sir, when are you going to pay me my bill?"

"Your bill, father? I don't know what you mean."

"Surgical attendance in mending your broken leg. That's been owing two years."

"When my ship comes in, father," cried Vince, laughing.

"But, I say, don't send me to a big school, father. I like being here so much."

"Yes: to waste the golden moments of boyhood, sir."

"But I don't, father," cried Vince. "I really do work hard at everything Mr Deane sets me, and get it all done before I go out. He never finds fault."

"Bah! You're getting too big to think of going out to play with Mike Ladelle."

"But you said, father, that you liked to see a fellow work hard at play as well as study, and that 'all work and no play made Jack a dull boy.'"

"Jack!" cried the Doctor, with his face wrinkling up, as he tried to look very severe. "Yes Jack. But you're not Jack: he was some common fisherman's or miner's boy, not the son of a medical man—a gentleman. There, go and dress that wound in his trousers, my dear."

"And you won't send me off to school, father? I do like private study at home so much better!"

"Humph! I don't know whether you're aware of it, sir, but you've got a very foolish, indulgent father, who is spoiling you."

"No, he did not know that," said Mrs Burnet, smiling, as she looked from one to the other proudly. "And it is not true, is it, Vince?"

"No, mother, not a bit of it," cried the boy.

"And I feel sure that father will not send you away if you try hard to master all your lessons with Mr Deane."

"Well, it isn't your father who is spoiling you now, Vince," said the Doctor. "There: I'll give you another six months' trial; and, here—which way are you going?"

"Round by the south cliff to look for Mike Ladelle."

"Ah, I daresay he's shut up in his father's study hard at work!"

"No, father; I've been up to the house, and they said he had gone out."

"There, go and get mended; and you may as well leave this medicine for me at James Carnach's. It will be ready for you by the time your mother has done."

"Yes, father—I'll come," cried the boy; and he hurried out of the surgery.

"Ah!" said the Doctor, "you undo all my work by your foolish indulgence."

Mrs Burnet smiled.

"I should be very miserable," she said, "if I could feel that all you say is true."

"But see what a reckless young rascal he grows."

"No, I cannot see that, dear," replied Mrs Burnet. "He is a thorough, natural boy, and I am glad to find him so fond of outdoor life."

"And not of his studies?"

"He works very hard at them, dear; and I'm sure you want to see him grow up manly."

"Of course."

"And not a weak, effeminate lad, always reading books over the fire."

"No, but—"

"Let him go on as he is, dear," said Mrs Burnet gently; "and show him that you take an interest in his sports."

"Spoil him more still?"

"No: encourage him in his love of natural history."

"And making the place untidy with his messing about. I say: by the way, have you been at that bottle of acid?"

"I? No, dear."

"Then he has, for some of his sham experiments."

"Mother!"

"Coming, my dear," cried Mrs Burnet, in answer to the call; and she hurried into the house, leaving the Doctor to write out the directions upon a label, so that Jemmy Carnach—fisherman when the sea was calm, and farmer when it was rough—might not make a mistake when he received his bottle of medicine, and take it all at once, though it would not have hurt him if he had.

"Nice boy!" muttered the Doctor, as he made a noose in a piece of twine and carefully tied the label to the bottle; "but I wish the young plague had been a girl."

At that moment Vince was standing with one foot upon a stool, so that the knee of his trousers was within easy reach of his mother's busy fingers, while the bright needle flashed in and out, and the long slit was gradually being reduced in extent.

"Mind, mother! don't sew it to the skin," he said laughingly; and then, bending down, he waited his opportunity, and softly kissed the glossy hair close to his lips.

"I say, mother," he whispered, "don't have me sent away. Father doesn't mean it, does he?"

"I don't think so, my dear; but he wants to see you try hard to grow into a manly, sensible lad."

"Well, that's what I am trying to do."

Mrs Burnet took hold of her son's none too clean hand, turned it over, and held up the knuckles, which seemed to have been cracked across, but were nearly healed.

"Well, I couldn't help that, mother," protested the boy. "You wouldn't have had me stand still and let young Carnach knock Mike Ladelle about without helping him?"

"I don't like fighting, Vince," said Mrs Burnet, with a sigh; "it seems to me brutal."

"Well, so it is, mother, when it's a big, strong fellow ill-using a small one. But it can't be brutal for a little one to stick up for himself and thrash the big coward, can it?"

"That is a question upon which I cannot pretend to decide, Vince. You had better ask your father."

"Oh, no! I shan't say anything about it," replied the boy, giving his short shock-brown hair a rub. "I don't like talking about it. Nearly done?"

"Yes, I am fastening off the thread."

There was a snip given directly after by a pair of scissors; Vince gave his leg a shake to send the trouser down in its place, and then stooped and kissed the sweet, placid face so close to his.

"There," he cried; "don't you tell me I didn't pay you for mending the tear."

"Ready, Vince?" said the Doctor, entering with the bottle neatly done up in white paper.

"Yes, father."

"Mind, sir! don't break it."

"No, father: all right."

The next minute Vince was trotting sharply down the road towards the rough moorland, which he had to partly traverse before turning down a narrow track to the cliff edge, where, in a gap, half a dozen fishermen's cottages were built, sheltered from the strong south-west wind.

"You will not send him away, Robert?" said Mrs Burnet.

"Humph! Well, no," said the Doctor, wrinkling up his brow; "it would seem so dull if he were gone."

# Chapter Two
# "Two for a Pair"

"Hullo, Cinder!"

"Hullo, Spoon!"

"Who are you calling Cinder?"

"Who are you calling Spoon?"

"You. Well, Ladle then, if you don't like Spoon."

"And you have it Scorcher if you like, old Burnet."

"Burnet's a better name than Ladelle."

"Oh, is it! I don't know so much about that, Vincey. And it isn't pronounced as if it was going into a soup tureen. You know that well enough. It's a fine old French name."

"Of course I know your finicking way of calling it *Lah Delle*; but, if you're English, it's Ladle. Ha, ha, ha! Ladle for frog soup, Frenchy."

"You won't be happy till I've punched your head, Vince Burnet."

"Shan't I? All right, then: make me happy," said Vince to another sun-browned lad whom he had just encountered among the furze and heather—all gold and purple in the sunny islet where they dwelt—and in the most matter-of-fact way he took off his jacket; and then began a more difficult task, which made him appear like some peculiar animal struggling out of its skin: for he proceeded to drag off the tight blue worsted jersey shirt he wore, and, as it was very elastic, it clung to his back and shoulders as he pulled it over his head, and, of course, rendered him for the moment helpless—a fact of which his companion was quite ready to take advantage.

"Want to fight, do you?" he cried: "you shall have it then," and, grinning with delight, he sprang upon the other's back, nipping him with his knees, and beginning to slap and pummel him heartily.

Vince Burnet made a desperate effort to get free, but the combination of his assailant's knees and the jersey effectively imprisoned him, and, though he heaved and tossed and jerked himself, he could not dislodge the lad, who clung to him like Sinbad's old man of the sea, till he fell half exhausted in a thick bed of heather, where he was kept down to suffer a kind of roulade of thumps, delivered very heartily upon his back as if it were a drum.

"Murder! murder!" cried Vince, in smothered tones, with the jersey over his head.

"Yes, I'll give you murder! I'll give you physic! How do you like that, and that, and that, Doctor?"

Each question was followed by a peculiar double knock on back or ribs.

"Don't like it at all, Mike. Oh, I say, do leave off!"

"Shan't. Don't get such a chance every day. I'll roast your ribs for you, my lad."

"No, no: I give in. I'm done."

"Ah! that sounds as if you didn't feel sure. As your father says to me when I'm sick, I must give you another dose."

"No, no, don't, please," cried Vince: "you hurt."

"Of course I do. I mean it. How many times have you hurt me?"

"But it's cowardly to give it to a fellow smothered up like I am."

"'Tisn't cowardly: it's the true art of war. Get your enemy up in a corner where he can't help himself, and then pound him like that, and that."

"Oh!—oh!"

"Yes, it is 'Oh!' I never felt any one with such hard, bony ribs before; Jemmy Carnach is soft compared to you."

"I say, you're killing me!"

"Am I? Like to be killed?"

"No. Oh! I say, Mike, don't, there's a good fellow! Let me get up."

"Are you licked?"

"Yes, quite."

"Will you hit me if I let you get up?"

"No, you coward."

*Bang, bang.*

"Oh! I say, don't!"

"Am I a coward, then?"

"Yes.—Oh!"

"Now am I a coward?"

"No, no. You're the bravest, best fellow that ever lived."

"Then you own you're beaten?"

"Oh yes, thoroughly. I say, Mike, I can hardly breathe. Honour bright!"

"Say, you own you're licked, then."

"Yes. Own I'm licked, and— Ah–h–ah!"

Vince gave a final heave, and with such good effect that his assailant was thrown, and by the time he had recovered himself Vince's red face was reappearing from the blue jersey, which the boy had tugged down into its normal position.

"Oh! won't I serve you out for this some day, Mikey!" he cried, as the other stood on his guard, laughing at him.

"You said you were beaten."

"Yes, for to-day; but I can't afford to let you knock me about like this. I say, you did hurt."

"Nonsense! I could have hit twice as hard as that. Pull your jersey over your head again, and I'll show you."

"Likely! Never mind, old chap," said Vince, giving himself a shake; "I'll save it up for you. Phew! you have made me hot."

"Do you good," said Mike, imitating his companion by throwing himself down at full length upon the elastic heath, to lie gazing at the brilliant blue sea, stretching far away to where a patch of amethyst here and there on the horizon told of other islands, bathed in the glowing sunshine.

The land ended a hundred yards from where the two lads lay as suddenly as if it had been cut sharply off, and went down perpendicularly some two hundred and fifty feet to where the transparent waves broke softly, with hardly a sound, amongst the weedy rocks, all golden-brown with fucus, or running quietly over the yellow sand, but which, in a storm, came thundering in, like huge banks of water, to smite the face of the cliff, fall back and fret, and churn up the weed into balls of froth, which flew up, and were carried by the wind right across the island.

"Where's old Deane?" said Vince suddenly.

"Taken a book to go and sit on the rock shelf and read Plutarch. I say, what a lot he does know!"

"No wonder," said Vince, who was parting the heather and peering down beneath: "he's always reading. I wish he was fonder of coming out in a boat and fishing or sailing."

"So do I," said Mike. "We'd make him do the rowing. Makes us work hard enough."

"I don't see why he shouldn't help us," continued Vince. "Father says a man ought to look after his body as well as his brains, so as always to be healthy and strong."

"Why did he say that?" said Mike sharply.

"Because it was right," said Vince. "My father's always right."

"No, he isn't. He didn't know what was the matter with my dad."

Vince laughed.

"What are you grinning at?"

"What you said. He knew well enough, only he wouldn't say because he did not want to offend your father."

"What do you mean?"

"That he always sat indoors, and didn't take enough exercise."

"Pish! The Doctor did not know," said Mike sharply, and colouring a little; "and I don't believe he wants people to be well."

"Hi! Look here!" cried Vince excitedly. "Lizard!"

A little green reptile, looking like a miniature crocodile, disturbed by the lad's investigating hands, darted out from beneath the heath into the sunshine; and Mike snatched off his cap, and dabbed it over the little fugitive with so true an aim that as he held the cap down about three inches of the wiry tail remained outside.

"Got him!" cried Mike triumphantly.

"Well, don't hurt it."

"Who's going to hurt it!"

"You are. Suppose a Brobdig-what-you-may-call-him banged a great cap down over you—it would hurt, wouldn't it?"

"Not if I lay still; and there wouldn't be a bit of tail sticking out if he did," said Mike laughing.—"I'm not going to hurt you, old chap, but to take you home and put you in the conservatory to catch and eat the flies and blight. Come along."

"Where are you going to put him?"

"In my pocket till I go home. Look here: I'll put my finger on his tail and hold him while you lift my cap; then I can catch him with my other hand."

"Mind he don't bite."

"Go along! He can't bite to hurt. Ready?"

"Yes," said Vince, stretching out his hand. "Better let him go."

"Yes, because you don't want him. I do. Now, no games."

"All right."

"Up with the cap, then."

Vince lifted the cap, and burst out laughing, for it was like some conjuring trick—the lizard was gone.

"Why, you never caught it!" he said.

"Yes, I did: you saw its tail. I've got it under my hand now."

"You've dropped it," cried Vince. "Lift up."

Mike raised his hand, and there, sure enough, was the lizard's tail, writhing like a worm, and apparently as full of life as its late owner, but, not being endowed with feet, unable to escape.

"Poor little wretch!" said Vince; "how horrid! But he has got away."

"Without his tail!"

"Yes; but that will soon grow again."

"Think so?"

"Why, of course it will: just as a crab's or lobster's claw does."

"Hullo, young gentlemen!" said a gruff voice, and a thick-set, elderly man stopped short to look down upon them, his grim, deeply-lined brown face twisted up into a smile as he took off an old sealskin cap and began to softly polish his bald head, which was surrounded by a thick hedge of shaggy grey hair, but paused for a moment to give one spot a rub with his great rough, gnarled knuckles. His hands were enormous, and looked as if they had grown into the form most suitable for grasping a pair of oars to tug a boat against a heavy sea.

His dress was exceedingly simple, consisting of a coarsely-knitted blue jersey shirt that might have been the great-grandfather of the one Vince wore; and a pair of trousers, of a kind of drab drugget, so thick that they would certainly have stood up by themselves, and so cut that they came nearly up to the man's armpits, and covered his back and chest, while the braces he wore were short in the extreme. To finish the description of an individual who played a very important part in the lives of the two island boys, he had on a heavy pair of fisherman's boots, which might have been drawn up over his knees, but now hung clumsily about his ankles, like those of smugglers in a penny picture, as he stood looking down grimly, and slowly resettled his sealskin cap upon his head.

"What are you two a-doing of?" he asked. "Nothing," said Mike shortly.

"And what brings you round here?"

"I've been taking Jemmy Carnach a bottle of physic; and we came round," cried Vince. "Why?"

"Taking Jemmy Carnach a bottle of physic," said the old fellow, with a low, curious laugh, which sounded as if an accident had happened to the works of a wooden clock. "He's mighty fond o' making himself doctor's bills. I'd ha' cured him if he'd come to me."

"What would you have given him, Daygo?"

"Give him?" said the man, rubbing his great brown eagle-beak nose with a finger that would have grated nutmeg easily: "I'd ha' give him a mug o' water out of a tar tub, and a lotion o' rope's end, and made him dance for half an hour. He'd ha' been 'quite well thank ye' to-morrow morning."

Vince laughed.

"Ay, that's what's the matter with him, young gentleman. A man who can't ketch lobsters and sell 'em like a Christian, but must take 'em home, and byle 'em, and then sit and eat till you can see his eyes standing out of his head like the fish he wolfs, desarves to be ill. Well, I must be off and see what luck I've had."

"Come on, Mike," cried Vince, springing up—an order which his companion obeyed with alacrity.

The old fellow frowned and stared.

"And where may you be going?" he asked.

"Along with you," said Vince promptly.

"Where?"

"You said you were going out to look at your lobster-pots and nets, didn't you?"

"Nay, ne'er a word like it," growled the man.

"Yes, you did," cried Mike. "You said you were going to see what luck you'd had."

"Ay, so I did; but that might mean masheroons or taters growing, or rabbit in a trap aside the cliff."

"Yes," said Vince, laughing merrily; "or a bit of timber, or a sea chest, or a tub washed up among the rocks, mightn't it, Mike? Only fancy old Joe Daygo going mushrooming!"

"You're a nice sarcy one as ever I see," said the man, with another of his wooden-wheel laughs. "I like masheroons as well as any man."

"Yes, but you don't go hunting for them," said Vince; "and you never grow potatoes; and as for setting a trap for a rabbit—not you."

"You're fine and cunning, youngster," said the man, with a grim look; and his keen, clear eyes gazed searchingly at the lad from under his shaggy brows.

"Sit on the cliff with your old glass," said Vince, "when you're not fishing or selling your lobsters and crabs. He don't eat them himself, does he, Mike?"

"No. My father says he makes more of his fish than any one, or he wouldn't be the richest man on the island."

The old man scowled darkly.

"Oh! Sir Francis said that, did he?"

"Yes, I heard him," cried Vince; "and my father said you couldn't help being well off, for your place was your own, and it didn't cost you anything to live, so you couldn't help saving."

A great hand came down clap on the lad's shoulder, and it seemed for the moment as if he were wearing an epaulette made out of a crab, while the gripping effect was similar, for the boy winced.

"I say, gently, please: my shoulder isn't made of wood."

"No, I won't hurt you, boy," growled the old fellow; "but your father's a man as talks sense, and I won't forget it. I'll be took bad some day, and give him a job, just to be neighbourly."

"Ha, ha!" laughed Vince.

"What's the matter?" growled the old man, frowning.

"You talking of having father if you were ill. Why, you'd be obliged to."

"Nay. If I were bad I dessay I should get better if I curled up and went to sleep."

"Send for me, Joe Daygo," cried Mike merrily, "and I'll bring Vince Burnet. We'll give you a mug of water out of a tar-barrel, and make you dance with the rope's end."

"Nay, nay, nay! don't you try to be funny, young Ladle."

"*Ladelle!*" shouted the boy angrily.

"Oh, very well, boy. Only don't you try to be funny: young doctor here's best at that."

All the same, though, the great heavy fellow broke into another fit of wooden chuckling, nodded to both, and turned to go, but back on the track by which he had come.

Vince gave Mike a merry look, and they sprang after him, and the man faced round.

"What now?"

"We're coming out with you, Joe Daygo."

"Nay; I don't want no boys along o' me."

"Oh yes, you do," said Vince. "I say—do take us, and we'll row all the time."

"I don't want no one to row me. I've got my sail."

"All right, then; we'll manage the sail, and you can steer."

"Nay; I don't want to be capsized."

"Who's going to capsize you? I say, do take us."

The man scowled at them both, and filed his sharp, aquiline nose with a rough finger as if hesitating; then, swinging himself round, he strode off in his great boots, which crushed down heather and furze like a pair of mine stamps. But he uttered the words which sent a thrill through the boys' hearts—and those words were:

"Come on!"

# Chapter Three
# A Day at Sea

Daygo's big boots crushed something beside the heather and little tufts of fine golden gorse; for as they went along a slope the sweet aromatic scent of wild thyme floated to the boys' nostrils; and the bees, startled from their quest for honey, darted to right and left, with a low, humming noise, which was the treble, in Nature's music, to the soft, low bass which came in a deep whisper from over the cliff to the right. And as the boys drew in long, deep draughts of the pure, fresh air which bathed their island home, their eyes were full of that happy light which spoke volumes of how they were in the full tide of true enjoyment of life in their brightest days.

They could not have expressed what they felt—perhaps they were unconscious of the fact: that knowledge was only to come later on, in the lookings-back of maturity; but they knew that the moor about them seemed beautiful, and there was a keen enjoyment of everything upon which their eyes rested, whether it was the purple and golden-green slope, or the wondrous lights upon the ever-changing sea.

"Hi! look! There goes a mag," cried Mike, as one of the brilliantly plumed birds rose suddenly from among some grey crags, and went off in its peculiar flight, the white of its breast of the purest, and the sun glancing from the purple, gold and green upon its wings and lengthy tail.

"Hooray!—another—and another—and another!" cried Vince, who the next moment passed from the enjoyment of the beautiful in nature to the grotesque; for he covered his lips with one hand to smother a laugh, and pointed with the other to a huge square patch of drugget laboriously stitched upon the back of the solid-looking trousers to strengthen them for sitting upon the thwart of a boat, a rock, or a bush of furze, which, when so guarded against, makes a pleasantly elastic seat.

But Vince's companion did not find it so easy to control his mirth; for, as he gazed at the gigantic trousers in motion along the slope, their appearance seemed so comic, in conjunction with Vince's mirthful face, that he burst into a hearty laugh.

Vince gave him a heavy punch in the ribs, which was intended to mean: "Now you've done it: he won't let us come!"

But old Daygo did not look round; he only shook his head and shouted:

"Won't do, young Ladle—*Ladelle*: you're thinking about the tar water, but you can't be so funny as he."

The boys exchanged glances, but did not try to explain; neither speaking till, to their surprise, the man turned suddenly to his right, and made for a huge buttress which ran out some fifty feet from the rugged edge of the cliff and ended in a soft patch of sheep-nibbled, velvet grass, upon which lay, partly buried, a couple of long iron guns, while the remains of a breastwork of stone guarded the edge of the cliff.

"I say! where are you going?" cried Vince.

"Eh? Here," said the man, sitting down astride of one of the old cannon. "Think I was going to pitch you off?"

"No," said Vince coolly, as he went close to the edge and looked down at the deeply-coloured purple, almost black, water at the foot of the cliff, where there was not an inch of strand. "Wouldn't much matter if you did: it's awfully deep there, and no rocks. I could swim."

"Swim? Wheer?" said the man sharply. "No man could swim far there. T'reble currents and deep holes, where the tide runs into and sucks you down if it don't take you out to sea. Nobody's safe there."

"Might go all right in a boat," said Vince, still gazing down, attracted by the place, where he had often watched before, and noted how the cormorants, shags, and rock-doves flew in and out, disappearing beneath his feet—for the great buttress overhung the sea, and its face could only be seen by those who sailed by.

"Nay, nay; no one goes in a boat along here, boy. There, I'm going to fill my pipe and light it, and then we'll go. Which o' you's got a sun-glass?"

"I have," said Vince quickly.

"Let's have it, then: save me nicking about with my flint and steel."

The rough black pipe was filled, and the convex lens held so that the sun's rays were brought to a focus on the tobacco, which dried rapidly, crisped up, and soon began to smoke, when a few draws ignited the whole surface, and the man began to puff slowly and regularly as he handed back the glass.

"It's nothing a boy could do," he said, with one of his fierce, grim looks, "so don't you two get a-glowering at a pipe like that."

"Get out!" said Vince quickly. "I wasn't thinking about that. I was wondering who first found out that you could get fire from the sun."

"Some chap as had a spy-glass," said the old fellow, "and unscrewed the bottom same as I do when I wants a light. Might ha' fired one o' these here with a glass if you put a bit o' tinder in the touch-hole."

"Yes," said Vince, "if the French had come."

"Tchah!" ejaculated the man contemptuously: "all fools who put the guns about the island! No Frenchies couldn't ha' come and landed here. Wants some one as knows every rock to sail a small boat, let alone a ship o' war. All gone to pieces on the rocks if they'd tried."

"Same as the old Spaniards did with the Armada," said Vince.

"Spannles! Did they come?"

"To be sure they did, and got wrecked and beaten and sunk, and all sorts."

"Sarve 'em right for being such fools as to come without a man aboard as knowed the rocks and currents and tides. Dessay I could ha' showed 'em; on'y there's nowhere for 'em to harbour."

"You'd better not try, if ever they want to come again," cried Vince, with animation. "Father says you are a Spaniard."

"Me?" cried the man, starting. "Not me. I'm English, flesh and bone."

"No: father says Spanish."

"Your father knows something about salts and senny," growled the old fellow, "but I know more about Joe Daygo o' the Crag than any man going. English right down to my boots."

"No: Spanish descent, father says," persisted Vince. "He says he goes by your face and your name."

"What does he mean?" said the man fiercely. "Good a face as his'n!"

"And principally by your nose. He says it's a regular Spanish one."

"He don't know what he's talking about," growled the old man, rubbing the feature in question. "How can it be Spanish when all the rest of me's English?"

"It's the shape," continued Vince; while Mike lay on his back, listened, and stared up at the grey gulls which went sailing round between him and the vividly blue sky. "He says there isn't another nose in the island a bit like it."

"Tell him he'd better leave my nose alone. But he is right there: there arn't a nose like it—they're all round or stunted, or turn t'other way up."

"Then he says your name Daygo's only a corruption of Diego, which is Spanish for James."

"Yah! It's Daygo—Joe Daygo—and not James at all. He's thinking about Jemmy Carnach."

"And he says he feels sure your people came over with the Spanish Armada, and you're descended from some sailor, named Diego, who was wrecked."

"You tell your father to mix his physic," grumbled the man sourly.— "Here, are you two going to stop here talking all day?"

"No," cried Mike, springing up, his example being followed by Vince, who was riding on the breech of the other gun.

"Then come on," growled the man, who made off now at a tremendous rate. Away over furze, and up and down over sunny slopes, where the fallow-chats rose, showing their white tail coverts; in and out among bare patches of granite, which rose above the great clumps of gorse; and still on, till all before them was sea. Then he began to rapidly descend a gully, where everything that was green was left behind, and they were between two vast walls of rock, almost shut-in by a natural breakwater stretching across, half covered by the sea and sand. Below them, in a natural pool, lay a boat which might have been built and launched to sail upon the tiny dock of stone; for there was apparently no communication with the sea, so well was it shut off from where, as the bare and worn masses of grey rock showed, the waves must come thundering in when the west wind blew.

Old Daygo went clumping down in his heavy boots, and the boys followed, soon to reach where stones as big as cheeses lay in a long slope, whither they had been hurled by the storms, and were rolled over till they were smooth and roughly round as the pebbles in a stream. Next they had to mount a great barrier, which now hid the boat, and then descended to its side, where it lay in the pool, only about twice as big as itself, but which proved now to be the widening out of a huge crack in the granite rocks, and zigzagged along to the sea, full of clear water at all times, and forming a sheltered canal to the tiny dock.

"Some on 'em 'd like to have that bit o' harbour," said the man, with a grin which showed his great white teeth; "but it's mine, and always will be. Jump in."

The boys obeyed, and the man fetched a boat-hook with a very sharp, keen point, from where it hung, in company with some well-tarred ropes, nets, and other fishing-gear, in a sheltered nook amongst the rocks, and then joined them, and began to push the boat along the narrow waterway.

At the first wave sent rippling outward by the movement of the boat, there was a rush and splash a dozen yards in front, as a shoal of good-sized fish darted seaward, some in their hurry leaping right out of the water, to fall in again with a plunge, which scared the rest in their flight.

The boys sprang up excitedly, and Daygo nodded.

"Ay," he said, "if we'd knowed they was there, we might ha' crep along the rocks and dropped a net acrost, and then caught the lot."

"Mullet, weren't they?" said Vince.

"Yes: grey ones," said Mike, shading his eyes, and following the wave made by the retiring shoal.

"Ay—grey mullet, come up to see if there was anything to eat. Smelt where I'd been cleaning fish and throwing it into the water."

The boat went on after the shoal of fish, in and out along the great jagged rift leading seaward, their way seeming to be barred by a towering pyramid of rock partly detached from the main island, while the sides of the fault grew higher and higher till they closed in overhead, forming a roughly-arched tunnel, nearly dark; but as soon as they were well in, the light shining through the end and displaying a framed picture of lustrous sea glittering in the sunlight, of which enough was reflected to show that the sides of the tunnel-like cavern were dotted with limpets, and the soft, knob-shaped, contracted forms of sea anemones that, below the surface, would have displayed tentacles of every tint, studded, as it were, with gems.

The roof a few feet above their heads echoed, and every word spoken went whispering along, while the iron point and hook of the implement old Daygo used gave forth a loud, hollow, sounding click as it was struck upon side or roof from time to time.

"I say," cried Vince suddenly, "we never tried for a conger along here, Mike."

"No good," growled Daygo.

"Why?" said Vince, argumentatively. "Looks just the place for them: it's dark and deep."

"Ay, so it is, boy; and I daresay there arn't so many of they mullet gone back to sea as come up the hole."

"Then there are congers here?"

"Ay, big uns, too; but the bottom's all covered with rocks, and there's holes all along for the eels to run in, and when you hook 'em they twist in, and you only lose your line."

He gave the boat a vigorous shove, and it glided out into the light once more, a hundred yards from the cliff, but with the rugged pyramid of granite through which they had passed towering up behind them, and its many shelves dotted with sea-birds lazily sunning themselves and stretching out their wings to dry.

A few flew up, uttering peculiar cries, as the boat darted out of the dark arch beneath them; but, for the most part, they merely looked down and took no further notice—the boat and its little crew being too familiar an object to excite their fear, especially as its occupants did not land, and the egg-time was at an end.

"Now, then, up with the mast, lads!" said the old man; and cleverly enough the boys stepped the little spar by thrusting its end through a hole in the forward thwart and down into a socket fixed in the inner part of the keel. Then the stays were hooked on, hauled taut, and up went the little lug-sail smartly enough, the patch of brown tanned canvas filling at once, and sending the boat gliding gently along over the rocks which showed clearly deep down through the crystal sea.

"Soon know how to manage a boat yourselves," said the old man grimly, as he thrust an oar over the stern and used it to steer.

"Manage a boat ourselves!" cried Mike. "I should think we could—eh, Vince?"

"Should think you could!" said the old man laughing. "Ah! you think you could, but you can't. Why, I hardly know how yet, after trying for fifty year. Wants some larning, boys, when tide's low, and the rocks are bobbing up and down ready to make holes in the bottom. Don't you two be too sure, and don't you never go along here far without me."

The boys said nothing; but they felt the truth of the man's words as he steered them in and out among the jagged masses of granite, around which the glassy currents glided, now covering them from sight, now leaving bare their weed-hung, broken-out fangs; while on their left, as they steered north toward a huge projection, which ran right out on the far side of a little bay, the perpendicular cliffs rose up grey and grand, defended by buttresses formed by masses that had fallen, and pierced every here and there by caverns, into which the water ran and rushed with strange, hollow, whispering noises and slaps and gurglings, as if there were peculiar creatures far up in the darkness resenting being disturbed.

Every now and then the sea, as it heaved and sank, laid bare some rounded mass covered with long, hanging sea-weed, which parted on the top and hung down on either side, giving the stone the appearance of some strange, long-haired sea monster, which had just thrust its head above the surface to gaze at the boat, and once this was so near that Mike shrank from it as it peered over the thwart, the boat almost grating against the side.

"Wasn't that too close?" said Vince quickly.

"Nay," said the old man quietly: "if you didn't go close to that rock, you'd go on the sharp rock to starboard. There's only just room to pass."

A minute later, as the two lads, were gazing in at the gloomy portals of a water-floored cave, in and out of which birds were flying, a dexterous turn of the oar sent the boat quickly round, head to wind, the sail flapped over their heads, and Vince seized the boat-hook without being told, and, reaching over the side, hooked towards him a couple of good-sized pieces of blackened cork, through which a rope had been passed and knotted to prevent its return.

This rope Mike seized, hauled upon it, drawing the boat along, till it was right over something heavy, which, on being dragged to the surface, proved to be a great beehive-shaped, cage-like basket, weighted with stones, and provided with a funnel-like entrance at the top.

"Nothing!" cried Mike; and the lobster-pot was allowed to sink back into the deep water among the rocks as soon as it had been examined to see if it contained bait.

Then there was another short run, and a fresh examination of one of these trap-like creels, with better success; for a good-sized lobster was found to be inside, and, after two or three attempts, Vince seized it across the back, and drew it out as it flicked its tail sharply, and vainly sought to take hold of its aggressor with its formidable, pincer-armed claws.

Old Daygo hooked the lobster towards him with the toe of his boot, clapped it between his knees, and cleverly tied its claws with pieces of spun yarn before dropping the captive into a locker in the stern, half full of water, which was admitted through holes in the side.

A couple more lobster-pots were tried, without success, as the boat glided along by the side of the great granite cliffs, where the many black cormorants, which made the shelves and points their home, gave ample reason for the solitary island, far out among the rushing waters of the fierce currents, to be named Cormorant Crag by all who sailed that way, and avoided as the most dangerous rock-bound place off the coast.

Then came a change, the boat being steered to a channel which ran between a mighty mass of piled-up granite and the cliffs. This gap was about forty yards wide, and the pent-up waters rushed through, eddying and rippling, and taking the boat along at a rapid rate. But Daygo steered close enough in to enable him to throw the little grapnel in the bottom of the boat on to the rocks nearest the cliffs. The iron caught at once, the line was checked and fastened, and the boat, swung now in the swift race close to a little keg, from which ran a row of corks, anchored in a calmer place across the tide.

"Down with the lug!" growled the old man. His crew lowered the sail quickly, and stowed it out of their way, for the chief feature of the little trip was close at hand. Old Daygo went forward now, shaking his head at the boys' progress of hauling in the trawl-net line themselves.

"Ay," he said; "you can take out the fish if there be any." And he methodically dragged the net, which had been stretched like so many walls of meshes overnight right across the swift waters of the tide, having been down long enough for the ebb and flow both to pass through it, with the consequence that, if fish had passed that way, they would have been pocketed or become netted among the meshes from either side. But a good deal of the net was dragged into the boat before the glittering scales of a fish were seen.

"Red mullet!" cried Vince, as he pounced upon two small ones, looking as if clothed in mother-o'-pearl, speckled and stained with scarlet.

These were taken out and thrown into the locker, with the result that the lobster flipped its tail and splashed about furiously. But by this time there was a golden gleam in the net drawn aboard; taking his turn, Mike dragged out a grotesque-looking, big-headed John Dory, all golden-green upon its sides, and bearing the two dark marks, as if a giant finger and thumb had been imprinted upon it. This, too, with its great eyes staring, and wide mouth gaping feebly, was thrown into the locker.

Then old Daygo began to growl and mutter: for the meshes showed the heads only of a fine pair of red mullet, the whole of the bodies having been eaten away; and a minute later up came the cause, in the shape of a long, grey, eely-looking fish, which writhed and struggled violently to get free, but only entangled itself the more tightly.

"Nay, nay! let me come," cried the old man, as he saw the boys whip out their knives. "I don't want my net cut to pieces; I'll do it myself."

He threw the portion of the net containing the captive on one side in the bottom of the boat, and hauled in the rest, which contained nothing but a sickly green, mottled-looking wrasse of about a couple of pounds weight. Then the lines, cords, and anchors were got on board, and, leaving the boat to drift with the sharp current which carried it onward, the old man drew a long, sharp-pointed knife from its sheath, and cautiously turned over portions of the net.

"Oh, murder!" said Mike.

"Well, how many poor fish has it murdered?" said Vince. "Mind it don't pike you, Joe!" he shouted.

"I'm a-goin' to, my lad; and you mind, too, when you ketches one. They'll drive their pike at times right through a thick leather boot; and the place don't heal kindly afterward. Ha! now I've got you," he muttered, as, getting one foot well down over the keen spine with which the fish was armed, and which it was striking to right and left, he held down the head, and, carefully avoiding the threads of the net, stabbed it first right through, and then dexterously divided the backbone just at its junction with the skull, before, with the fish writhing feebly, he gradually shook it clear of the net, and stood looking viciously down at his captive.

"Won't eat no more mullet right up to the head, will he, lads?"

"No; he has had his last meal," replied Vince, turning the fish over and displaying its ugly mouth. "Now, if it was six feet long instead of four, you'd call it a shark."

"Nay, I shouldn't; and he would be a dog-fish still. Well, he's eat a many in his time. Now his time's come, and something'll eat him. Hyste the sail."

The dog-fish—a very large one of its kind—was thrown overboard, the sail hoisted, and the boat began to glide onward toward the semicircular bay into which they were drifting, with the huge, massive promontory straight ahead. Then the oar was pressed down, and the boat began to curve round.

"Hi! stop! Don't go back yet!" cried Vince.

"Eh? Why not? No more lobster-pots down."

"I want to sail across the bay, and get round by the Scraw."

"What!" cried the old man, looking at him fiercely. "You want to go there? Well!"

He turned his eyes upon Mike, who encountered the fierce gaze, and said, coolly enough:

"Well, all right; I want to go too. I've only seen the place at a distance."

"Ay, and that's all you will ever see on it, 'less you get wings like one o' they shags," said the old man, pointing solemnly at a great black bird sunning itself upon an outlying rock. "They've seen it, p'r'aps; and you may go and lie off, if you're keerful, and see it with a spy-glass."

"And climb along to the edge of the cliff, and look over?" said Vince.

"What!" cried Daygo, with a look of horror. "Nay, don't you never try to do that, lad; you'd be sure to fall, and down you'd go into the sea, where it's all by ling and whizzing and whirling round. You'd be sucked down at once among the rocks, and never come up again. Ah! it's a horful place in there for 'bout quarter of a mile. I've knowed boats—big uns, too—sailed by people as knowed no better, gone too near, and then it's all over with 'em. They gets sucked in, and away they go. You never hear of 'em again—not so much as a plank ever comes out!"

"What becomes of them, then?" said Vince, looking at the rugged old fellow curiously.

"Chawed up," was the laconic reply, as the old fellow shaded his brow, and gazed long and anxiously beyond the headland they were leaving on their left.

"But I want to see what it's like," said Mike.

"Ay, and so has lots o' lads, and men, too, afore you, youngster," said the old man solemnly; "and want's had to be their master. It arn't to be done."

"Well, look here," continued Mike, for Vince sat very thoughtfully looking from one to the other as if he had something on his mind: "steer as close in as it's safe, and let's have a look, then."

"Do what?" roared the old man fiercely.

"Steer as close in as it's safe," repeated Mike. "We want to go, don't we, Vince?"

The lad nodded.

"Don't I tell you it's not safe nowhere? It's my belief, boys, as there's some'at 'orrid about that there place. I don't say as there is, mind you; but I can't help thinking as there's things below as lays hold o' the keel of a boat and runs it into the curren' as soon as you goes anywhere near—and then it's all over with you, for you never get back. Your boat's rooshed round and round as soon as you get clost in, and she's washed up again the rocks all in shivers, and down they goes, just as if you tied a little 'baccy-box at the end of a string, and turned it round and round, and kep' hitting it again the stones."

"Oh! I don't believe about your things under water doing that," said Mike—"only currents and cross currents: do you, Cinder?"

Vince did not answer, but sat gazing beyond the great headland, looking very thoughtful.

"Ah, my lad! it's all very well for you to talk," said the old man solemnly; "but you don't know what there is in the wast deep, nor I don't neither. I've heerd orful noises come up from out of the Scraw when the wind's been blowing ashore, and the roarings and moanings and groanings as come up over the cliffs have been t'reble."

"Yes, but it isn't blowing now," said Mike: "take us in a bit, just round the point."

"Nay," said the old man, shaking his head; "I won't say I won't, a-cause I could never face your fathers and mothers again, for I should never have the chance. I'm getting an old 'un now, and it wouldn't matter so much about me, though I have made up my mind to live to 'bout a hunderd. I'm a-thinking about you two lads, as is only sixteen or so."

"Vince is only fifteen," said Mike quickly, as if snatching at the chance of proving his seniority.

"On'y fifteen!" cried the old man. "Think o' that now—on'y fifteen and you sixteen, which means as you've both got 'bout seventy or eighty years more to live if you behave yourselves."

"Oh, gently!" cried Mike; but Vince did not speak.

"And do you think I'm a-going to cut your young lives short all that much? Nay. My name's Joe Daygo, and I'm English, and I won't do that. If I'd been what you two young fellows said—a Spannle—it might be different, but it arn't. There—let's get back; and one on you can have the lobster, and t'other the Dory and mullet."

"Then you won't take us round by the Scraw?"

"Right, my lad; I won't."

"Then I tell you what: Vince Burnet and I'll get a boat, and have a look for ourselves. You're not afraid of things catching hold of the keel, are you, Cinder?"

"No," said the lad quietly, "I don't think I am."

"Well, I've warned you both; so don't you blame me if you don't come back," growled the old man.

"Why, how can we if we don't come back?" cried Mike merrily.

The old man shook his head, and sat gazing straight before him from under his shaggy brows, steering carefully, as the boat now had to make zigzag tacks among the rocks which dotted the surface away from the cliffs. Then, in answer to a question from his companion, Vince shook off his fit of thoughtfulness, and sat chatting about the various objects they saw, principally about the caves they passed, some of which were low, arched places, excavated by the sea, whose entrances now stood out clear, now were covered by a wave which came back foaming from the compressed air it had shut-in. Then the conversation turned upon the birds, familiar enough to them, but always fresh and new. All along the face of these vast cliffs, and upon the outlying rocks, was a grand place for the study of sea-fowl. They were quite unmolested, save at nesting-time, and then interfered with but little. This was one of their strongholds, and, as the boat glided along back, the two lads set themselves to see how many kinds they passed. There were the two kinds of cormorant, both long, blackish-green birds, the one distinctive from the other by the clear white, egg-shaped marks on its sides close to the tail; rows of little sea-parrots, as they are familiarly called—the puffins, with their triangular bills; the terns, with their swallow-like flight; and gulls innumerable—black-headed, black-backed, the common grey, and the beautiful, delicately-plumaged kittiwakes, sailing round and round in the most effortless way, as if all they needed to do were to balance themselves upon widespread wing, and then go onward wherever they willed.

There was plenty to see and hear round Cormorant Crag as the boat sailed on over the crystal water, till the archway was reached in the pyramid of granite, when down went the sail, and the boat was thrust onward by means of the hitcher, the tide having risen so high that in places the boys had to bend down. Then once more they were in the long, canal-like zigzag, and soon after in the dock, where they loyally helped the old man carry up and spread the trammel net to dry, and turned to go.

"Here! stop a minute, youngsters," cried Daygo.

"What for?"

"Arn't got your bit o' fish."

"Oh, I don't want to take it, Joe," said Vince. "You've had bad luck to-day."

"Never you mind about that, my lad. I get lots o' fish, and I'm dead on some hammaneggs to-night. I said you two was to have that fish and lobster; so which is it to be? Who says lobster?"

Nobody said lobster, and the boys laughed.

"Well, if you two won't speak out like men, I must do it myself. Am I to divide the take, or are you?"

"You give us what you like, Joe," said Vince, who made up his mind to ask his mother for a pot of jam as a return present, knowing as he did that the old man had a sweet tooth.

"Right, then; I will," cried Daygo, rolling up his jersey sleeve, and thrusting a massive arm into the locker, out of which he drew the fish, the boat's stem having been lifted so that the water had run out. "There, look here: Doctor Burnet said as lobsters were undo-gestible things, so you'd better take that there one home with you, Ladle. You take the fish, Squire Burnet; your mar likes 'em fresh, as I well know."

Mike took the lobster; and the old fellow took a little willow creel from where it was wedged in a granite crevice, laid some sea-weed at the bottom, and then packed in the fish.

"Thankye, Daygo," said Mike. "Shall I pay you for it?"

"If you wants to be bad friends, lad," said the old man gruffly.

"Much obliged, Joe," said Vince. "My mother will be so pleased!"

"Ah! and you're a lucky one to have such a mother," growled the great fellow. "Wish I had."

This brought a roar of laughter from the lads, and Daygo looked fiercely from one to the other; then the bearing of his remark began to dawn upon him, and his countenance relaxed into a grim smile.

"Ah! I didn't see," he grumbled out. "Yes, I do look a nice sorter youngster to have a mother to wash my face, don't I? But here, I say," he continued sternly, "you two didn't mean it about getting a boat and trying to see the Scraw, did you?"

"Yes, to be sure," said Mike sharply.

"Then look here!" cried the old man, bringing his great doubled fist down into his left palm, with the result that there was a loud crack as of a mallet falling upon a board; "I've give you both fair warning, and you'd better take it. You don't know what may come to you if you try it. I tell you, once for all, that you can't get to see it from the sea, and you can't get to see it from the shore. Nobody never has, and nobody never can, and come back 'llve, as that there Johnny Dor'."

"I don't believe any one's had the pluck to try," said Mike stoutly.

"Ah! you're a unbelievin' young rip," growled Daygo fiercely. "But lookye here: you don't want to upset my lady your mother, Ladle, and you don't—"

"Look here, Joe Daygo, if you call me Ladle again I'll kick you!" cried Mike hotly.

"Nay, don't, lad—not yet, till you've practysed a bit on the rocks, 'cause you might hurten your toes. Look here, young Physic: you don't want to go and break your poor mother's heart, do you?"

"Of course not," said Vince.

"Then don't you go, my lad—don't you go. There—better be off, both on you. Weather's hot, and fish won't keep. Tell 'em to put some salt in the pot with that lobster, Ladle; and you'd better have your fish cooked to-night, Doctor."

Vince turned round and nodded; but the ladle was sticking in Mike's throat, and he stalked on without making a sign.

Daygo stood watching till the lads had climbed up out of his sight, and then he went and sat down on a block of granite, and began to rasp his nose on both sides with his rough, fishy finger, as if engaged in sharpening the edge of a feature which was sharp enough as it was; and as he rasped, he looked straight before him at the great rugged cliff. But he was not thinking of it in the least; his thoughts were half a mile away, at the most precipitous part of the coast—a spot avoided by shore-goer and seaman alike, from the ill name it bore, and the dangers said to attend those who ventured to go near, either climbing or in a boat.

"Nay," he said at last; "they won't go now."

# Chapter Four
# Cinder has Discovery on the Brain

"What are you thinking about, Cinder?" said Mike one day, when they were out together, after a long, hard morning's work up at the Ladelles, over algebra and Latin, with the tutor who was resident at the Mount, the Doctor sharing, however, in the cost. "You seem to have been so moony and stupid lately."

"Have I?" said Vince starting.

"Yes, always going into brown studies. I know: you can't recollect that problem in Euclid."

"What, the forty-seventh? Why, that's the one I recollect best. Guess!"

"What you were thinking about?"

Vince nodded.

"Give it up," said Mike.

"The Scraw."

"What about it? That it's guarded by water goblins and sea serpents and things, as old Joe calls them?"

"No," said Vince quietly: "I've been thinking about it ever since we were out with him that day in the boat."

"Well, and what do you think?" said Mike, who while he talked was trying how far he could jerk the flat pieces of oyster-shell, of which there were plenty near, off the cliff; but with all his skill—and he could throw far—they seemed, in the immensity around, as if they dropped close to the cliff foot.

"I think, as I thought that day, that old Joe doesn't want us to go there."

Mike was about to throw another shell, but he faced round at this with his curiosity roused.

"Why?"

"Ah! that's what I want to know; and I can't think of any reason why he shouldn't want us to go there. It seems so queer."

"Yes, it does seem queer," assented Mike.

"Of course the fishermen believe in all kinds of old women's tales about ghosts and goblins, and ill-wishing and that sort of nonsense, just as the women do about old Mother Remming's being a witch; but old Joe always seemed to me to be such a hard, solid old chap, who would laugh at a story about the fairies coming in the night and drying any one's cow."

"Well, I always thought something of that sort; but what he says must be right about the horrible currents among the rocks."

"Yes; there are fierce currents, I suppose, at some times of the tide."

"Well, that means it's dangerous."

"Of course it is, sometimes; but I'm not going to believe all he said."

"Nobody's ever been there."

"Indeed!"

"Oh yes, that's right," said Mike. "I've often heard the men talk about what an awful place it was, and say they wouldn't go on any account."

"And did that scare you?"

"Well, I don't think it did, because I always felt afterwards that I should like to climb somewhere along there till I could look over down to the sea. But of course you couldn't do it."

"I don't know," said Vince; "I should like to try."

"But after what old Joe Daygo said, you couldn't go there in a boat."

"Couldn't you?"

"No."

"Then how is it that old Joe himself can go?"

Mike dropped down on the cliff turf beside his companion and stared at him. "He never did go!"

"Yes, he did, for I was up on the Gull Cliff one day watching the birds, and I saw Joe go creeping round underneath in the boat, and sail across the bay, and then about the great point right in towards the Scraw."

"You mean it, Cinder?"

"Yes."

"It wasn't fancy?"

"No; I'm sure."

"Then there is some reason why he doesn't want us there. I say!"

"Well?"

"Let's go and see."

"You'd be afraid."

"No; I wouldn't if you wouldn't."

"I'll go if you will."

"Then we will. But how? Boat?"

"No; I say let's have a rope and try if we can't climb round by the cliff. It will be a jolly good adventure, and I keep feeling more and more as if I wanted to know what it all means."

"Then we will, and I'm ready to begin whenever you are. Why, we may find a valley of gold."

"Or get a bad tumble."

"We'll risk that."

"Then let's set to and make our plans."

The boys ceased speaking, and became very thoughtful; and, as if to sharpen their ideas, each took out his knife—a long-hafted jack knife such as a sailor uses, fastened by a lanyard to his waist. There was rather a rivalry between them as to which had the biggest, longest-bladed and sharpest knife—a point that was never decided; and the blades had rather a hard time of it, for they were constantly being opened and whetted so as to maintain a razor edge.

But, probably from not being expert, these razor-like edges were not maintained, and this was partly due to the selection of the sharpener upon which they were whetted. The sole of a boot is no doubt suitable, but not when it contains nails, which was the case with those worn by the lads. The rail of a gate is harmless, while a smooth piece of slate makes a moderately good enough soft hone. But when it comes to rubbing a blade upon a piece of gneiss, quartz crystal, or granite, the result is most unsatisfactory, the edge of the knife being prone to look like a very bad imitation of a miniature saw.

From force of habit each lad on opening his knife looked round for something upon which to give his knife a whet; but up there on the soft turf of a cliff slope whetstones were scarce. Down below on the wave-washed strand boulders and pebbles were plentiful enough, and in addition there was the rock; but from where they were it was a good quarter of a mile to the nearest place where a descent could be safely made. But the next moment Mike found an oyster-shell, upon which he began diligently to rub his blade; while, failing this, Vince pulled his foot across his knee, vigorously stropped his knife on the sole of his boot, and gave a finishing touch to the edge by passing it to and fro upon the palm of his hand.

This done, each looked out for something to cut, where there was for some distance round nothing but grass. This Vince began to shave off gently, with Mike watching him for a few moments; but the pursuit seemed to him too trivial, and, after wrinkling up his forehead for a few moments as if perplexed, an idea struck him, and he began to score the soft turf in regular lines, as if it were a loin of pork, but with this difference, that when he had made about a dozen strokes he commenced cutting between the marks, and sloping his blade so that he carved out the turf, leaving a series of ridges and furrows as he went on.

This was on his part an ingenious enough way of using the blade, out on an island cliff on a glorious sunny day; but at the end of a minute it became as monotonous as it was purposeless, and Vince shut his knife with a snap, after carefully wiping the blade; while Mike, who had been blunting the point of his by bringing it in contact with the granite, which, where they were, only lay three or four inches beneath the velvet turf, followed suit, after seeing that his knife point would need a good grinding before he could consider it to be in a satisfactory state.

"Well," said Mike, after they had looked at each other for a few moments, "how are we going to make our plans?"

"I dunno," replied Vince. "Yes, I do. You can't make plans here. Let's go and see what the place is like."

"No; that's wrong," said Mike, wrinkling his forehead again. "A general always makes his plans of how he'll attack a country before he starts, and takes what is necessary with him."

"Yes, but then he has maps of the country, and knows what he will want. We have no maps; but we've got the country, so I say let's go and see first—reconnoitre."

"Very well," said Mike, rising slowly.

"Don't seem very ready," said Vince. "Not scared about it, are you?"

"No, I don't think so," replied Mike thoughtfully; "only doesn't it seem rather—rather queer to go to a place that is strange, and where you don't know what there may be?"

"Of course it does," said Vince frankly; "and I am just a little like that. I suppose it's what the men here all feel, and it keeps them away."

"Yes, that's it," said Mike eagerly.

"But then, you know, they believe lots of things that we laugh at. There isn't a man or boy here in Crag would go and sit in the churchyard on a dark night."

"Well, you wouldn't either," said Mike.

"No, I suppose not," said Vince thoughtfully. "I don't think I believe in ghosts—I'm sure I don't; and I know that if I saw anything I should feel it was some one trying to frighten us. But I shouldn't like to go and sit in a churchyard in the dark, because—because—"

"You'd be afraid," said Mike, with a laugh.

"Yes, I should be afraid, but not as you mean," said the lad. "I should feel that it was doing a mocking, boasting sort of thing toward the dead people who were all lying asleep there."

"Dead," interposed Mike.

"No: father says asleep—quietly asleep, after being in pain and sickness, or being tired out from growing very old."

Mike looked at him curiously, and they were both silent for a few moments, till Mike said quickly:—

"I say, though, don't it seem queer to you that we've been here all our lives, and grown as old as we are, without ever going to the top of the cliff here and looking down into the Scraw?"

"Yes, that's just what I've been thinking ever since old Joe talked to us as he did. But I don't know that it is queer."

"Well, I do," said Mike: "it's very queer."

"No, it isn't. Ever since we can remember everybody has said that you can't get there, because nobody could climb up; and then while we were little we always heard people talk almost in a whisper about it, as if it were something that oughtn't to be named; and so of course we didn't think for ourselves, and took all they said as being right. But you know there may be whirlpools and holes and black caverns and sharp rocks, and I dare say there are regular monsters of congers down in the deep places that have never been disturbed."

"And sharks."

"No, I don't think there would be sharks. They live out in the open sea more, where it's not so rough."

"I say, how big have we ever seen a conger?"

"Why, that one Carnach brought in and said he'd had a terrible fight with: don't you remember?"

"Yes, I remember; he caught it on a dark thunderstormy day, and said when he hooked it first, baiting with a pilchard, it came so easy that he thought it was a little one, and swam up every time he slackened his line till he got it close to the top. But when he went to hook it in with his gaff he fell back over the thwart, because as soon as it saw him it opened its mouth and came over the gunwale with a rush, and hunted him round the boat till he hit it over the head with his little axe."

"Yes, I remember," said Vince, taking up the narrative; "and then he said they had a terrible fight, for it twisted its tail round his leg and struck at him, getting hold of his tarpaulin coat with its teeth and holding on till he got the blade of the axe into the cut he had made and sawed away till he got through the backbone. Oh yes, we heard him tell the story lots of times about how strong it was, and how it bruised his leg where it hit him with its tail, and how he was beginning to feel that, in spite of its head being nearly off, it seemed as if it would finish him, when all at once it dropped down in the bottom of the boat and only just heaved about. I used to believe it all, but he always puts more and more to it whenever he tells the tale. I don't believe it now."

"But it was a monster."

"Yes: two inches short of seven feet long, and as big round as a cod-fish; and I don't see why there mayn't be some twice as big in the Scraw. But I'm not going to believe in there being anything else, Mike; and we're going to see."

"Nothing horrid living in the caves?"

"Bogies and mermen and Goblin Jacks? No: stuff!"

"But up the cliff: you don't think there's anything there that makes it so that you can't go? I mean—"

"Dragons like father has in that old Latin book about Switzerland?"

"Yes; you've got pictures of them,—horrid things with wings, that lived in the mountains and passes."

"All gammon!" cried Vince. "People used to believe in all kinds of nonsense—magicians, and fiery serpents and dragons, and things that we laugh about now. There, one can't help feeling a bit shrinky, after all we've heard and been frightened with by people ever since we were little bits of chaps; but I mean to go. There's nothing worse about the Scraw than there is about other dangerous places."

"Ah! you say so now because it's broad daylight and the sun shines, but you'd talk differently if it was dark as pitch."

"Shouldn't go if it was dark as pitch, because we shouldn't know where we were going. I say, you're not going to turn tail?"

"No," said Mike, "I'll go with you; but one can't help feeling a bit shrinky. I'm ready: come on."

"Let's seem as if we were not going, then," said Vince.

"We shan't see anybody if we go round by the Dolmen," said Mike. "There isn't a cottage after you pass the one on the Crusy common."

"And nobody lives in that now."

"Why?" said Mike quickly. "Think they saw anything? It's nearest to the Scraw Cliff."

"See anything? No. But they used to feel—the wind. Why, it's the highest part of Crag Island! Come along."

"One minute," said Mike. "You said you thought old Joe didn't want us to go there."

"Yes," said Vince.

"Well, wasn't it because in his rough, surly way he likes us, and didn't want us to get hurt?"

"Perhaps!" said Vince laconically.

"Well, there couldn't be any other reason."

"Yes, there could. It might be a splendid place for fishing, and for ormers and queens and oysters, and he don't want any one else to find it out."

"Yes, it might be that," said Mike; and he set his teeth and looked as if he were going upon some desperate venture from which he might never return alive.

Vince looked a little uneasy too, but there was determination plainly written on his countenance as the two lads, after a glance round to see if they were observed, made off together; over the stony cliff.

# Chapter Five
## While the Raven croaked

It was getting well on in the afternoon, but they had hours of daylight before them for their task. To reach the spot would have been a trifle if they had possessed the wings of the grey gull which floated softly overhead as if watching them. A few minutes would have sufficed; for, as the boys had often laughingly said when at home in the centre of the island, where Sir Francis Ladelle's sheltered manor-house stood, near the Doctor's long granite cottage among the scattered dwellings of the fisher-farmers of the place, they could not have walked two miles in any direction without tumbling into the sea. But to reach the mighty cliffs overhanging the Scraw was not an easy task.

The way they chose was along the eastern side of the island, close to the sea, where from north point to south point the place was inaccessible, there being only three places practicable for a landing, and these lying on the west and south. There the mighty storm-waves had battered the granite crags for centuries, undermining them in soft veins till huge masses had fallen again and again, making openings which had been enlarged till there was one long cove; the fissure where they had taken boat with old Daygo; and another spot farther to the south.

The lads had not gone far before they curved suddenly to their left, and struggled through one of the patches of woodland that beautified the island. This was of oak trees and ilex, dwarfed by their position, tortured into every form of gnarled elbow and crookedness by the sea wind, and seldom visited save by the boys, who knew it as a famous spot for rabbits.

It was hard work getting through this dwarf-oak scrub, but they struggled on, descending now into a steep ravine quite in the uninhabited part of the island, and feeling that they might talk and shout as they pleased—for they were not likely to be heard. But they were very quiet, and when hawk or magpie was started, or an old nest seen, they instinctively called each other's attention to it in a whisper.

After a time they were clear of the sombre wood, and had to commence another fight in the hollow of the slope they had to climb, for here the brambles and furze grew in their greatest luxuriance, and had woven so sturdy a hedge that it was next to impossible to get through.

Perseverance, and a brave indifference to thorns, carried them along; and at the end of half an hour they were at the bottom of a gigantic precipice of tumbled-together masses of granite, suggesting that they were at the beginning of the huge promontory which jutted out into the sea, and round which Daygo had refused to take them; the beautiful little rounded bay which they had skirted being to their right; and forward toward the north, and lying away to their left, being the situation of the unknown region always spoken of with bated breath, and called The Scraw.

The lads stopped now, hot, panting and scratched, to stand gazing upward.

"Tired?" said Mike.

"Yes. No," replied Vince. "Come on."

But Mike did not move. He stood looking before him at the rugged masses of granite, grey with lichen and surrounded by brambles, reaching up and up like a gigantic sloping wall that had fallen in ruins.

Vince had begun to climb, and had mounted a few feet, but not hearing his companion following, he turned back to look.

"Why don't you come on?" he cried.

"I was thinking that we can never get up there."

"Not if you stand still at the bottom," said Vince, laughing; and his cheery way acted upon Mike's spirits directly, for he began to follow. It was strange, though, that the laugh which had raised the spirits of one depressed those of the other; for Vince felt as if it was wrong to laugh there in that wild solitude, and he started violently as something rushed from beneath his feet and bounded off to their right.

"Only a rabbit," said Mike, recovering from his own start. "But I say, Cinder, I never thought that there could be such a wild place as this in the island. Oh! what's that?"

They were climbing slowly towards a tall ragged pinnacle of granite, which rose up some ten or fifteen feet by itself, when all at once a great black bird hopped into sight, looking gigantic against the sky, gazed down in a one-sided way, and began to utter a series of hoarse croaks, which sounded like the barkings of a dog.

"Only a raven," said Vince quickly. "Why, I say, Mike, this must be where that pair we have seen build every year! We must find the nest, and get a young one or two to bring up."

"Doesn't look as if he'd let us," said Mike, peering round with his eyes for a stone that he could pick up and hurl at the bird. But, though stone was in plenty, it was in masses that might be calculated by hundredweights and tons.

They climbed on slowly, one helping the other over the hardest bits; the faults and rifts between the blocks of granite, which in places were as regular as if they had been built up, afforded them foothold; but their way took them to the left, by the raven, which gave another bark or two, hopped from the stony pinnacle upon which it had remained perched, spread its wings, and, after a few flaps to right and then to left, rose to the broken ridge above their heads, hovered for a moment, and then, half closing its wings, dived down out of sight.

"Pretty close to the top," cried Vince breathlessly; and he paused to wipe his streaming face before making a fresh start, bearing more and more to the left, and finding how solitary a spot they had reached—one so wild that it seemed as if it had never been trodden by the foot of man.

They both paused again when not many feet from the summit of the slope, their climb having been made so much longer by its laborious nature; and as they stopped, the action of both was the same: they gazed about them nervously, startled by the utter loneliness and desolation of the spot, which might have been far away in some Eastern desert, instead of close to the cliffs and commons about which they had played for years.

Granite blocks and boulders everywhere, save that in places there was a patch of white heather, ling, or golden starry ragwort; and in spite of their determination the desire was strong upon them to turn and hurry back. But for either to have proposed this would have been equivalent to showing the white feather; and for fear that Vince should for a moment fancy that he was ready to shirk the task, Mike said roughly, "Come on," and continued the climbing, reaching the top first, and stretching out his hand, which was grasped by Vince, who pulled himself up and sank down by his companion's side to gaze in wonder from the rugged ridge they had won.

It was not like the edge of a cliff, but a thorough ridge, steep as the roof of an old-fashioned house, down to where, some fifty feet below them, the slope ended and the precipice began.

It was rugged enough, but as far as they could see to right or left there was no way out: they were hemmed in by huge weathered blocks of granite and the sea. There was the way back, of course; but the desire upon both now was to go forward, for the curiosity which had been growing fast ever since they started was now culminating, and they were eager to penetrate the mystery of the place.

"What are we going to do next?" said Mike. "See if we can't get down to the shore, of course;" and Vince seated himself between two rugged, tempest-worn points of rock, and had a long, searching look beyond the edge of the precipice below him.

First he swept the high barrier of detached rock which stretched before him two hundred yards or so distant, and apparently shutting in a nearly circular pool; for he and his companion were at the head of a deep indentation, the stern granite cliffs curving out to right and left, and seeming to touch the rocky barrier, which swarmed with birds on every shelf and ledge, large patches looking perfectly white.

"Seems like a lake," said Mike suddenly, just as Vince was thinking the same thing.

"Yes, but it can't be," said Vince. "Look down there to the left, how the tide's rushing in. Looks as if a boat couldn't live in it a moment."

"And if the tide rushes in boiling like that, there must be a way out. Think there's a great hole right through under the island?"

"No; it looks deep and still there at the other end of the rocks, and—yes, you can see from here if you stand up. Why, Ladle, old chap, it is running."

Vince had risen, taken hold of one of the jagged pieces of rock, stepped on to a point, and was gazing down to his left at the pent-in sea, which was rushing through a narrow opening between two towering rocks, foaming, boiling, and with the waves leaping over each other, as if forced out by some gigantic power, but evidently hidden from the side of the sea by the great barrier stretched before them.

"I can't see anything," said Mike.

"Climb up a bit. Here—up above me."

Mike began to climb the rugged granite, and had just reached a position from whence he could stretch over and see the exit of the pent-in currents which glided round the little cove or bay, one strongly resembling the water-filled crater of some extinct volcano, when his left foot slipped from the little projection upon which he stood, and, in spite of the frantic snatch he made to save himself, he fell heavily upon Vince, driving him outward, while he himself dropped within the ridge, and for the moment it seemed as if Vince was to be sent rolling down the steep slope and over the edge of the precipice.

But the boy instinctively threw out his hands to clutch at anything to stop his downward progress, and his right came in contact with Mike's leg, gripping the trouser desperately, and the next moment he was hanging at the full extent of his arm upon the slope, his back against the rock, staring outward over the barrier at the sea, while Mike was also on his back, but head downward, with his knees bent over the strait ridge upon which they had so lately been standing.

For quite a minute they lay motionless, too much unnerved by the shock to attempt to alter their positions; while Vince felt that if the cloth by which he held so desperately gave way, nothing could save him, and he must go down headlong to the unseen dangers below.

There was another danger, too, for which he waited with his heart beating painfully. At any moment he felt that he might drag his companion over to destruction, and the thought flashed through his brain, ought he to leave go?

"The next moment he was hanging at the full extent of his arms upon the slope."

This idea stirred him to action, and he made a vain effort to find rest for his heels; but they only glided over the rock, try how he would to find one of the little shelf-like openings formed between the blocks, which often lay like huge courses of quarried stone.

Then, as he hung there breathing heavily, he found his voice:

"Mike!" he shouted; and the answer came in a smothered tone from the other slope of the steep ridge.

"Hullo!"

"Can you help me?"

"No: can't move; if I do you'll pull me over."

There was a terrible silence for what seemed to be minutes, but they were moments of the briefest, before Vince spoke again.

"Can you hold on?"

Silence, broken by a peculiar rustling, and then Mike said: "I think so. I've got my hand wedged in a crack; but I can't hold on long with my head down like this. Look sharp! Climb up."

"Look sharp—climb up!" muttered Vince, as, raising his left hand, which had been holding on to a projection in the rock at his side, he reached up, and, trying desperately, he managed to get hold of the doubled-over fold at the bottom of his companion's trouser, cramping his fingers over it, and getting a second good hold.

It does not seem much to read, but it took a good deal of his force out of him, and he lay still, panting.

"Pray look sharp," came from the other side.

"Yes. Hold on," cried Vince, as a horrible sensation began creeping through him, which he felt was preparatory to losing his nerve and falling: "I'm going to turn over."

"No, no—don't," came faintly. "I can't hold on."

"You must!" shouted Vince fiercely. "Now!"

Clutching desperately at the frail cloth, he gave himself a violent wrench and rolled himself right over upon his face, searching quickly with his toes for some support, and feeling them glide over the surface again and again, till a peculiar sensation of blindness began to attack him. Then a thrill of satisfaction ran through his nerves, for one boot toe glided into the fault between two blocks, and the tension upon his muscles was at once relieved.

"I can't help it," came faintly to his ears. "You're dragging me over. Help! help!"

*Croak*! came in a hoarse, barking note, and the great raven floated across them not a dozen feet above their heads.

"All right!" cried Vince. "I can manage now." And he felt about with his other foot, found a projection, and having now two resting-places for his feet, one higher than the other, he cautiously drew himself up, inch by inch, till his chin was level with his hands, when, taking a deep, long breath, he forced his toe well against the rock, trusting to a slight projection; and, calling to Mike to try and hold on, he made a quick snatch with one hand at the lad's leg a foot higher, but failed to get a good grasp, his hand gliding down the leg, and Mike uttered a wild cry.

For a moment Vince felt that he must fall, but in his desperation his teeth closed on the cloth beneath him, checking his downward progress; and as his feet scraped over the rock in his efforts to find fresh hold, he found his cliff-climbing had borne its fruits by hardening the muscles of his arms. How he hardly knew, he managed to get hand over hand upon Mike's leg, till he drew himself above the ridge, and in his last effort he fell over, dragging his companion with him, so that they rolled together down the inner slope twenty or thirty feet, till a block checked their progress.

Just then, as they lay scratched and panting, there was a darkening of the air, the soft whishing of wings, and the raven dropped on the big pinnacle close at hand, to utter its hoarse, barking croak as it gazed wickedly at them with first one and then the other eye.

"Ha! ha! ha!" laughed Mike, in a peculiarly hysterical tone; "wouldn't you like it? But not this time, old fellow. Oh, don't I wish I had a stone!"

The same memory had come to both, as they lay breathless and exhausted, of seeing this bird or one of its relatives rise from below the cliff edge one day as they approached; and, looking down, they saw upon a ledge, where it had fallen, a dead lamb, upon which the great ill-omened bird had been making a meal.

"Hurt?" said Vince at last, as he sat up and examined his clothes for tears.

"Hurt! why, of course I am. I gave my head such a whack against one of the stones.—Are you?"

"No," said Vince, making an effort to laugh at the danger from which he had escaped. "I say, though, your trousers are made of better cloth than mine."

"Trousers!" said Mike sourly: "you've nearly torn the flesh off my bones. You did get hold of a bit of skin with your teeth, only I flinched and got it away. I say, though—"

"Well? What?" said Vince; for the other stopped. "That's the way down to the Scraw; but you needn't have been in such a hurry to go."

Vince shuddered in spite of his self-control. "I wonder," he said softly, "whether it's deep water underneath or rocks?"

"I don't know that it matters," was the reply. "If it had been water you couldn't have swum in such a whirlpool as it seems to be. So you might just as well have been killed on the rocks. But oh! I say Cinder, don't talk about it."

The boy's face grew convulsed, and he looked so horrified that Vince cried eagerly —

"Here, I say, don't take it like that. It was not so bad as we thought. It wouldn't have happened if you'd held tight instead of blundering on to me."

"Let's talk about something else," said Mike, trying to master his feelings.

"All right. About that cove. You see the water comes rushing in at one side and goes out at the other, and I daresay when the tide turns it goes the other way. I should like to get right down to it, so as to see the water close to."

Mike shuddered. "You won't try again, will you?" he said.

"Try again? Yes. Why not? Why, we might come a million times and never slip again."

"Yes," said Mike, but rather shrinkingly. "Shall we go back home now?"

"No; not till we've had another good look down at the place. Here—hi! you be off, or next time we come we'll bring a gun."

*Croak!* said the raven, and it took flight—not, however, at the words, but from the cap sent skimming up at it where it perched watching them.

"Come on," cried Vince; and his companion sprang up as if ashamed of his weakness.

Then together they climbed back to the scene of their adventure, and had a good look down at the shut-in cove, calmly reconnoitring the danger through which one of them had passed; and, after gazing long at the entrance and place of exit of the tides, they climbed along the ridge for some distance to the right, and then back and away to the left, but they could see nothing more—nothing but the rock-bound bay shut-in from the sea, and whose shore, if there was any, remained hidden from their sight by the projecting edge of cliff at the bottom of the slope below them.

"There," said Vince at last,—"I know how I feel."

"So do I," said Mike: "that we've had all our trouble for nothing."

"No, I don't; I feel as if I shan't be satisfied till I've been right down there and seen what it's like."

"But we can't get there. Nobody could go in a boat."

"Perhaps not. We must climb down."

Mike suppressed a shudder. "Can't be done," he said.

"How do we know till we've looked right down over the edge?"

"Must bring a rope, then?"

"Of course, and one hold it while the other creeps to the edge and looks over."

Mike nodded, and they began to retrace their steps, talking thoughtfully as they went.

"Shall you say anything about our—accident?" asked Mike at last.

"No: only frighten my mother."

"Nor yet about the Scraw, and what we're going to try and do?"

"No: what's the good? Let's find what there is to see first. I say, Cinder, it will be as good as going to a foreign country seeking adventures. Who knows what we may find?"

"Raven's nest, for one thing."

"Yes, I expect that chap has got his wife and young ones somewhere about here. How about a rope? Have you got one at home?"

"Yes; but so have you."

"I'm not very fond of ours," said Vince thoughtfully. "It's a long time since it was new, and we don't want to have any accidents. You bring a coil of new rope from your boat-shed: we'll take care of it. And, I tell you what, I'll bring that little crowbar of ours next time, and a big hammer, so as to drive the bar into some crack. It will be better than holding the rope."

The talk of their future plans lasted till it was nearly time to part, and they were just arranging for their hour of meeting on the next day when they came suddenly upon old Daygo, at the corner of the lane leading down to his comfortable cottage.

"Art'noon," he said, with a nod, and fixing his eyes upon each of them searchingly. "Having a walk?"

"Yes," said Vince carelessly. "When are you going to take us fishing again?"

"Oh! one o' these fine days, my lads; but you're getting to be quite men now, and must think more about your books. Been on the cliffs?"

"Yes," said Vince. "Come on, Mike: it's tea-time."

The boys walked on in silence for some moments, and then Vince spoke.

"I say, Mike, do you think he's watching us?"

"No," said Mike shortly. "You fancy he is, because you've got some cock-and-bull notion that he don't want us to go to the Scraw."

"Perhaps so," said Vince thoughtfully; "but I can't help it. I do think so."

"Well, suppose he does; he said what was right: it is a horribly dangerous place, and all the people keep away from it because they've got ideas like his."

"Maybe," said Vince, with his brow all in puckers. "But never mind; we'll go and see."

# Chapter Six
# Haunted by the Scraw

The weather interfered with the prosecution of the boys' adventure for a week, and during that time, what with wind and rain, they had nothing to tempt them to the cliff but the sight of a large French three-masted lugger or *chasse-marée*, which was driven by the gale and currents dangerously near the Crag: so near, in fact, that old Daygo and nearly every fisherman in the place hung about the cliffs in full expectation of seeing the unfortunate vessel strike upon one or other of the rocks and go to pieces, when all on board must have inevitably been drowned, the height of the sea making it madness to attempt to launch a boat.

But, to the relief of all, the swift vessel was so cleverly managed that she finally crept through an extremely dangerous passage, and then, catching a cross current, was borne right out to where she could weather the northern point of the island, and disappeared into the haze.

"There, young gentlemen," said old Daygo in a stentorian voice, "that's seamanship! But she'd no business to come so near the Crag in weather like this. Wouldn't ha' like to be aboard o' she just now, would you?"

"No," said Vince; "nor you neither?"

"Hey? Why, that's just what I've been a-wishing these two hours past, my lad. I could ha' took her out o' danger long enough before; but them Frenchies don't know our island like I do. Why, I feel sometimes as if I could smell where the rocks are, and I could steer a boat by touch, like, even if it was black as the inside of a tar-barrel in the middle of the night."

It sounded like empty boasting, but the words were seriously received by the rough men around.

"Ay, ay," said one fat, heavy-looking fellow; "Joe Daygo knows. I wouldn't ha' been aboard her fer no money."

"Been thinking you'd eat no more byled lobster—eh, Jemmy Carnach?" said Daygo, with a hoarse laugh; and the man gave him a surly look and sauntered away.

"I say," said Mike, as soon as the lads were alone; "old Joe is really a good sort of fellow after all. He seemed a deal more troubled about that French boat than any one else."

"Yes; and I suppose he is a clever pilot, and knows all about the currents and the rocks; but I don't quite understand about his being so well off."

Mike began to whistle, and said nothing for a few moments.

"I don't see why he shouldn't be well off," he said; "he's getting old, and he's very mean, and never spends money upon himself."

Vince nodded, and remained silent.

Then came a lovely morning after the week's bad weather, and Vincent was just starting for Sir Francis Ladelle's rather unwillingly, to join Mike for the day's studies, when there was a cheery whistle outside and his fellow-pupil appeared.

"I say!" he cried, "father said it was a shame for us to lose such a fine day, and he told Mr Deane to give us a holiday."

"Eh? What's that?" cried the Doctor. "Here, I'm off up to the house to put a stop to that. I'm not going to pay half that tutor's expenses if this sort of idleness is to be encouraged."

Mike looked aghast.

"It's all right," said Vince merrily; "father doesn't mean it."

"Oh, don't I!" cried the Doctor, frowning.

"No: does he, mother?"

Mrs Burnet smiled and shook her head.

"Here, you boys, don't get into any mischief."

"No, father," said Vince, and the next minute they were outside.

"Scraw?" said Vincent; and his companion nodded unwillingly, as the boy thought, but he changed his opinion the next moment.

"I've got the hammer and bar ready, and a small rope; but we must have yours."

"Yes, of course."

"Well, run back and get it, and meet me out by the Dolmen."

"Brought it," said Mike: "tucked it under a furze bush out on the common."

Vince's face lit up with eagerness, and the pair were about to start when they saw old Daygo in the distance, and they turned back, went into the house, and waited till he had gone by.

Giving the fisherman time to get well out of sight, they sallied forth, and went to where the coil of rope was hidden—a thin, strong line that would have borne a couple of men hanging on its end—and as soon as this was brought out, and a glance round taken to make sure they were not watched, Mike cried—

"But what about the hammer and bar?"

Vince opened his jersey to show the head of the hammer on one side, the crowbar on the other, snugly tucked in the waistband of his trousers.

"Well done! that's capital!" cried Mike. And the two lads went off in the direction of the Scraw, but in a zigzag fashion, as if their intentions were entirely different; and this at Vince's wish, for he had a strong impression that old Daygo was keeping an eye upon their movements, though Mike laughed at the idea.

"I don't feel nervous about it now, do you?" said Vince, as soon as they were well under cover of the rugged ground.

"No; but I don't like to think about that ugly slip you had," said Mike thoughtfully.

"I didn't have an ugly slip: you knocked me over."

"Oh, well, I couldn't help it, could I? and I did hold on till you got out of it."

"Never mind that now," said Vince; "let's think about what we are going to do. There'll be no danger so long as we are careful—and I mean to be, very, and so I tell you. Wonder whether we shall see our black friend? I say, didn't it seem as if it was on the look-out for us to have a bad accident?"

"No: seemed as if it was on the look-out to keep us from finding its nest."

They chatted away merrily enough till they had nearly reached the chaos of tumbled-together rocks, when, in spite of the bright sunshine and blue sky overhead, the wildness of the place once more impressed them unpleasantly, and, instead of the cheery conversation and banter in which they had indulged, they became quiet, only speaking at intervals, and then in quite a low tone.

The bottom of the steep, rough slope was reached, and they paused to consider their plans. They had come out some fifty yards from where they made their former ascent to the ridge, for it was marked by the jagged sugar-loaf upon which the raven had perched. But the sloping wall of granite where they were presented just about the same aspect as that portion where they had struggled up before, and there was no reason for making a détour over very difficult ground, cumbered with huge blocks that must have fallen from above, and tangled in the hollows between with brambles; so they determined to climb from where they stood, and began at once, each selecting his own route, with the understanding that a pyramidal block eighty or ninety feet above their heads should be the meeting-place.

"Come on, then," cried Mike. "First up!"

"No, no," said Vince. "This must be done steadily. We shall want to be cool and fresh for anything we may have to do. One of us is sure to be obliged to go down by the rope."

"Very well," said Mike; and they commenced the ascent, each feeling the wisdom of the plan adopted, the climb being difficult enough, though there was not the slightest danger.

They were glad enough to rest and wipe their brows as they stood by the rough block, and upon which they found they could easily climb; but there was nothing more to see than at their former visit, save that the rocks looked far more rough, both at the torrent-like entrance and the narrow opening on their right, while even from the height at which they stood it was plain to see that the circular cove was in a violent state of ebullition.

But here, close in, was the slope which ran down towards the sea—very similar in character to that by which they had ascended, only that it was, as it were, chopped off short. In fact, they seemed to be on the summit of a stony ridge of granite mountains, one side of which had been nearly all gnawed away by the sea.

"Don't seem much choice of where to go down," said Vince, after a long scrutiny to right and left. "Shall we try here?"

"Just as well as anywhere else," said Mike. "Only what is it we are going to do? If it means creeping down with a rope round one, and then going over the edge to play chicken at the end of a roasting-jack, I feel as if I'd rather not."

"It means going carefully down to the edge and looking over first," replied Vince. "It may only be a place where we can get down easily enough."

"Or it may be a place where we can't," said Mike. "All right: I'll go, if you like."

"No: I'll go first," said Vince. And he drew out his hammer and crowbar; but a block of granite close by stood up so much like a thick, blunt post that there seemed to be no need for the crowbar to be driven in; so, making one end fast round the block with a well-tried mooring knot—one which old

Daygo had taught them might be depended upon for securing a boat—they calculated how much rope would be necessary to well reach the bottom of the broken-off slope, and at the end of this the line was knotted round Vince's chest and he prepared to descend.

"Ease it away gently, so that I'm not checked," said the lad, as Mike took hold close to him and knelt down ready to pay the rope out and so as to be able to tighten his grasp at any moment if there was a slip.

"Right! I'll mind; and you'll be all right: you can't fall."

"I know," was the reply; and trusting to his companion, while strengthened by the knowledge that at the very worst he must be brought up short by the granite block, Vince gave a sharp look downward, and, selecting a spot at the edge a little to his right for the point to make for, he turned his face to the slope and began to descend, carefully picking hand and foothold and helped by the steady strain upon the rope which was kept up by Mike, who watched every movement breathlessly, his eyes fixed upon his companion's head, and ready to respond to every order which was uttered.

Vince went down as calmly and deliberately as if the level ground were just below him till he was about two-thirds of the way, when he could not help giving a start, for Mike suddenly exclaimed:

"Here's that old raven coming!"

"Where?"

"Off to my right—in a hurry. You must be somewhere near the nest."

Vince hesitated for a few moments, for the thought occurred to him that the bird might make a swoop at him, as he had read of eagles acting under similar circumstances; but the next moment he had thought of what power there would be in the blow of a fist striking a bird in full career, and knowing full well that it must be fatal to the raven, he continued to descend, with the bird flying by some fifty feet overhead and uttering its hoarse croak.

"Lower away a little more," said Vince, as he drew nearer the edge of what might either be a precipice or an easy slope for aught he could tell.

"I'll lower," was the reply; "but I want to feel you well."

"That's right. I must have rope enough to move quite freely."

"Yes, that's all very well; but I don't feel as if I could haul you up if you slipped over the edge."

"Who's going to ask you to?" said Vince. "I should try and climb, shouldn't I? If you keep me tight like that I can't get down."

"Are you all right?" said Mike anxiously, for he was by far the more nervous of the two.

"Right?—yes; but I feel like a cow tethered to a picket, so that I can't reach the bit of grass sward. Now then, lower away."

Mike obeyed, with the palms of his hands growing very moist, as his companion drew closer to the brink.

"Lower away!" cried Vince.

"No: that's close enough," said Mike decidedly. "Look from where you are, and come back. Now then, what can you see?"

"A bit of moss and a patch of sea-pink just under my nose. Don't be so stupid! How am I to look over the edge if you hold me tight up like this? Ah!"

"What is it?" cried Mike, holding on to the rope with all his might, and keeping it resting on the rock, over which it had slowly glided.

"Only a loose stone gave way under my feet, and went down."

He remained silent, waiting to hear the fragment rebound and strike somewhere, but he listened in vain. The fall of the stone, however, had its effect, for a wild chorus of whistling and screaming arose, and an eddy of wings came up as a perfect cloud of white and grey birds rose into sight, and were spread to right and left.

"Hadn't you better come back now?" said Mike anxiously.

"If I do it will be to make you come down instead. Why, you're worse than I am, Mike! Now then, lower away! I only want about a fathom more, and then you may hold on tight."

"Very well, then," said the lad: "I'll give you just six feet, and not a bit more. Then you shall come up."

"Say seven," cried Vince merrily.

"No: six. That's what you said; so make much of it."

"Lower away, then!" cried Vince; and he carefully descended, after a glance over his left shoulder, creeping cautiously down, and edging to his left till he was just over the block at the edge which he had marked out for his goal.

"That's four feet, mind!" cried Mike: "only two more."

"Good little boy!" said Vince merrily. "Four and two do make six. I'll tell Mr Deane to-morrow. He was grumbling the other day about the muddle you made over your algebra."

"You look after your climbing, and never mind my algebra," said Mike huskily.

"Now, Mikey!" cried Vince; "hold on—tight as you can."

"Yes. Don't you want the other two feet?"

"Of course I do; but I'm going to turn over."

"No, no, I say—don't!" cried Mike. "Do think where you are! Have a good look, and then come up."

"Here, I say, you'd better come down instead of me. I can't see out of the back of my head if you can. Now, no nonsense. This is what I want to do: I'm going to turn over, with my back to the cliff, and then shuffle down that other two feet, with my legs on each side of that piece of stone."

"But it's at the very edge," said Mike. "Good boy again! How well you can see, Ladle! It is just at the edge; and, once I'm there, I can see down either way."

"But it isn't safe, Cinder. I can't help being anxious. Suppose the stone's loose, and gives way?"

"Why, then it will fall down and frighten more birds. Now then, don't fidget. If the stone goes, you'd still hold on by the rope, and I should be left sitting there all the same. I shouldn't do it if I didn't feel that I could. I'm not a bit nervous, so hold on."

"Very well," said Mike breathlessly: "I've got you."

"Ready?"

"Yes."

Vincent Burnet did not hesitate, but, with a quick movement, turned himself right over, dragging heavily upon the rope, though, and making his companion draw in his breath through his closed teeth with a hissing sound.

"There I am," said Vince coolly. "I could slip down into the place if I liked, but I won't try; so just ease the rope, inch by inch, as I shuffle myself lower. That's the way. Easy as kiss my hand. A little more, and a little more, and there we are. Why, Mike, old chap, it's just like sitting in a saddle—only it's so hard."

"Are your legs right over the side?"

"Yes, and the wind's blowing up the legs of my trousers like anything. Oh! you can't think what a sharp draught there is."

"Never mind the draught."

"No use to," said Vince.

"Oh, I say, do have a good look down, and then come up again. Now, then: does the cliff slope from where you are?"

"Yes, right down to the water."

"Steeply?"

"Yes."

"Could we climb down?"

"Yes, if we were flies: Mike, old chap, it's just awful!"

"What!" cried Mike breathlessly.

"Yes: that's it—awful," said Vince quietly, as he rested his hands on the block he bestrode, and looked over to his left. "It slopes down; but the wrong way. It goes right in as far as I can see, and— Yes, it does just the same on the other side. If I were to go down now I should plump right into black water, that's boiling up and racing along like it does where there's a rocky bottom, I do wish you were here to see."

"I don't," whispered Mike. "There—that'll do," he continued aloud. "Come up."

"Wait a bit. I must see a little more, now I am here. I say, it's awful!—it's grand! The rocks, as far as I can see, are as smooth as can be, and all sorts of colours, just as if they were often breaking away. Some are dark and some are browny and lavender, and there's one great patch, all glittering grey granite, looking as new as new."

"Yes, it must be very beautiful; but come back."

"Don't you be in such a hurry," said Vince. "You won't catch me sitting here again. I'll let you down if you like, but once is quite enough for me. I want to have a good look, though, so as to tell you all about it before I do come, for, on second thoughts, I shan't lower you down here—it's too horrid. I say: wherever I can see there are thousands of birds, but there are not many places where they can sit. I can see one raven, too—there are two of them sailing about just under me, with their backs shining in the sun. Oh, Mike: look at the cormorants! I never knew there were so many about the island. Big gulls, and puffins, and terns, and—I say, what a cloud of pigeons flying right out from under me: Why, there must be a cavern going right in. Hold tight! I want to lean out more to try and see."

"No!" shrieked out Mike. "Don't—don't! It's a hundred times worse kneeling here and seeing you than doing it oneself."

"But I only want to see if there is a cave."

"If the pigeons keep flying out there must be."

"Well, there they go, and here are some more coming, and they've flown right in somewhere, so I suppose there is. Want to hear any more about the place?"

"No, no. Come up now."

"All right, old chap; then I will, after one more look round and down below. The water is wild, though, and the rocks are grand; but old Joe is as right as can be: it's a terrible place, and unless any one likes to hang at the end of a three-hundred-feet rope he cannot get to the bottom here nor anywhere else along this cliff. It's just three parts of a round, and goes in all of a hollow below, where I am. There—that's all; and now I'm coming up."

"Hah!" ejaculated Mike, in a tone full of thankfulness; and as Vince shuffled himself a little way—not much, for there was not room—the rope tightened about his chest, giving him so strong a support that he leaned back, pressed his hands down on either side of him to steady himself, and drew up one leg till he could plant his heel on the stone where he had been seated. A steady draw up of the other leg, and it was beside its fellow; then, getting well hold of the nearest projections on either side, he shouted up to his companion to haul hard—shouted, though in the immensity of the place his words, like those which had preceded them, sounded weak and more like whispers.

"Right!" said Mike; and then he uttered a wild cry, for as Vince thrust with feet and hands together, straightening himself out, the rope tightened at the same moment, and then the lad hung motionless against the slope.

The rain and frost had been hard at work upon the edge of that precipice, as its sharply gnawed-off edge showed and the huge stone which the venturous lad had stridden was only waiting for the sharp thrust which it had received, for with a dull crack it was separated from the side, with an enormous mass beneath it, and went rushing down, leaving a jagged curve, as if the piece had been bitten out, just below the lad's feet.

Vince did not stir even to feel for a place to plant his hands, but remained motionless for some moments. Then there was a dull splash echoed from the barrier rock which shut-in the cove, and the rushing sound of wings, as the startled birds rose in clouds from their resting-places all around.

At last the full sense of his perilous position came to the boy, and with it his coolness; and he grasped the rock as well as he could, and called up to his companion.

"Grip hard, Ladle!" he cried. "I'm going to try and turn face to you."

There was no reply; but a thrill seemed to come down the fibres of the rope, and the strain upon the boy's chest to increase.

It was no easy task, for it was hard to find a resting-place on either side of the gap for his feet; but, full of trust in Mike's hold of the rope, and strengthened by the knowledge that it was secured to the granite block as well, Vince gave himself a quick writhe, and turned upon his face. Then, after a scrambling slip or two, his toes found a ledge, as his hands already had, and he climbed steadily up.

That task was not difficult, for the foothold was easy to select, the rope tightening still, and giving him steady help, while the distance, long as it had taken him to descend, was only short.

In another minute he was over the ridge, looking down on Mike, who, instead of hauling in the rope as he came up, had let himself glide down like a counterpoise, and as soon as he saw his companion in safety, he drew himself in a crouching position and stared up with his lips apart.

"It's all right," said Vince huskily. "Why, your face is white as white, and your hair's all wet."

"Yes," gasped Mike hysterically, "and so's yours. Oh, Cinder, old chap, I thought you had gone! Let's get away from this horrid place. Old Joe's right: there is something terrible about it after all."

"Wait a bit," said Vince, rather feebly, as he too crouched down upon a piece of rock. "I don't feel as if I could move much for a bit. I am so stiff and weak, and this rope's cut into my chest. Yes: old Joe's right; there's no getting down there. But it was awfully grand, Ladle, and I should have liked you to see it."

"And do you want to lower me down?" said Mike fiercely.

"No!" cried Vince sharply. "I wouldn't have you feel what I felt when that stone broke off and left me hanging there for all the riches in the world!"

# Chapter Seven
# The Pangs of Cold Pudding

"A burnt child fears the fire." So says the old proverb; and therefore it was quite reasonable for a couple of big lads to feel a certain sensation of shrinking when they talked about their adventure while trying to investigate the mysteries surrounding the portion of Crag, or Cormorant Island, as it was called, known as the Scraw.

For they did talk about it a great deal. Then, too, Vince had some *very* unpleasant dreams about hanging over a tremendous gulf. One night in particular he was especially bad.

It happened in this way: Mike came over to the Doctor's cottage one evening after tea—though this was no novelty, for he was always coming over to the cottage after tea, when Vince was not going over to Sir Francis Ladelle's quaint, semi-fortified house, which had stood there for hundreds of years, being repaired by its various occupants, but very little altered. In fact, when the little island was for sale, many years before this story commences, and the baronet became the purchaser, he was so pleased with the old place that he determined to keep up the traditions of the past, in spite of low ceilings, dark windows, and what Mike described to Vince as "the jolly old ghosts," which, being interpreted, meant rats.

So Mike came over one evening, after Vince had eaten a tremendous meal, and the two lads went out for a stroll to the cliff edge, where there was always something to see, returning after dusk by the light of the moon and glowworms, of which there were abundance. Then Vince had to see Mike up to the gates of the old house; and, to make things straight, Mike said he would walk back a few yards with him, the few yards being so elastic that they stretched out to five hundred, more or less.

At last Vince reached home and had his supper, which had been put out for him, and when he had finished, found that the sea air and exercise had made him ravenous.

"I must have something else to eat," he said to himself, and he was going into the parlour to speak upon this important subject to Mrs Burnet; but as he reached the door he could hear her pleasant voice, and he knew what was going on, though he could not see through the panels. For the picture rose plainly before his mind's eye of his father lying back in his easy chair, tired out with his round of the island and gardening, while by the light of a pair of mould candles—

*What*? You don't know what mould candles are? The happier you! People did fifty years ago, and they were largely used by those who could not afford wax or spermaceti; and they did what Vince heard the Doctor do from time to time—took up the old-fashioned, scissor-like snuffers from their plated tray, snuffed the candles, and laid them back with a sharp click. And let me tell you that there was an art in snuffing a candle which required practice and a steady hand. For if you of the present generation of boys who live in the days of gas, electric lights, spirit lamps, and candles ingeniously made after the analytical experiments of chemists on a material very different from the old-fashioned Russian tallow—if you, I say, were to try and snuff an old candle, the chances are that you would either cut the cotton wick too much or too little, if you did not snuff the light out. After a time these sources of light would grow lengthy of black, burnt wick, a curious mushroomy, sooty portion would grow on the top, and the flame of the candle would become dull yellow and smoky. Then, if you cut too little off, the light would not be much improved; if you cut too low down, it was worse; if lower still, you put the light out. But the skilful hand every few minutes cut to the happy medium, as the Doctor did, and the light burned up fairly white and clear; so that, according to the custom at the cottage, Mrs Burnet could see well to continue reading aloud to her weary husband, this being his one great enjoyment in the calm life on the island.

Now, it seems rather hard on Vince to keep him waiting hungrily at the door while the writer of this little history of boy life runs away from his narrative to begin prattling in print about candles; but what has preceded these lines on light, and the allusion to chemistry, does ask for a little explanation, for many of you who read will say, What can chemistry have to do with tallow candles?

A great deal. I daresay you have read a little chemistry, or heard lectures thereon. Many of you may have been bitten by the desire to try a little yourselves, as I was, and tried making hydrogen and oxygen gases, burning phosphorus, watch-spring and sulphur in the latter; and even tried to turn the salts of metals back into the metals themselves. But that by the way. Let us return to the candle—such a one as Vince had left burning, smoking and smelling unpleasantly, in the flat brass candlestick upon the little hall table, for it was time he was off to bed. Now, the chemists took the candle, and pulled it to pieces, just as the candle-makers took the loose, fluffy cotton wick metaphorically to pieces, and constructed another by plaiting the cotton strands together and making a thin, light wick, which, as it burned, had a tendency to curl over to the side of the conical flame where the point of the wick touched the air and burned more freely—so freely, in fact, from getting more oxygen from the air than the other part, as to burn all away, and never need snuffing. That is the kind of wick you use in your candles to-day; and the snuffers have gone into curiosity cases in museums along with the clumsy tinder-boxes of the past.

But that is to do with the wick, though I daresay some chemist or student of combustion gave the first hint to the maker about how to contrive the burning away of the unpleasant snuff.

Let us go back to the candle itself, or rather to the tallow of which it was made.

Now, your analytical chemist is about the most inquisitive person under the sun. Bluebeard's wife was a baby to him. Why, your A C would have pulled the Blue Chamber all to bits, and the key too, so as to see what they were made of. He is always taking something to pieces. For instance, quite lately gas tar was gas tar, and we knew that it was black and sticky, good for palings and horribly bad for our clothes, when, on hot, sunny days, we climbed over the said palings. But, all at once, the A C took gas tar in hand to see what it was made of, and the result is—what? I must not keep Vince and you waiting to tell all—in fact, I don't know, but may suggest a little. Gas tar now means brilliant aniline dyes, and sweet scents, and flavours that we cannot tell from pears and almonds, and ammonia and carbolic preparations good for the destruction of disease germs. But when the A C attacked the tallow of the candle he astonished us more.

For, so to speak, he took the tallow, and he said to himself, Now, here's tallow—an unpleasant animal fat: let's see what it is made of.

Years ago I should have at once told him that it was grease, obtained by melting down the soft parts of an animal. But the A C would have said to me: Exactly; but what is the grease made of?

Then he began making tests and analysing, with the result that out of candle fat he distilled a beautifully clear white, intensely sweet fluid, and made a name for it: glycerine, from the Greek for "sweet," for which, as Captain Cuttle would have said, consult your lexicon.

Then our friend the chemist tested the glycerine, and tried if it would burn; but it would not burn in the least, and he naturally enough said, Well, that stuff is no good for candles, so it may be extracted from the tallow. To make a long dissertation short, that was done at once, and the result was that, instead of the new tallow candles being soft, they were found to be hard, and to burn more clearly. Then chemicals were added, and they became harder still, and were called composites.

That was the beginning of the improvements, which subject I must carry no further, but return to our hungry lad, who, hearing the reading going on, would not interrupt his mother, but took up his candle and went to the larder to investigate for himself.

There was bread and butter, and bread and cheese, and a small piece of mutton—but this last was raw; and Vince was about to turn to the bread and cheese when his eyes lighted upon a wedge of cold apple dumpling, which he seized upon as the very thing, bore off to his bedroom, after putting his head in at the parlour door to say good-night, ate with the greatest of gusto, and then, thoroughly drowsy, tumbled into bed.

The next minute, as it seemed most vividly to Vince, the new rope that Mike took with them to the tempest-torn ridge above the Scraw was cutting into his chest and compressing it so that he could hardly breathe. But he would not complain, for fear his companion should think it was because he was too cowardly to go on down that steep slope of thirty or forty feet to look over the edge of the precipice. So he went on lower and lower, suffering horribly, but more and more determined to go on; and as he went the rope stretched out, and the slope lengthened, till he seemed to have descended for hours. Flocks of ravens came down, flapping their wings about him and making dashes with their great beaks at his eyes; while stones were loosened, rattled down into the gulf and startled clouds upon clouds of birds, which came circling up, their wings beating the air, till there was a noise like thunder.

Down to the stone at last; and upon this he sat astride, gazing at the vast gulf below, where the cove spread out farther than eye could reach, while the waters rushed by him like many cataracts of Niagara rolled into one. At last Mike's voice came to him, in imploring tones, sounding distant, strange and familiar, begging him to come up; and he drew himself up once more, and, with the rope tightening, gave that great thrust with his heels which sent the block upon which he had ridden falling down and down, as if for ever, into space, while he hung motionless, with the line compressing his chest so that he could not breathe. He could not struggle, he could not even stir—only hang there suffocating, till his senses were leaving him fast, and a burning light flashed into his eyes. Then the rope parted, the terrible tension about his chest was relieved, and he began falling more and more swiftly, with a pleasant feeling of restfulness, till a voice said loudly:

"Vince, Vince! What is it, boy? Wake up!"

Vince not only woke up, but sat up, staring at his father and mother, who were standing in their dressing-gowns on either side of his bed.

"He must have something coming on," said Mrs Burnet anxiously.

"Coming on!" said the Doctor, feeling the boy's temples and then his wrist; next, transferring his hand to where he could feel the pulsation of the heart, "Nightmare!" he cried.

"What's the matter?" said Vince confusedly. "Fire?"

"Any one would have thought so, and that you were being scorched, making all that groaning and outcry. What's the matter with you?"

"Nothing," said Vince, whose dreaming was all hidden now by a mental haze. "Is anybody ill, then?"

"I'm afraid you are, my dear," said Mrs Burnet anxiously; and she laid her cool hand upon her son's forehead. "His head is very hot and wet, dear," she added to the Doctor.

"Yes, I know," he said gruffly. "Here, Vince!"

"Yes, father."

"What did you have for your supper?"

"Oh! only a couple of slices of bread and butter, with a little jam on," said Mrs Burnet hastily. "I cut it for him myself."

"Nothing else?" said the Doctor.

"No, dear."

"Yes, I did, mother," said Vince, whose head was growing clearer now. "I was so hungry I went into the larder and got that piece of cold pudding."

"Wurrrh!" roared the Doctor, uttering a peculiar growling sound, and, to the astonishment of mother and son, he caught up the pillow and gave Vince a bang with it which knocked him back on the bolster. "Cold pudding!" he cried. "Here! try a shoe-sole to-morrow night, and see if you can digest that. Come to bed, my dear. Look here, Vince: tell Mr Deane to give you some lessons in natural history, and then you'll learn that you are not an ostrich, but a boy."

The next minute Vince was in the dark, but not before Mrs Burnet had managed to bend down and kiss him, accompanying it with one of those tender good-nights which he never forgot to the very last.

But Vince felt hot and angry with what had passed.

"I wish father hadn't hit me," he muttered. "He never did before. I don't like it; and he seemed so cross. I wonder whether he did feel angry."

Vince lay for some minutes puzzling his not quite clear brain as to whether his father was angry or pretending. There was the dull murmur of voices from the next room, as if a conversation were going on, but he could not tell whether his mother was taking his part or no. Then, all at once, there came an unmistakable "Ha, ha, ha!" in the Doctor's gruff voice, and that settled it.

"He couldn't have been cross," thought Vince, "or he wouldn't laugh like that. And it was only the pillow after all."

Two minutes later the boy was asleep, and breathing gently without dreams, and so soundly that he did not hear the handle of the door creak softly, nor a light step on the floor. Neither did he hear a voice say: "Asleep, Vince?" nor feel a hand upon his forehead, nor two soft, warm lips take their place as a gentle voice whispered: "God bless my darling boy!"

# Chapter Eight
# A Random Shot

"How about the cold pudding?"

"Look here, Ladle, if you say any more about that it means a fight."

"Ha, ha! Poor old Cinder riding the nightmare, and dreaming about the Scraw! Wish I'd been sleeping at the cottage that night. I'd have woke you up: I'd have given you cold pig!"

"Lucky for you that you weren't," said Vince. "I'd have given you something, my lad. But, I say, Ladle, drop it. I wouldn't have told you about that if I'd known you were always going to fire it off at me."

"Well it does seem so comic for a fellow to go stuffing himself with cold pudding, and then begin dreaming he was hanging at the end of our rope."

"Look here," said Vince sharply, "if you'd felt what I did that day, though I didn't say much, I'll be bound to say you'd have dreamed of it after."

"I felt bad enough," said Mike, suddenly growing serious, as they walked together over the heathery land, unwittingly taking the direction of the scene of their adventure; "and I don't mind telling you, Cinder, that I've woke up four nights since with a start, fancying I was trying to hold the rope, and it kept slipping through my fingers. Ugh! it was very horrid."

He laid his hand on Vince's shoulder, and his companion followed his example, both walking along very silently for a few minutes before Vince said quietly:

"I say, you won't grin if I tell you something?"

"No: honour bright."

"Well, let's see: it was last Thursday week we went, wasn't it?"

"Yes."

"I've been thinking about it ever since."

"So have I: not about the rope business, you know, but about that place. It's just as if something was always making me want to go."

Vince let his hand drop, shook himself free, and faced his companion.

"But that's just how I feel," he said. "I keep on thinking about it and wanting to go."

"Not to try and get down with a rope?" said Mike excitedly.

"Brrrr! No!" exclaimed Vince, with a shudder. "I don't say I wouldn't go down with a rope from the cliffs if it was to help some poor chaps who were wrecked and drowning, because that would seem to be right, I suppose, and what one would expect any fellow to do for one if being drowned. Why, you'd go down then, Ladle."

"I d'know. I shouldn't like to; but when one got excited with seeing a wreck, perhaps I should try."

"There wouldn't be any perhaps about it, Ladle," said Vince gravely. "Something comes over people then. It's the sort of thing that makes men go out in lifeboats, or swim off through the waves with ropes, or, as I've read, go into burning houses to get people out."

Mike nodded, and they went on very thoughtful and dreamy over the purple heather and amongst the golden furze till they reached the edge of the scrub oak wood, where they stopped short and looked in each other's eyes again.

"What do you say? shall we go and have another look at the place?"

"I feel as if I should like to," replied Mike; "and at the same time I'm a bit shrinky. You won't do anything risky, will you?"

"That I just won't," said Vince decisively.

"Then come on."

They plunged into the wood eagerly, and being more accustomed to the way they got along more easily; and decided as they walked that they would go to the southern end of the slope and then try and get up to have a look over the ridge from there, while afterwards they would make their way along the landward side of the jagged serrations of weather-worn granite points right to the northern end if they could get so far, and return at the bottom of the slope.

"That'll be more than any one in the Crag has ever done," said Vince, "and some day we'll bring Mr Deane, and see what he'll say to it."

Little more was said, but, being of one mind, they steadily went on fighting their way through the difficulties which beset them on all sides, till, hot, weary and breathless, they neared the slope some considerable distance from the spot where they had approached it first. Then, after a short rest, they climbed up, over and among the fallen rocks, with nothing more to startle them than the rush of a rabbit or two, which went scuttling away.

Half-way up they saw a couple of those fast disappearing birds, the red-legged choughs, and startled a few jackdaws, which went off shouting at them, Mike said; and then the top was won, and they had a long survey of the cove from another point of view.

But there was nothing fresh to see; all beneath them was entirely hid from view, and though they looked again and again as they continued their course along the ridge their patience and toil were not rewarded, for, save that they were from different standpoints, the views they obtained of the rocks and rushing waters were the same.

They continued along the ridge by slow climbing for a considerable distance, and then as if moved by the same spirit they stopped and looked at each other.

"I say," said Mike, "it don't seem any good to go any farther."

"No," was the reply, given in a very decisive tone. "The only way to see that place down below is to get there in a boat."

"And old Joe Daygo says it's not right to go, and we should never get back; so we shall never see it."

"I don't believe that," said Vince shortly.

"Well, I don't want to, but it seems as if he's right, and the more one looks the more one believes in him."

"I don't," said Vince. "The more I look the more I seem to want to go and have a thorough good search, and I can't help thinking he knows why."

"Shall we try him again?"

Vince thoughtfully shook his head, as he gazed down once more from between two pieces of granite that the storms of centuries had carved till they seemed to have been set upon edge.

"Might offer him some money."

"I don't believe he'd like it, and you know Jemmy Carnach once said that, though he always dressed so shabbily and never spent anything, he always was well off."

"Well, then, what are we to do? I want to see the place worse than ever. It looks so tempting, and as if there's no knowing what we might find."

"I don't think we should find anything about it but that it would be a good place for fishing. It must be if no one ever goes there. Why, Ladle, all the holes among the rocks must swarm with lobsters, and the congers must be as big as serpents."

Mike nodded.

"But how are we to get there to fish for them?"

"Don't know, unless we try it ourselves with a boat."

"Would you risk it?"

Vince did not answer for a few moments, but stood clinging to the rock, gazing down and searchingly examining the opening through which the tide poured.

"I'm not sure yet," he said; "but I begin to think I would. That narrow passage would look wider when you were right in it, and the way to do it would be to come in when the tide was high,—there wouldn't be so much rushing and tumbling about of the water then; and the way to get out again would be at high water too."

"But that would mean staying till the tide had gone down and come up again—hours and hours."

"Yes," said Vince, "that would be the way; but it would want ever so much thinking about first."

"Yes," replied Mike; "it would want ever so much thinking about first. Ready to go back?"

"May as well," said Vince; and he stepped down, after a farewell look down at the sheltered cove, fully realising the fact that any one passing it a short distance from the shore would take the barrier of rocks which shut it in for the continuation of the cliffs on either side; and as the place had a terrible reputation for dangerous reefs and currents, in addition to the superstitious inventions of the people of the Crag, it seemed highly probable that it had never been approached unless by the unfortunate crew of some doomed vessel which had been battered to pieces and sunk unseen and unheard.

"Shall I go first?" said Vince.

"Yes: you lead."

"Mean to go along among the bushes at the bottom, or would you like to slope down at once?"

"Oh, we'll go back the way we said, only we shan't have done as much as we promised ourselves."

Vince started off down the slope, and upon reaching the trough-like depression at the bottom he began to work his way in and out among the fallen blocks, leaping the hollows wherever there was safe landing on the other side. At times he had to stop to extricate himself from the brambles, but on the whole he got along pretty well till their way was barred by a deeper rift than they had yet encountered, out of which the brambles and ferns grew luxuriantly.

The easier plan seemed to be to go round one end or the other; but it only appeared to be the simpler plan, for on trying to put it to the test it soon proved itself to be the harder, promising as it did a long, toilsome climb, whichever end they took.

"Jump it," said Mike: "there's a good landing-place on the other side."

"Yes, but if I don't reach it I shall get a nice scratching. Look at that blackthorn covered with brambles."

"Oh, never mind a few thorns," said Mike, grinning. "I'll pick them all out for you with a packing needle."

"Thankye," said Vince, eyeing the rift he had to clear: "you'll have enough to do to pick out your own thorns, for if I go down I'm sure you will. Stand aside and let's have a good start."

There was no running, for it was a standing jump from one rugged block to another a little lower; and after taking a good swing with both arms, the lad launched himself forward, drawing his feet well up, clearing the mass of tangled bushes below, and just reaching the other side with his toes.

An inch or two more would have been sufficient; as it was, he had not leaped quite far enough, for his boots grated and scratched down the side facing him, the bushes below checked him slightly, and he tried to save himself with his hands and clung to the rough block for a few moments. Then, to Mike's great amusement, he slipped suddenly lower, right in among the brambles which grew from out of a rift, and looked matted enough together to support him as he hung now by his hands.

"Scramble up, Cinder!" cried Mike. "You are a jumper!"

"Wait till you try it, my lad," was the reply; and then, "Must drop and climb out at the end."

As Vince spoke his hands glided from their hold, and he dropped out of sight among the bushes, and at the same moment, to Mike's horror, there was the rushing noise of falling stones, increasing to quite an avalanche, and sounding hollow, echoing, and strange, as if descending to a terrific depth.

Mike's heart seemed to stand still as he craned forward, gazing at the slight opening in the brambles which his companion had made; and as he listened intently he tried hard to speak, but his mouth felt dry, and not a word would come.

It was horrible. They had both imagined that they were about to leap over a hollow between some masses of stone, probably two, perhaps three feet deep; but the bushes and brambles which had rooted in the sides had effectually masked what was evidently a deep chasm, penetrating to some unknown distance in the bowels of the earth.

What to do? Run for help, or try to get down?

Before Mike could decide, in his fear and excitement, which, he drew his breath heavily, with a gasp of relief, for a voice sounding hollow and strange came up through the bushes and ferns.

"Mike!"

"Yes. Hullo, are you hurt?"

"Bit scratched," came up.

"How far are you down? Tell me what to do. Shall I go for a rope?"

"Steady!" came up: "don't ask so much at once. Not down very far. I can see the light, and it's all of a slope here, but awful lower down. Did you hear the stones go with a rush?"

"Yes, yes; but Vince, old chap, tell me how I am to help you."

"I can't: I don't know. I think I can climb out, only I hardly like to stir for fear of a slip. Here goes, though. I can't stay like this."

Mike stood gazing down at the bushes, trembling with anxiety as he heard a rustling and scraping sound beneath, which made him long to speak and ask questions about how his companion got on, but he feared to do so lest he should take his attention from the work he had on hand. Then came the rattle of a falling stone going slowly down, as if there were a good, steady slope; and the boy listened for its plunge into water far beneath, but the falling of the stone ceased to be heard, while the rustling and scraping sound made by the climber increased. Then all at once the bushes began to move and a hand appeared at the far end.

"Take care! pray take care!" cried Mike. "Don't—pray don't slip back!"

"Oh, it's all right now," said Vince, to the watcher's great relief. "It's all of a slope here, as if it had once been a place where water ran down. Wait a moment till I get out my knife."

There was a pause, during which Mike climbed round to the end where Vince was trying to get out; and he was there by the time his companion began hacking at the brambles with his big knife, first his arm appearing and soon after his head, as he chopped away, getting himself free, and seizing the hand extended to him from where Mike knelt and reached down.

"Hah!" cried Vince, as he climbed on to one of the rugged blocks, "that wasn't nice. It slopes down from here, so that where I fell through I must have dropped a dozen feet; but I came down standing, and then fell this way on my hands and stopped myself from sliding, when a lot of stones that had been waiting for a touch went down."

"But are you hurt?" cried Mike anxiously.

"Not much: bit bruised, I suppose. But I say, isn't it rum? There must have been water running to make a place like that. It must have come all along the bottom, where we've been creeping, and run down here, eating its way, like your father and mine were talking about one evening."

"I'd forgotten," said Mike. "But if it ran down there, where did it go to?"

"Down to the sea, of course, and— I say, Mike, don't you see?" cried Vince excitedly.

"See? See what?" said the lad, staring.

"What I said."

"How could any one see what you said!" cried Mike, ready enough to laugh now that his companion was out of danger.

"Oh, don't be stupid at a time like this!" grumbled Vince excitedly. "Once water begins to eat away, it goes on eating a channel for itself, like it does at the waterfall over the other side of the island. Well, this must have cut itself a way along. It's quite a big, sloping passage, and it must go down to the shore. Can't you see now?"

"I don't know. Do you mean that hole leads down to the shore?"

"Yes, or into some cavern like the great holes where the stream runs out into the sea."

"Then it would be a way down into the Black Scraw?" cried Mike excitedly.

"Of course it would. Why, Mikey, we've found out what we were looking for!"

"You mean you tumbled upon it," said Mike, laughing.

"Tumbled into it," cried Vince, whose face was flushed with eagerness. "Come on down, and let's have a look if I'm not right."

"What, down there?"

"Yes, of course."

"But isn't it dark?"

"Black enough lower down; but you can see the top part, because the light shines through all these brambles and thorns."

"But hadn't we better wait till I've got a lanthorn and the rope?"

"Why, of course, before we try to explore it; but we might go and look a little way. You're not afraid?"

"No, I don't think I'm afraid," said Mike.

"Then come on."

Without a moment's hesitation Vince began to lower himself down where he had so lately emerged, and Mike followed; but in a few minutes they had decided that they could do nothing without a light. All they could make out was that there was a rugged slope, very steep and winding, going right away in the direction of the sea. They picked up the loose stones beneath their feet, and threw them into the darkness, and listened to hear them go bounding down, striking the sides and floor; but there seemed to be no precipitous fall, and at last, thoroughly satisfied with their discovery, they climbed back into daylight, and sat down on the stones to rest and think.

"I've got it!" said Mike suddenly. "It isn't what you think."

"What is it, then?"

"An old mine, where they bored for lead in the old, old days."

"No," said Vince stubbornly, "it's what I say—the channel of an old stream; and you'll see."

"So will you, my lad, when we bring a lanthorn. I say you'll find the walls sparkling with what-you-may-call-it—you know—that glittering lead ore, same as we've got specimens of in the cabinet at home."

"No," said Vince; "you'll find that it'll be all smooth, worn granite at the sides, where the water has been running for hundreds of years."

"Till it all ran away. Very well, then: let's go back at once and get a lanthorn and the rope."

Vince laughed. "We've got to get home first, and by the time we've done that we shan't want to make another journey to-day; but I say to-morrow afternoon, directly after dinner. Are you willing?"

"Of course."

"And you'll bring the rope?"

"To be sure; and you the crowbar and hammer?"

Vince promised, and sat there very thoughtful, as he gazed down at the hacked-away brambles.

"Let's put these away or throw them down," he said.

"Why?"

"Because if Old Daygo came along here, he'd see that some one had found a way down into the Scraw."

"Daygo! What nonsense! I don't believe he ever was along here in his life."

"Perhaps not; but he may come now, if he sees us spying about. I'm sure he watches us."

"And I'm sure you've got a lot of nonsense in your nut about the old chap. Now then, shall we go?"

"Yes; I'm willing. Think we can find it again?"

"Easily," said Mike. "Look up yonder: we can take those two pieces of rock up on the ridge for our bearings. They stand as two ends of the base A B, as Mr Deane would say, and if you draw lines from them they will meet here at this point, C. This hole's C, and we can't mistake it."

"No. But look here: this is better still. Look at that bit of a crag split like a bishop's mitre."

"Yes: I see."

"We've got to get this laid-down rock in a line with it, and there are our bearings; we can't be wrong then."

"No," cried Mike. "Who wouldn't know how to take his bearings when he's out, and wants to mark a spot! Now then, is it lay our heads for home?"

It was a long while before either of them slept that night for thinking of their discovery, and when they did drop off, the dark, tunnel-like place was reproduced in their dreams.

# Chapter Nine
## Study versus Discovery

"Dear, dear, dear, dear!" in a tone full of reproach, and then a series of those peculiar sounds made by the tongue, and generally written "tut-tut-tut-tut!" for want of a better way—for it is like trying to express on paper the sound of a Bosjesman's *click cluck* or the crowing of a cock.

The speaker was Mr Humphrey Deane—a tall, pale, gentlemanly-looking young university man, who, for reasons connected with his health, had arranged with Sir Francis Ladelle and the Doctor to come and stay at the Mount, where he was to have a comfortable home and the Doctor's attendance, a moderate stipend, and, in exchange, to help on the two lads in their studies every morning, the rest of the day being his own.

The plan had worked admirably; for Mr Deane was an earnest, able man, with a great love of learning, and always ready to display a warm friendship for boy or man who possessed similar tastes. The lads liked him: he was always firm, but kindly; and he possessed that wonderful power of imparting the knowledge he possessed, never seeming at a loss for means to explain some puzzling expression in classic lore, or mathematical problem, so as to impress it strongly upon his pupil's mind.

The morning he uttered the words at the beginning of this chapter he was seated with the two boys in the long, low library at the Mount, whose heavy windows looked out upon a great, thick, closely-cropped yew hedge, which made the room dark and gloomy, for it completely shut off all view of the western sea, though at the same time it sheltered the house from the tremendous gales which swept over the island from time to time.

It was the morning after the discovery in so unpleasant a manner of the hole at the foot of the slope, and their projected visit of investigation in the afternoon so filled the lads' heads that there did not seem to be any room for study; and, in consequence, after patiently bearing the absence of mind and inattention of his pupils for a long time, the tutor began to be fidgety and, in spite of his placid nature, annoyed.

The Latin reading and rendering went on horribly, and the mathematics worse. Vince tried hard; but as soon as he began to write down $a + b - c =$ the square root of $x$, his mind wandered away to the rocks over the Black Scraw. For that root of $x$ was so suggestive: $x$ represented the unknown quantity, and the Black Scraw was the unknown quantity of which he wanted to get to the root; and, over and over again, when the tutor turned to him, it was to find the boy, pen in hand, but with the ink in it dried up, while he sat gazing straight before him at imaginary grottoes and caverns, lit up by lanthorns which cast the black shadows of two explorers behind them on the water-smoothed granite floor.

But this did not apply only to Vince, for Mike was acting in a similar way; and at the end of an hour Mr Deane could bear it no longer, for it had happened at a time when he was not so well as usual, and it required a strong effort of will to be patient with the inattentive lads when suffering pain.

And so it was that at last he uttered the "dear dears" and "tut tuts," and roused the two boys from their dreams about what they would see in the afternoon.

"Are you unwell, Vincent Burnet?" he said.

"Unwell, sir?—oh no!" said the lad, colouring a little.

"You seem so strange in your manner this morning; and Michael Ladelle here is the same. I hope you are not both sickening for something."

"Oh, I'm quite well, sir," said Mike hurriedly. "Perhaps it's the weather."

"Perhaps it is," said Mr Deane drily. "Now, pray get on with those problems."

"Yes, of course," cried Vince; and he began to work away most industriously, till, as the tutor was resting his head upon his hand and looking down at the paper upon which he was himself working out the problem he had set the boys, so as to be able to show them, step by step, how it was best done, Mike scribbled something on a scrap, shut it in a book, and passed it to Vince, after glancing across the table and then giving him a nudge.

Vince glanced across too; but Mr Deane was apparently intent upon the problem, his delicate right-hand guiding the new quill pen, and forming a long series of beautifully formed characters which were always looked upon by the boys with envy and surprise.

Vince opened the book at the scrap of paper and read:

"I say: let's tell old Deane, and make him go with us."

Vince turned the paper over and wrote:

"What for? He'd spoil it all. Want to knock all the fun out of our discovery?"

The scrap was shut up in the book and pushed back to the sender; the work continued, and then came another nudge and the book once more, with a fresh scrap of paper stuck in.

"I say, I can't get on a bit for thinking about the Black Scraw."

Vince wrote on the back:

"More can I. Get on with your work, and don't bother."

This was forwarded by library table post, and then there was nothing heard but the scratching of the tutor's pen. But Mike's restlessness increased: he fidgeted and shuffled about in his chair, shook the table, and tried all kinds of positions to help him in solving his algebraic problem, but without avail. Scrub oaks, ravens and red-legged choughs danced before his eyes; great dark holes opened in the rocks, and the desire to finish work, get out in the bright sunshine, and run and shout, seemed more than he could bear.

At last, to relieve his feelings a little, he took a fresh piece of paper, laid it over his pluses and minuses and squares and cubes, and then wrote enigmatically:

"Lanthorn and rope."

This he blotted, glanced at the hard-working student across the table, and then thrust it sidewise to Vince, who took it, read it, and, turning it over, wrote:

"You be hanged!"

He was in the act of blotting it when the pen dropped from Mr Deane's fingers; he sat up, and extended his hand as he looked sternly across the table.

"Give me that piece of paper, Vincent," he said.

Vince hesitated; but the tutor's eyes gazed firmly into his, and wrong yielded to right.

He passed the paper across to Mr Deane, and then nearly jumped out of his chair, for Mike gave him a violent kick under the table.

"To be paid with interest," thought Vince.

"Oh! you jolly sneak, to give it up!" thought Mike, as the tutor read the paper on both sides.

"I am very sorry," he said, after coughing to clear his voice—"very sorry to have to exercise my authority towards you two, who have been acting this morning like a pair of inattentive, idle schoolboys; but when I undertook to act as your tutor, it was with the full understanding that I was to have complete authority over you, and that you were both to treat me with proper respect."

The boys sat silent and feeling horribly guilty. If Humphrey Deane had been an overbearing, blustering personage, they might have felt ready to resent his words; but the injured tone, the grave, gentle manner of the invalid went right home to both, and they listened, with their eyes upon their scanty display of work, as the tutor went on.

"You both know," he said, "that my health will not permit of much strain, but so long as you both work with me and try your best, it is a pleasure to me, and no one could feel more gratification than I do when you get on."

"Mr Deane," began Vince.

"One moment, and I have done," continued the tutor. "You well know that I try to make your studies pleasant."

"Yes, sir," said Mike.

"And that when the morning's work is over I am only too glad to join you in any amusement or excursion. I ask you, then, is it fair, when you see I am unwell, to make my endeavours to help you a painful toil, from your carelessness and inattention?"

"No, Mr Deane," said Vince quickly; "it's too bad, and I'm very sorry. There!"

"Thank you, Burnet," said the tutor, smiling. "It's what I expected from your frank, manly nature."

"Oh, and I'm sorry too," said Mike quickly; but he frowned slightly, for the speaker had not called him frank and manly.

"I have no more to say," said the tutor, smiling at both in turn; "and I suppose I ought to apologise for insisting upon seeing that paper. I am glad to find that it was not of so trifling a nature as I thought for on Michael Ladelle's part, though I am sorry that you, Burnet, treated the note he passed you in so ribald a way. 'You be hanged!' is hardly a gentlemanly way of replying to a historical memorandum or query such as this: 'Lanthorn and rope.' Of course, I see the turn your thoughts had taken, Michael."

The boys stared at him wonderingly. While they had been suspecting old Joe Daygo of watching them, had Mr Deane been quietly observing them unnoticed, and had he divined that they were going to take lanthorn and rope that afternoon?

"Of course, history is a grand study," continued the tutor, "and I am glad to see that you have a leaning in that direction; but I like to be thorough. When we are having lessons on history let us give our minds to it, but when we are treating of algebra let us try to master that. There—we will say no more. I am glad, though, that you recall our reading; but try, Michael, to remember some of the other important parts of French history, and don't let your mind dwell too much upon the horrors of the Revolution. It is very terrible, all that about the excesses of the mob and their mad hatred of the nobility and gentry—*A bas les aristocrates!* and their cry, *A la lanterne!* Yes: very terrible those ruthless executions with the lanthorn and the rope. But now, please, I have finished that compound equation. Pray go on with yours."

The two lads bent down now earnestly to their work, and with a little help mastered the puzzle which had seemed hopeless a short time before. Then the rest of the morning glided away rapidly, and Vince hurried off home to his midday dinner, after a word or two about meeting, which was to be at the side of the dwarf-oak wood, to which each was to make his way so as not to excite attention, and in case, as Vince still believed, Daygo really was keeping an eye upon their movements.

"I thought as much," said Vince aloud, as he reached the appointed place, with a good-sized creel in his hand, the hammer and crowbar being in a belt under his jersey, like a pair of hidden weapons. "I'd go by myself if I had the rope."

"And lanthorn," said Mike, raising his head from where he had been lying hidden in a clump of heather.

"Hullo, then!" cried Vince joyously. "I didn't see you there. But, I say: lanthorn and rope! I felt as if I must burst out laughing."

"Yes: wasn't it comic?"

"I felt that I must tell him—poor old chap!—and as if I was trying to cheat him."

"Oh no, it wasn't that! We couldn't help him taking the wrong idea. I'd have told him at once, only it seems to spoil the fun of the thing if everybody knows. But come on."

"Wait a minute," said Vince, sitting on a stone. "I want to look all round first without seeming to. Perhaps old Joe's watching us."

"If he is," said Mike sagely, "you won't see him, for he'll be squatted down by some block of stone, or in a furze bush. He's a regular old fox. Let's go on at once. But where's the lanthorn?"

"Never you mind about the lanthorn: where's the rope?"

"Lying on it. Now, where's the light?"

"In the creel here," was the reply. Then without further parley they plunged into the wood, and, profiting by former experiences, made their way more easily through it into the rocky chaos beyond; threaded their way in and out among the blocks, till at last with very little difficulty they found their bearings, and, after one or two misses in a place where the similarity of the stones and tufts of furze and brambles were most confusing, they reached the end of the opening, noted how the old watercourse was completely covered in with bramble and fern, and then stepped down at once, after a glance upward along the slope and ridge, to stand the next minute sheltered from the wind and in the semi-darkness.

# Chapter Ten
# A Venturesome Journey

"Mind how you go," said Mike in a subdued voice, for the darkness and reverberation following the kicking of a loose pebble impressed him.

"All right: it's only a stone. It was just down there that I slipped to. Ahoy!"

He shouted softly, with one hand to his mouth, and his cry seemed to run whispering away from them to echo far beneath their feet.

"I say, don't do that," said Mike excitedly.

"Why not? Nobody could hear."

"No; but it sounds so creepy and queer. Let's have a light."

It did sound "creepy and queer," for the sounds came from out of the unknown, which is the most startling thing in nature, from the fact that our busy brains are always ready to dress it up in the most weird way, especially if the unknown lies in the dark.

But no more was said, for Vince was busy opening his basket, out of which he drew an old-fashioned horn lanthorn and gave it to Mike to hold, while he took something else out of the creel, which rattled as it was moved.

"Why, you've only brought half a candle," said Mike, who had opened the lanthorn, and held it so that the rays which streamed down through the brambles overhead fell in its interior. "What shall we do when that burns out?"

"Light one of the pieces I've got in my pockets," said Vince coolly, as he sat down on the water-worn granite, and placed a round, flattish tin box between his knees. "Didn't bring a cushion with you, did you?"

"Cushion? No; what for?"

"One to sit on: this is precious hard."

And then *scratch, scratch*: a rub of a tiny wax match upon the sanded side of a box, and a flash of red, dim light followed by a clear white flame?

Nothing of the kind: matches of that sort had not been invented fifty or sixty years ago. Whoever wanted a light had to go to work as Vince prepared to do, after placing a thin slip of wood sharpened at each end and dipped in brimstone ready to hand. Taking a piece of steel or iron bent round so as to form a rough handle to be grasped, while the knuckles were guarded by the edge of the steel, this was held over the tin box, which was, on the inner lid or press being removed, half full of burned cotton ash now forming the tinder that was to catch the sparks.

Vince was pretty handy at the task from old experience, and gripping the box tightly between his knees he made the hollow, cavernous place echo again as he struck the steel in his left hand with a piece of sharp-edged flint held in his right.

*Nick, nick, nick, nick*—the nearly forgotten sound that used to rise in early morning from the kitchen before a fire could be lit—and *nick, nick, nick, nick* again, here in the narrow opening, where the rays of sunshine shot down and made the sparks which flew from flint and steel look pale as they shot downward at every stroke the lad gave.

Mike felt nervous at the idea of penetrating the depths below them, and to hide this nervousness he chattered, and said the first thing that came to his lips in a bantering tone:

"Here! you are a fellow to get a light. Let me have a try."

But as he spoke one spark fell upon the tinder and seemed to stay, while as soon as Vince saw this he bent down and blew, with the result that it began to glow and increase in size so much that when the brimstoned point of the match was applied to the glowing spot still fanned by the breath the curious yellow mineral began to melt, sputter, and then burst into a soft blue flame, which was gradually communicated to the wood. This burned freely, the candle in the lanthorn was lit, the door shut, and the tinder-box with flint and steel closed and smothered out and returned to the creel.

"You'd have done it in half the time, of course," said Vince, rising and slinging the creel on his back. "Now then, are you going to carry the lanthorn?"

"I may as well, as I've got it," said Mike.

"All right: then you'll have to go first."

Mike felt disposed to alter the arrangement, but he could not for very shame.

"You take the rope, then. But, I say, you needn't carry that creel as well," he said.

"I don't want to; but suppose the candle goes out?"

"Oh, you'd better take it," said Mike eagerly. "Ready?"

"Yes, if you are."

Mike did not feel at all ready, but he held the lanthorn up high and took a step or two forward and downward, which left the sunlit part of the place behind, and then began cautiously to descend a long rugged slope, which was cumbered with stones of all sizes, these having evidently fallen from the roof and sides, the true floor of the tunnel-like grotto being worn smooth by the rushing water which must at one time have swept along, reaching in places nearly to the roof just above the boys' heads.

The way was very steep, and winding or rather shooting off here and there, after forming a deep, wonderfully rounded hollow, in which in several cases huge rounded stones lay as they had been left by the torrent, after grinding round and round as if in a mill, smoothing the walls of the hollow, and at the same time making themselves spherical through being kept in constant motion by the water. These pot-holes, as a geologist would call them, are common enough in torrents, where a heavy stone is borne into a whirlpool-like eddy, and goes on grinding itself a deeper and deeper bed, the configuration of the rock-walls where it lies having prevented its being swept down at the first, while every year after it deepens its bed until escape becomes impossible.

Again and again, as they went on, places of this kind were met with; while twice over they had to pause at spots where the water must have sprung from a shelf ten or a dozen feet down into a basin which it had hollowed for itself in the course of time.

Upon the first of these sudden drops presenting itself Mike stopped with the lanthorn.

"Here's the end of it," he said. "Goes down into a sort of bottomless pit, black as ink. Let's go back."

Vince stepped close to his side and gazed down into the black depths with a feeling of awe, the place looking the more terrible from the fact that the tunnel had narrowed until there was only just room for them to stand between the smooth granite walls.

"Looks rather horrid," said Vince. "Worse than a big well. Let's see how deep it is."

He stepped back and picked up a stone that had fallen from the roof, returning to where Mike held up the lanthorn for him to see.

Down went the block of stone, and they prepared themselves to hear it go bounding and echoing far away in the bowels of the earth; but it stopped instantly with a loud clang, and Vince cried,—

"Why, it isn't deep at all! I can see it."

A ring or two of the rope was cast loose, passed through the handle of the lanthorn, and upon lowering it down block after block presented itself sufficient to enable them to descend into what proved to be quite a hollow, from which the stream must have leapt into another and again into another, each being a fall of only a few feet. After which there was another great pot-hole, like a vast mortar with a handleless pestle of rock remaining therein.

Beyond this the water had carved out a rugged trough, steep enough to form a slide if they had felt disposed to trust themselves to it, and Vince laughingly suggested that they should glide down.

"Only it wouldn't do," he added. "We can't tell what's at the bottom. Might mean a bad fall. Had enough of it?"

"Yes, ever since we started," replied Mike.

"Then you want to go back?"

"Oh no, I don't," retorted Mike. "One can't help feeling that one must keep on and see where it goes to, even if it does make you turn creepy. Doesn't it you?"

"Well, yes, I suppose so," replied Vince thoughtfully; "and I wouldn't go on, only it's so easy to climb back, and the air feels fresh and sweet, so that except that it's dark there's nothing to mind."

"But suppose the candle went out. How much is there left?"

As Mike spoke, he opened the door of the lanthorn and looked at the light anxiously, but they had not burned an inch.

"We could easily get another light," said Vince; "and we must go on now. Here, shall I go down first?"

"No; I'll keep to it," cried Mike. "I'm not going to have you jeering at me afterwards and telling me I was afraid. But look here, Cinder: you can't walk down—it really is too steep."

"Let's try the rope: I'll fasten it, and then you can hold on."

"Nothing to fasten it to."

"Soon get over that," said Vince; and, taking out the iron bar and the hammer, he found a crack in the rock directly, into which he drove the narrow edge till it was perfectly firm, the roof just overhead echoing the blows of the hammer so rapidly that in a short time it sounded as if a dozen smiths were at work.

"Stop a moment," cried Mike, as he held the light, and Vince began to tie the end of the rope to the strong iron peg he had formed.

"What for?"

"Suppose when we get down we want the rope for another place, what should we do if we leave it here?"

Vince took the lanthorn and held it out before him, so that he could examine the trough-like slope.

"I shouldn't like to trust myself to slide down here," he said; "but there's nothing to prevent our climbing up. Let's double the rope and hook the middle over the bar; then, when we're down, we can pull one end and get it free."

This was done, and, tying the lanthorn to his neck by means of his kerchief, Mike secured the doubled rope and let himself down, his companion soon after seeing him standing some thirty feet lower.

A minute later Vince was by his side, and they looked about them, but there was nothing fresh to see. The roof was only a foot above their heads. The width of the place averaged six or seven feet, and there was this to encourage them—no branches occurred to form puzzling labyrinths. If they had been overtaken by darkness there was nothing to prevent their feeling their way back into the sunshine. So, growing accustomed to the place, familiarity, if it did not breed contempt, made them cooler and more ready to go on descending over similar obstacles to those they had previously encountered, till all at once Mike stopped short, and held up the lanthorn beneath which he peered.

"What is it?" said Vince anxiously.

"Hark! What's that?" said Mike, in a whisper full of awe.

A dull rushing sound smote upon their ears, but in a muffled, strange way, that puzzled them to make out what it might be.

"I know," said Vince at last: "it's water."

"Think so?" said Mike dubiously.

"Yes. I've been puzzling ever so long to make out how it was that water could have run along here, and for there to be none now, but I see how it is. This was once the channel of the stream, till it ate its way down through the rock to a lower one, and that's it we can hear running somewhere below."

"Perhaps," said Mike; but his words implied doubt, and, after once more examining the candle in the lanthorn, he led on, but very cautiously and slowly now, though the passage was easier, and the slope less broken by step-like faults in the granite, over which the water must once have flowed.

At the end of a dozen yards Mike stopped again, and Vince quite as willingly, for the dull rushing sound continued, and they looked at each other by the light of the lanthorn.

"How far down are we, do you think?" said Mike.

"I dunno. Must be a long way below the sea."

Mike nodded, and Vince continued:

"I thought it led down into the Scraw cove, but we must be lower than that."

"Yes, ever so much; and it strikes me that we might go on down and down for hours. Haven't we done enough for this time?"

"Well, yes," said Vince, in a hesitating tone; "only I should have liked to find out something better than going on and on, just like in one of the caverns on the shore stretched out a tremendous way."

"Yes, I should have liked to see something more; but this is a curious place. Old Deane would like to come down here and see those round stones in the holes."

"We'll bring him some day," said Vince. "Well, suppose we'd better go back, for it seems to be all like this."

"Can't be all like this, because there's water rushing somewhere down below."

"Well, let's go on till we come to the water, and then turn back."

"But if it's very dangerous?"

"We won't go into danger. You keep the lanthorn well up, so that you can see where you go, and then you can stop."

"Suppose you lead now," said Mike: "my arm aches awfully with holding up the light."

"All right: I'll go first, then."

"But I'm not afraid to!" cried Mike hastily.

"Well, I am, Ladle," said Vince frankly; "and I shall go very slowly and carefully, I can tell you. Here, you carry the rope and hammer. Stop a minute, though: how's the light?"

He opened the lanthorn door now, and was surprised to see how little the candle was burned down, but there was a tremendously long snuff with a fungous top.

"I thought it was very dull," he said; and, moistening his fingers, he snuffed the candle. —"Now we shall have a better light."

But unfortunately he had moistened his fingers too much, and the result was that the shortened wick hissed, sputtered, burned blue, and then without further warning went out.

"Oh!" cried Mike, in tones of horror, as they stood there in profound darkness.

"Oh!" was echoed along the passage, and prolonged as if in a groan.

# Chapter Eleven
# The Sea Palace

For a few moments neither of the boys spoke, but stood listening to the dull roaring sound. Then Vince started, for he felt himself touched; and he nearly uttered a cry of horror, but checked it by setting his teeth hard as he grasped the fact that the touch came from Mike's hand, which he seized and found to be cold and damp.

"Let's get back—quick, somehow," gasped the lad.

"Yes: come on. We can feel our way," replied Vince. "Keep hold of hands. No, that would make it harder. Here, give me a piece of the rope, and I'll put it round my waist, then you can hold on by that and follow me. I think I can recollect exactly how it goes."

"Be quick!" said Mike, in an awe-stricken whisper, as he passed several yards of the rope to his companion in misfortune; and this Vince fastened round his waist, and then uttered an ejaculation.

"What is it?" cried Mike: "don't say something else is wrong."

"Wrong? No," cried Vince, whose hands had come in contact with the creel: "I forgot the tinder-box."

"Ah!" cried Mike joyfully; and he pressed close to Vince, as the latter sat down, took out the box, and began nicking away with the flint and steel, making the scintillating sparks flash and send their feeble light in all directions.

"Oh, do make haste!" panted Mike; "that dreadful roaring's coming nearer."

"I can hear it," muttered Vince, as he kept on nicking; but not a spark took hold of the tinder.

"Here, let me try," cried Mike.

"No, not yet: I'll do it. The tinder must have got damp."

"Turn it over, then," cried Mike piteously. "Oh, do make haste."

Vince thrust his fingers into the tinder-box to follow out his companion's instructions, and uttered an impatient sound.

"What is it now?"

"Such an idiot!" cried Vince. "I never took the tin off the top of the tinder."

And so it was that after the disk, which damped out the sparks after a light had been obtained, was removed, the first blow of the flint on the steel sent down a shower, a couple of which caught at once, and were blown into an incandescent state, the match was applied, began to melt, and after a little trouble the sputtering candle once more burned brightly behind the semi-transparent horn, while the roaring sound did not now seem to be so loud.

"I say," said Vince, with a forced laugh, "isn't it easy to feel scared when you're in the dark?"

"Scared? It was awful!"

"But we're not going to give up till we've seen where the water runs?"

Mike remained silent.

"We must do what we meant to do?"

"Very well," said Mike, drawing a deep breath, which was followed by a gasp.

"Come on, then, and let's get it over."

Setting his teeth firmly, Vince once more attacked the unknown, and came upon another sharp turn, where the water must have eddied round, and was reflected almost back upon itself, and then turned away, after another rounded hollow, almost at right angles.

Here the slope became a little more inclined, still not enough to make progress difficult; but as soon as the two windings had been passed, they knew that the goal they had marked out for themselves was at hand, for the noise suddenly became louder, and was unmistakably caused by water rushing over stones.

"Take care!" cried Mike warningly. "You're close to it."

"Yes," cried Vince excitedly; "we are close to it;" and he stopped and held up the lanthorn, so that his hand struck against the roof. "Look there!"

Mike pressed close, and looked at the object which had taken his companion's attention; but for a few moments he realised nothing save that the passage had grown more contracted, and that the roof seemed to be formed by two huge pieces of glistening granite leaning together. Then he looked down and saw that the floor, which was smoother than ever, ran down suddenly, while a faint, damp, salt odour of sea-weed struck upon his nostrils as a puff of air was suddenly wafted up.

"Mind, mind!" he shouted. "Ah!"

For the lanthorn was once more darkened, but not by the candle being extinct. On the contrary, it was burning brightly still, but hidden by Vince drawing his jersey suddenly over the sides.

"It's all right," cried Vince, for there before him was the shape of the end of the passage marked out by a pale, dawn-like light. "Can't you see? We've been fancying we've come down such a tremendous depth, and all the time we were right: the hole has led us to the shore."

But Vince was not quite right, for, upon his drawing the lanthorn out— and none too soon, an odour of singed worsted becoming perceptible—they found that the sudden sharp slope of the granite flooring went down some twenty feet, and upon lowering the light by means of the rope the lanthorn came to rest in soft sand.

"It isn't very light down there," said Vince, whose feelings of nervousness were being rapidly displaced by an intense desire to see more; "but light does come in, and there's the waves running in and out round here. You don't want to go back now, do you?"

"No," said Mike quickly. "Who's to go down first?"

"I will, for I found out what it was."

"All right," said Mike; "but we shall want the rope. How are we to fasten it?"

"There's plenty," said Vince, "and we'll go back and tie it round that last great stone in the hole."

This was done, Mike lighting him; and then, upon their returning, the rope coil was thrown down.

"Here goes!" cried Vince. "Hold the light high up."

Mike raised it on high, and leaned forward as far as he could; while, sitting down and grasping the rope, Vince let himself glide, and the next moment his feet sank deep in soft sand.

"Come on!" he shouted back to where Mike was anxiously watching from twenty feet or so above him. "It's easy as easy. Never mind the lanthorn."

He looked round as he spoke, to see that he was in a large cavern, floored with beautifully smooth, soft sand, and lit up by the same soft grey dawn that had greeted him at the end of the passage, but how it entered the place he could not make out, for no opening was visible, and the rushing, roaring sound of the water came from the lofty roof.

Vince's was only a momentary glance, for Mike was coming slowly down the smooth shoot, sliding on his back, but lowering himself foot by foot, as he held on to the rope.

"There!" cried Vince, as his companion stood beside him, gazing at the rugged walls and lofty roof of the great dry channel; "wasn't this worth coming to see?"

"Why, it's grand," replied Mike, in a subdued voice. "I say, what a place!"

"What a place? I should think it is. I say, Ladle, we've discovered this, and it's all our own. You and I ought to come and stay here when we like. I say, isn't it a size? Why, it must be thirty feet long."

He paced across the rugged hollow, tramping through the soft sand.

"Twelve paces," he cried from the other side. "It's splendid; but I wish it was a bit lighter. There must be somewhere for the light to come in. Yes, I see!"

Vince pointed up at the side farthest from him where he stood, and a little closer investigation showed that the pale soft light appeared to be reflected upward against the roof, coming from behind a screen of rock.

Crossing to this spot, they found that they could pass round the rocky screen, which reached half-way to the ceiling, and they now stood in a narrow passage lit by a soft green light, which came through a low arch, and on reaching and passing through this the boys uttered a shout of delight, for before them was another cavern of ample dimensions, whose low flattened roof was glorious with a lovely, ever-changing pattern, formed by the reflection of the sunlight from the waves outside. They were fascinated for the time by the appearance of the roof, which seemed to be all in motion— lights and shadows, soft as silken weavings, chasing each other, opening, closing, and interlacing in the most wonderful way, till they grew dazzled.

"It's too much to see at one time," whispered Mike at last. "I say! look at the arch with ferns hanging all round like lace."

"Yes, and what a colour the sea is!"

"And the anemones and limpets and coral! Look at those pools, too, among the rocks."

"Yes, and outside at the sea-birds. I say, Ladle! did you ever see anything like it?"

"Never thought there was such a beautiful place in the world," replied Mike softly. "Shall we go any farther?"

"Go any farther? I should think we will! Why, Mikey, this is all our own! Two beautiful caverns, one opening into the other, and all a secret, only known to ourselves. Talk about luck! But come on."

They passed under the arch, and stood in a cavern opening by another arch upon the sea, which rippled and played amongst the sand below, the mouth of the place being protected by ridge after ridge of rock just level with the surface, and sufficient to break the force of the wild currents, which boiled as they rushed by a short distance out. This cavern appeared as if, at some distant period, it had been eaten out of soft or half-decayed strata by the waves; and its peculiarity was the great extent of low, fairly level roof, which in places the lads could touch by tiptoeing and extending their fingers. It ran in at least a hundred feet; and apparently, from the state of the sand, was never invaded by the highest tides, which were pretty exactly marked by the living shells and sea-weed at the mouth.

Everywhere the place was carpeted with soft sand, through which stood up smooth blocks with flattened tops, readily suggesting tables, chairs and couches of the hardest and most durable nature.

They were not long in examining every cranny and crevice inward, fully expecting to find some low arch leading into another or a series of caverns; but they found nothing more, and did not spend much time in examining the place, for the great attraction was the mouth, through which, as if it were a frame, they gazed out at the glittering cove and the barrier of rock, dotted with sea-birds, which hid the open sea beyond.

Making their way, then, to the mouth, and hastily taking off shoe and stocking, they tucked up and began to wade, so as to get outside; but the huge buttresses which supported the rugged arch completely shut them in, running out as they did to where the sea swirled along with tremendous force, and looked so deep and formidable, that the two lads grasped in a moment what the consequences of a slip would be,—no swimmer could have stemmed such a rush.

"It's jolly—it's grand—it's splendid!" cried Vince at last, after they had been paddling about for some time in the shallow water, and stepping on to the low ridges of rock which barred the entrance; "but it's precious disappointing."

"Yes," said Mike; "for we can't see much now, shut-in like this."

It was quite true; for when they had stepped from rock to rock as far as they dared go, they were still in the mouth of the cave, which projected far out over them like a porch, and completely hid the cove on either side and the precipice extending upward to the ridge.

"I want to get round there to the left," said Vince, after gazing thoughtfully along the foot of one large buttress. "It looks shallow there, for the water's pale green. I can't see from here, but I don't believe it's up to one's knees."

"We'll try," said Mike, springing on to the rock, flush with the water, upon which Vince stood, with none too much room.

"Mind what you're doing!"

"Oh my! how sharp the rock is!" shouted Mike, who stood on one leg to pet and comfort an injured toe.

"I shall go along there," said Vince, "and then keep close to the wall."

"But you'll mind and not get in the current. It would take you away directly."

"Just as if it was likely I should risk it, with my clothes on!" said Vince scornfully. "Do you suppose I want a soaking? I think, you know, that if I get along there I shall be able to hold on and look up at this part of the cliffs. 'Tis a pity there isn't a narrow shore, so that you could walk right round."

"Well, take care," said Mike. "Mind, I'm not coming in after you, to get wet."

Vince laughed, and, picking his way, he stepped from stone to stone, till he was only a short distance from the massive wall of the buttress, and not far from where the sun shone upon the water.

"Why, it's as shallow as shallow!" he cried. "I thought it was, it looked so pale and green. I don't believe it's a foot deep, and it's all sand, just like a garden walk; you can wade right out here, Mike, and round by the corner, and I dare say all round the cove like this."

"Oh, do mind!" cried Mike.

"Of course I'll mind. Don't suppose I want to drown myself, do you? What are you afraid of?"

"I'm not afraid."

"Yes, you are. You keep thinking of old Joe's nonsense about the place being full of water bogies and things, when all the time there's nothing but some dangerous rocks, and the sharp eddies and currents. Why, I haven't even seen a fish!"

"Well, I have," said Mike. "I can see the mullet lying down here in the still black water, so thick that they almost touch one another."

"You can? Well, I'll come and have a look presently. Here goes for a wade."

Vince gave the bottoms of his trousers an extra roll, so as to get them as high as possible above his knees, and leaning forward from where he stood upon a detached block of stone, he rested his hands upon the side of the great buttress, and lowered one foot into the water over ankle, calf, and knee; and then he uttered a cry, and nearly went headlong, but making a violent effort, he wrenched himself back, thrusting the rock with all his might, and came down in a sitting position upon the great stone.

# Chapter Twelve
# Lost in the Darkness

"What was it?" cried Mike excitedly: "something get hold of your leg?"

"No," replied the boy, with a shiver, as his face turned clayey-looking. "Yes."

"What was it—crab or a conger?"

"Something ever so much worse," said Vince, with a shiver. "It looks quite hard down there, and all as tempting as can be; but it's loose quicksand, and my foot went down into it just as if it was so much sticky oil. There's no getting along there."

"Lucky you hadn't let go," said Mike sympathetically. "Good job we found out as we have. It might have been much worse."

"Worse? Why, I nearly went right in. And then I should have been sucked down. Ugh!"

Vince shuddered; but the colour began to come naturally again into his cheeks, and after a bit he laughed as they waded back into the cavern—being particularly careful, though, in spite of the roughness, to plant their feet on the pieces of shell-dotted stone beneath the surface.

"Yes, it's all very well to laugh," said Mike, in an ill-used tone; "but you're always running risks and getting into some hobble."

"Not such a good little boy as you, Ladle. You never do wrong, and—There, see what you've done now!" cried Vince, as he stood now in the soft, dry sand, and nestled his feet in it to take the place of a towel.

"What have I done now?"

"Come down and left the candle burning. I know you did; and it will have burned into the socket and melted it. How will you like going back in the dark?"

Mike stared at him aghast.

"You did forget, now, didn't you?"

"You never told me to put it out."

"I didn't tell you to eat your dinner to-day, did I?"

"No; but—"

"Where's your common sense? Now we shall have to go all through that dark hole like a couple of worms."

"No, we shan't," cried Mike. "I've got common sense enough to know you said you had some bits of candle in your pocket."

"Humph!" grunted Vince, whose eyes were wandering in all directions about the beautiful cave. "What's the good of candles without something to stick them in? That socket's melted off, I know."

"Soon manage that," said Mike, picking up a large whorled shell. "There's a natural candlestick; and if we hadn't found that, our fists would have done, or we could have stuck the candle on to the lanthorn with some of the grease."

"My word, he is a clever old Ladle!" cried Vince jeeringly. "I say, isn't this dry sand jolly for your legs? Mine are as right as can be."

"Capital," said Mike, who was pulling on his grey knitted socks. "I say, though, we have found out a place. I vote we come often."

"Yes," said Vince. "After a bit we shall be able to step through that dark hole as easily as can be."

"Yes, and in half the time. It's all very well to bounce, but it was queer work coming down."

"I don't bounce, Ladle; I felt squirmy enough. Of course you couldn't help feeling creepy when you didn't know where you were going next."

"Well, I daresay you felt so too."

"Of course I did," continued Vince. "I expected to put my foot in a great crack every minute, and fall right through to Botany Bay."

"Yes," said Mike seriously. "There's something about being in the dark that is queer."

"Till you get used to it," said Vince, jumping up, with his boots laced. "Now, then, look sharp. I want to have another good look round."

"Ready," said Mike. "I say, let's make a fireplace here, and bring wood, and get a frying-pan and a kettle, and cook fish and make tea and enjoy ourselves."

Vince nodded assent.

"Yes," he said; "might sleep here if you came to that. Sand would make a jolly bed and bed-clothes too. I say, we've found a place that some boys would give their heads to have. Why, there's no end to the fun we can have here. We can fish from the mouth."

"Yes, and I found some oysters—put my foot on them."

"And we can bring things by degrees: potatoes and apples and flour. Why, Ladle, old chap, we can beat old Robinson Crusoe all to nothing, and smugglers and robbers and those sort of people. But we must keep it a secret. If any one else knew of this place being here it would be spoiled at once. I say, what's that?"

"What?" said Mike.

"That dark bit there?" and Vince nodded to a spot in the gloomiest part of the cavern, right up in one corner, where the roof rose highest.

"Crack in the rock. There's another just beyond."

"Yes, a regular split. Hope it don't mean that the roofs going to tumble in."

"Not just yet," said Mike, gazing up curiously at the fault in the granite stratum. "We might try where it goes to."

"Want a ladder," said Vince; "and you may carry it, for I'm not going to try and bring that sort of thing down here. I say, there's the place to make a fire, just by the mouth, and then the smoke will all go up outside; and we can wash our fish and keep the place clean. Those pools will be splendid. There's one deep enough to bathe in."

"There, I tell you what," said Mike; "we've got about as splendid a place close to home as any fellows could find if they went all over the world. I say, though, how we could laugh at old Joe if we brought him down and showed him the Scraw has about as beautiful a cave as there is anywhere!"

"I say, don't talk about it. I wouldn't have any one know for the world; and do be careful about smuggling things down here."

"Don't you be afraid of that," said Mike. "Hi, look! There's a shoal of fish out there. Mackerel, I think."

"Oh, the place teems with fish, I'm sure," said Vince, as he watched the shimmering of the surface just in a smooth patch beyond where the sea was troubled. "Now, then, shall we go and look at the other place before we go back?"

"Yes," said Mike, but his tone suggesting no. "I feel as if I could sit down in the sand and look out at the sea and the birds on the rocks there opposite for ever."

"Without getting hungry, I suppose," said Vince. "Come on. It won't be long before we come down again. I say, Ladle, what a place to come to on wet days!"

"Splendid; and I shan't be satisfied till you and I have sailed round here to see if there isn't a way of getting into the bay with a boat."

"We might; but I daresay there isn't. Very likely it's such a race and so full of rocks that we should be upset directly. Come on."

They went down and peered through the low arch into the narrow way between the rocks, and onward into the other chamber, which looked black and dark to them as they entered from the well-lit outer cavern. But in a few minutes their eyes were accustomed to the gloom, and the place seemed filled with a soft, pearly light which impressed Mike, who was the poetical lad of the pair.

"I say," he said softly, "isn't this one beautiful?"

"Not half so beautiful as the other," said Vince bluntly.

"Oh yes, it is so soft and grey. It's just as if it was the inside of a great oyster-shell."

"And you were a pearl," cried Vince, laughing. "Never mind; it is very jolly, though, and if ever we slept here this place would do for bedroom, but I don't think that's very likely. Well, I suppose we'd better go. We've been here a precious long time, and I shall be late for tea."

"Never mind: come home and have tea with me. I don't feel in much of a hurry to go up through that black hole."

"We shan't mind it if it hasn't tumbled in since we came, and shut us up."

"I say, don't!" cried Mike, with a look of horror. "That might be true, you know."

"Yes; but pigs might fly," cried Vince, laughing. "I say, what a chap you are to take fright! Puzzle a stone place like that to tumble in. A few bits might come off the roof, but even then we could crawl over them, for they must leave a hole where they come from. Ready?"

"Yes," said Mike unwillingly, and they walked to the foot of the slide.

"I'll go first," cried Vince; and, seizing the rope, he held on by it, and, shortening his hold as he went, contrived to walk right up to the top, in spite of the great angle at which it stood.

"Try that way, Mike: it's as easy as easy."

The boy tried, and after a slip or two managed to reach the top pretty well. Here it was found that the candle had burned right out, but without injuring the socket; and a fresh piece having been set up, a light was soon obtained, and they started back, after deciding to leave the rope where it was, ready for their next visit, as they did not anticipate any difficulty about climbing back up the various step-like falls.

There was plenty to have detained them during their return journey, for the passage of the little underground river presented a wonderfully different aspect from the new point of view, and often seemed dimly mysterious by the feeble yellow light of the horn lanthorn; but there were no difficulties that a couple of active lads ready to help each other did not readily surmount; and they went on turning curves and loops and corners, mounting places that were once waterfalls, and steadily progressing, till Mike was horrified by one of his companion's remarks.

It was just as they had paused breathless before beginning to climb one of the great step-like impediments.

"I say, Ladle," he cried, "suppose the water was to come back all of a sudden, and begin rushing down here! What should we do?"

But Mike recovered his balance directly.

"Pooh!" he cried; "how could it? I don't believe there has been water along here for hundreds of years."

He began to climb, and they went on again, till it struck Vince seriously that they were a very long time getting out, and he cried, in alarm,—

"I say, we haven't taken a wrong turning, have we?"

His words struck a chill through both, and they stood there speechless for some moments, gazing in each other's dimly seen faces.

"Couldn't," cried Mike at last. "We did not pass a single turning."

"Didn't see a single turning?" said Vince. "No, we did not; but we might easily have passed one going sharply off to right or left, and come along it without noticing."

"I say, don't say that," whispered Mike hoarsely; "it sounds so horrible. Why, we may be going right away from the daylight into some horrible maze of a place underground."

"Seems as if that's what we are doing," said Vince sadly, "or we should have got out by now. We must have borne off to right or left, and—here we are."

"Yes; here we are," chorused Mike, rather piteously; "but it's no use to be dumpy, is it? Let's go back to the cave and start again, unless we can find out where we turned off as we go."

Vince did not reply, but opened the lanthorn, and raised his finger and thumb to his lips to moisten them before snuffing the candle, which was long-wicked, and threatened to gutter down.

"Mind!" cried Mike warningly, as he thought of their former fright.

"Well, I am minding. Didn't you see that I wouldn't wet my fingers? There! that's right."

He cleverly snuffed the candle, which flashed up brightly directly, and seemed to illumine the boy's brain more clearly, as well as the glittering roof and sides of the water-worn passage, for he spoke out sharply directly after.

"Look here, Ladle," he cried, "I don't believe we can have come wrong."

"Don't be obstinate," replied Mike; "we must have come wrong, or we shouldn't be here now."

"I don't know that."

"But I do. See what a while we have been climbing back."

"Yes; because it has all been uphill, and we had so much to think of going that we did not notice how far we went."

"But we've been hours coming back."

"Not we. You were tired, and that's made it seem so long. Come on: the way must be right."

"No; let's turn back. I'm tired, and don't want to do it, but it's the best way."

"But it will take so long," cried Vince.

"It'll take longer if we're going on walking we don't know where," said Mike ominously.

"Oh, come, I say, don't go on like that," cried Vince. "Fellows who are mates ought to try and cheer one another up, and you're doing nothing but cheer one down."

"I must speak the truth," said Mike gloomily.

"Here! do leave off! Why, you're as bad as that old raven out over the Scraw—all croak, croak, croak!"

"I don't want to croak; I only want for us to find the way out. Let's go back and make a fresh start."

"I shan't," said Vince: "we're right now, I'm sure, only we went wrong just now."

"There! I knew it! How far was it back?"

"Just where we took fright and began to fancy we were wrong. Now then, forward."

"No," said Mike firmly; "we'll go back. You are always so rash, and will not think."

"Yes, I will; I'm thinking now!" cried Vince warmly, "and I think that you're about the most pig-headed fellow that there ever was. Now, look here, Ladle, don't be stupid. I'm as sure as sure that we are going right after all, and all we've got to do is to go straight on."

"And I'm sure that we ought to go back."

"I shan't go back!"

"And I shan't go forward!" cried Mike angrily.

"All right, then: I shan't go back. Only mind how you go, old chap: those places where we had to creep down are rather awkward, and you may take the skin off your nose."

"What do you mean by that?" cried Mike.

"Only that I've got the candle," said Vince, laughing. "I'll come and see you to-morrow, and bring you something to eat, for you'll never find your way out again in the dark."

"But I'm not going in the dark, old clever!" cried Mike, snatching the lanthorn suddenly from his companion. "How now?"

"So how!" cried Vince, springing at him, and seizing the light structure of tin and horn.

Then there was a sharp struggle, the two lads swaying here and there in the narrow place, till Vince flung his companion heavily against the wall, giving him so violent a jar as he clung to the lanthorn that the candle was jumped out of its socket, fell over against the side, and before the boys could even think of getting the door open, the light flashed upon their startled faces and went out.

"You've done it now," cried Mike, in a dolorous tone.

"Oh, come, I like that," said Vince. "Who snatched the lanthorn away? Wait till we get out, and you'll see what I'll give you."

"Get out the tinder-box quickly," said Mike.

"What for? Suppose I want you to snatch it away? I'm going on in the dark, same as you're going back."

"Don't be an idiot," cried Mike, who was growing desperate. "Get out the tinder-box and strike a light."

"Good-night," replied Vince tauntingly; "I'm off. Shall I tell them you'll be home to-morrow?"

For answer Mike sprang at him and grasped him tightly.

"No, you don't play me that trick," he cried. "Get out that tinder-box at once."

"Not I," cried Vince.

"Get out that tinder-box at once!"

"Do you want to make me savage?" growled Vince. "I don't care what I make you now," cried Mike. "You're going to strike a light, so that we can find our way out."

"I'm not going to strike a light and go back to please you, Ladle, and so I tell you," said Vince, holding his companion at arm's length, with his teeth set, and a strong desire rising in him to double his fists and strike. "Give me the flint and steel," cried Mike fiercely. For answer Vince wrenched himself free, thrust out his hands, and, guiding himself by the wall, backed softly away and stood motionless, listening to Mike's movements. Then, stooping, he picked up a stone and pitched it over where he supposed Mike to be standing, with the result that it clattered down on the floor.

His anger had evaporated, and his face relaxed into a grin, for his ruse took effect directly. Judging that the noise was made by Vince backing from him, and in his horror and confusion mistaking his way, Mike thrust out his hands and went in the direction of the sound, while, under cover of the noise made, Vince backed still farther, moving as silently as he could.

"Now then," cried Mike, from fully thirty yards away, "it's of no use,—I have you. No more nonsense: take out that box and strike a light."

Vince turned aside to smother his laughter, then turned back to listen.

"Do you hear me?" cried Mike, in a hoarse, excited tone. "You'll be sorry for this. See if I come out with you again!"

Vince remained perfectly still, listening while he heard Mike make a short dash or two in the darkness as if to seize him, kicking up the stones on the floor and once more threatening what he would do when he got hold of his companion again.

Then he shouted louder, his voice echoing along the passage; and at last from far back in the darkness he groaned out:

"Vince! Vince, old chap, don't leave me here all alone!"

That appeal went home to Vince's heart at once.

"Who's going to?" he cried rather huskily. "Come on. This way, old obstinate. Mr Deane's quite right: he always said you would have your own way, even if you knew you were wrong."

"But I am so sure, Cinder—I am indeed," cried the lad, piteously. "It is this way—it is indeed! Oh, do strike a light!"

"There now! I'm going to show you how wrong you are," said Vince triumphantly.

"Not now: let's get out of this dreadful place."

"'Tisn't a dreadful place; it's only you scaring yourself about nothing, same as I did. It's this way. Come along."

"Yes, I'll come," said Mike meekly; "only don't go far, and then let's get back. But do strike a light."

"What for? There's no need. Come along, close up to me."

Mike came, blindly feeling his way, till he touched his companion, and his hands closed tightly upon Vince's shoulder and arm.

"There!" cried Vince, "look straight before you. What can you see?"

Mike uttered a cry of joy, for right upward, and apparently at a great distance, there was a feeble light, and a minute or two later the two lads were beneath the matted roofing of brambles, through which the bright evening glow was streaming. Directly after, they were out upon the surrounding stones, carefully scanning the ridge, to see if they had been observed. But the place was absolutely solitary, and, after hiding the lanthorn down in the rift, the lads started for home in silence, Mike feeling annoyed and aggrieved, while Vince's breast was full of triumphant satisfaction.

"I say," he said, as they reached at last a little opening in among the scrub oak trees, "are we two going to have it out before we go home?"

"No," said Mike shortly.

"Oh! all right, then; only you didn't speak or make any apology when you knew you were wrong."

"Yes," said Mike, after an interval, "I know I was wrong. I'm very sorry, Vince."

"So am I," said the latter, "and something worse."

Mike looked at him wonderingly.

"Yes, ever so much: I'm about half-starved."

Mike made no reply, but walked on in silence for some time, and it was not until they were near home that he turned again and held out his hand.

"I'm very sorry, Vince," he said.

"What about?" cried Vince.

"That we had such a row."

"Oh, bother! I'd forgotten all about it. Don't make any more fuss about that. I say, what a bit of luck! We must keep it quiet, though, eh?"

"Quiet? I wouldn't have any one know for the world!"

# Chapter Thirteen
## A Startling Discovery

The two lads were such close companions, and so much accustomed to wander off together of an afternoon, fishing, cliff-climbing, and collecting eggs, insects, minerals, or shells, that their long absences were not considered at all extraordinary, though they were noticed by both Mrs Burnet and Lady Ladelle, and one evening formed the subject of a few remarks at dinner.

The Doctor and his wife often dined at the old manor-house, and upon this occasion Mike's mother asked her visitors if they did not think they wandered too much.

"No," said Sir Francis, taking the answer out of his guests' mouths laughingly. "Mrs Burnet doesn't think anything of the kind, so don't you put such ideas in her head."

"But they are often so late, my dear."

"Well, it's summer-time, and cooler of an evening. Pleasantest part of the day. If they work well, let them play well. Eh, Burnet?"

"Certainly," said the Doctor, "so long as they don't get into mischief. But do they work well?"

"What do you say, Mr Deane?" said the baronet.

"Admirably," replied the tutor; "but I must say that I should like them to have a couple of hours' more study a day—say a couple of hours in the afternoon."

"No," said the Doctor emphatically. "You work them well with their English and classics and calculations every morning: let them have some of Nature's teaching of an afternoon, and strengthen their bodies after you've done strengthening their heads."

"I side with you, Burnet," said the baronet. "Let them go on as they are for a year or two, and then we'll see."

The tutor bowed. "I only thought I was not doing enough for them," he said apologetically.

"Plenty, my dear sir—plenty. I like to see them bringing home plenty of litter, as the servants call it."

"Yes," said the Doctor, "all's education. I see Lady Ladelle fidgets about her boy, just as my wife does. They'll be all right. They can't go very far from home."

"But I always dread some accident," said Mrs Burnet.

"Yes, my dear, you are always inventing something, and have been ever since Vince broke his leg."

"Through going into dangerous places," said Mrs Burnet.

"Well, yes, that was from a cliff fall; but he might have done it from tumbling off a wall or over a chair."

Just when this conversation was taking place the boys were slowly trudging home from their "retreat," as they called it—coming by a circuitous way, for the fact was very evident that old Daygo did spend a good deal of time in watching the boys' proceedings, and Vince was strongly of opinion that he suspected their discovery.

But Mike was as fully convinced to the contrary.

"He has no idea of it, I'm sure; but he is curious to know where we go. The old chap always talks as if the island belonged to him. He'd better not interfere with it if he does find out; but, I say, fancy old Daygo scrambling down through that passage. I should like to see him."

"I shouldn't," said Vince, "especially after all we've done."

For a month had glided away, and they had been pretty busy, during their many visits to the place, carrying all kinds of little things which they considered they wanted, with the result that the lanthorn and a supply of candles always stood in a niche a short distance down the passage; short ropes were fastened wherever there was one of the sharp or sloping descents, so that they could run down quickly; and in several places a hammer and cold chisel had been utilised so as to chip out a foothold.

In the caverns themselves there was a fireplace, a keg which they kept supplied with water, a small saucepan, a little frying-pan, and a common gridiron, all of which had been bought and brought for them by the skipper of the little smack which touched at the island like a marine carrier's cart once a week.

Then they had an axe and saw, and stored up driftwood for their fire; fishing lines and a good supply of hooks; a gaff and many other objects, including towels—for the pools in the outer cavern's mouth were now their regular places for bathing.

As the time went on the novelty of possessing such a curious secret place did not wear off. On the contrary, the satisfaction it afforded them grew, the more especially that the journey to and fro had become much more simple, for they had picked out the easiest way through the oak wood, knew the smoothest path among the granite blocks, and were always finding better ways of threading the rugged chaos at the bottom of the ridge slope.

As far as they could see ahead it seemed to them that there was nothing more to discover, and they might go on keeping the place entirely to themselves till they were grown up.

But at sixteen or so we do not know everything. It was the day after the conversation at the old manor-house that, after a long morning with Mr Deane, the two boys met as usual, and started in the opposite direction to that which they intended to take, for they had not taken many steps before Vince kicked out sidewise and struck Mike on the boot.

"What did you do that for?" said the other angrily.

"'Cause I liked;" and a tussle ensued, half serious on one side, jocular on the other.

"Now," whispered Vince, "break away and run towards that bay, and I'll chase you."

"What for? What's come to you this afternoon?"

"Don't look round. Old Daygo's sitting under a stone yonder smoking his pipe."

Mike obeyed, running off as hard as he could go, chased by Vince, till they were well out of sight, and then, by making a *détour* of a good half-mile, they reached the oak wood a long way north of their customary way of entrance, and began to plod onward towards their goal.

"That's what they call throwing dust in any one's eyes, isn't it?" said Mike, laughing.

"Yes," said Vince, "and we shall have to make it sand with old Joe. He's getting more and more suspicious, though I don't see why it matters to him. You see, we never go near him now to ask him to take us out fishing, or into one of the west bays to shell, and he thinks we have something else on the way."

"Well, so we have, and— Hullo, Joe! you there?"

"Yes, young gentleman, I'm here," said Daygo gruffly, as he suddenly came upon them in a little opening in the wood. "I thought you'd gone down to the west bays."

"Well, we did think of going; but it's cooler and more shady here. The sun does come down so strongly there under the cliffs. Seen any rabbits?"

"Two on 'em," said the man; "but you won't ketch them. Dog couldn't do it, let alone you. Ounce o' shot's only thing I know that runs fast enough to ketch them."

It was an awkward predicament, and both lads had the same feeling that they would like to go off at once in another direction, only that they shrank from leaving the old fisherman, for fear he should find the way down into the caves.

They wandered on in his company for a few minutes, and then Vince took the initiative and cried,—

"I say, I'm sick of this; it's dreadful. Come out on the common somewhere, so that we can get down to the sea."

"I don't think you can get down anywhere near here. Can you, Joe?" asked Mike.

"Oh yes," said the old man; "easy enough. I'll show you a place if you like."

"Come on, then!" cried Vince eagerly.

"Off here, then," said Daygo; "on'y I ought to tell you that you won't enjy yourselves, for it'll take Doctor Burnet all his time to pull you both together again."

The old fellow burst into a fit of chuckling at this, and looked from one to the other, thoroughly enjoying their disgusted looks.

"There, I knew he was making fun of us. Of course there's no way down," grumbled Mike. "Come on out of this scrimble-scramble place. What's the good of tiring ourselves for the sake of seeing a rabbit's white cotton tail."

Vince was about to follow his companion, but turned to shout after Daygo.

"I say, when are you going to take us fishing again?"

"When you two young gents likes to come; on'y you've both been so mortal proud lately. Never come anigh to me, and as to wanting a ride in a boat, not you. Got one of your own somewheres, I suppose. Hev yer?"

Mike shook his head, and they went on in silence for a few minutes before Mike whispered,—

"What shall we do: creep back and watch him?"

"No. If we did we should come upon him directly. He's watching us, I'm sure. Let's go to the cliff edge somewhere for a bit, and then go to the other side of the island. We shan't get down to the cave to-day."

As far as they could tell they were unobserved the next afternoon, and after exercising plenty of caution they reached the mouth of the little river tunnel and dropped down out of sight one after the other in an instant. In fact, so quick was their disappearance that it would have puzzled the keenest searcher as to where they had gone. For one moment they were standing upon a piece of lichen-covered granite, the next they had leaped in among the brambles, which parted for them to pass through and sprang up again, the lads dropping on to the old stream bed, which they had carefully cleared of stones. They left no footmarks there, and they were careful to preserve the thin screen of ferns and bramble, so that a watcher would have credited them with having ducked down and crept away.

This ruse, trifling as it may seem, added to their enjoyment of their hiding-place, and as soon as they were in darkness they struck a light and went on down to the caves, had a look round, and Mike immediately began to get down the fishing lines which hung from a wooden peg driven into a granite crack.

"Never mind the fish to-day," said Vince, who was busily fixing a fresh piece of candle in the lanthorn.

"Why? We're not hungry now, but we shall be before we go back. Hullo! what are you going to do?"

"Wait a bit, and you'll see," replied Vince, who now took a little coil of rope from where it hung, and then asked his companion's assistance to extricate something which he had placed in the belt he wore under his jersey.

"Why, whatever have you got here?"

"Grapnel," was the reply; and Vince began to rub the small of his back softly. "I say, how a thing like that hurts! It's worse than carrying a hammer. I'm quite sore."

Mike laughed, and again more heartily upon seeing Vince begin to secure the grapnel with a sea-going knot to the length of rope.

"Let those laugh that lose," cried Vince sententiously; "they are sure to who win."

"Enough to make any one laugh," cried Mike. "What are you going to bait with?"

"You, if you like," said Vince sharply, "Wonder what I should catch?"

"Here! no nonsense," cried Mike: "what are you really going to do?"

"What we've been talking about so long. Try and get up through that crack up there."

Mike whistled.

"Why, of course," he said. "What a good idea! But I don't believe it goes in above a foot or two."

"Oh yes, it does," said Vince decisively. "I thought so a little while ago, but last time we came I found out that it goes ever so far, and so I brought this hook."

"And never told me."

"Telling you now, aren't I?"

"But how did you know?"

"Saw a pigeon fly out."

"Well, that proves nothing. It only flew in to settle for a bit, and then came out again."

"That's what I fancied," said Vince, trying his knot by standing upon the grapnel and tugging hard with both hands at the rope; "but I watched while you were lying on your back asleep and saw others go in and come out."

"Well, that only shows that there are several nests there instead of one. I say, let's bring some paste next time we come and make a pigeon pudding of young ones. I'll get our cook to make us some. I'll tell her what we want it for, and she'll think we are going to make a sort of picnic dinner under a rock somewhere."

"Wait a bit, and let's try first," said Vince. "There, I'm ready now. We did talk about examining that great crack when we came, but I thought it wasn't worth the trouble till yesterday. I fancy it leads into another cave."

"Hope it does," said Mike. "Make this place all the more interesting."

"Couldn't," said Vince shortly. "Come along and let's see if I can catch a big fish without a bait."

They went to the darkest corner of the outer cave, where the roof was highest, and after laying the rope ready, Vince took hold of it about two feet from the large triple hook, swung it to and fro several times, and then sent it flying upward towards the roof, where it struck the edge of the jagged crack ten feet or so above their heads and came down with a loud clang.

"One," said Mike. "Three offers out."

"All right: you shall have your innings then," said Vince, picking up the hook, aiming more truly, and again sending it flying up.

This time it passed right up out of sight and fell back, striking the bottom of the crack and glancing off again to the floor, falling silently into the sand.

"Two," cried Mike. "He won't do it."

"Wait a bit," said Vince, and he swung the hook upward. There was a click, and it stayed just within the crack; while the lad laughed. "Now," he cried, "can't I do it?"

"No!" said Mike triumphantly, for at the first jerk of the rope the iron fell back into the sand.

"You don't know how to throw a grapnel," said Mike, picking up the rope. "There, stand aside and I'll show you."

Vince drew back, and after a good deal of swinging, Mike launched the grapnel upward, so that it passed right into the hole some distance from the length of rope which followed; then came a click, and the rope hung swinging from the sloping roof.

"There!" cried Mike.

"It'll come away as soon as you pull it."

Mike gave the rope a tug, then a sharp jerk, and another, before, raising his hands and grasping it as high as he could, he took a run, and then, raising his legs, let himself swing to and fro.

"Bear anything," he cried. "There, you'd better go first."

"You fastened it," said Vince, "so you've got first go."

"No, it was your idea. Up with you! but you've scared the pigeons away."

Vince seized the rope as high as he could reach, twisted it about his leg, pressing the strong strands against his calf with the edge of his shoe-sole, and then began to climb slowly, drawing himself up by the muscular strength of his arms, while the rope began to revolve with him slowly.

"Meat's burning," cried Mike, grinning. "Wants basting;" and he picked up handsful of sand to scatter over the climber's back.

But Vince was too busy to heed his interruption, and by trying hard he soon drew himself right into the narrow crack, and the next minute only his boots were visible, and they were drawn out of sight directly after.

"Well?" cried Mike; "what have you found?"

"Grapnel," panted Vince; for climbing a single thin rope is hard work.

"Yes, but what else?"

"Big crack, which goes right in. Light the lanthorn and fasten, it to the end of the rope."

This was soon done and the light drawn up.

"I say, play fair!" cried Mike, as the lanthorn disappeared; "don't go and do all the fun yourself."

For answer Vince threw him down the rope, which he had freed from the lanthorn.

"Come up," he said shortly; and Mike, who began to be deeply interested, his curiosity now being excited, seized the rope and began in turn to climb.

He was as active as his companion, and as much accustomed to rope work, the pair having often let themselves down portions of the cliff and climbed again in their search for eggs; so that in another minute he too was in the crack, dimly lit by the lanthorn, which Vince had set low down, where the fracture in the rock began to close in towards where it was again solid.

"Don't seem much of a place," said Mike, rising upright, but having to keep himself in that position by resting a foot on either side of the rift. "Goes in, though."

"Yes," said Vince, "and I was right, for the pigeons must have flown through."

"No," said Mike, looking about: "nests somewhere on one of the ledges."

"Are no ledges here," said Vince: "the top goes up to a point. Shall we go on?"

"Of course," said Mike; and, taking up the lanthorn, Vince began to shuffle himself along the narrow, awkward place, till, at the end of a dozen yards, in darkness which grew thicker as he went, the great crack turned suddenly right off to the right, and again directly after to the left.

"Why, it looks just the same shape as a flash of lightning," cried Mike. "Does it get any bigger?"

"Doesn't seem to," was the reply; "but there's plenty of room to walk along."

"Walk? I don't call this walking? I'm going along like a lame duck striddling a gutter. I say, think there's ever been water along here?"

"Sure there hasn't," said Vince, holding the light low down. "Why, you can see. The rock isn't worn a bit, but looks as sharp as if it had only lately been split."

"But what could split it? The lightning?"

"No: father says these rocks crack from the water washing the stuff away from beneath them, and then the tremendous weight does the rest. But I don't know. I say, though, I shouldn't wonder if this goes on into another cave. Look here."

Mike pressed forward, and found, as his companion held up the light, that the fault in the rock shot off sharply now to the left, and sloped up at an angle of some forty-five degrees.

"Looks awkward," said Mike. "Are we going up there?"

"Of course. Why not? We can climb it."

"Oh yes, I can get up there; but it isn't very good for the boots."

Good or bad, Vince did not hesitate, but, lanthorn in hand, commenced the ascent by climbing right in the narrow part of the rift, where each foot became wedged between the sides of the opening, and had to be dragged out again as the next foot was brought over and placed in front.

"Awkward travelling," said Vince; "but you can't slip."

"Begin to feel as if I can," replied Mike—"right out of my shoes. I say, it is awkward."

The distance they had to traverse here, however, was but short, and the next angle showed that the fault was at a much easier slope, while the opening was wider, so that they got along more pleasantly. But at the end of another twenty yards the walls began to close in, and the place looked so uninviting that Mike stopped. "Hadn't we better go back?" he said. "What for?" replied Vince. "Let's see the end of it. We can't make any mistake in going back. There's no roof to fall, and no pits or holes to drop into."

"But it may go on for ever so long; and, I say, I don't believe a pigeon ever flew through here."

"Well, I don't know," said Vince. "It seemed to me as if they did, and—Hurrah, Ladle! I can see light."

"Light? So there is. Look! it must come from round the next corner. That's reflection we can see."

And so it proved: for upon passing the next sharp angle Vince found himself facing the sea, which was visible through a great arch, far larger and more rugged than that in their own cavern mouth. Going on a little farther, he found himself at the end of the singular zigzag passage, which was an opening in the roof of another and larger cavern, and into which they looked down as from a window.

It was lighter and loftier than their own, and, like it, beautifully carpeted with sand; but, to the amazement of the lads, instead of this being smooth and wind-swept, as that of their own place when they first discovered it, the floor was covered with footmarks leading from the mouth inward to where the great cave grew dim and obscure. There were sails, too, and ropes. Several small yards and spars lay together by the side of the wall, and farther in were sails and three or four oars.

But what most took their attention was the fact that, dimly outlined in the higher part of the cave there were little stacks, which looked as if they were built up of packages or bales, side by side with which, carefully stacked in the sand, were dozens upon dozens of small kegs.

As their eyes grew more familiar with the gloom at the upper end, they realised that there were a great number of these bales and kegs, the former being of three kinds, varying a good deal in shape and size.

They neither of them spoke, not daring even to whisper, for the feeling was strong upon them that the next thing they would see must be the figure of some fierce-looking smuggler in big boots, belted, carrying cutlass and pistols, and crowned with a scarlet cap.

Then they started back in alarm, for there was the sharp whirring of wings, and half a dozen pigeons darted out of the cavern, seeming to come from far back beyond the stacks of kegs and bales, and rushing out into the bright light beneath the arch.

It was nothing to mind; but their nerves were on the strain, and they breathed more freely as soon as the birds were gone. It seemed to signify that no human beings were in the higher part of the cavern, and the solemn silence of the place encouraged them at last to speak, but only in whispers.

"Wish we'd brought the rope," said Vince; "we might have got down."

"Ugh! It wouldn't be safe. They might come and catch us."

"Who might?"

"The smugglers."

"Smugglers? There are no smugglers on the Crag."

"Well, those must be smuggled goods, anyhow," said Mike.

"Can't be."

"What are they, then? I'll be bound to say that those little kegs have all got 'Hollands' or French spirits in them, and the packages are silk and velvet, and the other parcels laces and things—perhaps tobacco."

"But we never heard of smuggling here. Who can it be?"

"Well, that's what they are, for certain," said Mike. "It's just like what one's read about. They must be ever so old—a hundred years, perhaps—and been put here and forgotten."

"Perhaps so," said Vince.

"Then we'll claim them for ours," said Mike decisively. "They can't belong to anybody else now. Nobody can be alive who brought them a hundred years ago."

"No," said Vince; "but I don't see how we can claim them. I say, though, it shows that boats can get into the cove."

"Or could at one time."

"Place wouldn't alter much in a hundred years. I do wish, though, we had brought the rope. Perhaps as soon as we touch those bales they'll all tumble into dust."

"And all the kegs have gone dry," said Mike.

"And all we can see before us only so much dust and touchwood. I say, Mike, we shan't be very rich from our find. I do wish we had brought the rope. Let's go back and get it."

"Let's go back soon," replied Mike; "but I don't think we'll come again to-day. My head feels all of a whizz."

"Yes, it is exciting," said Vince thoughtfully. "Perhaps you're right: we won't come back to-day." And, contenting themselves with a long, searching inspection from the window-like place they occupied, they soon after returned, and, after placing the grapnel so that it could be jerked out, went down the rope, got the iron hooks loose, and seated themselves to think.

That evening they got home early, each so full of the great discovery that, when they went to bed, it was long before they slept, and then their brains were busy with strange dreams, in which one was fighting for his life against a host of well-armed men, the victor taking a vessel with the treasure of valuable silks and spices, and making his parents rich people to the last.

But an idea was dominant with both when they woke, soon after sunrise. They must go back to the cavern soon, and probe the mystery to the very end.

# Chapter Fourteen
## Daygo describes Horrors

"Er-her! Going to school! Yer!"

Vince, who had some books under his arm, felt a peculiar twitching in the nerves, as he turned sharply upon the heavy-looking lad who had spoken the above words, with the prologue and epilogue formed of jeering laughs, which sounded something like the combinations placed there to represent them.

The speaker was the son of the Jemmy Carnach who was, as the Doctor said, a martyr to indigestion—a refined way of expressing his intense devotion to lobsters, the red armour of which molluscs could be seen scattered in every direction about his cottage door, and at the foot of the cliff beyond.

As Jemmy Carnach had thought proper to keep up family names in old-fashioned style, he had had his son christened James, like his father, grandfather and great-grandfather—which was as far as Carnach could trace. The result was a little confusing, the Crag island not being big enough for two Jemmy Carnachs. The fishermen, however, got over the difficulty by always calling the father Jemmy and his son Young 'un; but this did not suit Vince and Mike, with whom there had always been a feud, the fisherman's lad having constantly displayed an intense hatred, in his plebeian way, for the young representatives of the patricians on the isle. The manners in which he had shown this, from very early times, were many; and had taken the forms of watching till the companions were below cliffs, and then stealing to the top and dislodging stones, that they might roll down upon their heads; filling his pockets with the thin, sharply ground, flat oyster-shells to be found among the beach pebbles—a peculiarly cutting kind of weapon—and at every opportunity sending them skimming at one or other of the lads; making holes in their boat, when they had one—being strongly suspected of cutting two adrift, so that they were swept away, and never heard of again; and in divers other ways showing his dislike or hatred—displaying an animus which had become intensified since Mike had called in Vince's help to put a stop to raids and forays upon the old manor orchard when the apples, pears and plums were getting ripe, the result being a good beating with tough oak saplings.

Not that this stopped the plundering incursions, for Carnach junior told the two lads, and probably believed, as an inhabitant of the island, that he had as good a right to the fruit as they.

Of course the many assaults and insults dealt out by Carnach junior—for he was prolific in unpleasant words and jeers, whenever the companions came within hearing—had results in the shape of reprisals. Vince was not going to see Mike Ladelle's ear bleeding from a cut produced by a forcibly propelled oyster-shell, without making an attack upon the young human catapult; and Mike's wrath naturally boiled over upon seeing a piece of rock pushed off the edge of the cliff, and fall within a foot of where Vince was lying on the sand at the foot. But the engagements which followed seemed to do no good, for Carnach junior was so extremely English that he never seemed to realise that he had been thrashed till he had lain down with his eyes so swollen up that there was hardly room for the tears to squeeze themselves out, and his lips so disfigured that his howls generally escaped through his nose.

"I never saw such a fellow," Vince used to say: "if you only slap his face, it swells up horribly."

"And it's of no use to lick him, it doesn't do any good," added Mike. "Why, I must have thrashed him a hundred times, and you too."

This was a remark which showed that either Mr Deane's instructions in the art of calculation were faulty, or Mike's mental capacity inadequate for acquiring correctness of application.

Still there must have been some truth in Mike's words, for Vince, who was a great stickler for truthfulness, merely said:

"Ah! we have given it to him pretty often."

Vince and Mike did not take to Young 'un or Youngster, as a sobriquet for Carnach junior, and consequently they invented quite a variety of names, which were chosen, not for the purpose of distinguishing the fat, flat-faced, rather pig-eyed youth from other people, but it must be owned for annoyance, and by way of retaliation for endless insults.

"You see, we must do something," said Mike.

"Of course," agreed Vince; "and I'm tired of making myself hot and knocking my knuckles about against his stupid head; and besides, it seems so blackguardly, as a doctor's son, to be fighting a chap like that."

"Oh, I don't know," said Mike thoughtfully: "I shall be a Sir some day, I suppose."

"What a game!" chuckled Vince—"Sir Michael Ladelle!"

"I don't see anything to laugh at," said Mike; "but, as I was saying, if we don't lick him every now and then there'll be no bearing it. He'll get worse and worse."

So it was to show their contempt for the young lout that they invented names for him—weakly, perhaps, but very boylike—and for a time he was James the Second, but the lad seemed rather to approve of that; and it was soon changed for Barnacle, which had the opposite effect, and two fights down in a sandy cave resulted, at intervals of a week, one with each of his enemies, after which the Barnacle lay down as usual, and cried into the sand, which acted, Vince said, like blotting paper.

Tar-pot, suggested by a begrimed appearance, lasted for months, and was succeeded by Doughy, and this again by Puffy, consequent upon the lad's head having so peculiar a tendency to what home-made bread makers call "rise," and as there was no baker on Cormorant Crag the term was familiar enough.

A whole string of forgotten names followed, but none of them stuck, for they did not irritate Carnach junior; but the right one in the boys' eyes was found at last, upon a very hot day, following one upon which Vince and Mike had been prawning with stick and net among the rock pools under the cliffs,—and prawning under difficulties. For as they climbed along over, or waded amongst the fallen rocks detached from the towering heights above, Carnach junior, who had watched them descend, furnished himself with a creel full of heavy pebbles, and, making his way to the top of the cliffs, kept abreast and carefully out of sight, so as to annoy his natural enemies from time to time by dropping a stone into, or as near as he could manage to the little pool they were about to fish.

Words, addressed apparently to space, though really to the invisible foe, were vain, and the boys fished on; but they did not take home many prawns for Mrs Burnet to have cooked for their tea.

The very next day, though, they had their revenge, for they came upon the lad toiling homeward, shouldering a couple of heavy oars, a boat mast and yard, and the lug-sail rolled round them, and lashed so as to form a big bundle, as much as he could carry; and, consequent upon his scarlet face, Vince saluted him with:

"Hullo, Lobster!"

That name went like an arrow to the mark, and pierced right through the armour of dense stupidity in which the boy was clad. Lobster! That fitted with his father's weakness and the jeering remarks he had often heard made by neighbours; and ever after the name stuck, and irritated him whenever it was used.

It was used on the morning when Vince was thinking deeply of the discovery of the previous day, and going over to Sir Francis Ladelle's for his lessons with Mike. As we have said, he was saluted with coarse, jeering laughter, and the contemptuous utterance of the words "Going to school?"

Being excited, Vince turned sharply upon the great hulking lad, and his eyes began to blaze war, but with a laugh he only fell back on the nickname.

"Hullo, Lobster!" he cried: "that you?" and went on.

Carnach junior doubled his fists, and looked as if he were going to attack; but Vince, strong in the consciousness that he could at any time thrash the great lad, walked on with his books, heedless of the fact that he was followed at a distance, for his head was full of kegs and bales neatly done up in canvas, standing in good-sized stacks.

"I wonder how many years it has been there," he kept on saying to himself; and he was still wondering when he reached the old manor gates, went into the study, and there found Mike and their tutor waiting.

Both lads tried very hard to keep their discovery out of their minds that morning, but tried in vain. There it was constantly, and translated itself into Latin, conjugated and declined itself, and then became compound algebraic equations, with both.

Mr Deane bore all very patiently, though, and a reproachful word or two about inattention and condensation of thought upon study was all that escaped him.

At last, to Vince's horror, things came to a kind of climax, for Mike suddenly looked across the table at the tutor, and said quickly:—

"I say, Mr Deane!"

The tutor looked up at once.

"I want to ask you a question in—in—something—"

"Mathematics?" suggested the tutor.

"N–no," said Mike: "I think it must be in law or social economy. I don't know, though, what you would call it."

"Well: let me hear."

"Suppose anybody discovered a great store of smuggled goods, hidden in a—some place. Whom would it belong to?"

"To the people who put it there, of course." Vince's eyes almost blazed as he turned them upon the questioner.

"Yes," continued Mike; "but suppose there were no people left who put it there, and they had all died, perhaps a hundred years ago?"

"Oh, then," said the tutor thoughtfully, "I should think it would belong to the people upon whose ground it was discovered,—or no: I fancy it would be what is called 'treasure trove,' and go to the crown."

"Crown—crown? What, to a public-house?"

"No, no, my dear boy: to the king."

"Oh, I see," said Mike thoughtfully. "Is that all?"

"Yes, sir; that's all."

"Well, then, wasn't it rather a foolish question to ask, just in the middle of our morning's work? There, pray go on: we are losing a great deal of time."

The boys tried to get on; but they did not, for Mike was conscious of being kicked twice, and Vince was making up a tremendous verbal attack upon his fellow-student for letting out the discovery they had made.

It came to words as soon as the lessons were over, and Mike took his cap to accompany Vince part of the way home, and make their plans for the afternoon.

"I couldn't help it—'pon my word I couldn't," cried Mike. "I felt like that classic chap, who was obliged to whisper secrets to the water, and that I must speak about that stuff there to somebody."

"And now he'll go and talk to your father about it, and our secret place will be at an end. Why, we might have kept it all quiet for years!"

"So we can now. I put it so that old Deane shouldn't understand. I say, if he's right we can't claim all that stuff: it'll belong to the king."

"I suppose so," said Vince.

"Never mind: we'll keep it till he wants it. Hullo! what's old Lobster doing there?"

Vince turned in the direction pointed out; and, sure enough, there was Carnach junior sunning himself on a block of granite, which just peeped up through the grass.

"Got nothing to do, I suppose," said Vince. "I saw him when I was coming. But never mind him. And I say, don't, pray don't be so stupid again."

"All right. I'll try not to be, if it was stupid," said Mike. "Well, how about this afternoon?"

"I'll come and meet you at the old place, about half-past two."

This was agreed to; and, full of anticipations about the examination of the farther cave, they parted, leaving Carnach junior apparently fast asleep upon the grey stone.

Just as Vince reached home he came upon Daygo, who gave him a nod; and the lad flushed as he thought triumphantly of the discoveries they had made, in the face of the old fisherman's superstitious warnings of terrible dangers.

"Morn'—or art'noon, young gen'leman," said Daygo, by way of salutation. "Lookye here: I'm going out 'sart'noon to take up my pots and nets, and if you and young squire likes to come, I'll take you for a sail."

"Where will you take us?" said Vince eagerly.

"Oh, round and about, and in and out among the rocks."

"Will you sail right away round by the Black Scraw?"

"No, I just won't," growled the old man fiercely. "What do you want to go round about the Scraw for?"

"To see what it's like, and find some of the terrible currents and things you talked about, Joe."

"Lookye here, my lad," growled the old fellow, "as I told you boys afore, I want to live as long as I can, and not come to no end, with the boat bottom uppards and me sucked down by things in the horrid whirlypools out there. Why, what would your mars and pars say to me if I took you into dangers 'orrible and full o' woe? Nay, nay, I arn't a young harem-scarem-brained chap, and I shan't do it: my boat's too good. So look here, if you two likes to come for a bit o' fishing, I'll take the big scrarping spoon with me, and go to a bank I know after we've done, and try and fish you up a basket o' oysters. If you comes you comes, but if you arn't wi' me soon arter dinner, why, I hystes my sail and goes by myself. So what do you say?"

"I can't say anything without seeing Mike Ladelle first. Look here: I'm going to him this afternoon, and if he'll come, we'll run over to the little dock where your boat is."

"Very good, young gen'leman; on'y mind this: if you arn't there punctooal, as folks call it, I'm off without you, and you'll be sorry, for there's a powerful lot o' fish about these last few days."

"Don't wait if we're not there directly after dinner," said Vince.

Old Daygo chuckled.

"You needn't be afraid of that, my lad," he said; "and mind this,—if you're late and I've started, I'm not coming back, so mind that. D'reckly you've had your bit o' dinner, or I'm gone."

"All right, Joe," cried Vince; and he hurried in, feeling pulled both ways, for he could not help nursing the idea that, once out a short distance at sea, he might be able to coax the old fisherman into taking them as close as he could safely get to the ridge of rocks which hid the little rounded cove from passers-by.

# Chapter Fifteen
# A Spy on the Way

Punctual to the time the lads met; and Vince, who was full of old Daygo's proposal, laid it before his companion.

"What!" cried Mike; "go with him, when we've got such an adventure before us! You wouldn't do that!"

"Why not? We can go to the caverns any day, and this will be a chance to sail round and see what the outside of the Scraw is like."

"Did he say he would take us there?" cried Mike eagerly.

"No; but we'd persuade him."

"Persuade him!" cried Mike, bursting into a mocking laugh. "Persuade old Joe! Why, you do know better than that."

Vince frowned and said nothing, for he did know better, and felt that he had let his desires get the better of his judgment.

"Very well," he said. "You'd rather not go?"

"Well, wouldn't you rather go and have a look at those old things than see a few fish in a net?"

"Yes, if Joe wouldn't sail round where I want to go."

"Well, he wouldn't, and you know it. Why, this is a chance. You felt sure he was watching us; and he'll be off to sea, where he can't."

"Off, then!" said Vince; and, full of anticipations, they made for the oak wood, and were soon at the opening, into which, without pausing to look round, they leaped down quickly; and, after lighting the lanthorn, descended as rapidly as they could to the rope.

The place looked as beautiful as ever, as they slid down to the sandy floor of the inner cavern, and more than ever like the interior of some large shell; while the outer cave, with its roof alive, as it were, with the interlacing wavings and quiverings reflected from the sunny surface of the sea, would have made any one pause.

But the boys had no eyes for anything that day but the wonders of their new discovery; and, quickly getting to work with the rope and grapnel, Mike threw it up.

"Got a bite!" he cried. "No: he's off."

For, after catching, the grapnel gave way again.

The second time he missed; but the third he got another hold, and told Vince to climb first.

This he did, and in a very few seconds he was two-thirds of the way up, when with a scrape the grapnel gave way, and Vince came down flat on his back in the sand, with the iron upon him.

"Hurt?" cried Mike.

"Not much," said Vince, rubbing one leg, which the iron had struck. "Try again."

Mike threw once more, got a hold, and, to prove it, began to climb, and reached the opening safely. Then the lanthorn was drawn up, Vince followed, and this time taking the rope with them, they went along through the peculiar zigzag free from doubts and dread of dangers unknown, so that they could think only of the various difficulties of the climb.

Upon nearing the open end of the fissure they kept back the lanthorn and advanced to peer down cautiously; but, save a few pigeons flying in and out, there was no sign of life. Everything was just as they had seen it before; the footprints all over the trampled sand, which had probably been made ages before, so they thought; the boat mast, sails, and ropes, were at the side, and in the shadowy upper part there were the stacks of bales and the carefully piled-up kegs.

"Well?" said Mike; "shall we go down?"

"Of course."

"But suppose there is any one there?"

"We'll soon see," said Vince; and, placing his hands to his mouth, he gave vent to a hullo! whose effect was startling; for it echoed and vibrated about the great cave, startling a flock of pigeons, which darted out with a loud whistling of wings.

Then the sound came back in a peculiar way from the barrier of rocks across the bay, for there was evidently a fluttering there among the sea-birds, some of which darted down into sight just outside the mouth of the cave.

"Nobody at home," said Vince merrily, "and hasn't been lately. Now then: may I go first?"

"If you like," said Mike; and, after securely hooking the grapnel in a crevice, Vince threw the rope outward from him into the cavern, where it touched the sand some twenty feet below.

"There we are!" he said; "that's easier than throwing it up."

"Yes, but look sharp down. I want to have a good look."

"After me," said Vince mockingly; and, taking the rope, he lowered himself out of the crack, twisted his leg round the hemp, and quickly dropped hand over hand to the flooring of the cave.

"Ever so much bigger than ours, Mike," he shouted, and then turned sharply round, for a voice said plainly:

"Ours, Mike."

"I say, what an echo!"

"Echo!" came back.

"Well, I said so."

"Said so."

"Hurrah!" cried Mike, as he too reached the floor, and a soft "Rah" came from the other side.

Their hearts beat fast with excitement as they stood in the middle of the cave, looking round, and pretty well taking in at a glance that it was far larger and more commodious than the one they had just quitted, especially for the purpose of a store, having the hinder part raised, as it were, into a dais or platform, upon which the little barrels and packages were stored; while behind these they were able now to see through the transparent gloom that the place ran back for some distance till flooring and roof met. Instead, too, of the entrance being barred by ridge after ridge of rocks, there was only one some little distance beyond the mouth to act as a breakwater, leaving ample room for a boat to come round at either end and be beached upon the soft sand, which lay perfectly smooth where the water slightly rose and fell.

There was a fine view of the rounded cove from here; and the boys felt that if they were to wade out they would be able to get beyond the archway sufficiently to look up the overhanging face of the cliff; but, with the recollection of the quicksands at the mouth of their own cave, neither of them felt disposed to venture, and they were about to turn back and examine the goods stored behind them, when on their right there was a loud rush and a heavy splash, and Mike seized his companion's arm just as a head rose out of the water, and for a moment it seemed as if a boy was watching them, the face being only faintly seen, from the head being turned away from the light.

"Seal," said Vince quietly. "Shows how long it is since any one was here, for things like that to be about!"

He caught up a couple of handfuls of sand and flung it toward the creature, which dived directly, but rose again to watch them, its curiosity being greatly excited.

"Won't come ashore and attack us, will it?" said Mike.

"No fear. I daresay it would bite, though, if we had it in a corner, and it couldn't pass. Look! one must have come ashore there."

He pointed to a smooth channel in the sand, where one of the curious animals had dragged itself a few feet from the water, going back by another way, and so forming a kind of half-moon.

"Let it watch us: it don't matter," said Mike. "Come and have a look at the packages."

They walked up to the pile of kegs, and Vince took one down, to find that it was peculiar in shape and hooped with wood.

"Empty," he said; "it's light as can be."

"Try another," said Mike; and Vince put the one he held down, and tried one after another—at least a dozen.

"The stuff has all run out or evaporated," he said. "Hark here!"

He tapped the end of one with his knuckles, but, instead of giving forth a hollow sound, the top sounded dead and dull.

"They're not empty," he said, giving one a shake: "they must be packed full of something light. And I say, Mike, they look as if they couldn't be many years old."

"That's because the cavern's so clean and dry. Let's look at the packages. I say, smell this one. There's no mistake about it—cloves!"

Vince nodded, and they tried others, which gave out, some the same unmistakable odour, others those of cinnamon and nutmeg.

Further examination of some small, heavy, solid packets left little doubt in the lads' minds that they were dealing with closely folded or rolled pieces of silk, and they ended their examination by trying to interpret the brands with which some of the packages were marked.

"One can't be sure without opening them," said Vince eagerly; "but I feel certain that these are silk, the other packages spice, and the kegs have got gloves and lace in them. There are two kinds."

"Yes; some are larger than the others. Shall we open a few of them, to see if they've been destroyed by time?"

"No, not yet," replied Vince thoughtfully. "Let's go and have a look at that boat sail and the oars. Those oars ought to be old and worm-eaten— ready to tumble to pieces—and the sail-cloth like so much tinder!"

Mike nodded, and followed him rather unwillingly; for the keg nearest to his hand fascinated him, and he longed intensely to force out the head.

It was not many steps to where the boat gear stood and lay, and Vince began to haul it about after the first glance.

"Look here, Ladle!" he cried; "these things are not so very old. The canvas is as strong as can be, and it can't be so many years since these oars were marked with a hot iron."

"Oh, nonsense!" said Mike, who did not like to give up his cherished ideas; "it's because they're so dry and safe here."

"It isn't," said Vince impetuously; "and look here, at all these footmarks!"

"Well, what's to prevent them from being just the same after a hundred years?"

"The wind," cried Vince. "If those marks were old the sand would have drifted in and covered them over quite smooth, same as the floor was in our cave before we walked about it. Mike, all these things are quite new, and haven't been put here long."

"Nonsense! who could have put them?"

"I don't know; but here they are, and if we don't look out some one will come and catch us. This is a smugglers' cave."

"But there are no smugglers here. Who ever heard of smugglers at the Crag!"

"I never did; but I'm sure these are smuggled goods."

"Well, I don't know," said Mike. "It seems very queer. The cave can't be so dangerous to come to, if boats can land cargoes. Old Daygo's all wrong, then?"

"Of course he is; so are all the people. Every one has told us that the Black Scraw was a terrible place, and looked as if they thought it was haunted by all kinds of sea goblins. Let's get away."

"Think we'd better?"

"Yes; I keep expecting to see a boat come round the corner into sight. I shouldn't like to be here when they did come."

"But it's so disappointing!" cried Mike. "I thought we were going to have all this to ourselves."

"I don't think I did," said Vince thoughtfully.

"But I don't believe you're right, Cinder. These things can't have been put here in our time, or we must have known of it. See what a little place the Crag is."

"Yes, it's small enough, but the Scraw has always been as if it were far away, and people could come here and do what they liked."

"But they wouldn't be so stupid as to come here and leave things for nobody," said Mike. "Is there anybody here who would want them?"

"No," replied Vince; "but smugglers might make this a sort of storehouse, and some bring the things here from France and Holland and others come and fetch them away. There, come on, and let's get up into the crack. I don't feel safe. It has regularly spoiled our place, though, for whoever comes here must know of the other cave."

"Well," said Mike, as they stood by the rope, and he gazed longingly back at the rich store he was about to leave behind, "I'll come; but I don't believe you're right."

"You'll soon see that I am, Ladle; for before long all these things will be taken away—perhaps by the time we come again."

"If it's as you say we shan't be able to come again," replied Mike rather dolefully; and then, in obedience to an impatient sign from his companion, he took hold of the rope and climbed slowly up, passing in at the opening, and being followed by Vince directly after.

Then the rope was drawn up and coiled, and both took a long and envious look at the cargo that had been landed there at some time or other, before making their way along the fissure to their own place.

"I don't believe any one would do as we've done, and come along there," said Mike, as soon as they were safely back. "Perhaps, if you're right about that stuff being new, these smuggling people don't, after all, know of this cave."

"They must have seen it when they were going and coming in their boat, and would have been sure to land and come in."

"Land where?" said Mike scornfully. "No boat could land here, and nobody could wade in, on account of the quicksands. But I'm right, Cinder. These things are awfully old, and they'll be ours after all."

"Very well: we shall see," said Vince. "But I don't feel disposed to stop here now. Let's get back home."

"Yes," said Mike, with a sigh, "let's get back home;" and, after setting up a fresh bit of candle, they started for the inner cave, ascended the slope, and made their way along the black passage to the spot where they put out and hid their lanthorn.

This done, with the caution taught by the desire to keep their hiding-place secret, Vince stepped softly on to the opening, and was about to pass along to the end, but he paused to peer out through the briars to see if all was right, and the next moment he stood there as if turned to stone. Mike crept up to him and touched his shoulder, feeling sure from his companion's fixed attitude that something must be wrong.

"'He does not know that we are close to his feet.'"

The answer to his touch was the extension of Vince's hand, and he pointed upward and toward the side of the deep rift.

Mike turned his head softly, and gazed in the indicated direction. For some moments he could see nothing for the briars and ferns; but at last he bent a trifle more forward, and his fists clenched, for there, upon one of the stones beside the entrance to their cave, with his hand shading his eyes, and staring upward apparently at the ridge, was Carnach junior.

"Spying after us," said Mike to himself; "and he does not know that we are close to his feet."

# Chapter Sixteen
## Some Doubts about the Discovery

Certainly Lobster did not know how near the two boys were, and he soon proved it by coming closer, looking down, and then turning to reconnoitre in another direction.

Vince stared at Mike, and their eyes simultaneously said the same thing: "He must have been watching us, and seen us come in this direction."

It was evident that he had soon lost the clue in following them, although, judging from circumstances, he must have tracked them close to where they were.

They recollected now that they had not exercised their regular caution— though, even if they had, it is very doubtful whether they would have detected a spy who crawled after them, for the cover was too thick—and a feeling of anger troubled both for allowing themselves to be outwitted by a lout they both held in utter contempt.

They stood watching their spy for nearly a quarter of an hour, and were able to judge from his actions that he had seen them disappear somewhere in this direction; and in profound ignorance in this game of hide and seek that he was having, Carnach scanned the high slope and the ridge, and the bottom where the stones lay so thickly again and again, ending by ensconcing himself behind one of them, after plucking some fern fronds, and putting them on the top of his cap to act as a kind of screen in case those he sought should come into sight somewhere overhead.

The two boys hardly dared stir, but at last, with his eyes fixed upon Carnach to see if he heard their movement, Vince pointed softly back into the dark passage, and Mike crept away without making the slightest sound. Then, as soon as he was satisfied of the coast being clear behind him, Vince began to back away till he felt it safe to turn, and followed his companion some fifty yards into the darkness, which now seemed to be quite a refuge to them.

"Where are you?" whispered Vince.

A low cough told him that he was not yet far enough; and, keeping one hand upon the wall, he followed until he felt himself touched.

"I say," he whispered, "this is nice: smugglers at one end and that miserable Lobster at the other! What are we to do?"

"I don't know," said Mike dolefully. "He must have seen us go out of sight, and feels sure that we shall come back again, and he'll wait till we do."

"No, no; he'll soon get tired."

"Not he," said Mike; "he's just one of those stupid, heavy chaps who will sit or lie down and wait for us for a week."

"But I want to get home. I'm growing hungry."

"Let's go back and fish, and light a fire and cook it."

"What, for him to smell the frying? He would, as sure as could be. No; we must wait."

"I say, Cinder," whispered Mike, "what an unlucky day we are having! Everything seems to go wrong."

"It'll go worse still if you whisper so loud," said Vince; "the sound runs along the walls here, and gets stronger, I believe, as it goes."

"Well, I can't help it; I feel so wild. I say, couldn't we creep out without being seen, and get home?"

"Yes, when it's dark; not before."

"But that means waiting here for hours, and I feel as if I can't settle to anything now. Let's go back down to the cave. The smugglers can't come to-day. It would be too bad."

"Better wait here and watch till Lobster goes," said Vince; but, yielding at last to his companion's importunity, he was about to follow him back, when there was a loud rustling, a heavy thud, and then a dismal howl.

The Lobster had slipped and fallen into the rift while backing so as to get a better view of the ridge.

"Oh my! Oh my! Oh, mother! Oh, crikey! Oh my head—my head! Oh, my arm! Oh, it's broke! And I'm bleeding! Won't nobody come and help me?"

The above, uttered in a piteous, dismal wail, was too much for Vince's feelings; and, pushing his companion aside, he was about to hurry to the lad's help, but Mike seized him by the arm, and at the same moment they heard Carnach junior jump up and begin stamping about.

"Here, who did this?" he roared. "What fool's been digging stone here and left this hole o' purpose for any one to fall in? Wish he'd tumbled in himself, and broke his stoopid old head. Yah! Oh my, how it hurts!"

He stamped about in the hollow, and they heard him kick one of the stones with his heavy boots in his rage.

"Wish them two had tumbled in 'stead o' me. Oh dear, oh! Here's a mess I'm in! Making a great hole like this, and never leaving no stuff outside. Might ha' been deep, and killed a chap. It aren't broke through," he grumbled, after a pause. "Wonder where they've got to. Oh dear! oh dear! what a crack on the head! That comes o' going backwards. Yah!"

This last ejaculation was accompanied by the rattle of stones, as the great lad evidently kicked another piece that was in his way; and, feeling now that there was nothing serious in the fall, Vince gave Mike's hand a squeeze as they stood listening and expecting every moment to hear the young fisherman say something in the way of surprise as he saw the dark hole going downward. But they listened in vain,—full of anxiety, though, for it was like a second blow to find that their secret place was becoming very plain, known as it evidently was to people at the sea entrance, and now from the landward side discovered by the greatest enemy they had.

Vince felt this so strongly that, in spite of the risk of being heard, he put his lips to Mike's ear and whispered: "This spoils all."

Mike responded in the same way: "I say, what's he doing? Shall I go and see?"

"No, I will," whispered back Vince.

"Take care."

Vince's answer was a squeeze of the hand. Then, going down upon all fours, he crept silently and slowly up the slope till he could see the lad, expecting to find him peering about the mouth of the passage, and trying to see whether they were there.

But nothing of the kind. There was the young fisherman seated upon a piece of stone, with the light shining down upon him through the brambles, busily tying his neckerchief round his head, making it into a bandage to cover a cut somewhere on the back, and tying it in front over his forehead. Then, picking up his cap, which lay beside him, he drew it on over the handkerchief, having most trouble to cover the knot, but succeeding at last.

Then he stood up and began to examine his hands, which appeared to be scratched and bleeding; and making Vince start and feel that he was seen, for the boy turned in the direction of the dark passage and cried viciously:

"All right, Doctor: I'll let yer have it next time I ketches yer—and you too, old Squire. Oh my! how it smarts, though! Wonder wherever they got."

Those last words came like a fillip to Vince's spirits, for he felt now that there was nothing to mind, as he could not give the Lobster credit for knowing that they were close at hand and acting his part so as to make believe he was in ignorance.

Just then a light touch told Vince that Mike had crawled silently up behind him; and they both crouched there now, in the darkness, watching the lad, till he suddenly seemed to become impressed by the fact that the hole went right in underground, and he stood staring in till the two boys felt that he was looking at them and seeing them plainly.

"Goes right in," he said aloud—"ever so far, p'r'aps. Well, let it. I aren't going to get myself all wet and muddy. Oh! how it do hurt!"

He raised his hand to the back of his head; but he remained staring in, the boys hardly daring to breathe, as each doubled his fists, and prepared for an encounter.

"He must see us," thought Vince; and when he felt most certain, his heart gave a throb of satisfaction, for a slight movement on the lad's part brought his face more into the light, and Vince could see that there was a vague look in the lad's eyes, as if he were thinking; and then he turned slowly round and began to look about for the best way out of the trap into which he had fallen, proceeding to drag at the brambles in one spot where an exit seemed easiest; but a sharp prick or two made him snatch away his hands with an angry ejaculation, and, looking about again, he noticed that there was a simpler way out at the end—that used by the two boys for returning, their entries always now being by a sudden jump down through the pendent green shoots.

"I'll let 'em have it for this when I do find 'em," grumbled the lad. "Must ha' gone home'ards some other way." And they could hear him muttering and grumbling as the twigs and strands rustled where he passed, till they knew that he was well outside, for they heard him give a stamp on one of the blocks of granite.

Vince rose silently.

"Come on," he said,—"the brambles will screen us;" and he crept forward carefully, till he was close to the hole, and then cautiously advanced his head, to peer upward, raising his hand warningly to Mike, who was just behind. For the lad had not gone away, but was standing at the edge with his back to them, and his eyes sheltered, gazing upward at the ridge.

He remained there watching intently for quite ten minutes without moving, and then went off out of sight, the only guide to the direction he took being the rustling of displaced bushes and the musical clink of a loose block of stone moved by his passing feet.

They did not trust themselves to speak for some time after the last faint sound had died out, and then they began to discuss the question whether they could escape unseen.

"Must chance it," said Vince at last. "I'm tired of staying here. Come on."

Mike was evidently quite as weary, for he showed his agreement by following at once. They were both cautious in the extreme, going out on all fours, and then crawling in and out between the blocks of granite—a pleasant enough task so long as the growth between was whortleberry, heath or ferns, but as for the most part it was the long thorny strands of the blackberry, the travelling became more and more painful. At last, after progressing in this way some three hundred yards, a horribly thorny strand hooked Vince in the leg of his trousers and skin as well, with the result that he started to his feet angrily.

"Here, I've had enough of this," he cried. "Hang the old cavern! it isn't worth the trouble."

"Hist!" exclaimed Mike, seizing him by the leg and pointing straight away to their right.

Vince dropped forward, with his arms stretched over the nearest block of grey stone, staring at the object pointed out, and seeing Carnach junior right up close to the highest part of the ridge.

For a few moments he could not be sure whether the young fisherman was looking in their direction, or away; from them; but a movement on the part of the lad set this at rest directly after, and they saw him go slowly on, helping himself by clutching at the saw-like row of jagged stones which divided one slope from the other; and, satisfied that they had not been seen, they recommenced their crawl, till they reached the cover of a pile of the loose rocks, which were pretty well covered with growth.

Placing this between them and the lad, now far away upon the ridge, they made for the cover of the stunted oaks, and there breathed freely.

Mike was the first to speak, and he began just as if his companion had the moment before made his impatient remarks about the adventure not being worth the trouble.

"I don't know," he said. "This is the first time we have had any bother, and I don't see why we should give such a jolly place up just because that thick-headed old Lobster came watching us."

"Ah! but that isn't all," said Vince. "We can't go down there any more, on account of the smugglers."

"But I don't believe you are right. Those things looked new, I know; but they must be as old as old, for if any smuggling had been going on here we must have seen or heard of it."

"But the sand—the sand! Those footprints must be new."

"I don't see it," said Mike, rather stubbornly. "Because the wind blows into one cave and drifts the light sand all over, that's no reason why it should do so in another cave, which may be regularly sheltered."

"It's no good to argue with you," said Vince sourly, for he was weary and put out. "You can have it your own way, only I tell you this,—smugglers don't stand any nonsense; they'll shoot at any one who tries to stop them or find out where they land cargoes, and we should look nice if they suddenly came upon us."

"People don't come suddenly on you when they've been dead a hundred years," replied Mike. "Now, just look here: we must do it as if we took no interest in it, but you ask your father to-night, and I'll ask mine, whether they ever heard of there being smugglers in the Crag."

"Well, I will," said Vince; "but you must do the same."

"Of course I shall; and we shall find that it must have been an enormous time ago, and that we've as good a right to those things as anybody, for they were brought there and then forgotten."

"Well, we shall see," said Vince; and that night, at their late tea, he started the subject with—

"Have you ever known any smugglers to be here, father?"

"Smugglers? No, Vince," said the Doctor, smiling. "There's nothing ever made here that would carry duty, for people to want to get it into England free; and on the other hand, it would not be of any use for smugglers to bring anything here, for there is no one to buy smuggled goods, such as they might bring from Holland or France."

Somewhere about the same time Mike approached the question at the old manor house.

"Smugglers, Mike?" said Sir Francis. "Oh no, my boy, we've never had smugglers here. The place is too dangerous, and perfectly useless to such people, for they land contraband goods only where they can find a good market for them. Now, if you had said pirates, I could tell you something different."

"Were there ever pirates, then?" cried Mike excitedly. Sir Francis laughed.

"It's strange," he said, "what interest boys always have taken in smugglers, pirates, and brigand stories. Why, you're as bad as the rest, boy! But there, I'm running away from your question. Yes, I believe there were pirates here at one time; but it is over a hundred years ago, and they were a crew of low, ruffianly scoundrels, who got possession of a vessel and lived for years by plundering the outward and inward bound merchantmen; and being on a fast sailing vessel they always escaped by running for shore, and from their knowledge of the rocks and currents they could sail where strangers dared not follow. But the whole history has been dressed up tremendously, and made romantic. It was said that they brought supernatural aid to bear in navigating their craft, and that they would sail right up to the Crag and then become invisible: people would see them one minute and they'd be gone the next."

"Hah!" ejaculated Mike, and his father smiled. "All superstitious nonsense, of course, my boy; but the ignorant people get hold of these traditions and believe in them. Mr Deane here will soon tell you how in history molehills got stretched up into mountains."

"Or snowballs grew into historical avalanches," said the tutor.

"Exactly," said Sir Francis. "I fancy, Mike, that those people may have had a nest here. One of the men—Carnach I think it was—told me that they had a cave, and only sailed from it at night."

"Did he know where it was, father?"

"I remember now he said it was 'sumwers about,' which is rather vague; but still there are several holes on the west coast which might have been made habitable; though I have never seen such a cave on the island, nor even one that could have been serviceable as a store."

Mike winced a little, for he fully expected to hear his father say "Have you?" But then Sir Francis went off to another subject, and the boy nursed up his ideas ready for his next meeting with Vince, which was on the following day.

# Chapter Seventeen
# Pirates or Smugglers? How to prove it

"Pirates, Cinder!"

Mike was down at the gate waiting for Vince to come with his roll of exercises, ready for the morning's work; and as soon as Vince came within earshot he fired off the word that he had been dreaming about all night—

"Pirates!"

"Where?" cried Vince, looking sharply round and out to sea.

"Get out! You know what I mean. It's pirates, not smugglers."

Vince stared at him for a few moments, and then burst out laughing.

"Well, you've got it this time," he said, "if you mean the cave."

"And I do," said Mike quietly. "Pirates; and that's some of the plunder and booty they took from a ship over a hundred years ago. So now whose will it be?"

"Stop a moment," said Vince, looking preternaturally serious; "let's be certain who it was. Let me see: there was Paul Jones, and Blackbeard, and the Buccaneers. What do you say to its having belonged to the Buccaneers?"

"Ah! you may laugh, but my father said last night that he never knew of smugglers being on the island, but that there was a story about pirates having a cave here, and going out in their vessel to plunder the outward and homeward bound merchantmen."

"Humph!" grunted Vince, with a sceptical look.

"And look here: he said the people had a superstitious belief that the pirates used to sail towards the Crag, and then disappear."

"What!" cried Vince eagerly.

"Disappear quite suddenly."

"Behind that line of rocks when they sailed into the little cove, Mike?"

"To be sure. Now, then, why don't you laugh and sneer?" cried Mike. "Does it sound so stupid now?"

"I don't know," said Vince, beginning to be dubious again.

"Then I do," said Mike warmly. "I never knew of such an unbelieving sort of chap as you are. There's the cave, and there's all the plunder in it— just such stuff as the pirates would get out of a ship homeward bound."

"Yes; but why did they leave it there and not sell it?"

"I know," cried Mike excitedly: "because one day they went out and attacked a ship so as to plunder her, and found out all at once that it was a man-o'-war; and as soon as the man-o'-war's captain found out that they were pirates he had all the guns double-shotted, and gave the order to fire a broadside, and sank the pirate."

"That's the way," said Vince, laughing; "and the pirate captain ran up the rigging with a hammer and some tin-tacks, and nailed the colours to the mast."

"Ah! you may laugh," said Mike. "You're disappointed because you didn't find it out first. There it all is, as plain as plain. The people used to think the pirate vessel disappeared, because she sailed out of sight and used to lie in hiding till they wanted to attack another ship. Well, I shan't say any more about it if you are going to laugh, but there's the treasure in the cave: we found it; and half's yours and half's mine. Now then, what did the Doctor say?"

"That he never heard of any smugglers ever being here."

"There!" cried Mike triumphantly.

"He said there was no one here to buy smuggled goods, and nothing here to smuggle."

"Of course not: the other's the idea, and I vote we go down and properly examine our treasure after dinner."

"That is curious," said Vince, "about the tradition of the pirate ship disappearing, because it proves that there is a channel big enough for a small ship."

"Oh you're beginning to believe, then, now?"

"No, I'm not; for I feel sure those are smuggled goods. But, Mike, we must get old Joe to lend us his boat, and sail along there ourselves."

"He wouldn't lend it to us."

"Then I know what we'll do—"

"Now, gentlemen, I'm waiting," said a familiar voice.

"All right, Mr Deane; we're coming," cried Mike. "Now, Cinder, what shall we do?"

"Go and ask the old chap to lend us his boat, and if he won't we'll come back disappointed."

"And what's the good of that?"

"Slip round another way and borrow her. You and I could manage her, couldn't we?"

"Why, I could manage her myself."

"Of course you could. We shouldn't hurt the boat; and we could feel our way in, and see from outside whether it has been a smugglers' place or no."

"That's it," said Mike; and five minutes after they were working hard with the tutor, as if they had nothing on their minds.

That afternoon, with the sun brighter and the sea and sky looking bluer than ever, the two boys were off for their afternoon expedition, making their way along a rough lane that was very beautiful and very bad. It was bad from the point of view that the fisher-farmers of the island looked upon it as a sort of "no man's land," and never favoured it by spreading donkey-cart loads of pebbles or broken granite to fill up the holes trodden in by cows in wet weather, or the tracks made by carts laden with vraick, the sea-weed they collected for manuring their potato and parsnep fields. Consequently, in bad seasons Vince said it was "squishy," and Mike that it was "squashy." But in fine summer weather it was beautiful indeed, for Nature seemed to have made up her mind that it was nonsense for a roadway to be made there to act like a scar on the landscape, just to accommodate a few people who wanted to bring up sea-weed, sand and fish from the shore, and harness donkeys to rough carts to do the work when they might more easily have done it themselves by making a rough windlass, such as they had over their wells, and dragging all they wanted directly up the cliff face to the top—a plan which would have done in fifty yards what the donkeys had to go round nearly half a mile to achieve. As to the road being kept up solely because old Joe Daygo had a cottage down in a notch in the granite walls overlooking the sea, that seemed to be absurd.

Consequently, Nature went to work regularly every year to do away with that road, and she set all her children to help. The gorse bushes hung from the sides, thrusting out their prickly sprays covered with orange and yellow blossom and encroached all they could; the heather sprouted and slowly crept here and there, in company with a lovely fine grass that would have made a lover of smooth lawns frantic with envy. Over the heath, ling, and furze the dodder wreathed and wove its delicate tangle, and the thrift raised its lavender heads to nod with satisfaction at the way in which all the plants and wild shrubs were doing their work.

But there were two things which left all the rest behind, and did by far the most to bring the crooked lane back to beauty. They laughed at the two brionies, black and white; for though they made a glorious show, with their convolvulus and deeply cut leaves, and sent forth strands of wonderfully rapid growth to run over the sturdy blackthorn, which produced such splendid sloes, and then hung down festoons of glossy leaves into the lane that quite put the more slow-growing ivy to the blush, still these lovely trailing festoons died back in the winter, while their rival growths kept on. These rivals were the brambles and the wild clematis, which grew and grew in friendly emulation, and ended, in spite of many rebuffs from trampling feet, by shaking hands across the road; the clematis, not content with that, going farther and embracing and tangling themselves up till rudely broken apart by the passers-by—notably by old Joe Daygo, when he went that way home to his solitary cot, instead of walking, out of sheer awkwardness, across somebody's field or patch.

"I wish father would buy old Joe's cottage," said Vince, as the two lads trudged down the lane that afternoon. "We could make it such a lovely place."

"Yours is right enough," said Mike, pausing in whistling an old French air a good deal affected by the people.

"Oh yes, and I shouldn't like to leave it; but I always like this bit down here; the lane is so jolly. Look."

"What at?"

"Two swallow-tail butterflies. Let's have them."

"Shan't. I'm not going to make myself red-hot running after them if we're going out in the boat. Besides, we haven't got any of your father's pill boxes to put 'em in. I say, how the things do grow down here! Look at that fern and the bracken."

"Yes, and the old foxgloves. They are a height!"

"It's so warm and sheltered. What's that?"

They stopped, for there was a quick, rushing sound amongst the herbage.

"Snake," said Vince, after a pause; "and we've no sticks to hunt him out."

"Down his hole by this time. Come along. What a fellow you are! You always want to be off after something. Why can't you keep to one purpose at a time, as Mr Deane says, so as to master it?"

"Hark at old Ladle beginning to lay down the law," cried Vince merrily. "You're just as bad. I say, shall we stop about here this afternoon? Look at that gull—how it seems to watch us."

Vince threw back his head to gaze up at the beautiful, white-breasted bird, which was keeping them company, and sailing about here and there some twenty feet overhead, watching them all the time.

"Bother the gull!" said Mike. "Let's go on and speak to old Joe about the boat."

"Oh, very well," said Vince; "but what's the hurry? I hate racing along when there's so much to see. Here, Ladle: look—look! My! what a chance for a seine!"

They had just reached a turn in the lane where they could look down at an embayed portion of the deep blue sea, in which a wide patch was sparkling and flashing in the most dazzling way, and literally seeming to boil as if some large volcanic fire were at work below.

"Mackerel," said Vince.

"Pilchards," said Mike.

"'Taint: it's too soon. It's mackerel. What a chance!"

"Have it your own way," said Mike; "but a nice chance! Ha! ha! Why, if they surrounded them they'd get their nets all torn to pieces. There's sand all round, but the middle there is full of the worst rocks off the coast."

"Yes I s'pose it would be rocky," said Vince thoughtfully. "Well, do come on."

Mike turned upon him to resent the order, feeling that it was nice to be accused of delaying their progress; but the mirthful look on Vince's face disarmed him, and after a skirmish and spar to get rid of a little of their effervescing vitality, consequent upon the stimulating effects of the glorious air, they broke into a trot and went past a large patch where a man was busy hoeing away at a grand crop of carrots, destined for winter food for his soft-eyed cow, tethered close at hand; and soon after came in sight of a massive, rough chimney-stack of granite, apparently level with the road. But this latter made a sudden dip down into a steep hollow, and there stood the comfortable-looking cottage inhabited by the old fisherman, with its goodly garden, cow-shed, and many little additions which betokened prosperity.

The door was open, and, quite at home, the boys walked into the half parlour, half kitchen-like place, with its walls decorated with fishing-gear and dried fish, with various shells, spars, and minerals, which the old man called his "koorosseties," some native, but many obtained from men who had made long voyages in ocean-going ships.

"Hi, Joe! where are you?" cried Vince, hammering on the open door. But there was not a sound to be heard; and they came out, climbed up the rocks at the back till they were above the chimneys, and looked round, expecting to find that he had gone off to the granite-hedged field where he tethered his cows.

But the two sleek creatures were browsing away, and no one was in sight but the man, some hundred yards or so distant, hoeing the weeds from his carrots.

"How tiresome!" said Mike.

"All right: he'll know," cried Vince; and they trotted to where the man was very slowly freeing his vegetables from intruders.

"Hi, Jemmy Carnach!" shouted the lad, "seen Joe Daygo?"

"Ay,—hour ago," said the man, straightening himself slowly, and passing one hand behind him to begin softly rubbing his back: "he've gone yonder to do somethin' to his boat."

"Come on, Mike; we'll cut straight across here and catch him. It's much nearer."

"Going fishing, young sirs?" said the man.

"Yes, and for a sail."

"If you see that boy o' mine—"

"What, Lobster?" said Vince.

"Eh? lobster?" said the man eagerly. "Ay, if you ketch any, you might leave us one as you come back. I arn't seen one for a week."

"All right," said Mike, after a merry glance at Vince; "if we get any we'll leave you one."

"Ay, do, lad," said the man. "Good for them as has to tyle all day. If you see my boy, tell him I want him. I'm not going to do all the work and him nothing."

"We'll tell him," said Vince.

"And if he says he won't come, you lick him, mind. Don't you be feared."

The boys were pretty well out of hearing when the last words were spoken; and after a sharp trot, along by the side of the cliff where it was possible, they came to the rugged descent leading to old Daygo's tiny port.

This time they were not disappointed, for they caught sight of the old man's cap as he stood below with his back to them, driving a wooden peg into a crack in the rock with a rounded boulder, ready for hanging up some article of fishing-gear.

"You ask him," said Mike: "he likes you best."

"All right," said Vince; and, putting his hands to his lips, he shouted out, "Daygo, ahoy!"

"Ahoy!" cried the old man, without turning his head; and he kept on thumping away till the boys had reached him, when he slowly turned to face them, and threw down the great pebble.

Vince was too thorough to hesitate, and he opened the business at once, in his outspoken way:

"Here, Joe!" he cried; "we want you to lend us your boat to go for a sail."

"To lend you my boat to go for a sail?" said the old man, nodding his head softly.

"Yes; and we shan't be very long, because we must be back to tea."

"And you won't be very long, because you must be back to tea?"

"Yes; and we won't trouble you. We can get it out ourselves."

"And you won't trouble me, because you can get it out yourselves?"

"That's right."

"Oh, that's right, is it, Master Vince? That's what you thinks," said the old fisherman.

"But you'll lend it to us, won't you?"

"Nay, my lad—I won't."

"Why?"

"Why?" said Daygo, beginning to rasp his nose, according to custom, with his rough forefinger. "He says why? Mebbe you'd lose her."

"No, we wouldn't, Joe."

"Mebbe you'd run her on the rocks."

"Nonsense!—just as if we don't know where the rocks are. Know 'em nearly as well as you do."

Daygo chuckled.

"Oh, come, Joe, don't be disagreeable. We'll take plenty of care of it, and pay you what you like."

"Your fathers tell you to come to me?"

"No."

"Thought not. Nay, my lads, I won't lend you my boat, and there's an end on it. I'm not going to have your two fathers coming to ask me why I sent you both to the bottom."

"Such stuff!" cried Vince angrily. "Just as if we could come to harm on a day like this."

"Ah! you don't know, lad; I do. Never can tell when a squall's coming off the land."

"Well, I do call it disagreeable," said Vince. "Will you take us out?"

"Nay, not to-day."

"Oh, very well. Never mind, but I shan't forget it. Did think you'd have done that, Joe. Come on, Mike; let's go and get some lines and fish off the rocks."

"Ay, that's the best game for boys like you," said the old man; and, stooping down, he picked up the boulder and began to knock again at the wooden peg without taking any notice of his visitors.

"Come on, Vince," said Mike; and they walked back up the cliff, climbing slowly, but as soon as they were out of the old man's sight starting off quickly to gain a clump of rocks, which they placed between them and the way down. Here they began to climb carefully till they had reached a spot from whence they could look down upon the little winding channel leading from the tunnel to Daygo's natural dock.

They could see the old man, too, moving about far below, evidently fetching something to hang upon the great peg he had finished driving in; and, after disappearing for a few minutes, he came into sight again, and they saw him hang the something up—but what, at that distance, they could not make out.

At the end of a few minutes the old man went down to his boat, stayed with it another five minutes or so, and then stood looking about him.

"It's no go, Cinder," said Mike, in a disappointed tone; "we shan't get off to-day, and perhaps it's best. We oughtn't to take his boat."

"Why not? It's only like borrowing anything of a neighbour. He was sour to-day, or else he'd have lent it."

"But suppose he finds out?"

"Well, then he'll only laugh. You'll see: he'll be off directly."

Mike shook his head as they lay there upon their breasts, with their heads hidden behind tufts of heather; but Vince was right as to the old man soon going, for directly after they saw him begin to climb deliberately up to the level, look cautiously round, and then, bent of back, trudge slowly off in the direction of his home; while, as soon as he was well on his way, the boys crept downward till they were at the foot of the rocks, when Vince cried:

"Now then: lizards!" and began to crawl at a pretty good rate towards the way down to the natural dock, quite out of sight of the old man if he had looked back.

The rugged way down was reached, and here they were able to rise erect and begin to descend in the normal way, Vince starting off rapidly.

"Come on!" he cried; "old Joe will never know. I say, we have 'sarcumwented' him, as he'd call it."

"Yes, it's all very well," said Mike, whose conscience was pricking him, "but it always seems so precious easy to do what you oughtn't to."

"Pooh!" cried Vince; "this is nothing."

"Some one is sure to say he has seen the boat out."

"Well, I don't care if he does. Joe ought to have lent us the boat; I'm sure we've done things enough for him. There, don't talk; let's get her. He might come back for something, and stop us."

# Chapter Eighteen
# A Risky Trip

But the old fisherman did not return, and they took down mast, sail, oars, and boat-hook, cast the little craft loose, jumped in, and skilfully sent her along the channel, without startling any mullet this time. Then the tunnel was reached, passed through, a good thrust or two given, and the boat glided out over the transparent waves, Mike thrusting an oar from the stern and sculling her along till they were well out from the shelter of the rocks, when he drew in his oar and helped to step the little mast and hoist the sail. In a few minutes more they were gliding swiftly along, with Vince cautiously holding the sheet and Mike steering.

"As if we couldn't manage a boat!" cried Vince, laughing. "Starboard a little, Ladle. Rocks."

Mike knew the sunken rocks, though, as well as he, and carefully gave them a wide berth; while, as they reached out farther from the land and caught the full power of the soft south-westerly breeze, the boat careened over, the water rattled beneath her bows, and away they went, steering so as to clear the point and get well abreast of the Scraw before going in to investigate, and try if there was an easy way of reaching the sheltered rounded cove.

For some time every rock and point was perfectly familiar; they knew every cavern and rift, and talked and chatted about the days when they had fished here, gone egging there, and climbed up or descended yonder; but after a time the rocks began to look strange.

"Good job for us that Joe's place is on the other side of the island," said Vince cheerily. "I say, what a game if he saw the boat going along, and took out his old glass to try and make out what craft it was?"

"But he isn't this side," said Mike. "I say, think there are any rocks out here?—because I don't know them."

"I don't think there can be," said Vince. "Remember coming out here with your father a year ago?"

"Yes," said Mike; "but we were half a mile farther out, because he said something about the current."

"Well, of course I don't know," said Vince; "but the water looks smooth and deep. We should soon see it working and boiling up if there were any rough rocks at the bottom."

"Or near the top," said Mike thoughtfully. "Now, look: oughtn't we to be seeing the ridge over the Scraw by this time?"

"Not yet," replied Vince, who was carefully scanning the coast now. "We've only just passed the point; and it must be yonder, farther along."

They both scanned the cliffs very carefully, but they all looked much the same—grey, forbidding, and grand, as they towered up from the water, nowhere showing a place where any one could land.

"I say," cried Vince suddenly, "we're going along at a pretty good rate, aren't we?"

"Yes, I was thinking so. Too fast: take in a bit of canvas."

Vince did not speak for a few moments, but gazed from the sail to the surface of the smooth sea and back again two or three times.

"'Tisn't the sail that carries us along so," he said at last; "she only just fills, and hardly pulls at the sheet at all. Ladle, old chap, we're in a current that's carding us along at a tremendous rate."

Mike looked at him in alarm, but Vince went on coolly.

"There's nothing to mind, so long as we keep a sharp look-out for rocks. The old boat would crush up like an egg if she went on one now. Here, Ladle, quick! Look there!"

"What at?"

"The rocks. I mean the cliffs. Ah! port! port!—quick."

Mike obeyed, and none too soon, for as Vince was calling his attention to the shape of the cliffs ashore, a rough, sharp pinnacle of rock rose some ten feet out of the water just in front, with others to right and left, and the boat just cleared the principal danger by gliding through a narrow opening and then racing on upon the other side.

Here they found rock after rock standing out, some as much as twenty feet, whitened by the sea-birds, while others were just level with the surface and washed by foam.

The way was literally strewn with dangers, and prudence suggested lowering the sail; but prudence was wrong—quick sailing was the only way to safety, so that they might have speed enough to insure good steering in the rapid current.

"We must keep on going," said Vince, "or we shall be on the rocks, as sure as we live. I say, can you keep an eye on the shore?"

"No: I'm obliged to mind the rocks ahead. You look."

"I can't," said Vince; "it's impossible, with all these shoals about. Look out! here's quite a whirlpool. Port a little more—port!"

The eddy they had to pass was caused by a couple of rocks close to the surface; and in avoiding these they went stern over another, which appeared to rise suddenly out of the clear sea, and was so close that the wonder to them was that they did not touch it. But the little boat drew very little water, and probably they were a few inches above it as they glided on into deep water again.

"That was a close shave," cried Vince. "I say, it's impossible to try and find the way in there while we have to dodge in and out here."

"Think there would be less current closer in?" said Mike.

"No, I don't. Look for yourself: it's rushing along, and there are twice as many rocks. I say, Ladle, we had better get out of this as soon as we can."

Mike said nothing, but he evidently agreed, and sat there steering with his oar over the stern, his teeth set and his brow knit, gazing straight ahead for the many dangers by which they had to pass, before, to their great relief, the last seemed to be past, and they had time to turn their attention toward the shore.

"It's easy enough now," said Vince. "Why, that's North Point, and the Scraw must be half a mile behind!"

The current was now setting right in, as if to cross the most northern point of the island; and knowing from old experience that it was possible to get into a return current close beneath the north cliffs, they steered in, and, the breeze freshening a little, they gradually glided out of the swift race which had been bearing them along, and in a few minutes were about a hundred yards from the cliffs, in deep water, and were being carried slowly in the opposite direction—that is, back towards the place they sought to examine.

"Well, that's right enough," said Vince; "it's a regular backwater, and just what we wanted. We shall do it this time."

"Think there's any danger?" said Mike.

"Not if it keeps like this," replied Vince. "We'll go on, won't we?"

Mike nodded; and making short tacks, helped by the gentle current which was running well inside the rocks, about which they could see the tide surging, they by degrees approached the range of cliffs which they felt must be the outer boundary of the little cove.

"This is grand," said Vince, as they drew nearer. "Why, it's as easy as can be, and any one might have done it if they'd thought of coming here. I say, isn't it deep? This is a regular channel, and I shouldn't be surprised if it takes us straight to the way in, for it's perfectly plain that it can't be out there. No boat could get in—big or little."

"Yes, this seems to be right," said Mike. "See any rocks?"

"Only outside, and they keep off the tide. I say, Mike, there ought to be some good fishing here. I wonder nobody comes."

"Look!" cried Mike; "that is the ridge of rocks we can see across the cove."

"How do you know?"

"Because it's so covered with cormorants and gulls. Then there ought to be an opening somewhere a bit farther—"

"Look out, Mike! Starboard!—hard, or we shall be on that great snag."

As he spoke Vince seized the sail and swung it across, so as to send the boat upon another tack, and as he did so there was a jerk which nearly threw them overboard, a strange scraping, jarring sensation, and the boat's head was swung round, and she was borne rapidly along once more by the current which they had experienced before.

For the fierce race suddenly swept about the rock they had grazed, catching the boat and treating it as if it had been a cork, leaving the boys to devote all their energies to steering, to avoid the rocks which studded their course.

"Just the same game over again," said Vince, "only we're about a hundred yards nearer in, and the rocks are closer together."

Their experience of half an hour before was being repeated, but with added perils in the shape of larger rocks, while, to make matters worse, water was rapidly rising in the boat, one of whose planks had been started when they struck.

Vince was seaman enough to know what to do, and, warning his companion to keep a sharp look-out ahead, he took off his jacket, and then dragged the jersey shirt he wore over his head. Kneeling in the bottom of the boat, he proceeded to stuff the worsted garment into a jagged hole, through which the clear water came bubbling up like some spring.

Mike had glanced at the bubbling water once, and shuddered slightly; but he did not speak then, for there was a great rock right in front, towards which the boat was rushing, with the sail well-filled, and having the leeward gunwale low down by the surface.

But Mike did not even wince. The current was racing them along, while the wind was fresher now, and as the boy pressed down the blade of the oar he could feel that the boat was fully under his control—that it was like some great fish of which he was the tail, and that he had only to give one good stroke with the oar blade to send the prow to right or left as he willed.

And, as Vince patted and stuffed the woollen jersey as tightly as he could into the place where the water rushed up, Mike sat fast, till with a rush they glided by the dangerous rock, and the boy strained his eyes to catch the next danger.

Nothing was very near, and he spoke.

"Will she sink, Cinder?" he said; and it seemed a long time, in his terrible anxiety, before his companion spoke.

"No. There's a lot of water in, but if you can look out and steer, I can hold the sheet and bale."

He handed the sheet to Mike, crept forward, opened the locker in the bows, and took out an old tin pot kept for the purpose, crept back and took the sheet again, as he knelt down in the water and began to bale, scooping it up, and sending it flying over the side, but without seeming to make much impression.

"Another rock," said Mike.

"All right; you know how to pass it," said Vince, without ceasing his work, but sending the water flying to leeward; and for the next quarter of an hour he did not cease—not even turning his head when they went dangerously near rock after rock.

It was only when, with a deep, catching sigh, Mike said that the current did not seem so strong, that he looked up and saw that the rocky point of the island was nearly a couple of miles away.

"Which way shall I steer?" said Mike; and Vince stood up to take in their position.

"If we go round the point with the tide we shall have to fight against the wind and the current that sets along the west shore," he said. "That won't do. We must go back the way we came."

"What, against that mill race?" cried Mike in dismay.

"No: couldn't do it. We must stand out more to sea."

"Out to sea!" cried Mike, aghast: "with the boat filling with water?"

"Well, we can't go the other way. Besides, if we did old Joe would see us pass by, and there'd be a row."

"Well, he must know. He'll see the hole in the bottom,—if we get back," Mike muttered to himself. "But, Vince," he cried, "hadn't we better run ashore somewhere?"

"Yes: where's it to be?" said the boy, with a curious laugh. "Nonsense! We should only sink her at once. There, I must go on baling. It's the only thing we can do, Mikey. Turn her head to it, and run right across the tide. It's getting slacker here. Keep her head well to it. I won't let her sink."

Mike groaned.

"Hullo!" cried Vince cheerily, "is it hard work?"

There was no reply, but the boat careened over as from the fresh pressure of the oar the sail caught the full force of the wind, and they began to run swiftly towards the south-east, right out to sea, but with the intent of running back after reaching well out to south of the island.

It seemed like madness, with the boat leaking as she did, but Vince was right. It was their only chance; and after a few minutes he said, as if to himself:

"I'm going to do a stupid thing. I ought to hold that sheet in my hand, but I want both for baling. Be on the look-out, Ladle. Mind you throw her up in the wind if she goes over too much."

As he spoke he made the sheet fast, rolled up his sleeves, and, taking the pot in both hands, began to make the water fly over the side.

"I say, Ladle," he cried, "when I'm tired you'll have to take a turn; but don't she go along splendidly with all this water ballast in her?"

"Yes," said Mike huskily. "Are you getting it down?"

"Yes, a little. Not much; but if you sail her well we shall run in all right."

"Aren't we going out too far to sea?"

"No; just right. Now, then, don't talk. I want all my breath for working."

Setting his teeth, the boy baled away, and by slow degrees lowered the water a good deal; but he could not cease for a moment, for it surged in through the leak, nor did he dare to push the jersey farther, for fear of loosening the plank more and making a bigger hole.

This went on for fully half an hour, with the island getting more and more distant, and Mike twice over asked if it was not time to make for the shore.

But Vince shook his head, after a glance back at the south point, and worked away at the baling.

"Now," he said suddenly, "I want to go on, but I'm getting slow. Be ready to jump into my place and scoop it out. I'll catch hold of the oar. Ready?"

"Yes."

"Now then."

The exchange was quickly effected, the water sent flying with more energy, and Vince pressed upon the oar as he rested himself, and sent the brave little boat faster through the sea.

"You're giving it to her too hard," remonstrated Mike, as the gunwale went down dangerously near the surface.

"No, I'm not. You hold your tongue and bale," said Vince fiercely. "Keep it down."

Mike worked as he had never worked before, but he could not get the water an inch lower than Vince had left it. Still he never slackened his pace, though he felt sure that it was gaining upon him, and that before long the boat would begin to sink.

At last he could contain himself no longer, and with a hoarse gasp he cried:

"It's of no use, Vince; she's going down."

"No, she isn't," said the boy quietly; "and she can't go down if we pitch out those two big pieces of iron ballast. She'll go over on her side, and we shall have to hold on if it comes to the worst; but I think I can send her in, Ladle, if you can keep on baling."

"Yes, I can keep on," said Mike faintly.

"Tell me when you're beat out, and I'll begin again."

Mike nodded.

"But keep on till you're ready to drop, so as to give me all the rest you can, for my arms feel like bits of wood."

Mike jerked his head again, and the water went on flying out, looking like a shower of gold in the late afternoon sunshine, till Vince shouted to his companion, in regular nautical parlance, to stand by with the sail.

Mike sprang up and loosened the sheet, standing ready to swing the yard over to the other side. Vince threw the boat up in the wind, the sail swung over, filled for the other tack, and they both began to breathe freely as they glided now toward the south point of the island, where a jutting-up mass of rock, looking dim in the distance, showed where the archway and tunnel lay which led into old Joe's little natural dock.

"Shall we do it, Cinder?" said Mike faintly, as he made fast the sheet on the other side.

"Do it? —yes, of course," cried Vince stoutly. "There, my arms are not so numb and full of pins and needles now. Come here and steer."

"No, I can do a little more," said Mike.

"No, you can't. Obey orders always at sea," cried Vince fiercely; and the exchange of position was made; but there was a full two inches more water in the boat, and as Vince began to bale he did so from where he could at any time seize the pieces of pig iron and tilt them over. In fact, several times he felt disposed to do so, but shrank from it as being a last resource, and from dread lest the act should in any way interfere with the boat's speed.

Over went the water in the sunshine; and as the boy baled, from looking golden, it by slow degrees grew of an orange tint, and sparkled gloriously, but a deadly feeling of weakness fixed more and more upon Vince's arms, and as he toiled he knew that before long he must give up to his companion once again. But still he kept on, though it was more and more slowly; and the despair that he had kept to himself was not quite so terrible, for the south point gradually grew nearer, and he had the satisfaction of feeling that he could manage a boat at sea, and well too, for the course they were steering was dead for the tunnel rock, and, could he keep the boat afloat for another twenty minutes or half an hour, they would be safe.

"Come and steer now?" said Mike.

"No," was grunted out; and Vince baled away till the pot dropped from his hands, and he rose and took the oar, pressing it to his chest, and steering by the weight of his body.

Once more the water flew out faster; but Mike was only making a spurt, and his arm moved more and more slowly, till, with a groan, he said feebly:

"I can't do it any longer."

Vince made no reply, but gazed straight before him, seeing the jutting-up rock as if through a mist, while the water bubbled in through the leak, and rose, and rose, without an effort being made to lower it now.

Would she float till they were close in?—would she float till they were close in?—would she float till they were close in? It was as if some one kept on saying this in Vince's ears, as they rushed on, with the rock nearer and nearer, as if coming out of the mist, till it stood out bright in the setting sunlight, and the mental vapour was dispersed by the feeling of exultation which surged through the steersman's breast. For all at once it seemed that safety was within touch; and, turning the boat head to wind, she glided slowly up to the opening in the rock, while the sail flapped and the two boys quickly lowered and furled it, unstepped the mast, and then thrust her in with the boat-hook, reaching the little dock as if in a dream.

Vince staggered as he stepped out on to the granite stones to make the boat fast, and Mike was in little better condition; but by degrees the suffocating sensation which oppressed them grew less painful, and they slowly and laboriously carried oars, spars and sail up to their place of stowage. Then Vince returned to the boat, thrust down his hand and drew out his jersey, Mike taking hold of one end to help him wring it out.

They had neither of them spoken for some time; but at last Vince said: "We shall have to pay old Joe for the mending of the boat."

"I say, Vince," said Mike, in a low, husky tone, "oughtn't we to be thinking about something else? It was very near, wasn't it?"

"Yes," said Vince, with a passionate outburst, "I was thinking of something else;" and he threw himself down upon a huge piece of wave-worn granite and hid his face on his arm.

Half an hour later, the two lads walked slowly home, feeling as grave and sober as a couple of old men, knowing as they did that, though the evening sunshine had been full in their eyes, the shadow of death had hovered very near.

# Chapter Nineteen
## Having it out with the Enemy

The two boys were very quiet the next morning, on meeting, and their tutor rubbed his hands with satisfaction twice in the course of their lesson.

"Now, that is what I like," he said; "and how much happier you must feel when you have given your minds thoroughly to the work we have in hand!"

That was the only time during the study hours that anything approaching a smile appeared on Vince's face; but he did cock his eye in a peculiar way at Mike, only to receive a frown in return.

At last the lessons were over, and the boys went out into the garden, strolled into the small shrubbery and patch of woodland which helped to shelter the house from the western gales, and then, marvellous to relate, instead of running off to get rid of some of their pent-up vitality, they sat down upon a prostrate tree-trunk, which had been left for the purpose, and Vince began to rub his shins, bending up and down in a peculiar seesaw fashion.

"I am stiff and tired this morning as can be," he said.

"Oh! I'm worse," said Mike. "I feel just as if I were going to be ill. Haven't caught horrible colds through kneeling in the water so long, have we?"

"Oh no; it's only being tired out from what we did. I say, feel disposed to have another try to find the way in?"

"No," said Mike shortly: "I wouldn't go through what we did yesterday for all the smugglers' caves in the world."

"Well, I don't think I would!" said Vince thoughtfully. "I'm sure I wouldn't. I don't want all the smugglers' caves in the world. But it was risky! Every time I went to sleep last night I began dreaming that the boat was sinking from under me, and then I started up, fancying I must have cried out."

"I got dreaming about it all, too," said Mike, with a shudder. "It was very horrible!"

They sat thinking for some time, and then Vince tried to rouse himself.

"Come on," he said.

"No; I want to sit still."

"But you might walk half-way home with me."

"No," said Mike; "I feel too tired and dull to stir. Besides, if I come half-way with you, I shall have as far to walk back as you have to go. That's doing as much as you do. I'll come with you as far as the corner."

"Come on, then," said Vince; and they started, after groaning as they rose. "I feel stiff all over," sighed Vince, "and as if my head wouldn't go."

They parted at the corner, with the understanding that they were to meet as usual after dinner, and at the appointed time Vince came along the roadside to where Mike lay stretched upon the soft turf.

But there was not the slightest disposition shown for any fresh adventure, and the only idea which found favour with both was that they should stroll as far as the cliff known to them as Brown Corner, and sit down to go over the seascape with their eyes, and try and make out their course on the previous afternoon.

Half an hour later they had reached the edge of the cliff, sat down with their legs dangling over the side, and searched the sea for the rocks they had threaded and for signs of the swift current.

But at the end of some minutes Vince only uttered a grunt and threw himself backward, to lie with his hands under his head.

"I can't make anything of it, Ladle," he said impatiently; "and I'm not going to bother. It looked horribly dangerous when we were in it yesterday, but it only seems beautiful to-day."

"Yes," said Mike; "it's because we're so far off, and things are so much bigger than they look. But it was dangerous enough without having the boat leak."

"Horribly," said Vince. "I wonder we ever got back. Won't try it again, then?" he added, after awhile.

"No, I won't," cried Mike, more emphatically than he had spoken that day.

"Well, I don't think I will, Ladle; only I feel as if I had been beaten."

"So do I: as sore all over as sore."

"Tchah! I don't mean that kind of beating: beaten when I meant to win and sail right into the cove in front of the caves. I say, it wasn't worth taking old Joe's boat for and making a hole in the bottom."

"No; and we haven't said a single word about it yet."

"Felt too tired. I don't care. He'll kick up a row, and say there's ten times as much damage done to it as there really is, and it's next to nothing. Five shillings would more than pay for it. I'll pay part: I've got two-and-fourpence-halfpenny at home; but it's a bother, for I wanted to send and buy some more fishing tackle. Mine's getting very old."

"Well, I'll pay all," said Mike. "I've got six shillings saved up."

"No, that won't be fair," said Vince; "I want to pay as near half as I can."

"Well, but you want to buy some hooks and lines, and I shall use those as much as I like."

"Of course," said Vince, as Mike followed his example and let himself sink back on the soft turf, to lie gazing up at the blue sky overhead; "but it won't be the same. I helped poke the hole in the boat, and I mean to pay half. I tell you what: we'll pay for the damage together, and then you'll have enough left to pay for the fishing lines, and I can use them."

"Well, won't that be just the same?"

"No; of course not," said Vince. "The lines will be yours, and you won't be able to bounce about, some day when you're in an ill-temper, and say you were obliged to pay for mending the boat."

"Very well; have it that way," said Mike.

"And we ought to go over and see the old man, and tell him what we did."

"He doesn't want any telling. He has found it out long enough ago. There was the sail rolled up anyhow, too. I was too much fagged to put it straight. When shall we go and see him?"

"I dunno. I don't want to move, and I don't want to have to tell him. He'll be as savage as can be."

The boys lay perfectly still now, without speaking or moving; and the gulls came up from below, to see what was the meaning of four legs hanging over the cliff in a row, and then became more puzzled apparently on finding two bodies lying there at the edge; consequently they sailed about to and fro, with their grey backs shining as they wheeled round and gazed inquiringly down, till one, bolder than the rest, alighted about a dozen yards away.

"Keep your eyes shut, Ladle," said Vince. "Birds are coming to peck 'em out."

"They'd better not," said Mike.

"I say, couldn't we train some gulls, and harness them to a sort of chair, and make them fly with us off the cliff? They could do it if they'd only fly together. I wonder how many it would take."

"Bother the old gulls! Don't talk nonsense. When shall we go and see the old man?"

"Must do it, I suppose," said Vince. "Yes, we ought to: it's so mean to sneak out of it, else we might send him the five shillings. I hate having to go and own to it, but we must, Ladle. Let's take the dose now."

"Do what?" said Mike lazily.

"Go and take it, just as if it was salts and senna."

"Ugh!"

"Best way, and get it over. We've got to do it, and we may as well have it done."

"Yes."

"But I say, when are you going to the cave again? Not to-day?"

"No."

"To-morrow?"

"No."

"Next day?"

"Well, p'r'aps. See how I feel."

"Ready?"

"What for?"

"To go and see old Joe Daygo."

"Haven't got the money with me now."

"We'll go and fetch it, and then go to him."

Mike grunted.

"There, it's of no use to hang back, Ladle; we've got it to do, so let's get it done."

"Yes; you keep on saying we've got it to do, but you don't jump up to go and do it."

"I'm quite ready," said Vince; "and I'll jump up if you will. Now then, ready?"

"Don't bother."

"But we must go, Ladle."

"Well, I know that; but I haven't got the money, and it's so far to fetch it, and I ache all over, and I don't want to see old Joe to-day, and—"

"There, you're shirking the job," interrupted Vince.

"No, I'm not, for I want to get it over."

"Then don't stop smelling the stuff; hold your nose, tip it up, and you shall have a bit of sugar to eat after it if you're a good boy."

"Oh, Cinder, how I should like to punch your head!"

"No, you wouldn't. Come on and take your physic."

"I won't till I like. So there."

"'Cowardy, cowardy, custard, Ate his father's mustard,'" said Vince. "I say, I don't see that there was anything cowardly in eating his father's mustard. It was plucky. See how hot it must have been; but I suppose he had plenty of beef and vegetables with it. He must have had, because, if he hadn't, it would have made him sick."

"What, mustard would?" said Mike, who was quite ready to discuss anything not relating to the visit to old Daygo.

"Yes; mustard would."

"Nonsense. How do you know?"

"Father says so, and he knows all about those sort of things, including salts and senna. So now, then, old Ladle, you've got to get up and come and take your dose."

"Then I shan't take it to-day."

"And have old Joe come to us! Why, it would be disgraceful. You've got to come."

"Have I?" grumbled Mike; "then I shan't."

"''Day, young gen'lemen!"

Mike leaped to his feet in horror, and Vince pulled himself up in a sitting position, to stare wonderingly at the old fellow, who had come silently up over the yielding turf.

"You?" said Mike: "you've come?"

"Nay, I arn't, so don't you two get thinking anything o' the sort. I won't let you have it to go out alone."

"You—you won't let us have it to go out alone?" faltered Vince.

"That's it, my lad," said the old man.

"Then he hasn't found out yet," thought Vince; and he exchanged glances with Mike, who looked ready to dash off.

"Why, yer jumped up as if yer thought I was going to pitch yer off the cliff, Master Ladelle. Been asleep?"

"No, of course not," said Mike; and he looked at Vince, whose lips moved as if he were saying—"I'm going to tell him now."

"Might just as well have said 'yes' to you, though," grumbled Daygo.

"Just as well," assented Vince.

"Nice sort o' condition she's in now. One streak o' board nearly out. Cost me a good four or five shilling to get it mended, for I can't do it quite as I should like."

Four or five shillings! Just the amount Vince had thought would be enough.

"If I'd let you have it," continued the old man, "that wouldn't ha' happened. But I know: they can't cheat me. I'm a-goin' over to Jemmy Carnach to have it out with him, and first time I meets the young 'un I'm going to make him sore. See this here?"

Daygo showed his teeth in a very unpleasant grin, and drew a piece of tarry rope, about two feet long, from out of his great trousers, the said piece having had a lodging somewhere about his breast.

"Do you think Lobster—" began Vince.

"Ay, that's it: lobster," said Daygo. "Lobster it is: Jemmy Carnach would sell himself for lobster, but he arn't a-going to set his pots in my ground and go out to 'zamine 'em with my boat. I don't wish him no harm, but it would ha' been a good job if she'd sunk with him and his young cub. They're no good to the Crag—not a bit. Ay, I wish she'd sunk wi' 'em, only the boat's useful, and I should ha' had to get another."

Old Daygo ceased speaking, and after giving the rope a fierce swish through the air, as if he were hitting at Lobster's back, he put the end inside the top of his trousers, just beneath his chin, and gradually worked it down out of sight.

Vince coughed, and he was about to begin, after looking inquiringly at Mike, who shook his head, and turned it away. But Vince somehow felt as if it would be better to wait till the whole of the rope had disappeared, and Daygo had given himself a shake to make it lie comfortably. Then his lips parted; but the old man checked him by saying,—

"On'y wait till I meet young Jemmy. I've on'y got to slip my hand in here, and it's waiting for him. Yes, young gen'lemen, I'm a-going to make that chap sore as sore as sore."

"No, you're not, Joe," said Vince firmly.

"What? But I just am, my lad. If I don't lay that there piece on to his back, and make him lie down and holloa, my name arn't Daygo."

"But you are not going to thrash him, Joe," said Vince.

"Who'll stop it?"

"I will," said Vince. "It wasn't Jemmy Carnach and his boy."

"Eh? Oh yes, it was. Lobstering they were arter. I know."

"No, you do not, Joe. They didn't take it."

"What!" cried the old man. "Then who did?"

"Mike Ladelle and I."

"You did!" cried the old man, staring. "Why, I told you I wouldn't let you have it, and saw you both go home."

"But we didn't go home," said Vince. "We went and hid in the rocks, and watched till you'd gone away, and then we crept down to the boat and got her out."

"You did—you two did?" cried the old man; and his hand went into the top of his trousers.

"Yes," said Vince desperately, "and we had a long sail."

"Well!" growled the old man,—"well! And I thought it was him!"

"We're very sorry we scraped a rock, and made her leak."

"Made her leak!" roared the old man: "why, she's spyled, and I shall have to get a new boat."

"No, she isn't, Joe: you said it would cost four or five shillings to mend the hole."

"Eh? Did I?"

"Yes, you did; and Mike and I will give you five shillings to get it done."

The old man thrust out his great gnarled hand at once for the money.

"We haven't got it here, Joe," said Vince; "but we'll bring it to you to-night. Eh, Mike?"

"Yes; after tea."

"Honour?"

"Yes: honour."

"Honour bright—gen'leman's honour?"

"Yes," said Vince emphatically.

"Let him say it too," growled Daygo.

"Honour bright, Joe," said Mike.

"Oh, very well, then; I s'pose I must say no more about it," grumbled the old man; "but I'm disappynted—that I am. I thought it were they Carnachs, and I'd made up my mind to give it the young 'un and make him sore. It's such a pity, too. I cut them two feet o' rope off a ring a-purpose to lay it on to him. I owe him ever so much, and it seemed to be such a chance."

"Save it for next time, Joe," said Vince, as Mike looked on rather uneasily, for the old man kept on playing with the end of the rope.

"Eh? Save it for next time?" he said thoughtfully. "Well, I might do that, for the young 'un's sure to give me a chance, and then it won't be wasted. Yes, I'll hang it up over the fireplace at home, ready agen it's wanted. But you two'll bring me that five shilling to-night?"

"Yes, of course."

"Ay, course you will," said the old man slowly.

"There's one thing I likes in a gen'leman. Some chaps says they'll do something, or as they'll pay yer, and they swear it, and then most times they don't; but if a gen'leman says he'll do anything, thère yer are, yer knows he'll do it—without a bit of swearing too. But, haw—haw—haw—haw!"

The boys stared, for the old man burst out into a tremendous roar of laughter, and kept on lifting one leg and stamping it down.

"Why, what are you laughing at?" said Mike, gaining courage now that the trouble was so amicably settled.

"What am I laughin' at?" roared the old fellow, stamping again: "why, at you two! Comes to me and wants to borrow my boat, and boasts and brags and holloas about as to how you knows everything. We can sail her, says you; we knows how to manage a boat as well as you do, and, haw, haw,

haw! you helps yourselves and goes out, and brings her back with a hole in her bottom. Here! where did you go?"

"Oh, along where you took us," said Vince quickly.

"And which rock did you run on?"

"Oh, I don't know what rock it was, only that it was just under water."

"'Course not. Says to me, says you, that you knows all the rocks as well 's me, and goes and runs her on one on 'em fust time."

"Well, it was an accident, Joe."

"Ay, my lads, it were an accident; but you've got to think yourselves very lucky as she didn't founder. Did you have to bale?"

"Yes, all the way home, as hard as ever we could go."

"Ay, you would, with a hole in her like that. Well, I arn't got no time to stand a-talking to you two here; but I just tells you both this: that there boat, as soon as she's mended and fresh pitched, 'll be a-wearing a great big padlock at her stem and another at her starn.—I shall be at home all evening waitin' fer that five shilling."

He gave them both a peculiar wink, stood for a few moments shading his eyes and looking out to sea, and then, giving his head a solemn shake, he went off without another word.

"Feel better, Mike?" said Vince, as soon as the old man was out of hearing.

"Better? Ever so much. I'm glad we've got it over. I say, Cinder, nothing like tipping off your dose of physic at once."

"But I had to take it," cried Vince. "You wouldn't do your share."

That evening after tea they kept their word. Vince handed Mike his two-and-fourpence-halfpenny, and Mike gave him the five shillings which he was to pay.

They found the old man standing outside his cottage, with his old spy-glass under his arm, waiting for them, and apparently he had been filling up the time by watching three or four vessels out in the offing.

"Let's have a look, Joe," said Vince, as soon as the business was over and the money lodged in a pocket, access to which was obtained by the old man throwing himself to the left nearly off his balance, and crooking his arm high up till he could get his fingers into the opening.

The telescope was handed rather reluctantly, and Vince focussed it to suit his sight as he brought it to bear on one of the vessels.

"Brig, isn't she, Joe?" said Vince.

"Ay, my lad; looks like a collier."

"Schooner," said Vince; and then, running the glass along the horizon, he took a long look at a small, smart-looking vessel in full sail, her canvas being bright in the evening glow.

"Why, she's a cutter!" said Vince, rather excitedly: "Revenue cutter."

"Nay, nay, my lad, only a yawrt."

"I don't think she is, Joe; I believe it's a king's ship."

"Tchah! what would she be doing yonder?"

"I don't know," said Vince.

"Done with my glass?" growled the old man.

"Directly," replied Vince; and he swept the sea again.

"Hullo!" he said suddenly: "Frenchman."

"Eh? Where?" said Daygo quickly.

"Right away, miles off the North Point."

The old man took the glass, altered the focus again, and took a long, searching look.

"Bah!" he exclaimed; "that's not a Frenchman, my lads," and he closed the glass with a smart crack. "I say, lookye here."

He led the way to the door, grinning tremendously, and pointed in to where, hanging over the fireplace, was the piece of well-tarred rope, hanging by a loop made of fishing line.

"Ready when wanted—eh?"

The boys laughed and went off soon after towards home.

"Five shillings worse off," said Mike, when they parted for the night; "but I'm glad we got out of all that so easily.—I say, Cinder!"

"Well?"

"It would have been rather awkward if he'd taken it the other way and been in a rage."

"Very," said Vince, before whose eyes the two feet of rope seemed to loom out of the evening gloom.

"And it would have been all your fault."

"Yes," said Vince shortly. "Good-night: I want to get home."

They parted, and as he walked back Vince could not help thinking a good deal about the previous afternoon's experience, and he shook his head more than once before beginning to think of the cavern.

# Chapter Twenty
## Fresh Pulls from the Magnet

A week elapsed; the weather had been stormy, and a western gale had brought the sea into a furious state, making the waves deluge the huge western cliffs, and sending the churned-up foam flying over the edge and inland like dingy balls of snow.

And the boys were kept in by the gale?

Is it likely? The more fiercely the wind blew, the more heavily the huge Atlantic waves thundered against the cliffs and sent the spray flying up in showers, the more they were out on the cliffs searching the dimly seen horizon, watching to see if any ship was in danger.

But it was rare for a ship to be seen anywhere near Cormorant Crag when a sou'-wester blew. Its rocks and fierce currents were too well known to the hardy mariner, who shook his head and fought his way outward into deep water if he could not reach a port, sooner than be anywhere near that dangerous rock-strewn shore.

Vince and Mike had long known that when the wind was at its highest, and it was hard work to stand against it, there was little danger in being near the edge of some perpendicular precipice, and that there, with the rock-face fully exposed to the gale, and the huge waves rushing in to leap against the towering masses with a noise like thunder, they could sit down in comparative shelter, and gaze with feelings akin to awe at the tumult below.

Why? For the simple reason that, after striking against a high, flat surface, the swift current of air must go somewhere. It cannot turn back and meet the winds following it, neither can it dive into the sea. It can only go upward, and sweeps several feet beyond the edge of the cliff before it curves over and continues its furious journey over the land, leaving at the brink a spot that is undisturbed.

These places were favoured always by the boys, who would generally be the only living creatures visible, the birds having at the first breaking out of the storm hastened to shelter themselves on the other side of the island.

"Sea's pretty busy cave-making to-day," said Vince, on one of these stormy mornings. "I wonder what it's like in the cave in front of our place."

"All smooth, of course," said Mike. "It's on the other side, and it's shut-in, so I daresay it doesn't make a bit of difference there. I say, oughtn't we to go there again?"

"You want to open some of those packages," said Vince, as he reached his head a little way over the side of the cliff to gaze down at an enormous roller that came plunging through the outlying rocks a couple of hundred feet below. "Well, what of that?"

"Phew! My!" cried Vince, drawing back breathlessly and wiping the blinding spray from his face. "You can't do that, Ladle. I believe you might try to jump down there and find you couldn't. The wind would pitch you up again and throw you over into the fields."

"Shouldn't like to try it," said Mike drily. "But I say, why shouldn't I want to open the bales and kegs and see what's in them?"

"Because they belong to somebody else, as I told you before."

"If they belong to anybody at all they belong to my father, and he wouldn't mind my opening them."

"Don't know so much about that," said Vince stolidly. "I'll ask him."

"No, no; don't do that," cried Mike, in alarm; "you'll spoil all the fun."

"Very well, then: you ask him what he thinks, then we should know."

"There's plenty of time for that. I never did see such a fellow as you are, Cinder. What's the matter with you?"

"Wet," said Vince. "It was just as if some one with an enormous bucket had dashed water into my face."

"Then you shouldn't have looked over. You might have known how it would be. But look here: never mind the sea."

"But I do mind it. Hear that? Oh, what a tremendous thud that wave came with!"

"Well, of course it did."

"Wonder how many years it will be before the sea washes the Crag all away."

"What nonsense!"

"It isn't. I was talking to Mr Deane about it the other day, and he says it is only a question of time."

"What, before the Crag's washed away? I should think it would be. I'll tell you the proper answer to that—Never."

"Oh, indeed," said Vince: "then how about the caves in under here? Haven't they all been hollowed out, and aren't they always getting bigger? That's how those on the other side must have been made. I shouldn't wonder if they are full of water now."

"What, with all those things in!" said Mike, in alarm. "Oh, I don't believe that. When shall we go and see?"

"It would be horrible to go across the common on a day like this, and we should be soaked getting through the ferns and brambles."

"Yes; it wouldn't be nice now. But will you come first fine afternoon?"

"Well, I don't know."

"Oh, I say," cried Mike reproachfully—"you are getting to be a fellow! You thought the caves grand at first."

"So I did, when we could go there and fish, and cook our tea, and eat it, and enjoy ourselves like Robinson Crusoe; but when it comes to finding the other cave and all that stuff there, it makes one uncomfortable like, and I don't care so much about going."

"Why?"

"I don't know. I can't explain it, but it seems queer, and as if we ought to tell my father or yours. I felt like you do at first, and it seemed as if we'd found a treasure and were going to be very rich."

"So we have, and so we are," said Mike. "I don't see why you should turn cowardly about it."

"I didn't know that it was cowardly to want to be honest," said Vince quietly.

"Only hark at him!" cried Mike, as the waves came thundering in, and the wind roared over them. "You are the most obstinate chap that ever was. Why won't you see things in the right light? Don't those things belong to my father?"

"I don't know."

"Yes, you do. If they were brought and hidden there a hundred years ago, and everybody who brought 'em is dead, as they're on father's land, mustn't they be his?"

"Or the king's."

"The king don't want them, I know. By rights they're my father's, but he won't mind our doing what we like with them, as we were the finders. Now then, don't be snobby; will you come first fine afternoon?"

Vince was silent.

"I won't ask you to meddle with anything—only to keep it all quiet."

Vince picked up a stone and threw it from him, so that it should fall down into the raging billows below, but he made no reply.

"I say, why don't you speak?" cried Mike.

"Who's to talk here in this noise, with the wind blowing your words away?"

"You could just as easily have said you would come as have said that," shouted Mike.

"All right, then, I'll come," said Vince; and Mike gave him a hearty slap on the back. "But look here, Mikey," he continued, "don't you ever think about it?"

"About what?"

"The caves, and all that."

"Of course I do: I hardly think of anything else."

"Yes; but I mean about that young Carnach watching us and old Joe hanging about after us."

"Thought it rather queer once or twice, but of course it was only because we were so suspicious. If we hadn't had the cave and been afraid of any one knowing our secret, we might have met them a hundred times and never thought they were watching us."

"Yes, we might," said Vince thoughtfully. "I don't know, though: they certainly did watch us."

"Then, if they did, it was because we looked as if we wanted to hide something."

"Yes, that sounds right," said Vince. "I never looked at it in that way, and it has bothered me a good deal. Why, of course that is it! I'm all right now, and I'll go with you whenever you like; only we ought to tell them soon. We have known it all to ourselves for some time now."

"Very well, then, we'll tell them soon; and I know my father will say that all the treasure there is to be divided between us two."

"Will he?" said Vince, laughing, for he was far from taking so sanguine a view of the case as his companion; and the matter dropped. They stopped watching the roll and impact of the waves till they were tired, and then went home to wait for the fair weather, which was to usher in their next visit to the caves.

# Chapter Twenty One
# The Mystery unrolls

Four more days passed before the weather broke, and then two more when they were not at liberty. But at last came one when their tutor announced that they could have the whole day to themselves, and it was not long before each announced at home that he was off out for a good long cliff ramble.

This meant taking a supply of provisions, with which each was soon furnished, so as not to break into the holiday by having to come back to dinner.

No questions were asked, for it was taken for granted, both at the Mount and at the Doctor's cottage, that they would be going fishing or collecting; and the boys set off in high glee, meaning to supplement their dinner with freshly cooked fish, and plenty of excitement by climbing about the rocks at the entrance of the caves.

Everything seemed gloriously fresh and bright after the late rains: the birds were circling overhead, and the sea was of a wonderfully vivid blue. In fact, so bright was the day that Vince said,—

"I say, isn't it a shame to go and bury ourselves underground?"

"Not a bit of it," cried Mike; "it's glorious! Why, it's a regular treat, after being away so long. Have you enough wood for cooking?"

"Plenty."

"And what about water?"

"We took a big bottle full last time."

"That's right. I say, keep your eyes open. See anything of old Joe Daygo? Don't seem to be looking on purpose."

They both kept their eyes well open, but there was no sign of the old fisherman; and before long the reason why was plain, for on their coming a little nearer to the cliff edge, on their way to where they struck off for the oak wood, Vince suddenly pointed outward:—

"There he goes."

"Who?" said Mike.

"Old Joe. He has got his boat mended, then."

"That can't be his boat."

"It is. Why, look at that patch on the sail. It's a long way off, but I'm sure it's the boat. He's gone out a long way, seemingly."

"Yes: going out to the sands, I suppose, to try if he can't get some soles."

"Well, we shan't have him playing the spy to-day," said Vince, who was in capital spirits. "Now, if we could see old Lobster going too, we should be all right."

"I dare say his father's got him hoeing carrots or something. We shan't see him."

They did not see Jemmy Carnach's hopeful son, nor any other living being but a cow, which raised its soft eyes to gaze at them sadly, and remained looking after them till they plunged into the scrub-wood, and, once there, felt safe. Then, after their usual laborious work beneath the trees, they reached the granite wilderness, clambered in and out and over the great blocks, keeping an eye as much as they could on the ridge up to their right, in case of the Lobster being there, and finally reached the opening, jumped down through the brambles, and at once made for the spot where the lanthorn and tinder-box were stowed.

"I say, isn't it jolly?" cried Mike eagerly. "Just like old times, getting back here again. What a while it seems!"

"Yes, it does seem a good while," said Vince, beginning to strike a light. "I hope nothing has happened since we were here."

"Eh?" cried Mike excitedly. "What can have happened?"

"Sea washed the place out, and taken all our kitchen and parlour things away."

"Nonsense!" said Mike contemptuously. "Oh, it might, you know; there would have been no waves, but there might have been a high tide. There must have been tremendously high tides down there at one time, so as to have washed out those caves."

"Ah! it's a precious long time since they've been washed out, I know," said Mike, laughing. "They don't ever get swept out now."

"No, but they're kept neat, with sand on the floor," said Vince, snapping to the door of the lanthorn and holding it up for the soft yellow light to shine upon the granite walls. "I say, Mike, don't you think we're a pair of old stupids to make all this fuss over a hole in the ground?"

"No: why should we be?"

"Because it doesn't seem any good. Here we take all this trouble hiding away and going down the hole like worms, so as to crawl about there in the sand."

"And what about the beautiful caves, and the rocks where we sit and watch the sea-birds?"

"We could see them just as well off the cliffs."

"But the cove with the great walls of rock all round, and the current racing round like a whirlpool?"

"Plenty of currents and eddies anywhere off the coast."

"But the fishing?"

"We could fish in easier places," said Vince, talking loudly now they were well down in the passage. "Why, we've had better luck everywhere than here."

"Oh, you are a discontented chap!" said Mike. "You ought to think yourself wonderfully well off, to be able to come down to such a place. See what jolly feasts we've had down here all alone."

"Yes, but it seems to me sometimes like nonsense to be cooking potatoes and frying fish down in a cave, when we could sit comfortably at a table at your house or ours, and have no trouble at all."

"Well, you are a fellow!" cried Mike. "You said one day that the fish we cooked down there tasted twice as good as it did at home."

"Yes, I did one day when we hadn't got it smoky."

"We don't often get it smoky," protested Mike. "But I say, don't talk like that. You were as eager to make our little secret place there as I was. You don't mean to say you're getting tired of it?"

"I don't know," said Vince. "Yes, I do. No, I'm not getting tired of it yet, for it does seem very jolly, as you say, when we do get down here all alone, and feel as if we were thousands of miles from everywhere. But I shall get tired of it some day. I don't think it's half so good since we found the way into the other cave."

"I do," said Mike. "It's splendid to have made such a discovery, and to find that once upon a time there were pirates or smugglers here."

Meanwhile they were slowly descending the bed of the ancient underground rivulet, so familiar with every turn and hollow that they knew exactly where to place their feet when they reached the little falls, and never thinking of stopping to examine the pot-holes, where the great rounded boulders, that had turned and turned by the force of the falling water, still remained. Vince's light danced about in the darkness like a large glowworm, and Mike followed it, humming a tune, whistling, or making a few remarks from time to time; but he was very thoughtful all the same, as his mind dwelt upon the packages in the far cavern, and he felt the desire to examine them increase, till he was quite in a state of fever.

"Pretty close, aren't we?" said Mike at last, to break the silence of the gloomy tunnel.

"Yes, we shall be there in five minutes now. But, I say, suppose we find that some one has been since we were here?"

"Well, whoever it was, couldn't have taken the caves away."

"No; but if Lobster has found out the way down?—and I dare say he has, after tumbling into the front hall."

"'Tisn't the front hall," said Mike laughingly; "it's the back door. Front hall's down by the sea, where the seal cave is."

"Have it which way you like," said Vince, giving the lanthorn a swing, "but it seems to me most like the back attic window. I say, though, if Lobster has found it out, he'll have devoured every scrap we left there, and, I daresay, carried off the fishing tackle and pans."

"A thief! He'd better not," cried Mike.

"Ha—ha—ha!" laughed Vince. "I do call that good."

"What? I don't know what you mean."

"Your calling him a thief for taking away the things he discovered there."

"Well, so he would be. They're not his."

"No," said Vince, laughing; "and those things in the far cavern aren't ours, but you want to take them."

"That's different," said Mike hastily. "We only put our things there a few weeks ago; those bales and barrels have been there perhaps hundreds of years."

"Say thousands while you're about it, Ladle," cried Vince cheerily. "Hold hard. *Puff!*"

The candle was blown out through a hole in the lanthorn, and the latter lowered down to the usual niche close to the cavern wall, where they were accustomed to keep it.

"Down with you!" cried Vince; and Mike required no second telling, but glided down the slope so sharply that he rolled over in the sand at the bottom.

"Below!" shouted Vince; and he charged down after him, sitting on his heels, and also having his upset. "I say, though, I hope no one has been."

They walked across the deep, yielding sand, with the soft pearly light playing on the ceiling; peered through into the outer cave; and then Mike, who was first, darted back, for there was a loud splash and the sound as of some one wallowing through the water at the cave mouth.

"Only a seal," cried Vince. "There goes another."

He ran forward over the sand in time to see a third pass out of a low, dark archway at the right of the place where the clear water was all in motion from the powerful creatures swimming through.

"I say, Mike, why don't we take the light some day and wade in there to see how far it goes?" said Vince, as he looked curiously at the doorway of what was evidently a regular seal's lurking-place.

"Because it's wet and dark; and how do we know that we could wade in there?"

"Because you can see the rock bottom. It's shallow as shallow."

"And how do you know that it doesn't go down like a wall as soon as you get in?"

"We could feel our way with a stick, step by step; or, I know, we'd get the rope—bring a good long one—and I'd fasten it round your waist and stand at the door and send you in. Of course I'd soon pull you out if you went down."

"Thank you," cried Mike, "you are kind. My mother said you were such a nice boy, Cinder, and she was glad I had you for a companion, as the Crag was so lonely. You are a very nice boy, 'pon my word."

"Yes; I wouldn't let you drown," said Vince.

"Thank ye. I say, Cinder, when you catch me going into a place like that, just you tell me of it, there's a good fellow."

Vince laughed.

"Why, who knows what's in there?" said Mike, with a shiver.

"Ah! who knows?" said Vince merrily. "I tell you what it is, Ladle: that must be the place where the things live that old Joe talked about."

"What things?"

"Those that take hold of a boat under water, and pull it along till it can't come back and is never heard of again."

"Ah, you may grin, Cinder," said Mike seriously; "but, do you know, I thought all that when we were out yonder in the boat. It felt just as if some great fish had seized it and was racing it along as hard as it could, and more than once I fancied we should never get back."

"Did you?" said Vince quietly.

"Yes, you needn't sneer. You're such a wooden-headed, solid chap, nothing ever shakes you; but it was a very awful sensation."

"I wasn't sneering," said Vince, "because I felt just the same."

"You did?"

"Yes, that I did, and though I wanted to laugh at it because it was absurd, I couldn't then. But, I say, though, we might try and get to the end of that cave, just to see how far it goes."

"Ugh! It's bad enough going through a dark hole with a stone floor."

"Till you're used to it. See how we came down this morning."

"Yes, but we weren't wading through cold, black water, with all kinds of live things waiting to make a grab at you."

"Nonsense! If there were any things there they'd soon scuttle out of our way."

"Ah, you don't know," said Mike. "In a place like this they grow big because they're not interfered with. Those were the biggest seals I ever saw."

"Yes, they were tidy ones. The biggest, I think."

"Yes, and there may be suckers there. Ugh! fancy one of those things getting one of his eight legs, all over suckers, round you, and trying to pull you into his hole."

"Take out your knife and cut the arm off. They're not legs."

"I don't know what they are: just as much legs as arms. They walk on 'em. Might be lobsters and crabs, too, as big as we are. Think of one of them giving you a nip!"

"Wish he would," said Vince, with a grin. "We'd soon have him out and cook him."

"Couldn't," said Mike. "Take too big a pot."

"Then we'd roast him; and, I say, fancy asking Jemmy Carnach down to dinner!"

"Yes," cried Mike, joining in the laugh. "He'd eat till his eyes would look lobstery too, and your father would have to give him such a dose."

"It don't want my father to cure Jemmy Carnach when he's ill," said Vince scornfully. "I could do that easy enough."

"And how would you do it, old clever?"

"Tie him up for two or three days without anything to eat. Pst! Hear that?"

"Yes," said Mike, in a whisper, as a peculiar hollow plashing sound arose some distance down the low dark passage, and the water at the mouth became disturbed. "Shoal of congers, perhaps—monsters."

"Pooh! It was another seal coming out till it saw or heard us, and then it gave a wallop and turned back. Look here, I'll wade in this afternoon if you will."

Mike spun round on his heels. "No, thank you," he cried. "Come on, and let's look round to see if all's right."

A few minutes proved that everything was precisely as they had left it; and as soon as they had come to this conclusion, they found themselves opposite the fissure which led into the other cavern.

Mike glanced at the rope and grapnel, and then back inquiringly at his companion.

"No!" said Vince, answering the unspoken question that he could plainly read in Mike's eyes; "we can have a good afternoon without going there."

"How? What are we going to do?"

"Fish," said Vince shortly.

"But I should like to go and see if everything is there just the same as it was."

"If it has been there for a hundred years, as you say, it's there all right still. Come on."

"But I should just like to have a peep in one or two of the packages, Cinder."

"Yes, I know you would; but you promised not to want to meddle, or I wouldn't have come. Now didn't you?"

"All right," said Mike sulkily; "but I did think you were a fellow who had more stuff in you. There, you won't do anything adventurous."

"Yes, I will," cried Vince quickly: "I'll get the lanthorn and go and explore the seal's hole, if you'll come."

"And get bitten to death by the brutes. No, thankye."

"Bitten to death! Just as if we couldn't settle any number of seals with sticks or conger clubs!"

"Ah, well, you go and settle 'em, and call me when you've done."

"No need to. You wouldn't let me go alone. Now then, we'll get some fish, and have a good fry."

Vince ran to the wall, where their lines hung upon a peg; and now they noticed, for the first time, that there had been a high tide during the late storm, for the sand had been driven up in a ridge at one side of the cave mouth, but had only come in some twenty or thirty feet.

Their baits, in a box pierced with holes to let the water in and out, were quite well and lively; and putting some of these in a tray, they went cautiously out from rock to rock in the wide archway till there was deep water just beyond for quite another twenty feet; then rocks again, and beyond them the gurgling rush and hurry of the swift currents, while the pool before them, though in motion, looked smooth and still, save that a close inspection showed that the surface was marked with the lines of a gentle current, which apparently rose from below the rocks on the right.

It was an ideal place for sea-fishing, for the great deep pool was free from rocks save those which surrounded it, and not a thread of weed or wrack to be seen ready to entangle their lines or catch their hooks; while they knew from old experience that it was the sheltered home of large shoals, which sought it as a sanctuary from the seals or large fish which preyed upon them.

In addition, the place they stood upon was a dry, rocky platform, shut off from the cave by a low ridge, against which they could lean their backs, whilst another much lower ridge was just in front, as if on purpose to hide them from the fish in the crystal water of the great pool.

Partly behind them and away to their right was the entrance to the seals' hole, from which came a hollow splashing from time to time, as something moved; every sound making Mike turn his head quickly in that direction, and bringing a smile to Vince's lips.

"Ah! it's all very well," said Mike sourly, "but everybody isn't so brave as you are."

"Might as well have lit our fire before we came here," said Vince, ignoring the remark.

"What's the good of lighting the fire till we know whether we shall get any fish?" said Mike. "We didn't catch one last time, though you could see hundreds."

"To boil the kettle and make some tea," replied Vince; and he rose to get hold of the bait, pausing to look back over the ridge which shut him off from the cave, and hesitating.

"I think I'll go back and light the fire," he said, as he fixed his eyes on the dark spot which they made their fireplace, it looking almost black from the bright spot they occupied, which was as far as they could get out towards the open cove.

"No, no; sit down," said Mike impatiently. "We didn't catch any last time because you would keep dancing about on the rocks here, and showing the fish that you were come on purpose to hook them. We can get a good fire in a few minutes. There's plenty of wood, and we're in no hurry."

"You mean you kept dancing about," retorted Vince. "Very well," he added, seating himself, "it shan't be me, Ladle: I won't stir. But it's the wrong time for them. If we were to come here just before daylight, or to stop till it was dark, we should be hauling them out as fast as we could throw in our—our" —*splash*—"lines."

For as Vince spoke he had resumed his seat, deftly placed a lug-worm on his hook and thrown the lead into the water, where it sank rapidly, drawing after it the line over the low ridge of rock.

"There," said Vince, as his companion followed his example, "I won't move, and I won't make a sound."

"Don't," said Mike: "I do want to catch something this time."

"All right: I won't speak if you don't."

"First who speaks pays sixpence," said Mike.

"Agreed. Silence!"

The fishing began, but fishing did not mean catching, and the time went on with nothing to take their attention but an unusual clamouring on the part of the sea-birds, which, instead of sitting about preening and drying their plumage, or with their feathers almost on end, till they looked like balls as they sat asleep in the sun, kept on rising in flights, making a loud fluttering whistling as they swept round and round the cove, constantly passing out of sight before swooping down again upon the great rocks which shut out the view of the open sea.

Lines were drawn up, rebaited, and thrown in again, with the faint splashes made by the leads, and they tried close in to the side, to the other side, to right and left; but all in vain,—the baits were eaten off, and they felt that something was at their hooks, but whether they struck directly, or gave plenty of time, it was always the same, nothing was taken and the hours passed away.

They were performing, though, what was for them quite a feat, for each boy had fully made up his mind that he would not have to pay that sixpence. They looked at each other, and laughingly grimaced, and moved their lips rapidly, as if forming words, and abused the fish silently for not caring to be caught, but not a word was spoken; till all at once, after a tremendous display of patience, Vince suddenly struck and cried:

"Got him at last!"

"Sixpence!" said Mike.

"All right!" said Vince quietly: "I was ready to pay ninepence so as to say something. I've got him, though, and he's a big one too."

"Be steady, then. Don't lose him, for I'm sick of trying, and I did want for us to have something for tea."

"Oh, I've hooked him right enough; but he don't stir."

"Bah! Caught in the bottom."

"Oh no, I'm not. He was walking right away with the bait, and when I struck I felt him give a regular good wallop."

"Then it's a conger, and it's got its tail round a rock."

"May be," said Vince. "Well, congers aren't bad eating."

"B–r–r–ur!" shuddered Mike. "I hate hooking them. Line gets twisted into such a knot. You may cut it up: I shan't."

"Yes, I'll cut him in chunks and fry him when I get him," said Vince. "He's coming, but it isn't a conger. Comes up like a flat fish, only there can't be any here."

"Oh, I don't know," said Mike. "I daresay there's plenty of sand down below."

"Well, it is a flat fish, and a heavy one too," said Vince, as he hauled in cautiously, full of excitement, drawing in foot after foot of his line; and then he cried, with a laugh, "Why, it's a big crab!"

"Then you'll lose it, for certain. 'Tisn't hooked."

"Shall I lose him!" said Vince, with another laugh, as he lifted out his prize for it to come on to the rock with a bang. "Why, he has got the line twisted all round his claw, and— Ah! would you bite! I've got him safe this time, Mike."

Safe enough; for, after the huge claws of the monstrous crab had been carefully tied with a couple of bits of fishing line, it was quite a task to disentangle the creature, which, in its eagerness to seize the bait, had passed the line round and under its curious armoured joints, and in its struggles to escape, made matters worse.

"This is about the finest we've seen, Mike," said Vince. "Well, I'm sorry for him, and we'll try and kill him first; but his fate is to be cooked in his own shell, and delicious he'll be."

"I should like to take him home," said Mike, as he wound up his line.

"So should I; but if either of us did we should be bothered with questions as to where we got it, and we couldn't say. We shall have to cook it and eat it ourselves, Ladle. Come on; we don't want any more fish to-day."

They stepped back over the rocks, and while Mike hung up the lines Vince thrust his prize into the big creel they had close to the place they used for their fire, and then hurried towards the inner cave to fetch the tinder-box and a portion of the wood they had stored up there for firing, as well as the extra provisions they had brought with them that day.

"It strikes me, Mikey, that we're going to have a regular feast," said Vince. "Lucky I caught that fellow!—if I hadn't we should have come short off."

"Hark at him bragging! I say, why didn't you catch a lobster instead?"

*Phew*! came a soft whistle from the opening into the passage—a whistle softened by its journey through the subterranean place; but sounding pretty loudly in their ears, and as if it had been given by some one half-way through.

"Lobster!" ejaculated Vince excitedly. "Why, there he is coming down."

"Oh, Vince!" cried Mike, "that spoils all. I felt sure he would, after falling in as he did. He saw the hole, and he is searching it."

"Yes, and he'll come right on, feeling sure we're here."

"What shall we do? I know: frighten him."

"Frighten him? How?"

"Go up and stand at the bottom of one of the steep bits, and when he comes up, throw stones at him and groan."

"Bah!" ejaculated Vince contemptuously; "that wouldn't frighten him. He'd know it was us. I say, it's all over with the place now."

"Yes, for he'll tell everybody, and they'll come and find the outer cave with all the treasure in it."

"Yes, that won't do, Ladle. There's no help for it now; there'll be no secret caves. You must tell your father to-night, and he'll take proper possession of the place. If he don't, every one in the island will come and plunder."

"Yes, that's right," said Mike; "but it's a horrible pity. I am sorry. But what shall we do now?"

"There's only one thing I can think of now—yes, two things," whispered Vince: "either go up and stop him, fight for it and not let him come; or hide."

"Hide?" said Mike dubiously.

"Yes, down here in the sand. It's dark enough. We could cover ourselves."

"Or go and hide in the other cave," said Mike. "Yes, we'll get the rope and grapnel, and get up into the great crack, pull the rope up, and we can watch from there."

"That's it," said Vince. "We only want to gain time till Sir Francis knows."

"And your father," said Mike. "Fair play's a jewel, Cinder. Look sharp! Come on!"

They listened in the gloom of the inner cave for a few moments, and then Mike led the way to the opening between the two caves, passing behind the rock, and as he did so he turned to whisper to his companion—

"Perhaps he won't find this way through."

Then he stepped on over the deep, soft sand, and was about to pass through into the outer cavern, when he saw something which made him dart back, to come heavily in collision with Vince; but not until the latter had seen that which startled Mike.

For there, standing in the sand, gazing up at the fissure, was a heavy, thick-set, foreign-looking man, with short black hair, a very brown skin, and wearing glistening gold earrings, each as far across as a half-crown piece. The glance taken by the boys was short enough, but they saw more than that, for they caught sight of a rope hanging down and a man's legs just appearing.

"*Vite! vite!*" cried the foreign-looking fellow. "*Dépêchez*; make you haste, you slow swab you."

There was a growl from above, and something was said, but the boys did not hear what. They heard the beating of their hearts, though, and a choking sensation rose to their throats as they stood in the narrow way between the two caverns, asking themselves the same question—What to do?

For they were between two fires. The caves were in foreign occupation, that was plain enough; and the whistle had not come from young Carnach, but from some one else.

There could be no doubt about it: these were not strangers, but the smuggling crew come to life again after being dead a hundred years, if Mike was right; a crew of the present day, come to see about their stores, if Vince's was the right version.

Whichever it was, they seemed to be quite at home, for a second whistle came chirruping out of the long passage, as the boys hurried into the gloomy inner cave for safety, and this was answered by the Frenchman, who roared:

"Ah, tousan tonderres! Make you cease if I come;" but all the same an answering whistle came from the outer cave.

What to do? Where to hide? They were hemmed in; and it was evident that either the party in the long passage was coming down, and might even now be close to the slope, or the Frenchman and the others were going to him.

It took little time to grasp all this, and almost as little to decide what to do. The boys had but the two courses open to them—to face it out with the foreign-looking man, who seemed to be leader, and his followers; or to hide.

They felt that they dared not do the former then, and on the impulse of the moment, and as if one spirit moved them both, they decided to hide—if they could!

The inner cavern was gloomy enough, and they could only dimly make out the top of the opening above the slope; all below was deep in shadow, for the faint pearly light only bathed the roof. But still they felt sure that if they entered from the upper entrance or from below they must be seen, unless they did one thing—and that was, carried out the idea suggested for hiding from young Carnach.

They had no time for hesitation; and any hope of its being still possible to escape by the upper passage was extinguished by a clinking noise, as of a big hammer upon stone, coming echoing out of the opening, suggestive of some novel kind of work going on up there; so, dashing to the darkest part of the cave—that close down by where the slope came from above—the boys thrust the lanthorn and tinder-box on one side and began to scoop away at the deep, loose sand near the wall. Then, shuffling themselves down something after the fashion of a crab upon the shore, they cast the sand back over their legs and then over their breasts and faces, closing their eyes tightly, and finally shuffling down their arms and hands.

Anywhere else the manoeuvre would have been absurd to a degree; but there, in the gloom of that cavern, there was just a faint chance of any one passing up or down the slope without noticing that they were hiding, while all they could hope for now was that the heavy, dull throb, throb, of their hearts might not be heard.

Vince had covered his face with sand, but a few laboured breathings cleared his nostrils, and one of his ears was fully exposed; and as he lay he longed to do something more to conceal both himself and his companion; but he dared not stir, for the people in the outer cave were moving about, and their leader could be heard in broken English cursing angrily whoever it was that had dared to come down into his cave.

They heard enough to make them lie breathlessly, almost, waiting, while the moments seemed to be terribly prolonged; and at last Vince found himself longing for the time to come when they would be discovered, for he felt that if this terrible suspense were drawn out much longer he must spring up and shout aloud.

Possibly the two lads did not lie there much more than two minutes, but they were to Vince like an hour, before he heard the rough, domineering voice in the outer cavern cry out—

"Now, *mes enfans*, forvard march!" And there was a dull sound following, as of men's heavily booted feet shuffling and ploughing up the sand.

# Chapter Twenty Two
## Two Boys in a Hobble

Five men, headed by the heavy fellow who spoke in broken English, passed silently before the boys through the soft sand, their figures looking black against the beautiful light which seemed to play on the ceiling of the place. Then the leader stopped, and he gazed sharply round for a few minutes, his eyes seeming to rest for some time upon the sand which the boys had strewed over themselves and burrowed into as far as they could get.

Vince shivered a little, for he felt that it was all over and that they must be seen; but just as he had come to the conclusion that the best thing he could do would be for them to jump up and throw themselves upon the man's mercy, the great broad-shouldered fellow spoke.

"Dere sall not be any mans here. Let us go up and see vat they do—how they get on."

Apparently quite at home in the place, he walked to the foot of the slope, and for the first time saw the rope, and was told that it was not theirs.

"Aha!" he cried, "it vas time to come here and look. *En avant!*"

He seized the rope, and in spite of his size and weight he went up skilfully enough, the others following as actively as the boys would have mounted; and while Vince and Mike lay perspiring beneath the sand, they heard the next order come from the opening on high.

"Light ze lanthorn," said the Frenchman sharply; and, trembling now lest the light should betray their hiding-place, the boys lay and listened to the nicking of the flint and steel, heard the blowing on the tinder, saw the faint blue gleam of the match, and then the gradually increasing light, as the wood ignited and the candle began to burn; but throwing the rays through into the cavern, they passed over the corner where the boys lay, making it intensely dark by contrast, and they breathed more freely as the dull sound of the closing lanthorn was heard and the Frenchman growled out—

"*Vite! vite!* I have to lose no time."

People seemed to be doing something more, far in the passage, which evoked the sharply spoken words of their leader; but what it was the boys could not make out, though they heard a strange clinking, as of pieces of iron being struck together, and then there was a loud clang, as if a crowbar or marlinspike had fallen upon the stony floor.

"*Ah, bête* with the head of an *Anglais cochon*—pig! You always have ze finger butter. Now, *en avant*, go on—*dépêchez*, make haste."

There was the sound of footsteps, the shuffling over stones, as if the men were not accustomed to the way; and then the light rapidly grew more feeble, and finally died out.

"Phew!" sighed Vince, expiring loudly and blowing away the sand which had trickled about his lips, but not without first more firmly closing his eyes.

"Hist!" whispered Mike; and then he sputtered a little and whispered the one word "Sand."

There was no need to say more; the one word expressed his position, and Vince knew all he suffered, for the sand was trickling inside his jersey round the neck, and if he had not raised his head a little it would have been in his eyes, of which he naturally had a horror.

The two boys lay perfectly still in their corner, listening with every sense upon the strain; and for some little time the movements of the men could be heard very plainly, every step, every stone that was dislodged sending its echo whispering along the narrow passage as a voice runs through a speaking tube.

At last all seemed so still that they took heart to whisper to each other.

"What shall we do, Cinder?" said Mike.

"I don't know, unless we go through into the other cave."

"What's the good of that?—they'll come back soon and find us."

"Unless we can hide somewhere among the bales, or right up in the back, where it's dark."

"That might do," said Mike. "But, I say, what have they gone after?"

"To try and find us."

"But they don't know us."

"Well, the people who are using this cave, and they must know of the way up to the top. Ah! that's it."

"Yes; what?" cried Mike excitedly.

"Hist! don't speak so loudly. They've gone up there to loosen some of the stones and block the way, so as to put an end to any one coming down; or else to lay wait and trap us."

Mike drew a long, deep breath; and it sounded like a groan.

"Oh dear!" he said; "whatever shall we do? Perhaps we had better get through into the other cavern. They'll search this thoroughly, perhaps, when they come back; but they mayn't search that."

"That's what I thought," said Vince. "Yes, it's the only thing for us to do, unless we go into the seals' cave and try and hide there."

"Ugh!" said Mike, with a shudder. "Why, it may be horribly deep, and we should have to swim in ever so far in the darkness before we touched bottom; and who knows what a seal would do if it was driven to bay?"

"Better have to fight seals than be caught by these men, Ladle," said Vince. "But we ought to have something to fight the seals with. There's the big stick in the other cavern, and your knife."

"And yours."

"Yes; there's mine," said Vince thoughtfully. "Ah! of course there's the conger club with the gaff hook at the end."

"To be sure. But, oh no, we couldn't do that. It would be horrible to wade or swim into that hole without a light."

"We'd take a light," said Vince.

"Yes, but we'd better try the other cave," said Mike hurriedly. "I feel sure we could hide in the upper part. Draw a sail over us, perhaps: they'd never think we should hide in an open place like that, where they landed."

"Very well, then: come on. Here's the lanthorn and the tinder-box."

Vince secured these from where they lay half buried in the sand; and then, rising quickly out of their irritating beds, and scattering the loose fine dry grit back, they hurried into the outer cave, seized the rope and grapnel, and Mike was swinging it to throw up into the opening, when his arm dropped to his side, and he stood as if paralysed, looking wildly at his companion.

For that had occurred upon which they had not for a moment counted. They had seen the party of men pass them, and it never struck either that this was not all, till they stood beneath the opening in the act of throwing the grapnel. Then, plainly heard, came a boisterous laugh, followed by the murmur of voices.

They looked at each other aghast, as they saw that their escape in that direction was cut off. There was no seeking refuge among the bales, and in despair the grapnel was thrown down in its place; while, in full expectation of seeing more of the smuggler crew come through the fissure, they were hurrying back to the inner cave, when Vince turned and caught up the conger club and the heavy oaken cudgel, holding both out to Mike to take one, and the latter seized the club.

Enemies behind them and enemies in front, they felt almost paralysed by their despair and dread, half expecting to find the party that had ascended already back. But on reaching the dark cave all was perfectly still for a few moments, during which they stood listening.

"Think we could find a better place to hide in here?" said Mike, in a husky whisper.

"No; they had that lanthorn with them."

"But if we shuffle down in the sand again?"

"It's of no use to try it," said Vince sharply. "Once was enough. We must try the seal cave."

"Then why did you come in here?" whispered Mike petulantly.

"Because you were afraid to go into that black hole in the dark."

"And so were you," said Mike angrily.

"That's right, Ladle—so I am," whispered Vince coolly; "and that's why I came in here for the moment, to think whether we could possibly hide."

"Hist! I can hear them coming."

Vince stood listening to the murmur of voices coming out of the opening above them.

"Ever so far back yet," he whispered; and he dropped upon his knees and opened the tinder-box and the lanthorn, which he had placed before him on the sand.

"No, no; don't do that," protested Mike, who was half wild with alarm.

"Can't help it: we must have a light," said Vince; and the cavern began to echo strangely with the nicking of the flint and steel.

"Then come in the other cavern," said Mike, as he stood holding the club and cudgel.

"Don't bother me. Other fellows would hear me there, and the wind blows in."

And all the time he was nicking away, and in his hurry failing to get a spark to drop in the tinder.

"Oh! it's all over," said Mike. "They're close here."

"No, they're not. Ah! that's it at last."

For a spark had settled on the charred linen, and was soon blown into a glow which ignited the brimstone match; but, quick as Vince was in getting it to burn and light the candle, it seemed to both an interminable length of time before he could close the door of the lanthorn and shut the half-burned match in the tinder-box.

This last he was about to hide in a hole he began to scratch in the sand; but on second thoughts he thrust the flat box, with its rattling contents, under his jersey, and caught up the lanthorn, which now feebly lit the cavern.

"Yes," said Vince; "they're pretty close now, for the voices sound very distinct. Come on."

He turned into the narrow passage to enter the outer cave, and they stopped short in horror as they stood in the full light there, for a loud chirruping whistle came suddenly from the fissure before them and up to the left; and it had hardly ceased echoing when it was answered from the inner cave behind them, and was followed by a shout, which sounded as if the men were sliding down the rope and close at hand.

"Not much time to spare," said Vince, in a hurried whisper. "Come on, Ladle." And, lanthorn in hand, the light invisible as he hurried to the mouth of the cave, he stepped into the water, and, wading to the low arch on their right, stooped low and went in, closely followed by Mike; and, as they passed on, with the lanthorn light showing them the dripping walls and root of the place, covered with strange-looking zoophytes, there was a loud flopping, rushing, and splashing, which sent a wave above their knees, and made Mike stop short and seize his companion.

"Only a seal. Come on," said Vince; and he pressed forward, with the water getting deeper instead of more shallow, and a doubt rising in his mind as to whether they would be able to get in far enough to be safe.

"Hist! Quiet!" he whispered, for the sound of voices came to where they stood, and Vince felt that if sound was conveyed in one direction it certainly would be in the other.

"Mustn't say a word, or they'll hear us and be in and fetch us out in no time. Come on, or they'll see the reflection of the light."

"Can't," whispered back Mike faintly. "I've got my boot down a crack, wedged in."

Vince seized him sharply by the shoulder, and Mike nearly fell back into the water; but this acted like a lever, and the boot was wrenched free, just as another whistle was heard and its answer, both sounding strangely near.

Quite certain that if they did not get in farther the reflection from the lanthorn must be seen, Vince waded on, with the water rising from his knees to his thighs, and then, feeling terribly cold, nearly to his waist.

"We mustn't go any farther," said Mike in an excited whisper, "or we shall have to swim."

"Very well, then, we must swim," said Vince, holding the light well up above the water, and looking anxiously along the dark channel ahead, the roof not being two feet above their caps.

Deeper still—the water above their waists—but the cavern went nearly straight on, and Vince was about to open the door and blow out the light, when Mike caught his arm.

"Don't do that," he whispered: "it would be horrible here, with those beasts about. There, you can hear one swimming, and we don't know what else there may be."

"But they'll see the light."

"Well, let them," said Mike desperately. "I'd rather wade out."

"I'll risk it, then," said Vince; and then he drew a breath of relief, for at the end of a couple of yards the depression along which they had passed was changing to a gradual rise of the cavern floor, and the water fell lower and lower, till it was considerably below their waists, and soon after shallow in the extreme.

They went on with mingled feelings, satisfied that they were getting where they would not be discovered, and also into shallow water, that promised soon to rise to dry land; but, on the other hand, they kept having hints that they were driving back living creatures, which made known their presence by wallowing splashes, that echoed strangely along the roof, and made the boys grasp club and cudgel with desperate energy.

To their great joy, now, on looking back they found that they could not see the daylight shining in from the mouth upon the water, and as, in consequence, any one gazing into the cave was not likely to see the dim rays of their lanthorn, the boys paused knee-deep, glad to find that they need go no farther along the narrow channel—one formed, no doubt, by the gradual washing away of some vein of soft felspar or steatite.

"Pretty safe now," whispered Vince.

*Plash!*

"Ugh!" ejaculated Mike. "What's that?"

"Seal or some big fish," said Vince: "something we've driven in before us."

"I don't want to be a coward, Cinder," whispered Mike; "but if it's a great conger, I don't know what I should do."

"Hit at it," replied Vince. "I should, even if I felt in a regular squirm. But we needn't mind. The things we've driven up before us are sure to be in a horrible flurry, and all they'll think about will be of trying to get away."

"Think so?"

"Why, of course. You don't suppose there are any of the things that old Joe talked about, do you?"

"No, of course that's nonsense; but the congers may be very big and fierce, and isn't this the sort of place they would run up?"

"I dunno. S'pose so," said Vince. "They get in holes of the rocks, of course; but I don't know whether they'd get up such a big, long cave as this. Wonder how far it goes in? Pst!"

Vince grasped his companion's arm tightly, for they were having a proof of the wonderful way in which sound was carried along the surface of the water, especially in a narrow passage such as that in which they had taken refuge.

For all at once the murmur of voices sounded as if it were approaching them, and their hearts seemed to stand still, as they believed that they were being pursued.

But the next minute they knew that the speakers were only standing at the mouth of the cave and looking in, one of the men apparently whispering close to them, and with perfect distinctness: —

"Seals," he said. "I came and listened last time I was here, and you could hear 'em splashing and walloping about in the water. Like to go on in?"

"No," said another voice. "Get 'em up in a corner and they'll show fight as savage as can be; and they can bite too."

"Good polt on the head with a club settles them, though, soon enough."

"Ay, but who's to get to hit at 'em, shut up in a hole where you haven't room to swing your arm? 'sides, they're as quick as lightning, and they'll come right at you."

"What, attack?"

"Nay, I don't say that: p'r'aps it's on'y trying to get away; but if one of they slippery things comes between your legs down you must go."

"Think there's any in now?"

"Bound to say there are. They comes and goes, though. Listen: p'r'aps you'll hear one."

As it happened, just then there was a peculiar splashing and wallowing sound from some distance farther in, and it ended with an echoing report, as if one of the animals had given the surface of the water a heavy blow with its tail.

"No mistake—eh?" said one of the voices.

"Let's get the lanthorn and go in," said one eagerly.

"Nay, you stop wheer you are. Old Jarks is wild enough as it is about some one being here. If he finds any of us larking about, he'll get hitting out or shootin', p'r'aps."

"I say," said another voice—all sounding curiously near, and as if whispering for the two fugitives to hear—"think anybody's been splitting about the place?"

"I d'know. Mebbe. Wonder it arn't been found out before. My hye! I never did see old Jarks in such a wax before. Makes him sputter finely what he does blaze up. I don't b'lieve as he knows then whether he's speaking French or English."

"Well, don't seem as if we're going to ketch whoever it is."

"What! Don't you be in a hurry about that. If old Jarks makes up his mind to do a thing, he'll do it."

"Think he'll stop?"

"Stop? Ay, for a month, but what he'll ketch whoever it is. Bound to say they've been walking off with the silk and lace at a pretty tidy rate."

"They'll be too artful to come again, p'r'aps."

"Ah! that's what some one said about the mice, but they walked into the trap at last."

"What'll he do if he does ketch 'em?"

"Well, there, you know what old Jarks is. He never do stand any nonsense. I should say he'd have a haxiden' with 'em, same as he did with that French *douane* chap. Pistol might go off, or he might take 'em aboard and drop 'em—"

*Murmur, murmur, murmur*—and then silence.

The speakers had evidently turned away from the mouth of the seal hole, and the boys did not hear the end of the sentence.

"Oh!" groaned Mike faintly.

"I say, Ladle, if you make a noise like that they'll hear you, and come and fetch us out."

"I couldn't help it. How horrid it sounds!"

"Yes," said Vince very softly, "but he has got to catch us yet. Who's old Jarks? Here, I know: they mean the Frenchman: Jacks—Jacques, don't you see?"

"Yes, I see," said Mike dismally.

"He's the skipper, of course. French skipper with an English crew. They must be a nice set. I say, do you feel cold?"

"Cold? I don't feel as if I had any feet at all."

"We must have some exercise," said Vince grimly; and he uttered a faint chuckling sound. "I say, though, Mike don't be down about it. He's only a Frenchman, and we're English. We're not going to let him catch us, are we?"

"It's horrible," said Mike. "Why, he'll kill us!"

"He hasn't caught us yet, I tell you, lad. Look here: we know everything about the caves now, and we can go anywhere in the dark, can't we?"

"Yes, I suppose so," said Mike dismally.

"Very well, then; we must wait till it's dark, and then creep out and make for the way out."

"Is no way out now: it's either stopped up or watched."

"Well, then, we'll get out by the mouth of the smugglers' cave, and creep up on to the cliffs somewhere."

"Current would wash us away; and if we could get to the cliffs you know we shouldn't be able to climb up. We're not flies."

"Who said we were? Well, you are a cheerful sort of fellow to be with!"

"I don't want to be miserable, Cinder, old chap, but it does seem as if we're in a hole now."

"Seem? Why we are in a hole, and a good long one too," said Vince, laughing softly.

"Ah, I can't see anything to joke about. It's awful—awful! Cinder, we shall never see home again."

"Bah! A deal you know about it, Ladle. That French chap daren't shoot us or drown us. He knows he'd be hung if he did."

"And what good would it do us after he had killed us, if he was hung? I shouldn't mind."

"Well, you are a cheerful old Ladle!" said Vince. "Why don't you cheer up and make it pleasanter for me?"

"Pleasanter?" said Mike. "Oh!"

"Be quiet, and don't be stupid," said Vince. "Look here: don't forget all you've read about chaps playing the hero when they are in great difficulties."

"Who's going to play the hero when he's up to his knees in cold water?" cried Mike bitterly.

"Well, he has a better chance than if he was up to his neck; same as that fellow would have a better chance than one who was out of his depth."

"I say," cried Mike excitedly, "does the tide run up here and fill the cave?"

"No. It was high water when we came in, wasn't it? We never saw it more than half-way up the arch. Now look here, Ladle: we're in a mess."

"As if I didn't know!"

"And we've got to get ourselves out of it, because nobody knows anything about this place or our having come here. Think Lobster will say he has seen us come this way once? He's sure to hear we're missing and that they're looking for us."

"I don't suppose he will," said Mike dismally. "If they came this way they wouldn't find the hole. They'll think we've gone off the cliff and been drowned. What will they say! what will they say!"

These words touched Vince home, and for a few minutes a peculiar feeling overcame him; but the boy had too much good British stuff in him to give way to despair, and he turned angrily upon his companion:

"Look here, Ladle," he said: "if you go on like this I'll punch your head. No nonsense—I will. I don't believe that French skipper dare hurt us, but we won't give him the chance to. We can't see a way out of the hobble yet, but that's nothing. It's a problem, as Mr Deane would say, and we've got to solve it."

"Who can solve problems standing in cold water? My legs are swelling already, same as Jemmy Carnach's did when he was swept out in his boat and nearly swamped, and didn't get back for three days."

"You're right," said Vince. "I can't think with my feet so cold. Let's get into a dry place."

"What, go out?"

"No," said Vince; "we'll go in."

# Chapter Twenty Three
# A Strange Night's Lodging

Mike shrank from attempting to penetrate farther into the narrow hole; but Vince's determination was contagious, and, in obedience to a jog of the elbow, he followed his companion, as, with the lanthorn held high enough for him to look under, the cudgel in his right-hand, he began to wade on, finding that the passage twisted about a little, very much as the tunnel formed by the stream did—of course following the vein of mineral which had once existed, and had gradually decayed away.

To their great delight, the water, at the end of fifty yards or so, was decidedly shallower; the walls, which had been almost covered with sea anemones, dotted like lumps of reddish green and drab jelly, only showed here, in company with live shells, a few inches above the water, which now, as they waded on, kept for a little distance of the same depth, and then suddenly widened out.

Vince stopped there, and held up the lanthorn, to see the darkness spread all around and the light gleaming from the water, which had spread into a good-sized pool.

"Mind!" cried Mike excitedly: "there's something coming."

He turned to hurry back, but Vince stood firm, with his cudgel raised; and the force of example acted upon Mike, who turned towards him, grasping the conger bat firmly, as the light showed some large creature swimming, attracted by the light.

But the boys did not read it in that way. Their interpretation was that the creature was coming to attack them; and, waiting till it was within reach, Vince suddenly leaned forward and struck at it with all his might.

The blow only fell upon the water, making a sharp splash; for the lad's movement threw the lanthorn forward, and the sudden dart towards the animal of a glaring object was enough. The creature made the water surge and eddy as it struck it with its powerful tail, and went off with a tremendous rush, raising a wave as it went, and sending a great ring around to the sides of the expanded cavern, the noise of the water lapping against the walls being plainly heard.

This incident startled, but at the same time encouraged the lads, for it gave them a feeling of confidence in their own power; but as soon as they recommenced their advance, there was another shock,—something struck against Vince's leg, and in spite of his effort at self-command he uttered a cry.

There was no real cause for alarm, though; and they grasped the fact that the blow was struck by one of a shoal of large fish, or congers, making a rush to escape the enemies who had invaded their solitude, and in the flurry one of them had struck against the first object in its way. "I'm sure they were congers," whispered Mike. "I felt one of them seem to twist round me."

"Never mind: they're gone," replied Vince. "Come on. I fancy there must be a rocky shore farther on, as it's so shallow here, and it's all sand under foot."

"Not all: I've put my feet on rock several times," whispered Mike.

"Well, that doesn't matter. There's plenty of sand. Look out!"

There was a tremendous splashing in front, and the water came surging by them, while they noticed now that the sides of the place were once more closing in as they advanced.

"Shall we go back?" said Vince; for the sudden disturbance in front, evidently the action of large animals, or fish, had acted as a check to him as well as his companion.

Mike was silent for a few moments. Then he said hoarsely: "I'll stick to you, Cinder, and do what you do."

"Then come on," said the boy, who felt a little ashamed of his feeling of dread.

"Can't be sharks, can it?" whispered Mike, as, in addition to the lapping and sucking noises made by the water, there was a peculiar rustling and panting.

"Sharks, in a cave like this? No. They're seals, I'm sure, four or five of them, and they've backed away from us till they've got to the end. Hark! Don't you hear? There is a sort of shore there, and they are crawling about."

He waded forward two or three steps, holding up the light as high as he could; but the feeble rays, half quenched by the thin, dull horn, did not penetrate the gloom, and at last, as the strange noises went on, the boy lowered the lanthorn, opened the door, and turned the light in the direction just before them.

They saw something then, for pairs of eyes gleamed at them out of the darkness, seen vividly for a moment or two, and disappearing, to gleam again, like fiery spots, somewhere else.

Mike wanted to ask if they really were seals; but in spite of a brave effort to be firm, his voice failed him, the surroundings were so strange, and, standing there in the water, he felt so helpless. Every word about the horrors of the Black Scraw told to them by old Daygo came to him with vivid force, and his tongue clove to the roof of his mouth, and there was a sensation as of something moving the roots of his hair.

Then he started, for Vince closed the lanthorn with a snap and said hoarsely:—

"Hit hard, Mike. They must go or we must, and I'm growing desperate."

"Go on?" faltered Mike.

"Yes, and hit at the first one you can reach. They're lying about there, on the dry sand."

His companion's order nerved Mike once more; and, drawing a deep breath, he whispered "All right," though he felt all wrong.

"Don't swing the club, or you may hit me," said Vince. "Strike down, and I'll do the same. Now then, both together, and I'll keep the lanthorn between us. Begin."

They made a rush together through the water, which, after a few steps, grew rapidly shallow; and then they were out upon soft sand, striking at the dim-looking objects just revealed to them by the light; and twice over Vince felt that he had struck something soft, but whether it was seal or sand he could not tell. Violent strokes had resounded from the roof of the echoing cavern, as Mike exerted himself to the utmost, hitting about him wildly in despair, while every few moments there was a loud splashing. Then Mike fell violently forward on to his face, for one of the frightened creatures made a dash for the water. The panting, scuffling, splashing, and wallowing ceased, and Vince held up the light.

"Where are you?" he cried, forgetting the necessity for being silent.

"Here," said Mike, rising into a sitting position on a little bank of coarse sand, which was composed entirely of broken shells.

"Hurt?"

"Yes;—no. I came down very heavily, though."

"Fall over one of the seals?"

"No, it went between my legs, and I couldn't save myself. Well, we've won, and I'm glad we know now they were only seals. It was very stupid, but I got fancying they were goodness knows what horrible creatures."

"So did I," said Vince, with a faint laugh. "Old Joe's water bogies seemed to be all there, with fiery eyes, and I hit at them in a desperate way like. I say, you can't help feeling frightened at a time like this, specially when one of them fastens on you like a dog."

"What!"

"Yes," said Vince quietly, and without a tinge of boasting in his utterances. "I was whacking about at random, when one came at me, and made a sort of snip-snap and got hold, and for a bit it wouldn't leave go; but I whacked away at it as hard as I could, and then it fell gliding down my leg, and the next moment made another grab at me, but its head was too far forward, and it only knocked me sidewise. Such a bang on the thigh: I nearly went down."

"But where are you bitten?" cried Mike excitedly.

"Here," said Vince, laughing, and holding the lanthorn to his side. "Only my jacket, luckily. Look, it tore a piece right out. What strength they've got! I felt it worrying at it, wagging its head like a dog. I say, Mike!"

"Yes."

"I was in a stew. I wasn't sorry when the brute dropped down."

"It's horrible," said Mike.

"Oh, I don't know. I don't feel a bit scared now. I tell you what, though: it has warmed me up. I'm not cold now. How are you?"

"Hot."

"Then let's have a look round."

Raising the lanthorn, the two prisoners cautiously advanced for about twenty feet, and then were stopped by solid rock, forming a sharp angle, where the two walls of the cave met. Their way had been up a slope of deep, shelly sand, which crushed and crunched beneath their feet, these sinking deeply at every step. Then the light was held higher, with the door open; and by degrees they made out that the pool was about fifty or sixty feet broad, and touched the rock-walls everywhere but out by this triangular patch of sand, which was wet enough where the seals crawled out, the hollows here and there showing where one had lain; but up towards the angle it was quite dry, and the walls were perfectly free from zoophyte or weed—ample proof that the water never rose to where they stood.

"Well," said Vince, setting down the lanthorn close to the wall, "we've won the day, the enemy is turned out of its castle, and the next thing, I say, is to get off our wet, cold things."

"I can't take matters so coolly as you do," said Mike bitterly. "I was only thinking of getting away out of this awful place."

"Oh, it isn't so awful now you know the worst of it," said Vince coolly, though a listener might have thought that there was a little peculiarity in his tone. "One couldn't help fancying all sorts of horrors, but when you find there is nothing worse than seals—"

"And horrible congers: I felt them."

"So did I," said Vince; "but I've been thinking since. The congers wouldn't live in a place where seals were. There'd be fights, and perhaps the seals would get the best of them."

"But don't I tell you I felt one swim up against me and lash its great body half round my leg?"

"I believe those were young seals, swimming for their lives to get out to sea. There, take off your wet things and wring them out. I'm going to fill my boots with fine sand. It's not cold in here, and I dare say the things will dry a bit."

"But suppose the seals come back."

"They won't come back while we're here, Ladle—I know that. They're full of curiosity, but as shy as can be. They can see in the dark, and—"

"Dark!" cried Mike.

"To be sure. We mustn't go on burning that candle."

"But—"

"Look here, old chap," said Vince quietly: "there are only about two inches of it left. That wouldn't last long, and I'm sure it's better to put it out and save it for some particular occasion than to burn it now."

"But there's just enough to light us to the mouth of this terrible hole."

"And give ourselves up to old Jarks, as that fellow called him, whose pistol might go off by accident, or who might take us on board his vessel and let us fall overboard."

"That was only what the man said," argued Mike petulantly. "If we go boldly up to this smuggler captain and tell him that we only found out the caves by accident, and that we haven't touched any of the smuggled goods—"

"Pirates!"

"Smuggled."

"You stuck out it was pirates."

"But I didn't believe it then. Well, if we go to him and say that we have always kept the place a secret, and that we'll go on doing so, and swear to it if he likes, he will let us go."

"Go out boldly to him, eh?" said Vince.

"Yes, of course."

"Ah, well, I can't. I don't feel at all bold now. It all went out of me over the fight with the seals. That one which fastened on my jacket finished my courage."

"Now you're talking nonsense," said Mike angrily.

"Very well, then, I'll talk sense. If that captain was an Englishman perhaps we would do as you say; but as he's a Frenchman of bad character, as he must be, I feel as if we can't trust him. No, Ladle, old chap, I mean for us to escape, and the only thing we can do now is to wait till it's dark and then try. We mustn't run any risks of what Mr Jarks might do. Now then, you do as I've done before I put out the light."

"You're not going to put out the light."

"Yes, I am."

"I won't have it. It shall burn as long as I like. Besides, you couldn't light it again."

"Oh yes, I could. I've got the tinder-box, and it has always been too high up to get wet."

"I don't care," said Mike desperately; "it's too horrible to be here in the dark."

"Not half so horrible as to be in the dark not knowing that you could get a light if you wanted to. We could if I put it out. We couldn't if it was all burned."

"I don't care, I say once more—I say it must not be put out."

"And I say," replied Vince, speaking quite good-humouredly, while his companion's voice sounded husky, and as if he were in a rage—"and I say that if you make any more fuss about it I'll put it out now."

As Vince spoke he made a sudden movement, snatched the lanthorn from where it stood by the wall, and tore open the door.

"Now," he cried, catching up a handful of sand, "you come a step nearer, and I'll smother the light with this."

Mike had made a dart to seize the lanthorn, but he paused now.

"You coward!" he cried.

"All right: so I am. I've been in a terrible stew to-day several times, but I'm not such a coward that I'm afraid to put out the light."

Mike turned his back and began to imitate his companion in stripping off his wet lower garments, wringing them thoroughly, and spreading them on the dry sand, with which he, too, filled his saturated boots.

Meanwhile Vince was setting him another example—that of raking out a hole in the softest sand, snuggling down into it and drawing it over him all round till he was covered.

"Not half such nice sand as it is in our cave, Ladle," he said.

There was no answer.

"I say, Ladle, don't I look like a cock bird sitting on the nest while the hen goes out for a walk?"

Still there was no reply, and Mike finished his task with his wet garments.

"Sand's best and softest up here," said Vince, taking out the tinder-box from the breast of his jersey and placing it by the lanthorn.

Mike said nothing, but went to the spot Vince had pointed out, scraped himself a hollow, sat down in it quietly, and dragged the sand round.

"Feels drying, like a cool towel, doesn't it?" said Vince, as if there had been no words between them.

"You can put out the light," said Mike, for answer.

"Hah, yes," replied Vince, taking the lanthorn; "seems a pity, too. But we shan't hurt here. Old Jarks won't think we're in so snug a spot."

Out went the light, Vince closed and fastened the door, and then, settling himself in his sandy nest, he said quietly,—

"Now we shall have to wait for hours before we can start. What shall we do—tell stories?"

Mike made no reply.

"Well, he needn't be so jolly sulky," thought Vince. "I'm sure it's the best thing to do.—Yes, what's that?"

It was a hand stretched out of the darkness, and feeling for his till it could close over it in a tight, firm grip.

"I'm so sorry, Cinder, old chap," came in a low, husky voice. "All this has made me feel half mad."

There was silence then for a few minutes, as the boys sat there in total darkness, hand clasped in hand. Then Vince spoke.

"I know," he said, in a voice which Mike hardly recognised: "I've been feeling something like it, only I managed to stamp it down. But you cheer up, Ladle. You and I ought to be a match for *one* Frenchman. We're not beaten. We must wait."

"And starve," said Mike bitterly.

"That we won't. We'll try to get right away, but if we can't we must get something to eat and drink."

"But how?"

"Find where those fellows keep theirs, and go after it when it's dark. They won't starve themselves, you may be sure."

Mike tried to withdraw his hand, for fear that Vince should think he was afraid to be in the dark; but his companion's grasp tightened upon it, and he said softly,—

"Don't take your fist away, Ladle; it feels like company, and it's almost as good as a light. I say, don't go to sleep."

"No."

Mike meant to sit and watch and listen for the fancied splash that indicated the return of the seals. But he was tired by exertion and excitement, the cavern was warm and dry, the sand was become pleasantly soft, and all at once he was back in the great garden of the fine old manor-house amongst the flowers and fruit, unconscious of everything else till he suddenly opened his eyes to gaze wonderingly at the thick darkness which closed him in.

Vince had fared the same. Had any one told him that he could sleep under such circumstances, in the darkness of that water den, the dwelling-place of animals which had proved to him that they could upon occasion be desperate and fierce, he would have laughed in his face; but about the same time as his companion he had lurched over sidewise and fallen fast asleep.

# Chapter Twenty Four
## Getting Deeper in the Hole

For some moments Mike sat up, gazing straight before him, dazed, confused, not knowing where he was. Time, space, his life, all seemed to be gone; and all he could grasp was the fact that he was there.

At last, as his brain would not work to help him, he began to try with his ringers, feeling for the information he somehow seemed to crave.

He touched the sand, then a hand, and started from it in horror, for he could not understand why it was there.

By degrees the impression began to dawn upon him that he had been awakened by some noise, but by what sound he could not tell. He could only feel that it was a noise of which he ought to be afraid, till suddenly there was something or somebody splashing or wallowing in the water.

That was enough. The whole tide of thought rushed through him in an instant, and, snatching at the hand, he tugged at it and whispered excitedly, —

"Cinder — Vince! — wake up. They've come back."

"Eh? What's the matter? Come back? What, the smugglers? Don't speak so loud."

"No, no — the seals. Light the lanthorn. Where did you put the club and stick?"

"Stop a moment. What's the matter with you? I've only just dropped asleep. Did you say the seals had come back?"

"Yes: there, don't you hear them?"

"No," said Vince, after a few moments' pause, "I can't hear anything. Can you?"

"I can't now," said Mike, in a hoarse whisper; "but they woke me by splashing, and then I roused you."

"Been dreaming, perhaps," said Vince. "I suppose we must have both dropped asleep for a few minutes. Never mind, we can keep awake better now, and — Hullo!"

"What is it?"

"Here: look out, Mike—look out!"

There was no time to look out, no means of doing so in the darkness, and after all no need. Vince had placed his hand upon something hairy and moist, and let it stay there, as he wondered what it was, till that which he had felt grasped the fact that the touch was an unaccustomed one, and a monstrous seal started up, threw out its head and began to shuffle rapidly away from where it had been asleep. The alarm was taken by half a dozen more, and by the time the two boys were afoot and had seized their weapons—*splash, splash, splash!*—the heavy creatures had plunged back into the pool from which they had crawled to sleep, and by the whispering and lapping of the water on the walled sides of the cave the boys knew that the curious beasts were swimming rapidly away towards the mouth.

"Nice damp sort of bedfellows," said Vince, laughing merrily. "I say, Mike, I'm all right. I don't know, though—I can't feel my legs very well. Yes, they're all right."

"What do you mean?" said Mike. "I meant they haven't eaten any part of you, have they?"

"Don't talk stuff," said Mike, rather pettishly. "How could we be so foolish as to go to sleep?"

"No foolishness about it," said Vince quietly. "We were tired, and it was dark, and we dropped off. I say, I'm hungry. Think we've been to sleep long?"

"I don't know. Perhaps. There's only one way to find out: go to the mouth of the hole."

"Yes—that's the only way," said Vince; "and now the use of the candle comes in. I don't know, though: it seems a pity to light the last bit. Shall we go and see?"

Mike suppressed a shiver of dread, and said firmly,—"Yes."

Another point arose, and that was as to whether they should put on their clothes again.

It seemed a pity to do so and again get them wet; but both felt repugnant to attempting to wade back without them, and they began to feel about, half in dread lest the seals which had visited them in the night should have chosen their clothes for a sleeping place.

They were, however, just as they had been left, and, to the astonishment of both, they were nearly dry.

"Why, Mike," cried Vince, "we must have slept for hours and hours."

"We can't. The cave's warm, I suppose, and that accounts for it. How are your trousers getting on?"

"Oh, right enough, only they're very gritty. Glad to get into them, though."

In a very short time they were dressed, and it being decided that they would not return here if it were possible to avoid it, the lanthorn and tinder-box were taken, and they made up their minds to make the venture of wading back in the dark.

Mike was rather disposed to fight against it, but he yielded to his companion's reasoning when he pointed out that before long they would be able to see the light, and their lanthorn would be superfluous.

Vince rose, and starting with the cudgel outstretched before him, he stepped down into the water and began to wade.

His first shot for the opening in front proved a failure, for he touched the wall across the pool, but finding which way it trended he was not long in reaching the place where it gradually narrowed like a funnel—their voices helping, for as they spoke in whispers the echoes came back from closer and closer, the water deepened a little, and then Vince was able to extend the cudgel and touch the wall on either side.

Once only did he feel that they must have entered some side passage, and he stopped short with the old feeling of horror coming over him as the thought suggested the possibility of their wandering away utterly and hopelessly lost in some fearful labyrinth, where they would struggle vainly until they dropped down, worn out by their exertions, to perish in the water through which they waded.

"What's the matter?" said Mike, in a quick, sharp whisper; and Vince remained silent, not daring to speak, for fear that his companion should detect his thoughts by the tremor he felt sure that there would be in his voice.

"Do you hear? Why don't you speak?" said Mike. "Don't play tricks here in the dark."

"I'm not playing tricks," replied Vince roughly, after making an effort to overcome his emotion. "I'm leading, and I must think. Are we going right?"

"You ought to know. I trusted to you," said Mike anxiously, "and you wouldn't light the candle."

"Yes, it is all right," said Vince; and, mastering the feeling of scare that had come over him, he passed his hand along the wall, feeling the slimy cold sea anemones and the peculiar clinging touch of their tentacles. Then he pressed steadily on, till all at once there was a faint dawning of light. They turned one of the bends, and the dawn, became bright rays, which rapidly increased as they softly waded along, being careful now to speak to each other in whispers, and to disturb the water as little as possible; till at last there in the front was the low arch of the cave, framing a patch of sunny rock dotted with grey gulls, and an exultant sensation filled Vince's breast, making him ready to shout aloud.

The sensation of delight was checked by feeling Mike's hand suddenly upon his shoulder tugging him back, and at the same moment he saw the reason. For there, in the opening, evidently standing up to his shoulders in water, was some one gazing straight into the narrow cavern, and Vince felt that they must have been heard and a sentry placed there to watch for their coming out.

"But it is impossible for him to see us," thought Vince; and he stood there pondering on what it would be best to do, while a feeling of hope cheered him with the idea that perhaps after all they had not been heard, and that it was by mere accident that the man was gazing in.

The next moment he felt again ready to utter an exultant cry, for there was a sudden movement of the watching head, a dive down, and the water rose and fell, distinctly seen against the light.

"Bother those old seals!" he said: "they're always doing something to scare us. I really thought it was a man."

"Looked just like it," said Mike, making a panting sound, as if he had been holding his breath till he had been nearly suffocated.

"That chap must have been able to see us though we are in the dark. What wonderful eyes they have!"

"Perhaps the light shines on us a little," replied Mike.

"Very likely; but it's curious what animals can do. I wonder at their coming and lying down so near us."

"That was because we lay so still, I suppose. But we oughtn't to talk."

"No; come along: but what are we going to do? We shan't be able to stand in the water very long."

They waded very slowly on, hardly disturbing the surface, and straining their ears to catch the slightest sound; but the faint roar of the currents playing among the rocks, and the screams and querulous cries of the sea-birds which flew to and fro across the mouth of the cavern were all they could hear.

They were pretty close to the entrance now, but they hesitated to go farther, and remained very silent and watchful, till a thought suddenly struck Vince, who placed his lips close to Mike's ear.

"I say," he said, "oughtn't it to be this evening?"

"Of course."

"Then it isn't. It's to-morrow morning."

"Nonsense!"

"Well, I mean it's morning, and we've slept all night."

"Vince!"

"It is, lad. Look—the sun can't have been up very long; and oh, Mike, what a state they must have been in at home about us!"

Mike uttered a faint groan.

"It's horrid!" continued Vince passionately. "What shall we do?"

Mike was silent for a few minutes, and then said sadly,—"They won't have slept all night."

"No," said Vince wildly; "and they've been wandering about the place with people searching for us. Mike, it's of no use, we mustn't try to hide any longer. That Jarks daren't hurt us, and we had better go out boldly."

"Think so?"

"Yes. You see, we can't stay here standing in the water, and if we go back to the sand in there—"

Mike shuddered. "I can't go back there," he said.

"That's just how I feel," said Vince, speaking in a low, excited tone. "I didn't say much, but I couldn't help being horribly frightened."

"It was enough to scare anybody there in the dark, not knowing what might happen to us next," sighed Mike. "We can't go back. If we do we should soon starve. Think we could go to the mouth here and wade out, and then swim to that opening we saw?"

"No," said Vince decidedly, as he recalled the aspect of the turbulent cove from where he sat astride the stone; "no man could swim there, and I don't believe that a small boat could live in those boiling waters."

"Then we must go boldly out," said Mike. "Who's this fellow? He has no right to come here. Why, my father would punish him severely for daring to do it!"

"If he could catch him, Ladle, old fellow. But the man knows it, and that's what frightens me—I mean, makes me fidgety about it. But we must go."

"There is one chance, though," said Mike eagerly: "he may have taken fright and gone with all his smuggled stuff."

"Of course he may," said Vince eagerly. "Why, here are we fidgeting ourselves about nothing. While we've been sleeping in this seal cavern, he has had his men working away to carry off all that stuff to his ship. Poor old Ladle! He won't even get enough silk to make his mother a dress. Well, are you ready?" he continued, with forced gaiety. "I'm hungry and thirsty, and my poor feet feel like ice."

Mike hesitated.

"We must go," said Vince, changing his tone again. "Mike, old chap, it's too horrid to think of them at home. Come on."

Mike did not speak, but gave a sharp nod; and, summoning all their resolution, and trying hard to force themselves to believe that the smugglers had gone, they waded carefully on, now breathing more freely as they reached the mouth, with the bright light of morning shining full in to where they were, and sending a thrill of hope through every fibre and vein.

They paused, but only for a few minutes; and then, after a sign to Mike, Vince took another step or two, and leaned forward till he could peer round the side of the low arch and scan the interior of the outer cave.

Then, slowly drawing back, after a couple of minutes' searching examination, he spoke to Mike in a whisper.

"There isn't a sign of anybody," he said; "and I can't hear a sound. Come on, and let's risk it."

Their pulses beat high as, bracing themselves together, they stepped right from the low archway, moving very cautiously, so as to gaze out as far as they could command at the cove.

They fully expected to see some good-sized vessel lying there, or at least a large boat; but there were the sea-birds and the hurrying waters—nothing more. "They must have gone," whispered Vince. "Unless they are where we can't see—round by their cave."

"I believe they've gone," said Vince; and they stepped in on to the soft, loose sand, to find everything belonging to them untouched. Then, gaining confidence, Mike stepped boldly inward, right up to the right-hand corner beneath the fissure, and stood listening, but there was not a sound.

"Right," he whispered, as he stepped back: "they have gone."

But the boy's heart beat faster as he led the way now to the entrance of the inner cave; for there was the possibility of the passage being blocked, and, another thing, it was early morning, and the smugglers might be sleeping still in the soft sand.

Vince whispered his fears, and then, going first, he passed into the narrow passage without a sound, and stole cautiously along it till he could crane his head round and look.

For some moments he could see nothing, but by degrees his eyes grew accustomed to the soft gloom, and the walls and roof and sandy floor gradually stood out before his eyes, and the next minute, to his great joy, he could see the rope running up into the dark archway and disappearing there.

Nothing more: no sound of heavy breathing but his own—no trace of danger whatever.

He drew back again and placed his lips to his companion's ear.

"It's all right," he whispered; "they must have gone. Shall we step back and go to the far cave and see?"

"No," said Mike decisively. "Home."

"Yes: home!" said Vince. "Come on."

Leading once more, he stepped into the cavern, whose interior now grew plainer and plainer to their accustomed eyes, and, crossing at once to the bottom of the slope, he seized the rope and gave it a sharp tug.

"Will you go first?" he whispered.

"I don't mind," replied Mike. "No,—you;" and Vince tightened the rope again, feeling that in a very short time they would be able to set the anxieties of all at rest.

"Father won't be so angry when he knows," thought the boy; and, hanging there to the rope, he was about half-way up when he let go and dropped to the sand, for a figure suddenly appeared in the dark opening over his head, and before he could recover from his astonishment a piercingly shrill whistle rang through the inner cave.

# Chapter Twenty Five
# Trapped Birds

"Quick back to the seal hole!" whispered Vince; and the boys darted to the dark passage leading to the outer cave, and then stopped short, for the way was blocked by a man with a drawn cutlass, and two others were running up, while another was in the act of sliding down a rope from the fissure.

Directly after, *thud, thud, thud* came the sound of men dropping down into the inner cave, and in another moment there was a rude thrust from behind which drove Mike against Vince, and the two boys were forced onward through the opening to the outer cave, the man with the cutlass giving way sufficiently to let them enter, but presenting the point at Vince's chest, while one of his comrades performed the same menacing act for Mike, the other two taking up a position to right and left, and effectually cutting off escape.

The next instant the figure of the big, broad-chested leader came out into the light, and upon the boys facing round to him his features were pretty well fixed upon their brains as they noted his smooth, deeply-lined brown face, black curly hair streaked with grey, dark, piercing eyes and the pair of large gold earrings in his well-formed ears. "Aha!" he cried, showing his white teeth, "*bonjour, mes amis*. Good-a-morning, my young friends. I hope you sal have sleep vairy vell in my hotel. Come along vis me: ze brearkfas is all vaiting."

This address, in a merry, bantering tone, so different from the fierce burst of abuse which he anticipated, rather took Vince aback; and he was the more staggered when the man held out his hand naturally enough, which Vince gripped, Mike doing precisely the same.

"Dat is good, vairy good," said the man, while his followers looked on. "You vill boze introduce yourself. You are—?"

He looked hard at Mike.

"Michael Ladelle," said the owner of the name.

"And you sall be—?"

"Vincent Burnet."

"Aha, yaas. I introduce myself—Capitaine Jacques Lebrun, at your sairvice, and ze brearkfas vait. You are vairy moshe ready?"

"Yes," said Vince boldly; "I want my breakfast very badly."

"Aha, yaas; and *votre ami*, he vill vant his. You do not runs avay?"

"Not till after breakfast," said Vince, smiling.

"No? Dat is good. You are von brave. Zen ve vill put avay ze carving knife and not have out ze pistol. *En avant!* You know ze vay to ze *salle-à-manger*. You talk ze Français, bose of you. Aha?"

"I can understand that," said Vince. "So can he. *N'est-ce pas*, Mike?"

A short nod was given in response, and the French captain clapped them both on the shoulders, gripping them firmly and urging them along.

"It is good," he said. "I am so *bien aise* to see my younger friend. Up vis you!"

"Come along, Mike," said Vince, in a low voice; "it's all right."

Mike did not seem to think so, but he followed Vince up the rope into the fissure, after one of the armed men; the captain came next, and he kept on talking in his bantering tone as they crept along the awkward rift.

"The way was blocked by a man with a drawn cutlass."

"Vairy clever; vairy good!" he cried. "I see you know ze vay. It is *magnifique*. You see, I find I have visitor, and zey do not know ven ze *déjeuner* is *prêt*, so I am oblige to make one leetle—vat you call it—trap-springe, and catch ze leetle bird."

A rope was ready at the other end of the fissure, and as Vince dropped down it was into the presence of half a dozen more men, while in the rapid glance that he cast round, the boy saw that a boat was drawn up on the sand and a fire of wood was burning close down to the water's edge. Vince noticed, too, that one of the men who followed stopped back by the rope, with his drawn cutlass carried military fashion; and his action gave a pretty good proof that everything had been carefully planned beforehand in connection with the "trap-springe," as the Frenchman called it.

Preparations had already been made for breakfast, one of the men acting as cook; and in a short time kegs were stood on end round a beautifully clean white tablecloth spread upon the soft sand; excellent coffee, good bread-and-butter, and fried mackerel were placed before them, and the French captain presided.

The boys felt exceedingly nervous and uncomfortable, for they could see plainly enough that their captor was playing with them, and acting a part. They knew, too, that they were prisoners, and shivers of remorse ran through them as the thought of the anxious ones at home kept troubling them; but there was a masterfulness about their fierce young appetites, sharpened to a maddening desire by long fasting, which, after the first choking mouthful or two, would not be gainsaid; and they soon set to work voraciously, while the captain ate as heartily, and his men, all but the sentry, gathered together by themselves to make their breakfast alone.

"Brava!" cried the captain, helping them liberally to the capital breakfast before them: "I can you not tell how vairy glad I am to see my young *amis*. My table has not been so honour before."

At last the meal was at end, and the captain clapped his hands for the things to be cleared away, a couple of the men leaping up and performing this task with quite military alacrity.

The boys exchanged glances, and, without communicating one with the other, rose together; while the captain raised his eyebrows.

"Aha!" he said: "you vant somesings else?"

"Only to say thank you for our good breakfast, and to tell you that we are now going home."

"Going home?" said the captain grimly. "Aha, you sink so. Yaas, perhaps you are right. You *Anglais* call it going home—*à la mort*—to die."

"No, we don't," said Vince sharply. "We mean going home. We have been out all night."

"Aha, yaas; and the *bon* papa and mamma know vere you have come?"

"No," replied Vince quickly; "no one knows of this but us."

"*Vraiment?*" said the captain, and he looked searchingly at Mike. "No one knows but my young friend?"

"No," said Mike. "We found the cave by accident; we fell into the way that leads down, and kept it a secret."

"Good boy; but you can keep secret?"

"Yes," said Mike; "of course."

"Aha! so can I," said the captain, laughing boisterously. "Suppose I send you home my vay, eh? No one know ze vay to ze cavern."

"I don't understand you," said Mike sturdily.

"*Ma foi!* vy should you understand? I send you home, and nobody know nosings. *Les gens*—ze peoples—look for you; they do not find you, and zey say—Aha, *pauvres garçons*, zey go and make a falls off ze cliff, and ve nevaire see them any more!"

Mike turned pale; Vince laughed.

"He does not mean it, Mike," said the boy. "We know better than that, Captain Jacques."

"Aha, you are so clever a boy. You vill explain how you know all ze better zan me, le Capitaine Lebrun."

"There's nothing to explain," said Vince sturdily. "You don't suppose we believe you would kill us because we came down here,—here, where we have business to come, but you have not?"

"*Aha! c'est comme ça*—it is like zat, my friend? You may come here, and I must not?"

"Of course," said Vince. "This land belongs to his father, and you have no right to put smuggled things here."

"Aha! you sink it ees like zat, eh, *mon ami*? Ve sall see. You vill put yourselves down to sit."

"No, thank you," said Vince. "We must go now."

"To fetch ze peoples to come and fight and be killed?"

"No," said Vince; "we will not say a word about where we have been."

"But we must, Vince," said Mike. "They will ask us; and what are we to say?"

"To be certain, my friend—of course," said the captain, showing his teeth. "You see it is so. Zey vill ask vere you go all night, and you vill say to see le Capitaine Lebrun and his cargo of silk and lace and glove and scent bottaile and ze spice; and vat zen?"

Vince had no answer ready.

"You do not speak, my friend. Zen I vill. I cannot spare you to go and speak like zat. Nobodies must know that I have my leetle place to hide here. No, I cannot spare you. You will not go back *chez vous*—to your place vere you live. You understand?"

Vince looked at the man very hard, and he nodded, and went on:

"I am glad to see you bose. I make myself very glad of vat you call you compagnie. But I do not ask you to come; and so I say you go back nevaire more."

"You don't mean that!" said Vince, with a laugh that was very artificial.

"Aha! I do not mean? You vill see I mean. I sall see you vill sit down."

"No," said Vince firmly. "I am not frightened, and I insist upon going now."

"It is so? How you go?"

"Out by the passage yonder."

"Faith of a good man, no. I say to myselfs, 'People have come down zere, and it muss not be,' so ze place is stop up vis big stone—so big you nevaire move zem. But zere's ze ozaire vay."

"Well, we will go the other way," said Vince firmly. "Ready, Mike?"

"Yes, I'm ready," said Mike, pressing to his side.

"You know ze ozaire vay, my young friend?" said the captain.

"No: how do you go?"

"You take a boat, and a good pilot. You have ze good boat and pilot?"

"No," said Vince, who had hard work to be calm, with a great fear coming over him like a cloud; "but you will set us ashore, please."

The captain laughed in a peculiar way, and he was about to speak, when one of his men came up and said something.

"Aha!" he cried, "but it is good. You go, my young friends, and stay behind my cargo zere. You vill not come till I say you sall."

He pointed to the upper part of the cavern, but Vince said firmly:

"We cannot stay any longer, sir. We must go now."

The captain turned upon him savagely, and the next moment a couple of the men had seized the boys and run them up behind the pile of bales, and then stood on either side, with drawn cutlasses, to act as guards.

"What are we to do, Vince?" said Mike.

"I don't know. It seems like nonsense, and playing with us; but we are prisoners, and— Who's that?"

They both listened in wonder, for they heard their names mentioned angrily by the captain, who was speaking threateningly to some one who replied in a tone that they recognised directly.

"Aha! you lie to me. Ve sall see. Here, you two boy, come here, *vite— vite!*"

The guards made way for them, and followed just behind, as they marched back to where the captain was seated, with old Daygo standing before him.

The old man gave each of them a peculiar look, and then turned to the captain again.

"Now zen," cried that individual, "you 'ave seen zis man. Him you know?"

"Yes," said Vince; "of course we do."

"Aha! ze old friend. And he tell you of ze cavern and ze smuggling, and how you find ze vay here?"

"No, not a word," said Vince stoutly. "But I can see now why you wouldn't bring us round by the Black Scraw, Joe."

"Aha! ze vairy old friend. It is Joe!" said the captain fiercely.

"Well, why not?" said Vince quickly. "Old Joe has taken us in his boat scores of times fishing and sailing."

"And told you of ze goods here in my cavern?"

"Not a word," said Vince.

"I do not believe," said the captain.

"'Course I never told 'em," growled Daygo. "I dunno how they come here. I watched 'em times enough, and when I couldn't watch I set a boy to see wheer they went. I couldn't do no more, Capen."

The Frenchman looked at them all in turn fiercely, and then he fixed his eyes on old Daygo again.

"And ze peoples up above, zey are look for zem—ze boy?"

"I dunno," said Daygo. "I didn't know they were here, and I dunno how they come. Dropt down with a rope, young gen'lemen?"

"No, zay come anozaire vay, my friend. It is good luck for you I do not find zey know how of you. But sink no one on ze island know?"

"I dunno," said Daygo. "They don't know from me."

"You can go," said the captain sharply, and the old fisherman thrust his hands very deeply down in the pockets of his huge trousers and was turning slowly away when Mike cried:

"Stop!"

Daygo turned slowly back, and the captain watched the boy with his dark eyes glittering as he sat facing the light.

"Are you going back home?" cried Mike.

"Ay, m'lad, when the skipper's done with me."

"Then never mind what he says: you go straight to the Mount and tell my father everything, and that we are kept here like prisoners."

"Nay, young gen'leman," said Daygo, rolling his head slowly from side to side, "I warnt you both agen it over and over agen, when you 'most downed on your knees, a-beggin' and a-prayin' of me to bring you round by the Scraw; but I never would, now would I, Master Vince?"

"No, you old scoundrel!" cried Vince hotly. "I can see now: because you're a smuggler too."

Old Daygo chuckled.

"Didn't I tell you both never to think about it, because there was awful currents and things as dragged boats under, and that it was as dangerous as it could be? Now speak up like a man, Master Vince, and let Capen Jarks hear the truth."

"Truth!" said Vince scornfully; "do you call that truth, telling us both a pack of lies, when you must have been coming here often yourself?"

"Eh? Well, s'pose I did, young gen'leman: it was on my lorful business, and you fun out fer yourselves as it's no place for boys like you."

"Look here," said Vince fiercely: "you've got to do what Michael Ladelle says, and to tell my father too."

"Nay, my lad; that arn't no lorful business of mine."

"Do you mean to say that you will not tell?"

"Ay, my lad: I'm sorry for you both, proper lads as you are; but you would come, and it's no fault o' mine."

"You Joe," cried Vince angrily: "if you do not warn them above where we are, you'll never be able to live on the island again, and you'll be severely punished."

"Who's to tell agen me?" said the old man sharply.

"Why, I shall, and Mike here, of course."

"When?" said Daygo, in a peculiar tone of voice.

"As soon as ever we get back; and you'll be punished. I suppose Captain Jacques here will have sailed away."

"Soon as you get back, eh, young gen'lemen? Did Capen Jarks say as he was going to send you home?"

"No," said Vince; "but he will have to soon."

"I'm sorry for you, my lads—sorry for you," growled Daygo; and a chill ran through both the boys, as they saw the Frenchman looking at them in a very peculiar way. "Sorry—yes, lads, but I did my best fer you, and so good-bye."

"No, no," cried Mike excitedly; "don't go and leave us, Joe. Tell the captain here that if we say we'll promise not to speak to any one about the place we'll keep our words."

Daygo shook his head.

"It's o' no use for me to say nothin', Master Mike: he's master here, and does what he likes. You hadn't no business to come a-shovin' yourself into his place."

"It is not his place," cried Mike indignantly; "it is my father's property."

"I arn't got no time to argufy about that, my lad. He says it's his, and all this here stuff as you sees is his too. Here, I must be off, or I shall lose this high tide and be shut-in."

"No, no, Joe—stop!" cried Mike. "I'll—"

"Hold your tongue, Ladle," whispered Vince. "Don't do that; they'll think we're regular cowards. Here you, Joe Daygo, if you go away and don't give notice to Sir Francis or my father about our being kept here by this man—"

"Say the Capen or the skipper, my lad," growled Daygo. "Makes him orkard if he hears people speak dis-speckful of him."

"Pooh!" exclaimed Vince hotly. "I say, you know what the consequences will be."

"Yes, my lad; they won't never know what become of you."

Vince winced, in spite of his determination to be firm, on hearing the cold-blooded way in which the old fisherman talked, but he spoke out boldly.

"Do you mean to say he will dare to keep us here?"

"Yes, my lad, or take you away with him, or get rid of you somehow. You see he's capen and got his crew, and can do just what he likes."

"No, he can't," said Vince; "the law will not let him."

"Bless your 'art, Master Vince, he don't take no notice o' no law. But I hope he won't drownd you both, 'cause you see we've been friendly like. P'r'aps he'll on'y ship you off to Bottonny Bay, or one o' they tother-end-o'-the-world places, where you can't never come back to tell no tales."

"I don't believe it: he dare not. Don't take any notice, Mike; he's only saying this to scare us, and we're not going to be scared."

"Now, *mon ami*," cried the captain, "you vill not get out if you do not depart zis minute. I cannot spare to have you drowned. I sall sail to-night, and you vill be here ready?"

"Ay, ay, I'll be here," growled Daygo.

"Then you are coming back?" said Vince quickly.

"That's so, Master Vince. How's he going to get the *Belle-Marie* out without me to pilot him? Yes, I'm comin' back to-night, my lad; and I hope I shall see you agen."

He said these last words in a whisper, which sent a chill through the lads, for that he was serious there could be no doubt.

By this time two men were down by the boat, that was now half in the water, which had risen till she was rocking sidewise to and fro; and smartly enough the old fisherman turned and trotted over the sand to join in thrusting the boat out, and then sprang in.

This was too much for Mike, who made a sudden dash after him.

"Come on, Vince," he cried; and the boy followed, but only to catch hold of his companion as he clung to the bows of the boat.

"Don't I don't do that, Mike," cried Vince; "you couldn't get away."

Three men who had rushed after them, and were about to seize the prisoners, refrained as soon as they saw Vince's action; and the boat with old Daygo on board glided out among the rocks, and then passed off out of sight, round the left buttress of the cavern mouth.

This was enough: Mike turned furiously upon Vince and struck him, sending him staggering backward over the thick sand; and, unable to keep his balance, the lad came down in a sitting position.

"You coward!" cried Mike: "if it hadn't been for you we might have got away."

"Coward, am I?" cried Vince, as he sprang up and dashed at his assailant, with fists clenched and everything forgotten now but the blow. He did not strike out, though, in return, for an arm was thrown across his chest and a gruff voice growled out,—

"Are we to let 'em have it out, Capen Jarks?"

"No; *mais* I sink zey might have von leetle rights. *Non, non, non!* You do not vant to fight now, *mes enfans;* you have somesings else to sink. You feel like a big coward?"

"No, I don't," said Vince, to whom the words were addressed: "I'll let him see if you'll make this man let go."

"*Non, non, non!*" said the captain, raising his hand to tug at one of the rings in his ears. "You do not vant to fight. Let me see."

He began to feel the muscles of Vince's arms, and nodded as if with satisfaction.

"It seem a pity to finish off a boy like you. I sink you vould make a good sailor and a fine smugglaire on my sheep. Perhaps I sall not kill you."

"Bah!" cried Vince, looking him full in the face. "Do you think I'm such a little child as to be frightened by what you say?"

"Leetle schile? *Non, non. Vous êtes un brave garçon*—a big, brave boy. Zere, you sall not fight like you *Anglais* bouledogues, and vat you call ze game coq. You *comprends, mon enfant.*"

"Then you'd better take him away," cried Vince, who was effervescing with wrath against his companion.

"Aha, yaas," said the Frenchman, grinning. "You sink I better tie you up like ze dogue. But, faith of a man, you fly at von and anozaire I sall—"

"*He drew a small pistol, giving both lads a significant look.*"

He drew a small pistol out of his breast, and, giving both lads a significant look,—

"Zere," he continued, "I sall not chain you bose up. You can run about and help vis ze crew. I only say to you ze passage is block up vis big stone, ze hole vere ze seal live is no good—ze rock hang over ze wrong vay. You try to climb, and you are not ze leetler *mouche*—fly. You fall and die; and if you essay to svim, ze sharp tide take you avay to drown. Go and svim if you like: I sall not have ze pain to drown you. But, my faith! vy do I tell you all zis? You bose know zat you cannot get avay now ze passage is stop up vis stone, and I stop him vis a man who has sword and pistol as vell. Go and help ze men."

He walked away, leaving the boys together, carefully avoiding each other's eyes, as they felt that they were prisoners indeed, and wondered what was to be their fate.

Vince took a few turns up and down upon the sand with his hands deep in his pockets. Mike seated himself upon the keg he had occupied over his breakfast, for in their frame of mind they both resented being ordered to go and help the men; but at that time the worst pang of all seemed to be caused by the fact that, just at the moment when they wanted each other's help and counsel, with the strength of mind given by the feeling that they were together, they were separated by the unfortunate conduct of one.

# Chapter Twenty Six
# The Pirate Captain of their Dreams

The walk did Vince good, for the action given to his muscles carried off the sensation which made his fists clench from time to time in his pockets and itch to be delivering blows wherever he could make them light on his companion's person.

He did not notice that he was ploughing a rut in the sand by going regularly to and fro, for he was thinking deeply about their position; and as he thought, the dread that the captain's words had inspired, endorsed as they were by Daygo's, began to fade away, till he found himself half contemptuously saying to himself that he should like to catch the skipper at it—it meaning something indefinite that might mean something worse, but in all probability keeping them prisoners till he had got away all his stores of smuggled goods.

Then, as the rut in the sand grew deeper from the regular tramp up and down, Vince's thoughts flitted from the trouble felt by his mother, who must be terribly anxious, to his companion, whose back was towards him, and who with elbows on knees had bent down to rest his chin upon his hands.

Vince was a little surprised at himself, and rather disposed to think that he was weak; for somehow all the hot blood had gone out of his arms and fists, which were now perfectly cool, and felt no longer any desire to fly about as if charged with pugno-electricity, which required discharging by being brought into contact with Mike's chest or head.

"Poor old Ladle!" he found himself thinking: "what a temper he was in! But it was too bad to hit out like that, when what I did was to help him. But there, he didn't know."

Vince was pretty close to his fellow-prisoner now; but he had to turn sharply round and walk away.

"Glad I didn't hit him again, because if I had we should have had a big fight and I should have knocked him about horribly and beaten him well, and I don't want to. I'm such a stupid when I get fighting: I never feel hurt—

only as if I must keep on hitting; and then all those sailor fellows would have been looking on and grinning at us. Glad we didn't fight."

Then Vince began to think again of their position, which he told himself was very horrible, but not half so bad as that of the people at both their homes, where, only a mile or two away from where they were, the greatest trouble and agony must reign.

"And us all the time with nothing the matter with us, and sitting down as we did and eating such a breakfast! Seems so unfeeling; only I felt half-starved, and when I began I could think of nothing else.—Such nonsense! he's not going to kill us, or he wouldn't have given us anything to eat. Here, I can't go on like this."

Vince stopped his walk to and fro at the end of the beaten-out track in the sand, and turned off to stand behind Mike, who must have heard him come, but did not make the slightest movement.

Then there was silence, broken by the voice of the French captain giving his orders to his men, who were evidently rearranging the stores ready for removal.

"I say, Mike," said Vince at last.

No answer.

"Michael."

Still no movement. "Mr Michael Ladelle."

Vince might have been speaking to the tub upon which his fellow-prisoner was seated, for all the movement made.

"Michael Ladelle, Esquire, of the Mount," said Vince; and there was a good-humoured look in his eyes, which twinkled merrily; but the other did not stir.

"Ladle, then," cried Vince; but without effect,—Mike was still gazing at the sand before him.

"I say, don't be such a sulky old Punch. Why don't you speak? I want to talk to you about getting away. Mike—Ladle—I say, you did hurt when you hit out at me. I shall have to pay you that back!"

No answer.

"Look here: aren't you going to say you're sorry for it and shake hands?"

Vince waited for a while and then burst out impatiently,—

"Look here, if you don't speak I'll kick the tub over and let you down."

All in vain: Mike did not move, and Vince began to grow impatient.

"Here, I say," he cried, "I know I'm a bit of a beast sometimes, but you can't say I'm sulky. I did nothing; and if it was I, you know I'd have owned I was in the wrong and held out my fist—open; not like you did, to knock a fellow down."

Another pause, and Vince exclaimed,—

"Well, I *am*—"

He did not say what, but stood with extended arm.

"I say, Mikey," he said softly, "I know you haven't got any eyes in the back of your head, so I may as well tell you. I'm holding out my hand for a shake, and my arm's beginning to ache."

"Don't—don't!" said Mike now, in a low voice, full of the misery the lad felt. "I feel as if you were jumping on me for what I did."

"Do you? Well, I'm not going to jump on you. Come, I have got you to speak at last, and there's an end of it. I say, Ladle, it's too stupid for us two to be out now, when we want to talk about how we're stuck here."

"I feel as if I can't speak to you," said Mike huskily.

"More stupid you. Didn't I tell you it's all over now? You were in a passion, and so was I. Now you're not in a passion, no more am I; so that's all over. You heard what the pirate captain said about us?"

"Yes," said Mike dolefully.

"Well, he and old Joe— Here, Ladle: I'm going to kick old Joe. I don't care about his being old and grey. A wicked old sneak!—I'll kick him, first chance I get, for leaving us in the lurch; but that isn't what I was going to say. Here, why don't you turn round and sit up? Don't let those beggars think we're afraid of them. I won't be,—see if I am."

Mike slowly changed his position, turning round and sitting up.

"Now, then, that's better," said Vince. "What was I going to say? Oh! I know. The pirate captain and old Joe wanted to make us believe that we were to be taken out to sea, to walk the plank or be hung or shot or something."

"Joe said something about Botany Bay and sending us there."

"No, he didn't; he said Bottonny, and there is no such place. He couldn't do it, and he couldn't keep us prisoners here."

"He might kill us."

"No, he mightn't. Bah! what a silly old Ladle you are! He couldn't. People don't do such things now, only in stories. I tell you what I believe."

"What?" said Mike, for Vince paused as if to think.

"Well, I believe he feels that his old smuggler's cave is done for now we've found out the way down to it, so he's going to clear it out and start another somewhere else. He means to keep us prisoners till the last keg's on board, and as soon as this is done he'll go to his boat and take his hat off to us and tell us we may have the caverns all to ourselves."

"Think so?" said Mike, looking up at his companion for the first time.

"Yes, I believe that's it, Ladle; and if it wasn't for knowing how miserable they must be over yonder I should rather like all this—that is, if you're going to play fair and not get hitting out when we ought to be the best of friends."

"Don't—don't, Cinder: I can't bear it," groaned Mike, letting his head drop in his hands. "I hurt myself a hundred times more than I hurt you."

"Oh, did you! Ha! ha!" cried Vince. "Come, I like that: why, I shall have a bruise as big as the top of my hat! Oh, I say, Ladle, old chap, don't—don't talk like that! It's all right. You thought I was fighting against you. Sit up. Some of the beggars will see."

Mike sat up with his face twitching, and kept his back to the upper part of the cavern.

"That's better. Well, I say I should really like it if it wasn't for them at home. I call it a really good, jolly adventure, such as you read of in books. Now, what we've got to do is to wait till they're asleep, cut off all their heads with their own cutlasses, seize the boat, row off to the lugger, wait till old Joe comes back, and then spike him with the points of cutlasses till he pilots us out safely. Then we've got to sail home as prize crew of the lugger, which would be ours. Stop! there's something we haven't done."

Mike stared.

"Old Joe. As soon as we're out of the dangerous passages we've got to batten him down in the hold, and that's the end of the adventure."

"How can you go on like that?" said Mike piteously. "Making fun of it all, when we're so miserable."

"That's why: just to cheer us up a bit, and set us thinking about what's next to do."

"I can't think," said Mike. "It's a pity we didn't stop in the seal hole."

"Stop there? We should have felt nice by now. Why, our legs would be all swollen, and we should be so hungry that— Here, I say, Ladle, you wouldn't have been safe. I wonder how you'd taste?"

"I say, do be serious, Cinder. It's too horrible to laugh at it."

"Well, so it is, old chap, but I am thinking hard all the time, yet I can't see any way out of it. I know we could swim almost like seals; but look at the water out there,—we couldn't do anything in it."

"No, we should be sucked down in five minutes."

"Yes. The old pirate knows it, too, and that's why he leaves us alone. I say, he does look like a pirate, though, doesn't he? with that pistol, and the rings in his ears."

"Oh! I never saw a pirate, only on those pictures we tried to paint. But what about the cliffs?"

"No good. They're either straight up and down or overhanging. We couldn't do it."

"We might get over the other side and make signals."

"Yes; there is something in that. But don't you think we might get away by the passage? The sentry may go to sleep."

"No good," said Mike bitterly. "Those fellows daren't."

"S'pose not," said Vince thoughtfully. "Old Jarks is the sort of chap to wake 'em up with his pistol. It's of no use yet, Ladle; the idea hasn't come. Yes, it has! Why can't we wait our chance and seize the boat and get it off? We could manage."

"Hush!" whispered Mike.

The warning was needed, for the captain came from the back of the stack of packages, and marched down towards where they were.

# Chapter Twenty Seven
# What will he do with us?

"Aha!" he cried. "So you sall not try to escape any more?"

"No," said Vince coolly, looking the speaker full in the face. "I say, what time do you have dinner?"

The Frenchman stared at him for a few moments fiercely, and then burst into a boisterous fit of laughter.

"You are a *drôle de garçon*" he said. "You are again hungry?"

"I shall be by the time it's ready. But, I say, captain, how much longer are you going to keep us here?"

"Aha!" he said, with a shrug of the shoulders and a peculiar gesticulation with his hand, as if he were throwing something away, while he looked at them both sidewise through his half-closed eyes: "You are fatigue so soon? You vant to go somevere else?"

"We want to go home."

"Good leetler boy: he vant to go home. But not yet, *mes amis*. You give the good capitain all zis pains to move his cargo, and you vill not help."

"Oh, I'm ready enough to help," said Vince. "So's he; but they will be very anxious about us at home."

"Ta ta ta ta ta!" cried the captain. "Vy, you sink so mosh of your selfs. Ze *bon papa* vill say to *la maman*, 'Ah! *ma chère*, dose boy go and tomble zem selfs off ze cliff;' and ze *maman* sall wipe her eye and say, '*pauvre garçon*—poor boy, it is vat I expect.'"

"And instead of that," said Vince, "you are going to send us home, and then they will not be fidgeting any more."

"Aha! you sink so. Vell, ve sall see. So I go to be vairy busy, and it is better zat you two do not fight any more. So come vis me."

"Where?" said Vince suspiciously.

"Vere? Oh! you sall see, *mon brave*, vairy soon."

The boys exchanged glances, but feeling that it was hopeless to resist, they followed the captain down to where the boat was lying, just as she had returned a few minutes before, without Daygo.

The men in her were just keeping her afloat, but they ran her stern on to the sand as they saw the captain coming, and one of them leaped out to hold her steady.

"In vis you!" said the captain sharply.

"All right, Mike," whispered Vince. "Come on, and don't seem to mind."

He set the example by putting one foot on the gunwale and springing in lightly. Mike followed, and then the captain; while the man standing ankle-deep in the water waited till they were seated, and then, giving the boat a good thrust out, sprang on the stern, and climbed in as they glided over the transparent water, stepping forward quickly to seize an oar, and pulling sharply with his companion.

The boys gazed eagerly upward as soon as they were clear of the great overhanging archway, and saw the impossibility of escape by any cliff-climbing; for the mighty rocks were at least twenty feet out of the perpendicular, leaning over towards the little bay, whose waters were running, eddying and boiling like a whirlpool as they raced along, seizing the boat's head and seeming about to drag her right along towards a jagged cluster of rocks, standing just above the surface, and amidst which the current raged and foamed furiously.

But the men knew their work. One pulled hard, the other backed water, and by their united efforts the boat was forced into an eddy close under the cliff; and to their amazement the boys found that they were being carried in the opposite direction to that in which the main body of the water was racing along.

"You vill escape and climb ze cliff? No, *mes enfans*," said the captain: "you cannot climb. You vill take my boat to go avay? Aha! you sink so? No, it is not for you to manage ze boat. She vill capsize herself if you try."

Vince said nothing, but eagerly looked around; but it was everywhere the same—the roaring waters tearing wildly along in the crater-like cove, and from their seat in the boat no entrance, no exit, was visible.

"Now I take you bose and drop you ovaire-board: you sink, you go home?" said the captain, showing his teeth. "Yaas, you go home, but not to see ze *bon papa*, ze *belle maman*. It is not possible. Von of my men say von day he have sick of me, and he vill go. He shump ovaire-board to svim, and he svim vis his arm and leg von, two, twenty stroke, and zen he trow *les mains* out of ze vater, and he cry for ze boat; but zere vas no boat, and he turn round upon himself two time, and go down a hole in ze vater. I stand and look at him, but he came up again nevaire. He vas a good man—*bon matelot*—but he go. You like to shump in and svim? *Eh bien*, you shake ze hand, shump in. *Au revoir*, but ve shall meet again nevaire. You go? *Non? Eh bien!* I make you ze offaire."

The boys felt that it was all true, and marvelled where they were going, for the eddy was taking them along by the mighty rocks, which were overhanging them again; and, as far as they could make out, the cliffs under which they passed and the ridge away facing the cavern mouth, which they had imagined to be an island, were all one.

The captain seemed to be paying little heed to them, sitting with his eyes half-closed; but he was watching them all the time closely, and noted their astonishment as the men suddenly began to tug at their oars with all their might, apparently to avoid a rock, round one side of which the water was rushing with tremendous force, just as if the eddy stream along which they had been riding suddenly curved round it. The men were making for the other end, and as they drew nearer the water roared and splashed up, and it appeared to both that they must be carried right upon it by some undertow.

But every foot of the place, and all its difficulties, were perfectly familiar to the captain's crew, and by making use of the many cross streams and eddies, they were able to guide the boat into safety, as in this case; for just as Mike seized the gunwale with one hand, to be prepared for the shock, and Vince clenched his fists and gave a glance to the left, the boat's prow passed the end of the detached rock, they glided into an opening like a gash cut down through the massive rock-wall, and the next minute were swept into a comparatively calm pool, surrounded by towering cliffs, which seemed to overlap on their right; and there, right before them, rode by a couple of hawsers attached to great rings fixed in the rock-face behind, a long, low three-masted lugger of the kind known as a *chasse-marée*.

Vince looked sharply round for the channel by which this vessel must come and go—for it seemed certain that such a way must exist, since so large a boat could not by any means have entered the circular cove facing the cavern; and he was not long in seeing that, some twenty or thirty feet beyond her bow, the water was coming swiftly in round the cliff, which lapped over another to its right, but so calmly did the tide run that at the first its motion was unperceived.

Vince had hardly grasped this fact, when the boat was run up alongside, one of the men sprang into the lugger with the boat's painter and made it fast, while the boat seemed to tug to get away, and the captain turned to his prisoners.

"Aboard!" he said sharply; and as there was nothing for it but to obey, Vince made a virtue of necessity, and going forward, climbed up and over the bulwark, to stand upon a beautifully white deck, and see that rigging, sails and spars were all in the highest state of order.

Six or eight men were waiting, and they came aft at once, to stand as if waiting for orders, while Mike and the captain stepped on board.

"Back at once!" said the Frenchman to a stern-looking, red-faced man, who appeared to be the mate. "All ze boats; and work hard to get all on board."

This order was given in a low tone, but Vince's ears were sharpened by his position, and he divined its full meaning.

The men hurried to the side, and rapidly began to lower one of the boats hanging to the davits; while in his close scrutiny Vince grasped the fact that they were upon no peaceful vessel: there being a couple of longish guns forward, and another pair aft, all evidently in the best of trim, and ready for use at a very short notice.

While the men were busy the captain came to where the boys were standing together aft, and laying his hands upon their shoulders, he led them forward to where one of the stout hawsers ran over the side to the great ring secured in the rock.

"You see zat hawser, *mon ami*?" he said.

"Yes," said Vince wonderingly.

"Look you zen at ze ozaire."

"Yes, I see it," said Vince.

"Vat you make of zem?"

"They look strained too much, and as if they would part."

"Good boy! You vould make a good sailor. Zey vill not part, for zey are new, and *très fort*—strong. Now you look here, *mon ami*."

As he spoke he picked up a heavy dwarf bucket, with its rope attached, raised it above his head, and hurled it some twenty feet into the smooth water between the lugger and the high cliff face.

The water was like glass, and streaked with fine threads apparently; and the next minute the lads grasped the reason why, for the bucket had hardly touched the water when it began to be borne towards the lugger's side, striking it directly after sharply, and then diving down out of sight.

Vince ran across the deck instantly to see it rise; and Mike followed, the captain joining them to lay his hands upon their shoulders once more.

"Aha! you see him come up again? No? Look *encore* and *encore*, and you nevaire sall see him. Vat you say to zat?"

"There must be a tremendous current," said Vince. "Yais,—now," said the captain. "*Après*, some time he run all ze ozaire vay and grind ze sheep close up right to ze rock. Vat you sink now? You shump ovaire, and svim avay? You creep along ze hawser and try to climb up ze cliff? No, I sink not now. You stay here on ze deck and vait till I vant you—ven ze boat come back. Dat is vy I show you how go avay ze bucket. Look now again."

One of the boats was ready, and two men in her. The rope that held her to the side was cast off, and in an instant she glided away across the pool, towards an opening that had been unnoticed before, was deftly steered, and passed out of sight.

"Why, she must come out where we saw the water rushing at the other end of the rock!" thought Vince; and he stood watching while the other boats left the side of the lugger, to be cleverly guided to the same spot, and glide out of sight directly.

A feeling of helplessness came over the boys as they saw all this, and realised that now they were, beside the captain and a man who kept going in and out of a low, hutch-like place forward, the only occupants of the vessel; and that if their captor had any particular designs upon them, this would be the likely time for their happening. But they now had proof that this was not going to be the case, for the Frenchman took no further heed to them. He went to the cabin-hatch and descended, leaving them with the deck to themselves.

"What do you think of it now?" asked Mike dolefully.

"I don't know," said Vince, gazing up at the towering rocks, dotted with yellow ragwort and sea-pink, by which they were surrounded; "but it's a change. I wouldn't care if they only knew at home about our being safe. I say, isn't it likely that some one may come along the cliffs and be searching for us, and then we can signal to him?"

"Who ever came along the cliffs and looked down here?" said Mike. "We've been about as much as any one, but we never looked down into this pool."

"No," said Vince thoughtfully: "it puzzles me. I hardly make out whereabouts we are. I say, though, look forward: that's the galley, and the chap we saw is the cook."

"Of course," said Mike; "there's the chimney, and the smoke coming out."

"Let's go and see what there is for dinner."

Mike's forehead wrinkled up, and he felt disposed to say something reproachful; but he was silent, and followed his companion to the galley door, where the man they had seen looked up at them grimly, and as if resenting their presence.

"What's for dinner, old chap?" said Vince coolly.

The sour look on the man's face passed away. Vince's countenance, and his free-and-easy way, seemed to find favour, and he said gruffly,—

"Lobscouse."

"What, for the skipper?" said Vince, who had a lively memory of the captain's breakfast.

"Men," said the man laconically.

"And for the skipper?"

The man smiled grimly, and took the lid off a pot, which arose an agreeable steam, that was appetising and suggested good soup. Then, without a word, he pointed to a dish upon which lay a pair of thick soles, and to another, on which, ready egged and crumbed, were about a dozen neatly prepared veal cutlets.

"Got any potatoes," said Vince.

The man raised a lid and showed the familiar vegetable, bubbling away on the little stove, which was roaring loudly, and put the saucepan down again.

"Well, we shan't starve," said Vince, as they each gave the cook a nod and walked as far forward as they could. "Captain hasn't a bad notion about eating and drinking."

"And smuggling and kidnapping," said Mike bitterly.

"Kidnapping!" said Vince cheerily. "Ah, to be sure, that's the very word: I thought something had been done to us that there's a proper word for. That's it, Ladle—kidnapped. Yes, we've been kidnapped.—I say!"

"Well?"

"Look here: are we two chaps worth anything?"

"I don't feel to be now," said Mike; "I'm too miserable."

"Well, so am I miserable enough, but I suppose we must be worth something, and that's why the skipper's going to feed us well."

"What nonsense have you got in your head now?"

"Nonsense? I call it some sense. For that's it, Ladle, as sure as you stand there; he has kidnapped us, and he's going to take us right away somewhere. Ladle, old chap, I feel as sure of it as if he'd told us. It is all nonsense about making an end of us. I was sure it only meant trying to frighten us; but we're two big, strong, healthy lads, and he's going to take us right away."

"Do you mean it? What for?"

Vince looked sadly at his companion in misfortune for a few moments, and then he said huskily,—

"To sell!"

# Chapter Twenty Eight
# Prisoners, but not of War

Michael Ladelle was a good-looking lad, as people judge good looks; but at that moment, as he stood with his hand resting on the bulwarks of *La Belle-Marie*, he was decidedly plain, so blank and semi-idiotic did he seem, with his eyes dilated, his jaw dropped and his brains evidently gone wool-gathering, as people say, so utterly unable was he to comprehend his companion's announcement.

Still it was only a matter of moments before he shut his mouth, and then nearly closed his eyes, wrinkled up his face, and burst into a fit of laughter, which, however, was of so hysterical a nature that for a time he could not check it. At last, though, he mastered it sufficiently to say,—

"To do what with us?"

"To sell," said Vince again, as he gazed sadly in his companion's face.

"To sell!" cried Mike, growing more calm now; and his voice had a ring of contempt in it as he said,—

"Why, any one would think this was Africa, and we were blacks. What nonsense!"

"It isn't nonsense," said Vince. "That man will do anything sooner than have it known where his hiding-place is; and he won't kill us—he dares not on account of his men; but he'll get us out of the way so that we shan't be able to tell."

"Oh, I won't believe it!" cried Mike angrily. "Such a thing couldn't be done."

"But it has been done over and over again," said Vince: "I've read of it. They used to sell men and boys to sea-captains to take out to the plantations; and once they were there, they had no chance given them of getting back for years and years."

"I don't believe it," said Mike sharply. "It might have been in the past, but it couldn't be done now."

"That's what I've been trying to think," said Vince sadly; "but this wouldn't be done in England. This is a Frenchman, and the French have colonies abroad, the same as we have. How do we know where he'll take us?" Mike started at this, and looked more disturbed. "I say," he said at last, "you don't really think that, do you, Vince?"

"I wish I didn't," replied the boy sadly; "but it's what has seemed to come to me, since we've been on board here. I don't know where this man comes from, but he's a regular smuggler, and there's no knowing where he'll take us."

"But my father—your father—you don't suppose they'll stand still and let us be taken off without trying to stop it. Father's just like a magistrate in the island."

"Of course they wouldn't stand still and allow it to be done; but how will they know?"

Mike was silent, and his face now began to look haggard as he stared at his companion.

"Whoever knew that this Captain Jacques had a place in the island where he stored rich cargoes of foreign things? Why, he may have been doing it for years, and your father, though he is like a magistrate, hasn't known anything about it."

"No, nor your father either," said Mike sadly. "I don't think anything of that," continued Vince; "what I do think a great deal of is that neither you nor I, who've always been climbing about the cliffs and boating shouldn't have found it out before."

"But surely now we're missing they'll find it out," cried Mike, who was ready to snatch at any straw of hope.

"I don't see how," said Vince. "They're sure to think that one of us met with an accident, and that the other was drowned in trying to save him."

Mike was silent for some moments, during which he stood gazing wistfully at his fellow-prisoner.

"That would be very nice of them to think that of us," he said at last, slowly. "But do you think they would believe us likely to be so brave?"

"Oh yes, they'd think so," said Vince quickly—"I'm sure they would; but I don't know about it's being brave. It's only what two fellows would do one for the other. It's what English chaps always do, of course, but it's like making a lot of fuss about it to call it brave. I should say it's what a fellow should do, that's all."

"And no one knows—no one saw us go to the hole," said Mike bitterly. "Oh, I say, Vince, we have made a mess of it to keep it a secret."

"Yes, we have, and no mistake."

"And no one knows," repeated Mike thoughtfully. "Don't you think Lobster might know, and tell them?"

"No, I'm sure he can't. Of course old Joe knows; but he won't speak, because if he did, and told the truth, the captain here would be ready to shoot him."

"And my father would have him locked up, and tried for what he has done."

"Yes," said Vince, nodding his head; "Joe won't speak—you may depend upon that. Why, Mike, while we were fishing for that crab, and were so still, some one must have come across the cave behind us and never known we were there."

"Yes, and then we were caught as fast as the crab was and—"

"*Eh bien, mes enfans,* my good boy, are you hungry for your dinner?"

"Not very," said Vince, turning sharply as the skipper came silently up behind them. "We feel as if we should like to dine at home."

"Aha! You not mean zat, my *bon garçon*. Not ven I ask you to have dine vis me. Let us go and demand vat ze cook man—ze *chef*—have to give us, for it is long time since ze *déjeuner* and ve have much to do after. Come, sheer up, as ze sailor *Anglais* say. You like ze sea?"

"Yes," said Vince; "both of us do."

"And you can reef and furl ze sail?"

"Yes, we've often been in a boat."

"Brava! it is good; and, aha! ze brave cook go to prepare ze cabin for ze dinnaire. You sall bose be my compagnie *cet*—to-day."

Just then Vince caught sight of one of the lugger's boats, and noticed that it was particularly broad and punt-like in make, evidently so that it should carry a big load and at the same time draw little water—a shape that would save it from many dangers in passing over rocks, and also be very convenient for running in and landing upon the sands.

This boat was very heavily laden with bales, carefully ranged and stacked, while the boat's gunwale was so close to the surface that a lurch would have caused the water to flow in.

But the men who managed her seemed to be quite accustomed to their task; and after a sharp look directed at them by the skipper, he paid no more attention, but walked away.

It was different, though, with the boys; who, having ideas of their own connected with escaping from their position, watched the approach of the boat with intense curiosity, wondering how it could be rowed so easily against a current which ran with such tremendous force.

"I can't make it out," said Vince, as the boat came closer, and apparently with very little effort on the part of the men after they had passed out by the opening by which the prisoners had been brought on board.

"How is it, then?" said Mike.

"I suppose it's because they know all the currents so well. It's very hard to see; but I think that, as the water rushes round this cove and goes right across, most of it passes through the openings into our bay and makes all that swirling there."

"Of course it does," replied Mike. "I can see that."

"Well, you might let me finish," said Vince. "All this water flows right across."

"You said that before."

"And then," continued Vince, without noticing the interruption, "part of it which there isn't room for at the openings strikes against the rocks, and can't get any farther."

"Of course it can't."

"Well, it must go somewhere: water can't be piled-up in a heap and stay like that; so it's reflected—no, you can't call it reflected—it's turned back, and forms another stream, which flows back this way."

"It couldn't be," said Mike shortly.

"Well, that's the only way I can see, and that boat has come as easily as can be. Yes, I'm sure that's it, Ladle; and you may depend upon it that three or four feet down the water's rushing one way, while on the surface it's flowing in the other direction."

"Ah, well, it doesn't matter to us," said Mike bitterly, as the boat was brought up alongside cleverly, made fast, and her crew began to rapidly pass the bales over on to the deck, all being of one size, and, as Vince noticed, of a convenient size and weight for one man to handle.

"But it does matter to us, Mike," whispered Vince eagerly.

"Why?"

"Because you and I couldn't manage one of those big boats unless the currents helped us; but if we knew how these men managed them—"

"We could slip into one of them in the dark and get away."

Vince nodded, and Mike drew a deep breath.

"Don't look like that," whispered Vince; "here's Jacques coming to ask us why we don't help."

But they were wrong, for the captain took them each by the shoulder, his hands tightening with a heavy grip, which seemed to suggest that he could hold them much harder if he liked; and in this way he marched them before him to the cabin-hatch.

"Down vis you!" he said. "To-day you sall be vis me; to-morrow vis ze crew."

"Aren't you going to let us go back to-morrow?" said Vince quickly.

"*Non*! Go down."

That first word was French, but any one would have understood what it meant—the tone was sufficient.

The boys gave a sharp look round the little cabin, which was plain enough, with its lockers for seats, and narrow table, which just afforded room for the three who entered the place.

"Sit," said the captain shortly; and, directly after, "*Mangez*—eat. You do not understand—*comprends*—ze *Français*?"

"We do—a little," said Mike.

"Aha! zat is good," said the captain, with a peculiar laugh. "Zen ve sall be *bons amis*—good friend, eh? Now eat. You like soup, fish, eh?"

"We don't like to be taken off like this, sir," said Vince, who turned away from the food, good as it was, with disgust, wondering the while how he could have eaten so hearty a meal with the captain before. "We want to know what you are going to do with us."

"Ah, truly you vant to know," said the captain, partaking of his soup the while. "But ze ship boys do not ask question of ze *capitaine*."

"But we're not ship's boys," said Mike haughtily. "We are gentlemen's sons, and we want to know by what right you drag us away from home."

"Aha! yes; you eat your soup, *mon* brave boy, vile he is hot. Perhaps ze storms come to-morrow, and you are vere you get no soups no more, eh?"

"Look here, sir," said Mike, flushing in his excitement, "will you set us ashore somewhere if we promise not to tell?"

"*Non*," said the captain shortly. "Ve talk about all zat before! Eat your soup."

For answer Mike dropped his spoon upon the table, and the captain glared at him viciously, but passed his anger off with an unpleasant laugh.

"Aha," he said, "you vill not eat. I know. Ze *souris*—ze mouse, you know, valk himselfs into ze trap and spoil ze appetite. Ze toast cheese is not taste good, eh?"

Vince had his own ideas, and he ate a few spoonfuls of the soup and took some bread; but it seemed to choke him, and he soon put down his spoon, and the man, who seemed to act as cook and steward, took away the tureen and brought in the fish—the soles they had seen—well cooked and appetising; but the boys could not eat, in spite of the easy banter with which the captain kept on addressing them, and the fish gave way to cutlets and vegetables.

"Ah, I see," said their captor at last: "you vill not eat, and I know ze reason. *Ma foi*, and it is too late to make ze *amende* you call him. You bose mean to eat ze grand krebs you 'ave catch and 'ave give him to ze men. *Hélas!* it is, as you say, a pity. Now you forget him, and eat ze cotelette. To-morrow you not like ze dinner vis ze crew, and," he added, with a grin, "you may bose be vairy sick—*malade-de-mer*, eh?"

"Aha,' he said, 'you vill not eat."

He helped them both liberally, but they could not eat; and soon after they followed their host on deck, to find that the hatches were off, and the bales all carefully stacked below, while the emptied boat had disappeared and another was on the way, Vince paying great heed to the manner in which she glided up to the lugger just about amidships.

By the time it was dusk five heavy loads had been brought on board, and the hatches were then replaced, the boats all but one being hoisted to the davits, the other left swinging by its painter from a ring-bolt astern; and from the number of men aboard the boys judged that no one was left at the caves. They noticed too that, contrary to custom, no light was hoisted anywhere about the vessel, and that, though there were lanthorns in the men's cabin forward, and in the captain's aft, no gleam shone forth to play upon the water.

No one seemed to pay any heed to the prisoners, who went from place to place to gaze now up at the darkening rocks, with the stars above them beginning to twinkle faintly here and there, now down at the black waters, which, as the night deepened, began to reflect the bright points of light from the heavens. But soon after, to take their attention a little from their cares, they began to notice that the dark depths below them were alive with light—little specks, that looked like myriads of stars in motion, rising from below the vessel's keel, coming rapidly towards the surface and then gliding rapidly away. Every now and then there was a flash of light, just as if a pale greenish-golden flame had darted through the water from below; and, after noticing this several times, Vince said quietly—

"Fish feeding."

"Don't," said Mike petulantly. "Who's to think about fish feeding, when we're like this? You don't seem to mind it a bit."

"Don't I?" said Vince quietly; "but I do. Every time I see one of those little jelly-fish sailing along there, it makes me think of the light in our window at home—the one mother always puts there when I'm up at your place, so that I may see it from ever so far along the road. Father always jokes about it, and says it's nonsense, but she puts it there all the same; and it's there now, Mike, for she's sure to say I may have been carried out to sea in some boat and be coming back to-night."

"Oh, don't—don't!" groaned Mike: "it seems too horrid to hear."

"Hush! what's that?" said Vince. "Only a seabird calling somewhere off the water."

"No, it isn't," whispered Vince. "One of the men wouldn't have answered a seabird like that. It's a boat coming from somewhere out yonder."

"No boat would come through such a dark night, with all these dangerous currents among the rocks."

But a minute later a boat did glide out of the darkness, a rope was thrown over the bulwarks, made fast, and as a man climbed over on to the deck the captain came out of his cabin and went forward to where the fresh comer was standing.

It was so dark that they could not make out what he was like, but in the stillness every word spoken could be heard; and they recognised the voice directly, as, in answer to a growl from the captain about being late, the man said,—"Been here long enough ago, Skipper Jarks, if it had been any good, but she don't rise to it to-night. I've been hanging about ever so long, but she don't touch what she should. There won't be enough water for you on the rocks to-night by a foot."

"*Peste!*" ejaculated the captain; "and I vant to go. But after an hour, vat den?"

"Be just as she is now, skipper. Wind's been agen it since sundown, and kep' the water back: you won't get off to-night."

"Bah!" ejaculated the captain angrily; but he changed his manner directly: "Ah, vell, my friend Daygo, ve must vait, eh? You vill stay vis me here?"

"Nay," said the man. "I'll have to go back. I'm cruising about round the island a-looking for them two young shavers."

The captain turned his head sharply round and looked aft; but, keen as his sea-going eyes were, the presence of the boys passed unnoticed, and, probably concluding that they were farther aft, the captain said in a lower tone, but still perfectly audible.

"Dey look for zem?"

"Look for 'em? The whole island's been at it 'bout the rocks and cliffs, and with every boat out; but do you know, Skipper Jarks, they arn't fund 'em."

The old scoundrel chuckled, and Mike heard Vince's teeth grate together; and then directly after, he drew a deep breath, like a sigh, for the captain said softly,—

"And zey vill not find zem, eh?"

"They've been all day a-looking for their corpusses—for they're dead now."

"Aha! so soon?"

"Ay, skipper; they say they've gone off the rocks and been drownded, and when they told me I says I wondered they hadn't been years ago, for they was the owdaciousest pair as ever I see. They'd do anything they took in their heads."

"Aha! is it so?" said the captain.

"Ay, Skipper Jarks, it's so; but I'm 'fraid I shan't find their corpusses to-night. What do you say?"

"Nosing, *mon ami*: I on'y sink zat ze brave pilot. Josef Daygo, who know evairy rock and courant about ze island, vill find zem if any ones do. But, my friend, vat you sink? Zey find ze vay down to ze cave?"

"Nay, not they. Nobody can climb down they rocks."

"And you sink zere is no one who find ze leetler passage?"

"Sure of it, skipper. If any one had found that there way down do you think he'd ha' kep' it to hisself? Nay, I should ha' been sure to ha' heered it, and if I had I'd ha' done some'at as 'd startled him as tried to go down. On'y one man in the Crag know'd of that till they two dropped upon it somehow. I dunno how. It's been a wonder to me, though, as nobody never did. Well, I must be going back: I've got a rough bit to do 'fore I gets home, and then I've got to go up to the Doctor's."

"Vell, you vill eat and drink somesing," said the captain. "Come to ze cabin, and ve sall see."

As it happened, he led the way across the deck, and then along the port side aft to the cabin-hatch, from whence came soon after the call for the cook, who went to and fro carrying plates and glasses, while the two boys still stood in their former places, leaning over the bulwarks and apparently watching the phosphorescent creatures in the sea, but seeing none.

It was some time before either of them spoke, and then it was Vince who broke the silence.

"So we're both dead and swept out to sea, are we?" he said.

He waited for a few moments, and then, as Mike did not speak, he said, in a low whisper:

"I say, Mike, shouldn't you like to take a piece of rock and drop it through old Joe's boat?"

"No."

"Well, I should. Of all the old rascals that I ever heard of he seems to be about the worst. Why, he's regularly mixed up with this gang. Did you hear? It seems that you can only get in and out at certain times of the tide, and nobody knows how to pilot any one in but old Joe Daygo."

"Did you understand it to be like that?" said Mike eagerly.

"Yes, he seems to be the regular pilot, and comes to take this French lugger in and to steer it out among the rocks. Oh, it's terrible; and we've got old Joe to blame for all our troubles. I wish we'd sunk his boat."

"Shouldn't we have sunk ourselves too?"

"Well, perhaps. I should like to drop something through its bottom."

"I shouldn't," said Mike quietly. "Why not? It would serve him well right."

"Because I should like to use it ourselves."

"Eh? What do you mean?" said Vince excitedly. "Now, younkers," said a voice behind them, "skipper says I'm to show you two to your bunks."

It was a rough, hairy-faced fellow who spoke to them, though in the darkness they did not get a very good view of his features.

"To our bunks?" said Vince.

"Yes; come along. You're lucky: you've got a place all to yourselves."

He led them aft, to where a small hatchway stood, close to that of the captain's cabin, from whence the sound of voices came so loudly that, regardless of his companions' presence, the man stood and listened.

"But I tell you I must go back, skipper," said Daygo, "and it's getting late."

"*Oui*—yais, I know zat, *mon ami*," said the captain; "but I have ze good pilot on board, and it is late and ver' bad for him to go sail among ze rock and courant. I say it is better he sall stay all ze night, and not go run ze risk to drown himselfs. I cannot spare you. I have you, Daygo. You are a so much valuable mans. So I sall keep you till I sail."

"Keep me?" growled Daygo.

"Yais. You sall eat all as mosh as you vish, and drink more as you vish, but you cannot go avay. It is not safe."

There was the sound of a heavy fist brought down upon the table, and then the man, who had picked up a lanthorn, turned to them and said,—

"Down with you, youngsters!"

The boys obeyed, and the man followed.

"Old Daygo don't like having to stay," he said laughingly. "There you are, lads!—just room for you both without touching. Shall I leave you the lanthorn?"

"Please," said Vince. "Thank you.—I say—"

"Nay, you don't, lad," said the man, with gruff good humour; "you've nothing to say to me, and I've nothing to say to you. I don't want the skipper to come down on my head with a capstan bar. Here, both on you: just a word as I will say—Don't you be sarcy to the skipper. He's Frenchy, and he's got a temper of his own, so just you mind how you trim your boats. There, good-night."

"One moment," said Vince, in a quick whisper.

*Bang*! went the door, and they heard a hasp put over a staple and a padlock rattled in.

"Here, youngsters!" came through the door.

"What is it?"

"Mind you put out that light when you're in your bunks. Good-night!"

"Good-night," said Mike.

"Bad night," said Vince. And then: "Oh, Ladle, old chap, what shall we do?"

# Chapter Twenty Nine
# Longings for Liberty

It was easier to ask that question than to answer it, and they cast a brief glance round the bare, cupboard-like place, with its two shelves, which represented the prisoners' beds, each bearing a small horsehair mattress and a French cotton blanket.

"Put out the light," was all the answer Vince received; and, after holding it to the side of the place for a moment or two, he opened the lanthorn door and blew the candle out.

"No good to keep that in. Only makes the place hot and stuffy. I'm going to open that light."

The "light" was a sort of wooden shutter, which took the place of an ordinary cabin window, and as soon as he had drawn it wide open the soft night air entered in a delicious puff.

"Hah! that's better," sighed Vince. "Come here and breathe, Ladle, old chap. It's of no use to smother ourselves if we are miserable. I say, isn't it a beautiful night?"

"Who's going to think anything beautiful when one's like this? It's horrible!"

"Pst!" whispered Vince, for the voice of the captain was plainly heard overhead, and the deep growl of old Daygo in answer, the way in which the tones grew more subdued suggesting that the speakers had gone right forward.

"I should like to pitch that old villain overboard," said Mike, in a fierce whisper.

"Well, if you'd let me tie a rope round him first I'd help you, Ladle; but I shouldn't like him to drown till he'd had time to get a little better."

"Better?" said Mike: "he'll never grow any better."

"Well, never mind him," said Vince. "Now then, let's look the state of affairs in the face. You won't tell us what to do, so I must see what I can think of."

"Have you thought of anything?" cried Mike eagerly.

"If you shout like that, it won't be much good if I have," said Vince, in an angry whisper.

"I'm very sorry, Vince," said Mike humbly. "I'll be more careful."

"We shan't get away if you're not."

"Get away? Then you see a chance?" cried Mike eagerly.

"Just the tiniest spark of one if you're ready to try."

"I'll try anything," whispered Mike.

"Wouldn't mind going into the seal hole again?"

"Vince, old chap, I'd do anything," said Mike, seizing his fellow-prisoner's arm and holding him tightly. "What shall we do?"

"I'm afraid it's going to be very risky, for we don't know anything about the rocks and currents, and we may be upset. Now do you see?"

"I see: you mean escaping in a boat," said Mike eagerly; "but how?— what boat?"

"Don't take much thinking to know that," replied Vince; "the only thing that puzzles me is how they could be so stupid as to leave a boat there swinging to a painter."

"Old Joe's boat!" cried Mike joyously; and Vince clapped a hand over his mouth in anger, for just then they heard the voices of the captain and old Daygo as they walked forward again; and as far as the prisoners could make out, the two men were walking up one side of the deck and down the other, talking earnestly, but what was said the boys could not catch.

"Yes, old Joe's boat," said Vince in a subdued voice; "but if you're going to shout we may as well go to bed and have a night's rest."

"I really will mind, Cinder—I will indeed," whispered Mike. "I couldn't help that, old chap. But tell me, how are you going to manage it?"

"There's only one way," replied Vince, with his lips close to his fellow-prisoner's ear; "climb out of the window, and then over the bulwark to get down inside it where it's dark; then creep along till we can feel the painter."

"Then creep over the bulwark and drop down one after the other."

"Cut the painter," said Vince.

"And then we're free."

There was a pause, during which Mike got tight hold of Vince's hand, and the latter felt that it was cold and wet from the boy's excitement.

"I don't know so much about being free," whispered Vince. "We should be away from this wretched old lugger; but where should we be going then? Didn't I warn you about the rocks and currents?"

"Yes; but we should have old Joe's boat, and we can manage that easily enough."

"Yes, if we're in the open sea, even if she's sinking, Ladle; but shut-in here among the rocks I don't know how we should get along. But anything's better than sitting down and not having a try."

"Yes, anything," said Mike, in a low, excited whisper.

"Yes, anything. We must try for the sake of those at home. I know my father is sure to say to me, 'Didn't you try to escape?'"

"So will mine," said Mike. "Oh yes, we must have a good try. Think we can climb up?"

"I'm just going to try," said Vince, kneeling down to take off his boots. "If you like to try you can. If not, you've got to go down on all fours under the window, so that I can step on your back and climb out."

Mike was silent for a few moments, and then he said softly, —

"I'll do which you like, Cinder."

"Then I think I'll try first. If I can't manage it you can."

"But stop a moment: suppose there's any one on deck?"

"It will be very dark."

"But there'll be lanthorns burning and a watch kept."

"I feel sure there'll be no lights, because they might be seen from the cliffs; and as they know they're so safe here, I don't believe there'll be any watch kept."

"I wish I'd got a head like yours, Cinder."

"Do you? Well, we can't change. That's it. My! how tight my boots were! It's getting them wet and letting them dry on one's feet.—Pst! Slip into your berth."

Their needs and experience were beginning to make them obey a sharp order without question; and as Vince lowered down the shutter Mike crawled into the lower bunk silently enough, while, almost without a sound, Vince crept into the one above, stretched himself upon his back, and placed his hands together under his head.

The reason for this sudden action was that he had seen a gleam of light play for a moment beneath the rough door; and they were hardly in their places when there was the sound of descending steps on the ladder, the shape of the door marked out plainly by the light all round. Then came the rattling of a key in the padlock, which was drawn out of the staple, the door was flung open, and the hutch of a place was filled with the dull, soft light of a lanthorn, as a man stepped in.

It was hard work to lie there with the lanthorn held close up to them, but the boys both stood the ordeal. Mike was lying with his face close to the bulkhead, and of course with his back to their visitor and his features in the shade; but Vince's was the harder task, for he had assumed his attitude as being the most sleep-like, and to give better effect to his piece of acting, he had opened his mouth, and went on breathing rather heavily, while the fact of his having his boots off, and one foot sticking out over the bunk side, helped materially over the bit of deception.

"I wonder who it is," thought Vince; and, as if in answer, a familiar voice said, in a low tone,—

"Aha! *Vous êtes* not too much frighten to go fast asleep?"

Vince did not need to open his eyes, for he could see mentally vividly enough the swarthy, brown, deeply-lined face, with the keen dark eyes, and the crafty look about the mouth, drawn into an unpleasant smile, while the big earrings seemed to glisten in the soft light.

"You are fast asleep—*hein*?" said the man, rather sharply; but no one stirred, though Vince could feel the perspiration standing in a fine dew upon his forehead and by the sides of his nose.

"I came to see if you are good boys, and sall put out your light quite safe; for all ze powder is down underneas you, and you muss not blow yourselfs up and spoil my sheep. You hear, big, stupede boy?"

Vince gave vent to a low, gurgling sound, and made up his mind to babble a few words about the caverns; but his throat was dry, and his tongue refused to act.

Perhaps it was as well, for in doing so he might have overdone his part, which was perfect.

Then the light was withdrawn, the captain went out, and the door was carefully fastened, the light fading from round the door while something shook loudly as he ascended the ladder and dropped the trap down with a snap, which was followed by the crash of iron, as if another loop were passed on a staple.

"Hasn't dropped any sparks, has he, Vince?" whispered Mike, turning softly in his bunk.

"Can't see any," was the reply. "Oh, I say, Ladle, and I blew out our candle and saw them fly!"

"But do you think it's true? Is the powder here, or did he only say it to frighten us?"

"I don't know," whispered Vince. "There must be a powder magazine, for he has cannon on deck. But I didn't see any trap door: did you?"

"Yes—just as you put out the light. You knelt on it when you took off your boots."

"Oh dear!" sighed Vince. "I'm all dripping wet. Isn't this place horribly hot?"

"Hot? I feel as if my things were all soaked."

"Don't talk. We must lie still now, and wait. I don't think he'll come again."

"I do," said Mike. "He'll never be such a noodle as to believe we two will stop here without trying to escape."

"I don't know," sighed Vince. "I'm afraid we're quite safe?"

"What, to escape?"

"No—to stop in prison; for I expect we shan't be able to get on deck."

"But we're going to try?"

"Yes," said Vince through his closely set teeth; "we're going to try."

# Chapter Thirty
# A Bold Dash for Freedom

As the boys lay perfectly still in their bunks, gradually growing cooler, and feeling that even if they were over the part of the hold used as a powder magazine there was nothing to fear so long as there was no light near, they heard a step twice overhead, then all was perfectly still but the faint rippling of the swift current as it passed under the vessel and glided on across to the rocks.

They whispered to each other from time to time; Mike being impatient to begin their attempt, but Vince always refusing till he felt satisfied that all was still.

At last this feeling of satisfaction came, and, passing his legs out of his bunk, he dropped lightly on to the floor to begin feeling about, till his hand touched a rough hinge, and on the other side a ring which lay down in the woodwork of a trap door.

But he did not say anything, only rose and pulled open the light again, keeping it in that position by passing the leather strap which formed its handle over a hook in the ceiling, a slit having been cut in the piece of leather.

"Now, Ladle," whispered Vince, "come and kneel here, then I can stand on your back."

Mike obeyed at once, and then whispered quickly,—

"Vince, there is a trap door here: I'm right on it."

"I know,—I touched it; but there's no candle. Ready?"

"Yes."

Vince took hold of the opening frame, which was only just big enough for him to pass through, stepped lightly on to his companion as he stiffened himself on all fours, and then began to creep out.

For a few moments he hesitated, for there was the black water beneath him, full of sparks, gliding rapidly along, so brightly that he felt that if any one were on deck looking over the bulwark he must be seen; but the thought of freedom and those at home nerved him, and as soon as he was in a sitting position, with his legs inside, he bent down and whispered to his companion, who had risen,—

"Take tight hold of my legs till I give a jerk, which means let me loose."

Mike seized the legs firmly; and, thus secured, Vince stretched out his arms and began to feel about overhead, to find that the top of the light was just below the projecting streak, which runs, iron-bound, round the most prominent part of a vessel, from stem to stern, to protect the side from injury when it glides up to wharf, pier, or pile. This stood out about a foot, and Vince felt that if he could only climb on this, the rest would be easy.

He passed his hands cautiously over it, and, reaching in, found to his great delight a ring-bolt, through which it was possible to pass two or three fingers. Jerking his leg, he felt himself free, and rose up, getting first one foot and then the other on the sill of the opening.

There was no difficulty in standing like this, and as he did so he felt Mike's arms tightly embracing his legs, an act which hindered further progress if he had meant to climb higher.

But he was satisfied with what he had done; after peering about a little, and listening for some minutes, he jerked one leg again, felt them freed, and began to descend.

To an active boy, whose nerves were firm, this was easy enough; and directly after he stood in the little cabin, breathing hard, but able to find words, and whisper to his anxious fellow-prisoner.

"It's as easy as easy," he said: "nothing to getting up a bit of stiff cliff;" and he then described what he had found, and how all seemed as still as could be. "Couldn't you hear any watch on deck?"

"Not a sound of them. I believe every one's below; and I say, Mike, we needn't get over on deck at all. There's plenty of room to take hold of the top of the bulwarks and walk along. All we've got to do is to mind the stays when we come to them, and step round carefully."

"Yes, I understand perfectly," said Mike. "Come on, and let's get it over."

"Wait till I've put on my boots. I shall want them." The boy knelt down and hurriedly drew them on, and laced them as well as he could in the dark; then raising himself on to the window-sill without assistance, he drew himself into his old position, and reaching up and over the streak, found the ring-bolt, which rattled faintly, and, passing his fingers through, stood up on the sill, and then drew himself on to the projecting woodwork.

Here he crouched for a few moments listening, before rising erect, with one hand upon the top of the bulwark, over which he looked; but all was dark, and there was not a sound to be heard save the faint rustling below him made by Mike.

This was the most nervous part of the business. A certain amount of tremor had troubled the lad as he climbed out, and the thought of having a slip did once bring the perspiration out upon his forehead; but the effort needed dulled the fear, and he soon stood where he was in safety. But to listen to a companion undergoing the same trial in the darkness was another thing; and Vince felt ten times the dread as he listened and shivered to hear the ring-bolt seized and his companion slowly drawing himself upward so that he could stand.

Suppose he lost his nerve—suppose he slipped and tell with a splash into that black, spangled water—what could he do? Poor Mike would be swept away directly, and his only chance of life would be for him to swim steadily till he reached the rocks, and then try to find one to which he could cling, and draw himself up.

But Vince did better than think: he tightened his grasp of the bulwark rail by crooking his hand, and softly extended one leg over the streak.

This had the effect he desired. The next moment it was struck by a hand feeling about. Then the trouser was tugged at, and directly after the bottom was turned over and over, so as to form a good roll to grip. Then, with this for a second hand-hold, Mike was helped, and his climb on to the shelf-like projection became easier for the aid afforded, and he too rose to stand panting beside Vince.

They felt that everything depended upon their coolness, and hence they stood there, facing inward, holding on to the bulwark and listening.

But all was still; and at last, satisfied that it was time to move, Vince whispered "Now," and began to edge himself along to the right—that is, towards the forward part of the boat.

Mike started at the same moment, taking step for step, their hands touching at every movement. It was an easy enough task this, for there was plenty of hold and standing room—the only danger being that they might be heard by some one on the watch, while there was the chance that they had been heard and this was a new trap to re-catch them.

But their hearts rose as they crept slowly and silently along in the silence, and then went down deeply into a sense of despair, for a thought suddenly struck Vince which made him stop and place his lips close to his companion's ear, and whisper,—

"Suppose, as Joe is going to stop, they have hoisted the boat on deck?"

Mike replied promptly, and with a decision that was admirable under the circumstances,—

"Don't make bugbears. Go on and try."

It was rude enough to have brought forth a sharp retort at any other time; but then Vince felt its justice, and he went on again, and his hand touched the shrouds which held the mainmast in place, and a little care had to be exercised to pass round. But this was silently achieved by both; and Vince was gliding his right-hand along the top of the bulwarks once more, when it was as if an electric shock had passed through him, for he had suddenly touched something unmistakably like a man's elbow.

For a few moments he was ready to doubt this; but the doubt passed away directly, for from close to him a heavy, snoring breath was drawn, and as he gazed with starting eyes he made out dimly the head and shoulders of a man who was evidently the watch, but who conducted his watching by folding his arms upon the bulwarks, laying his head thereon, and going off fast asleep.

Vince felt that all was over unless they went back some little distance, climbed over and crossed the deck to the other side; and once more placing his lips to Mike's ear, he told him of the obstacle in the way, and suggested this plan.

Then Mike's lips were at his ear,—

"Take too much time—may tumble over another—go on."

The proposal almost took the boy's breath away, but he was strung up by his companion's firmness to do anything now, and, drawing a deep breath, he prepared to advance; but paused again, with his blood running cold, for there was an uneasy movement on the part of the watch and a low, growling muttering.

Silence once more; and then, nerving himself, Vince advanced his left hand till it was close to the sleeping man's elbow, then, edging along a little, he reached out his right-hand till he could grasp the bulwark beyond the other elbow; but the position brought his face down close to the back of the sleeper's head, and he could feel the warmth emanating from it and the man's rising breath, while he trembled as he dreaded lest the man should feel his.

Then Vince felt that he ought to step back and tell Mike how to manage—as he was acting; but, knowing that all this meant delay and that speed was everything, and might mean success instead of failure, he knew that he must trust to his comrade's own common sense. And now, with the feeling upon him that if the man awoke suddenly he would start and fall back into the sea, he tightened his hold of his right-hand, relaxed that of his left, edged along, and was safely past.

Naturally all these thoughts darted almost instantaneously through his mind, and a few moments only elapsed between Mike's words and his being safe upon the other side; while now, as he stood thus, after leaving ample room for his companion, the strain upon his nerves seemed to be greater, for he had to try and see Mike's movements, and listen in agony to the faint rustling sound he made.

Poor Mike had a harder test of his courage than that which had fallen to Vince's lot; for as by instinct he took the same means of getting by the obstacle as the former, and was standing with arms outstretched, the man made a sudden movement and growled out some tongue-blundered word, at the same time raising his head and striking Mike's chin slightly, to make the boy's teeth go together with a sharp click.

"It's all over," thought Vince. But he was wrong: the man settled his head down again in a more satisfactory position, and uttered a low, grumbling sigh of resting weariness.

Then Mike was alongside of his partner in the flight, and they edged themselves rapidly along to the foremast shrouds—so short a distance, but to them, with their nerves on the strain, so far.

Now came another heart-compressing question to Vince. The boat, when Joe Daygo arrived, had been made fast a short distance in front of the foremast: was it there now?

A strange hesitation came over the lad; he did not like to pass beyond the fore-chains to test this, for he felt that if it had been removed and hoisted on board the disappointment would be so keen as to be almost unbearable, for to let it down unheard would be impossible; but once more mastering himself he passed on, holding by the light shrouds which gave at his touch, and then began to run his hand once more along the bulwark to feel the line, which had been passed over and twisted to and fro over one of the belaying pins.

No—no—no.

*Yes!*

There it was, and as he grasped it the boat answered to his touch as it swung alongside and grazed softly against the copper sheathing.

"Got it?" was whispered.

"Yes;" and Vince's hand went to his pocket for his knife, as his busy, overstrung brain asked why it was that they had not been searched and their knives taken away.

But he did not withdraw the knife, for he found that it would be easy enough to cast the rope loose, and he turned to Mike.

"Down with you!" he said.

"No: you first."

A noise as of a heavy blow.

A savage yell, followed by a scuffling sound from where the sleeping man had been standing, and the boys stood holding on there, paralysed for the moment.

"Curse you if you hit me!" began a rough voice from out of the darkness; but the speech was cut short by a sharp clicking, and the familiar voice of the French captain arose, sharpened by rage and sounding fierce and tigerish in spite of the peculiarity of his broken English, mingled with words in his native tongue.

"Dog! *Canaille! Vite* sleep-head fool! Anozaire vord I blow out you brain and you are ovaire-board."

The sleeper growled something, which was again cut short by the French skipper.

"Vat? How you know zat ze boy do not get on deck to take a boat and go tell of my store *cachette*? To-morrow you are flog by all ze crew, and zey sall sare all ze monnaies zat vould come to you."

Vince drew on the painter, and then pressed Mike's shoulder for him to descend, while he began softly to cast off the rope.

Mike did his best to go down in silence, and Vince his to cast off without making a sound; but the boat ground against the side, the belaying pin rattled, and there was a rush from where the captain stood.

Mike was in the boat as the last turn was cast off from the belaying pin; and then, without a moment's hesitation, Vince leaped down, fortunately alighting beyond his companion upon one of the thwarts, and then falling forward upon his hands just as there was a flash of light and a loud report.

The thrust given by Mike and the impetus of Vince's leap sent the boat out to where it was caught by the current; but, instead of its bearing them away from the lugger, it seemed to keep them back for a few moments, but only for the bows to be seized by an eddy just as there was another flash, report, and simultaneously a dull thud, as of something being hit. Then the shouting of orders, the appearance of a light, and the hurrying of feet was more distant, as if the lugger had suddenly been snatched away; but the two lads knew that they were in one of the terrible rushing currents, and were being borne along at a tremendous rate. Where? In what direction?

They could not tell, for the tide had turned.

# Chapter Thirty One
# The Perils of the Scraw

In the hurry and confusion the boys crouched in the bottom of the boat for some minutes, gazing at the lugger, and seeing lanthorn after lanthorn dancing about. Then one descended like a glowworm apparently on to the surface of the water, and they knew that a boat had been lowered and that there would be pursuit. And all the time they felt that without effort on their part they were being borne rapidly along as fast as any one could chase them; but they were in a boat familiar to them, and furnished with oars and sails if they could only reach the open water. Then a despondent feeling came over them as they realised that they were surrounded by towering rocks, and as they crouched lower they fully expected from moment to moment to hear a grinding sound, and feel a sharp check as a plank was ripped out by some sharp granite fang, and then hear once more the rippling of the water as it rushed into the boat.

And this in the darkness; for the bright stars above and the phosphorescent atoms with which the black waters were dotted did not relieve the deep gloom produced by the overhanging cliffs.

"Hurt, Vince?" whispered Mike at last.

"Yes, ever so."

"Oh! Want a handkerchief to bind it up?" cried Mike, in horror.

"Well, it does bleed—feels wet—but it don't matter much."

"But it does," said Mike excitedly. "Where did it hit you?"

"On the shin; but it didn't hit me—I hit it."

"What! The bullet?"

"Go along! don't joke now. I came down against an oar. Oh, I see: you thought he hit me when he fired."

"Of course."

"Pooh! he couldn't aim straight in the dark. I'm all right. But I say: there's water in the boat. Not much, but I can hear it gurgling in. Why,

Mike," he cried excitedly, after a few moments' search, "here's a little round hole close down by the keel. There, I've stopped it up with a finger; it's where his bullet must have gone through. Got your handkerchief?"

"Yes."

"Tear off a piece, to make a plug about twice as big as a physic-bottle cork."

There was the sound of tearing, and then Mike handed the piece of cotton, which was carefully thrust into the clean, round hole, effectually plugging it; after which Vince proposed that they should each take an oar.

"Can't row," said Mike shortly.

"No, but we may want to fend her off from a rock. Hullo! where are the lanthorns now? I can't see either the lugger or the boat."

Mike looked back, but nothing was visible.

"We've come round some rock," said Vince. "We shall see them again directly."

But the minutes glided on, and they saw no light—all was black around as ever, but the loud, hissing gurgle of the water told that they were being borne along by some furious current; and at last came that which they had been expecting—a heavy bump, as the prow struck against a rock-face so heavily that they were both jerked forward on to their hands, while the boat was jarred from stem to stern.

They listened with a feeling of expectant awe for the noise of water rushing in; but none came, and a little feeling about was sufficient test to prove that there was no more than had come in through the bullet hole. But while they were waiting there came another heavy blow, and their state of helplessness added to their misery.

"Oh, if it was only light!" groaned Mike.

"Yes, we could use the oars or hook to fend her off."

Bump went the boat again, and they caught at the side to save themselves, conscious now, in the thick darkness, that they were being whirled round and round in some great whirlpool-like eddy, which dealt with the boat as if it were a cork.

"Don't seem as if we can do anything," said Vince at last, as the boat swept along, with the water lapping and gurgling about them just as if it were full of hungry tongues anticipating the feast to come as soon as they were sucked down.

"No," said Mike, "it doesn't seem as if we can do anything."

"'Cept one thing, Mike," said Vince in a low deep tone, which did not sound like his own voice.

"What?"

"Say our prayers—for the last time."

And in the midst of that intense darkness, black as ebony on either side, while above and below there were still the bright glittering and softened streaks of light, there was an interval of solemn silence.

Vince was the first to break that silence, and there was something quite cheerful in his tones now as he said,—

"Shake hands, Mikey: I'm sorry you and I haven't always been good friends. I have often been a regular beast to you."

Mike grasped the extended hands in a firm grip with both of his, as he said, in a choking voice,—

"Not half so bad as I've been to you, Cinder. I've got such a hasty temper sometimes."

"Get out!" cried Vince sharply. "There, I'm better now. I'm afraid we're going to be drowned, Ladle, but I feel as if we ought to be doing something to try and save ourselves. It's being so cowardly to sit still here. They wouldn't like it at home."

"But what can we do? I'm ready."

"So am I; but it's so dark. I say, though, we must be going round and round in a sort of hole."

"Then we shall be drawn right down somewhere into the earth."

"Not that! I tell you what, it's like one of those great pot-holes in the big passage, only a hundred times as big; and the water's sweeping the boulders round, and grinding it out and carrying us along with it. Look here, we shall be kept on going round and round here, if we don't get smashed, till daylight; and then old Jarks'll come and find us, and we shall be worse off than ever. I say, though, don't you think we could do something with the boat-hook?"

"What?"

"Wait till we bump against the rocks again, and then try and hold on."

"If you did the water would come over the stern."

"I don't know. Well, look here: I'll try. If it does I'll let go directly."

Taking hold of the boat-hook Vince knelt down right forward, thrust the iron-armed pole over the bows, and holding it like a lance in rest he waited, but not for long. Very soon after the iron point touched against stone, and he was thrown backward, nearly losing the pole, while the boat was sent surging along on one side for a few moments, bumped on the other side, then back again as if she were being sent from side to side, and directly after the keel came upon a rock which seemed to slope up like a great boulder standing in their way. There for a brief moment or two it was balanced, and made a plunge forward like a dive, the water came with a rush over the bows, and surged back to where Mike was kneeling, and then they were rushing onward again more swiftly than ever.

For a few moments the pair were too breathless to speak, but Vince recovered from the confusion caused by the shock and the rapidly following exciting incidents, and he shouted aloud, —

"Bale, Mike, bale! It's all right: we're out of that whirlpool, and we're going along again."

"You've got the baler forward," said Mike huskily.

"Eh? So I have in the locker here. I say, how deep do you make the water? There's hardly any here."

"Only a few inches."

"Then we're all right yet; but we may as well have that out."

He felt for the locker, and drew out the old tin pot, crept aft to where his companion knelt, and, after lifting the board which covered in the keel depression, he began to toss out the water rapidly, and soon lowered it so that the pot began to scrape on the bottom, while Mike listened with a feeling of envy attacking him, for he felt that it must be a relief to be doing something instead of kneeling there listening and wondering whether the pursuing boat was anywhere near.

"There!" said Vince at last, in a triumphant tone; "that's different to baling when you feel that the water is coming in as fast as you throw it out. I haven't got it all, but as much as I can without making a noise."

He replaced the bottom board and then returned the pot to the locker, and Mike moved a little forward now to meet him half-way.

"Think we're going as fast now as ever?" whispered Mike.

"Eh? I don't know. I was too busy to think about it. No, not quite, and — I say, are we going right?"

"Right?"

"Well, I mean as we were. We seemed to be going south, as far as I could make out by the stars; and now we're going north."

"Nonsense! impossible!"

"Look, then! I'm sure we had our backs to the pole star, and that meant going south, and out to sea; but now we've got our faces due north."

"Yes," said Mike, after a few moments' pause; "that's right: we're going north."

"Well, that isn't out to sea."

"No," replied Mike thoughtfully.

"And running along at such a rate as we are, we ought to have been ever so far away by this time, instead of rushing along here deep down among the rocks, as if we were in a narrow channel. I can't make it out: can you?"

Mike remained thoughtful and silent again for a time, and then said wearily,—

"No; I can't understand it. It gives me the headache to think; and being whirled along like this is so confusing. My thoughts go rushing along like the water."

"Don't talk so loud, Mike," said Vince, after a pause, "or we shall be heard. But we must have left them a long way behind, or else they've covered over their lanthorn so as to come upon us by surprise."

"Think they are near us, then?"

"Must be, because the tide would carry them along as fast as it does us; and they have the advantage of knowing the way. Oh! I do wish we could get out in the open sea; and then, once we were clear of the rocks, we'd show them what the boat could do. It would puzzle them to—"

He was going to say "catch us then," but he stopped short, gazing upward, out of the black chasm in which they were, at the stars.

"What is it? See the light?" whispered Mike.

"No: I was trying to make out our course. The passage has wound off to the right, and we're going east."

"Of course it would zigzag and turn about," said Mike wearily; "but we're in deeper water here, for we don't seem to go near any small rocks."

"No; but we're going by plenty of big ones on the left. The current runs close to them, I'm sure, though it's ever so much wider now. I believe I could almost have touched either side with the boat-hook a bit ago; now I can only touch one side."

"It's more ripply, too, now, isn't it?"

"Ever so much: seems to boil up all about us, and you can't see the bright specks sailing about so fast. The top of the water was as smooth as glass when we were in the great lugger."

"That's a sign we are near the sea, then," said Mike, with more confidence in his tones.

"Yes, and I don't like it," said Vince thoughtfully.

"Why?"

"Because I've been thinking that there must be another way out; and knowing all about it, as they do, they'll be waiting at the mouth of this horrible zigzag place along which we're dodging all this time, and catch us after all."

"Oh, Cinder!" cried Mike passionately, "don't say that: it would be too hard. It may be too dark for them to see us if we lie close and don't make a sound. And look," he said joyfully: "we really are close to the sea now, for we're going due south."

"Due south it is," assented Vince, as if he were standing at a wheel steering. "Yes, I suppose you're right, for I can hear the sound of surf. Listen."

"Yes, I can hear," replied Mike; "but it sounds smothered-like."

"Rocks between us, perhaps. Now then: only whispers, mind!—close to the ear. Don't let's lose our chance of getting away by telling them where we are. I say!"

"Yes."

"If there was a boat anywhere near us, could you see it?"

Mike turned his eyes to right and left before answering:

"Sure I couldn't on that side, and I don't think I could on this."

"That's what I felt, and if we're lucky we'll escape them after all. Now then, silence, and let's get the oars across and each take his place on the thwarts, ready to row hard if we are seen."

Each from long practice felt for the thole-pins and placed them in their proper holes; then, softly taking up their oars, they laid them right across the boat, with handle standing out on one side, blade on the other, and waited in silence, with the boat gliding on.

At the end of about a quarter of an hour, during which minute by minute they had expected to be swept out into open water where the great Atlantic tide was rolling along by the solitary island, Mike whispered,—

"I say, the boat has turned quite round more than once. Doesn't that account for the stars seeming different?"

"No, because we can tell we are sometimes going forward and sometimes back."

"But look! we're going north now."

"Yes, I know we are," said Vince; "and I'm beginning to know how it is."

"Well, tell me. It's so horrible to be puzzled like this."

Vince was silent.

"Why don't you speak?"

"Because I was thinking. Ladle, old chap, we've gone through too much, what with the seals' cave, and being caught and then put down in that stifling hole over the gunpowder. We're both off our heads—in a sort of fever."

"I'm not," said Mike shortly. "You are, or else you wouldn't talk such stuff."

"I talk such stuff, as you call it, because my father's a doctor, and I've heard him tell my mother about what queer fancies people have when their heads are wrong."

"Two people couldn't be queer in the same way and with the same things. What's the good of talking like that?"

"Very well: you tell me how it is. I can't understand it, and the more I try the more puzzled I am. It's horrible, that's what it is, and I feel sometimes as if we had been carried away by the tide to nowhere, or the place where the tides come and go in the hollows of the earth."

"We shall be out at sea directly, and then we shall be all right."

"No, we shan't be out at sea directly, and we shan't be all right; for we've got into some horrible great whirlpool."

"What!" cried Mike excitedly. "A whirlpool?"

"Yes, that's it; and we're going round and round, and that's why it is that we are sometimes looking south and sometimes north."

"But you don't think—if it is as you say—that at last we shall be sucked down some awful pit in the middle?"

"I don't know," said Vince. "I can't think properly now. I feel just as if my head was all shut up, and that nothing would come out of it. I say, Mike!"

There was no reply, for Mike was gazing wildly up at the stars, trying to convince himself of the truth or falsity of his companion's words; but he only crouched lower at last, with a feeling of despair creeping over him, and then he turned angrily, as Vince began to speak again, in a low, dreamy voice.

"That's it," he said: "we are going round and round. I wish we'd had some more of old Jarks' dinner, and then gone to sleep quietly in our bunks. We couldn't have been so badly off as we are now."

"Then why did you propose for us to escape?"

"Because I thought we ought to try," said Vince sharply, as he suddenly changed his tone. "There, it's of no use to talk, Mike. We're in for it, and I'm not going to give up like a coward. I don't know where we are, and you don't; but we're in one of those whirls that go round and round when the tide's running up or down, and we can't be any worse off than we are now, for there are no rocks, seemingly."

"But the middle — the hole."

"They don't have any hole. Why, you know, old Joe sailed us right across one out yonder by the Grosse Chaine, and we went into the little one off Shag Rock. It's one like that we're in, and I daresay if it was daylight we could see how to get out of it by a few tugs at the oars, same as we got out of that one when we went round and round before. Oh, we shall be all right."

Mike did not speak, for the words seemed to give him no comfort.

"Do you hear, Ladle?" continued Vince. "If we had been likely to upset, it would have been all over with us long ago; but we go on sailing round as steadily as can be, and I feel sure that we shall get out all right. What do you say to lying down and having a nap?"

"Lie down? Here? Go to sleep?" cried Mike in horror. "I couldn't."

"I could," said Vince. "I'm so tired that I don't think I could keep awake, even if I knew old Jarks was likely to come and threaten me with a pistol. But, I say, Ladle, that wretch shot at us twice. Why, he might have hit one of us. Won't he have to be punished when we get away and tell all about him?"

"Yes, I suppose so — if ever we do get away," said Mike sadly.

Then they relapsed into silence, both watching the stars to convince themselves that they were going round and round, making the circuit of some wide place surrounded by the towering rocks, which made the sea look so intensely black.

At last, thoroughly convinced, the strain of thinking became too great, the motion of the boat and the constant gliding along in that horrible monotonous whirl began to affect Mike as it had affected Vince, and, in spite of his energetic struggles to rouse himself from it, was now attacking him more strongly than ever. They were surrounded by dangers, the least of which was that of the pursuing boat with the exasperated captain; for so surely as the boat grazed upon a rock just below the surface she would capsize. But all this was as nothing to the mentally and bodily exhausted lads. Nature was all-powerful, and by degrees the head of first one then of the other drooped, and sleep, deep and sudden, fell upon them.

But the sleep was not then profound. The mind still acted like the flickering of a candle in its socket, and urged them to start up wakeful and determined once more. And this happened again and again, the sufferers telling themselves that it would be madness to go to sleep. But, madness or no, Nature said they must; and almost simultaneously, after seating themselves in the bottom of the boat, so as to prop themselves in the corners between the thwart and side, they glided lower and lower, and at last lay prone in the most profound of slumber, totally unconscious of everything but the great need which would renew with fresh vigour their exhausted frames.

# Chapter Thirty Two
# A Strange Awakening

The grey gulls were wheeling round and round, dipping down from time to time to pick up some scrap of floating food or tiny fish from out of a shoal; the cormorants and shags were swimming here and there, and diving down swift as the fish themselves, in chase of victim after victim for their ravenous maws, and the fish, crowded together, were playing about the surface, and leaping out at times like bars of silver, to fall back again with a splash, while the sun made the water sparkle as it rippled and played and foamed among the rocks.

It was a glorious morning; and the heather, gorse and purple-hued lavender blossomed, sea-pinks glistened and flashed, as the sun played and sent off rays of dazzling iridescent hues from the evanescent gems with which the night mists had bedewed them.

Everywhere all was life and light, save where a boat went gliding along upon a swift current stem first, stern first, or broadside on, as the various curves and jutting rocks at the foot of the huge cliffs affected the hurrying waters and made them react upon the boat.

All at once there was a desperate quarrel and screaming for as a diver rose from its plunge, and was flying towards one of the cliff shelves to enjoy its morning meal in the shape of a large, newly caught fish, it was attacked by a huge pirate of a black-backed gull, which pounced down upon it with open beak, secured the fish, and as it flew off was followed and mobbed by a score of other birds, when such a wild clamour of sharp metallic screams arose, that it startled one of the occupants of the boat, making him spring up, rub his eyes, stare, and then bend down to rouse his companion.

"Here! Hi! Mike! Ladle! Wake up!"

The other obeyed, sprang to his feet, and stared wildly at his companion, with that dull, heavy, dreamy look in the eyes, which tells that though the muscular energy of the body may be awake, the mind is still fast plunged in sleep.

Then both rubbed their eyes, and Vince did more: he knelt down, leaned over the side of the boat, and plunging both hands in, scooped up the cool sparkling water, and bathed face and temples till his brain grew clearer, and he stood up again, dabbing his face with his handkerchief.

"Do as I do. Do you hear, Mike? I say, you're asleep!"

"Sleep?" said Mike, looking at him vacantly.

"Yes, asleep. Rouse up and look! It's wonderful! Here, if you won't, I must. Kneel down."

He pressed upon the boy's shoulders; and Mike, without making the slightest resistance, knelt in the bottom of the boat. He yielded too as Vince pressed a hand upon the back of his head, and then splashed some water in his face.

The effect was electrical. The next minute Mike was bathing his brows, throwing up the water with both hands; and as he felt the refreshing coolness send an invigorating and calming thrill through every nerve, he rose up and stood drying himself and gazing round, wondering whether he was yet awake, or this was part of some strange, wild dream.

Vince did not speak, but stood there watching him, while the boat glided on, as it had all through the night, with unerring regularity; and there before them was the great watery oval they had gone on traversing, dotted with sea-birds, while now, instead of the mighty cliffs around, looking black, overhanging and forbidding, they were beautiful in the extreme, both in the morning light and their deep empurpled shades.

Mike looked and looked up at the highest cliffs on his left, over the rapidly gliding water to his right, where the great ridge was dotted with sea-birds, and away to fore and aft, where the lofty overhanging rocks were repeated.

"I say," cried Mike at last, "am I awake?"

"If you're not, I'm fast asleep," said Vince.

"But how did we get here?"

"I don't know. Through some narrow passage, I suppose; and then, as soon as we got in, we must have been going on round and round, and round and round, thinking that we were getting out to sea. I say, no wonder it seemed so far!"

"Then it is true," said Mike excitedly. "I don't know that cave, though."

"No, we never saw that before," said Vince, as they were swept by a low archway, and then onward by a broad opening, which, seen from their fresh point of view, looked beautiful but strange.

"Is that—" began Mike, in a dubious, hesitating way.

"Yes, of course. Look: we don't know it from out here, but there's the seal hole and our fishing place, where we caught the crab. It's all shadowy inside, or we could see our kitchen and fishing tackle."

"No, no; it can't be," said Mike despairingly: "if it was, we should come directly upon the smugglers' place."

"Yes, you'll see: we shall be carried by directly."

"But there'll be some one there. Here, quick: let's row away,"—and Mike seized an oar.

"You can't row against a current like this," said Vince quietly; "and if anybody had been in there they would have been awake and seen us long before this."

"Then I don't believe this is the cove, and that can't be our cavern," cried Mike sharply.

"Very well; but you soon will. Now look: here we go. I say, how smooth the walls of rock are worn by the water!—that accounts for our never having been upset in the night. We shall see the big cave directly. Shall we try and land?"

"Yes; no; I don't know what will be best to do. Yes; but let's make sure first."

"And land when we come round again?" said Vince.

"Yes, if you like. I don't know what to say."

"Seems best way," said Vince thoughtfully. "And yet I don't know. We might hide, for they've blocked up the passage; but they'd hunt us out, as we couldn't keep hidden very long. And they'd know we were there, because they'd find the boat."

"Perhaps they'd think we were drowned," said Mike; and then, excitedly, "Why, it is the big cavern, Cinder!"

"Yes, it's the big cavern, sure enough; and if it wasn't so dark inside we could see the stack of kegs."

There was no room for further doubt, as they glided by the mouth of the great opening, with its wonderful beach of soft sand, and directly after began to recognise the piled-up masses of rock. As they went on, they saw the outlying masses round which the waters foamed and bubbled, but became quite bewildered as they tried to make out which was the outlet by which the smuggler crew had taken them and the captain through on the previous day. They passed narrow rifts, but the water always seemed to be flowing swiftly into the great basin in which they were and joining the seething waters in their continuous round.

Vince pointed to this and then to that gap between the rocks, as the one through which they must have come overnight, but he could never be in the least sure; and as they went on, he had to content himself with looking up at the ridge which faced the caverns, and beyond which they believed the sea to be.

Everywhere at the foot of the cliffs the water was deep, and so clear that they could see the rocks at the bottom, smooth, and treacherous-looking, apparently rising up to capsize the boat; but they glided over all in safety, the great basin being worn smooth by the constant friction of the currents, and at last began to approach the end opposite to where they had been deftly taken out by the men.

Here they looked eagerly for another way of getting out—the rift through which the waters must pass back into the sea—but, if it existed, it was shut from their sight by the heaped-up rocks, and the current carried them on and on with unchecked speed.

"No wonder I thought we were a long while getting out to sea!" said Vince at last: "we can't have gone near the big channel through which the lugger must come and go."

"Never mind that," said Mike impatiently; "there must be another way out from this basin. We saw signs of it from up above, when you sat up there and I held the rope."

"Yes," said Vince gloomily; "but sitting up there's one thing, and sitting down here's another. Think we shall find another way out this end? Must, mustn't we?"

Mike nodded as he stood up and searched the rocks for the opening that was hidden from their eyes, from the fact that it was behind one of the barriers of rock and far below the surface current which swept them along.

As far as they could judge, they were going on for half an hour, making the complete circuit of the great watery amphitheatre; and then, as they passed the caverns again, they determined to examine the other end more carefully, for the exit used by the smugglers, which must, they knew, be ample and easy if they could master the knack of getting the boat in. For they had some hazy notion of learning how it was done and then hiding till night, when they might manage perhaps to pass out unseen.

"But if we did," said Mike despondently, "we should perhaps be swept in here again, or be upset and drowned. I say, Cinder, did you ever see such an unlucky pair as we are?"

"Never looked," said Vince; "but I tell you what: we shall have to land in the big cave, and get through to ours."

"What for?"

"Breakfast. There's all our food, if they haven't found it."

"Could you eat now?" said Mike, with a look of horror.

"Eat? I could almost eat you," replied Vince.

"Ugh!" said Mike, with a shudder. "I feel so faint and sick and sinking inside, I couldn't touch anything."

"Shouldn't like to trust you," said Vince, whom the bright sunshine and the beauty of the place were influencing in his spirits. "But now, then, let's have a good look this time."

They were going round swiftly enough, and noted the entrance to the first low, arched cavern, which was some forty or fifty yards to the westward of the seal hole; then they glided by the others in turn, and tried hard to make out how the men had managed to thrust the big boat through the running waters beyond that great beach and into the eddy which bore them in the other direction.

"Do you see?" asked Mike.

"No, not yet; but perhaps I shall when we come round again. But, I say, we can't keep on sailing round like this. We must land."

"But Jacques and his men, they won't be gone till to-night. You heard what was said by old Joe?"

"Don't mention his name," cried Vince passionately. "I should like to see the old wretch flogged."

"I should like to do it," said Mike grimly. "They'll come back and find us here, for certain, if we don't hide," said Vince; "but I don't know that I shall much mind now, for I'm afraid we shan't get away."

They glided round again, and in passing the spot where they believed the exit to be, Vince fancied he detected an eddy among some rocks, but he could not be sure; and at last they were once more approaching the cavern, with its low arch, when Vince, who was watching the far end and trying to fit together the means for getting away, suddenly snatched up the boat-hook, thrust it out, and, leaning over the stern, caught hold of a projecting rock, some two feet above the water. Then hauling hard, hand over hand along the ash pole, he checked the progress of the boat and drew it close in. Next, quick as lightning, he made another dash with the hook and caught at another projection, missed, and, as the boat was gliding back again, made another—a frantic—dash, and caught the hook in a rift, while Mike thrust out an oar against a rock to help.

This time he drew the boat right up to the mouth of the new cavern, and whispered sharply to his companion:

"Now—quick! help me run her in. Mind! duck down!"

Mike obeyed, and the boat glided in under the low arch, which just cleared their heads as they sat in the bottom of the boat, and passed on out of the bright sunshine into the chill darkness of the cave.

"Think they saw us?" whispered Vince.

"They? Saw us?"

"Didn't you see them coming through among the rocks quite quickly?"

"No: did you?"

"Just the tops of their caps: they were behind one of those low rocks where the water rushes round."

"Are you sure, Vince?"

"Sure?—yes. Ah, mind! that oar!" cried the boy.

He crept past Mike, after seizing the boat-hook, and, reaching over the stern, made a dash at the oar his companion had been using to thrust with against the rocks, and which had been laid-down when they passed right in, so that Mike could use his hands.

How it had slipped over the gunwale neither could have said; but when Vince caught sight of it, the oar was floating just in the entrance, and the sharp dash he made at it resulted in the hook striking the blade so awkwardly that he drove it farther out, where it was caught by the current and drawn swiftly away.

"Gone!" said Mike despairingly.

"Gone! Yes, of course it's gone; and now they'll find out where we are."

"No, they're not obliged to," said Mike; "that oar may have been washed from anywhere, and they haven't found it yet."

"Oh no," said Vince bitterly—"not yet; but you'll see."

Mike made no reply, but helped, without a word of objection, to thrust the boat farther in along the passage, which greatly resembled the seal hole, as they called it, but was nearly double the width, and afforded plenty of room for the boat.

As soon as they felt that they were far enough in to be hidden by the darkness, they sat watching the entrance, through which the bright morning light poured, and listened intently for some sound to indicate that the smugglers' boat was near.

But an hour must have passed, and Vince was fidgeting at something which took his attention, when Mike suddenly whispered,—

"I say, do you notice anything strange about the way in yonder?"

Vince was silent.

"Why don't you speak?" said Mike sharply. "You have seen it. Why didn't you speak before?"

"Felt as if I couldn't," said Vince hoarsely.

"Then it is so," said Mike. "The tide is rising, and the hole's getting smaller. Come on: we must get out at once."

"Too late," replied Vince gloomily. "The water's too high now. If we tried we should be wedged in."

"But— oh! we must try, Vince, or we shall be drowned! Why didn't you speak before?"

"I wasn't sure till it began to run up so quickly; and what could we do? If we had gone out we should have been seen directly. Perhaps it won't rise any higher now. It never covered the seal cave."

"That was twice as high," groaned Mike. "Look at the limpets and mussels on the roof: this must be shut right in at every tide."

# Chapter Thirty Three
## Re-Trapped

Misfortunes, they say, never come singly, and these words had hardly been uttered when voices were heard, and directly after a familiar voice said loudly, the words coming in through the low passage and quite plainly to the boys' ears, —

"Made the oar myself, Skipper Jarks, and I ought to know it again. What I say is as they must ha' managed somehow to ha' got in here."

The boat darkened the entrance for a few moments, and then glided by; while the cavern kept closing like some monstrous eye whose lid was pressed up from below, opening again fairly widely, enough almost to suggest the possibility of their passing under; but closing again as the tide rose and sank in slow, regular pulsations.

But as they watched they could make out that the soft wave rose higher and higher and sank perceptibly less, while the prisoners' eyesight became so preternaturally sharp that they could detect the gradual opening of the sea anemones, as they spread out their starry crowns of tentacles after the first kiss of the water had moistened them. The many limpets, too, which had been tight up against the smooth rock, like bosses or excrescences, were visibly raising their shells and standing up, partly detached.

Then a new horror attracted the boys, and made them almost frantic for the moment; for, as they crouched there in the bottom of the boat, watching the slowly diminishing amount of light which came in through the archway, the water softly and quickly, welled up, nearly shut the entry, and a wave ran up the passage and passed under the boat, which was heaved up so high that the gunwale grated against the roof, and they had to bend themselves down to avoid being pressed against the rock.

Then, as they lay there, they heard the wave run on and on, whispering and waking up the echoes far inside, till the whole of the interior seemed to be alive with lapping, hissing sounds, which slowly died away as the boat sank to nearly its old level, and the light flashed in once more.

"That's a hint to do something," said Vince, as he rose up, finding that his head nearly touched the shell-encrusted roof.

"Yes; to force our way out," said Mike excitedly. "We must before it's too late."

"It is too late, as I told you before," said Vince sharply. "Look for yourself. Can't you see that the arch is too small for the sides of the boat to get through? and at any moment another of those waves may come in. It's all right, Ladle, if you'll only be firm."

"I'll be as firm as you are," said the boy angrily.

"Then help me push her along."

Mike pressed his hands against the roof, Vince did the same; and they both thrust hard, but in spite of all the boat did not stir.

"Why, you're pushing to send it in," said Mike.

"And you to drive it out! What nonsense! This place is sure to get bigger inside, where the water has washed it out. We must get right in, beyond where the water rises."

Mike shuddered; for the silence and darkness of the place would, he felt, be horrible, and all the time he knew that the water would be gradually chasing them, like some terribly fierce creature, bent on suffocating them in its awful embrace.

Vince's was the stronger will; and his companion yielded, changing his tactics, and forcing the boat along for some distance before there was any change in the roof, which crushed down upon them as low as ever, and Mike began once more to protest.

"It's of no use," he said: "we may as well be smothered where we can see as here, where it is so dark. Let's go back as far as we can."

"No; I'm sure this place will open out more if we go farther in."

At that moment there was a loud, plashing noise far inward, and this raised such loud reverberations that Mike was fain to confess that the roof must be far higher.

Vince took advantage of this to urge his companion on; and a minute later they could not touch the rock above them with their hands, while a little farther on it could not be reached with an oar.

"Yes, it's bigger," granted Mike; "but we shall be suffocated all the same. There can't be enough air to last us till the tide goes down."

"We shall see," said Vince; and then, quite cheerily: "I say, this is better than wading, the same as we did in the seal hole."

"Yes, but there are seals here. I heard them."

"Yes, so did I, but what of that? We mustn't interfere with them, and they won't with us. Besides, we're in a boat now, recollect."

Mike recollected it well enough, but it did not comfort him much; however, he kept his thoughts to himself, and proposed that they should keep as near the light as they could.

"Better keep where the roof's highest," suggested Vince. "We shall be able to breathe more freely then."

After that they were both very silent, for they suffered horribly from the dread that as soon as the entrance was entirely closed up by the tide, they would be rapidly exhausting all the pure breathable air shut-in; and so deeply did this impress them, that before long a peculiar sensation of compression at the chest assailed them both, with the result that they began to breathe more hurriedly, and to feel as if they had been running uphill, till, as it is called, they were out of breath.

Neither spoke, but suffered in silence, their brains busy with calculations of how long it would be before it was high water, and then how long it would take before the tide sank low enough for the mouth of the cave to be open once more.

Vince probably suffered the more keenly after the light was shut out entirely; but his sufferings were the briefer, for just when his breath was shortest, and he was feeling that he must breathe more rapidly if he wished to keep alive, he heard a loud plashing and wallowing some distance farther in.

That it was a party of seals playing about he was certain, and in imagination he saw them crawling up on to some piece of rock by means of their flappers and plunging down again. Once he heard a pair of them swimming in chase one of the other, blowing and uttering loud, sighing noises as they came near, and then appeared to turn and swim back, to climb up on the rock again, with the effect of dislodging others, which sprang heavily into the water, sending little waves along big enough to make the boat rock perceptibly.

This was just when Vince felt at his worst, and Mike was lying back in the boat breathing hard and in the most hurried way.

It was singular that just then the recollection of a story he had once read in a work belonging to his father came to Vince's mind. True or false, it had been recorded that some French surgeons had been discussing the effect of the imagination upon the human mind, and to test for themselves whether its effects could be so strong as some writers and experimentalists had declared, they obtained permission to apply a test to a condemned convict.

Their test was as follows: It had been announced to the man that he was to die, and that his execution was to be the merciful one of being bled to death. So at the appointed time the culprit was bound and blindfolded in the presence of the surgeons, who then proceeded to lance his arm and allowed a tiny jet of warm water to trickle over the place and down to the wrist.

It is said that, though the man had not lost a drop of blood, he began, as soon as he had felt the lancet prick and the trickling of the warm water, to grow faint, and after a time sank and sank, till he actually died from imagination.

"And that's what we're doing," thought Vince, as he drew slowly a long, deep breath, and then another and another.

The first was very catchy and strange, the second caused him acute suffering, and the third was deep, strong, and life-inspiring.

"That's it," said Vince to himself—"it is imagination; for if the seals, which are things that have to come up to the surface to breathe, can live in here, why can't I?"

Vince again took a deep breath, and another, and another, and so great a feeling of vigour ran through him that he laughed aloud, and Mike started up.

"What is it?" he said.

"Listen," cried Vince; and he loudly drew breath, and expressed it as loudly, then, "Do that," he cried.

"I—I can hardly get mine. This place is stifling."

"Try," said Vince. "That's right. Again! Better. Now take a long pull. How are you now?"

"Oh, better—better," said Mike eagerly.

"Breathe again."

"Yes, yes; I am breathing better and better. Then the air is coming now?"

"Yes," said Vince drily; "the air is coming fast, and the light can't be very long. There—it's all right, Ladle; we shan't hurt now. But I don't know how we're going to manage when the tide falls, for we shan't dare to go out."

"No," said Mike, whose spirits sank again at these words, "we shan't dare to go out. Do you know, I wish, as you did, that we had stopped on board."

"And not taken all this trouble for nothing. How long should you say it would be before the light comes again?"

"Hours," said Mike; "but I don't mind it so much now that we can breathe better."

"No; it is better," said Vince drily. "I say, I wonder what they are doing at home?"

Vince wished the next moment that he had not said those words, for they had the effect of sinking his companion into a terrible state of depression, while, in spite of his efforts, he was himself nearly as bad.

But then it was before breakfast, and they had hardly touched a mouthful since the morning before.

At last, after what seemed to be a full day in length of time, there was afar off a faint soft gleam of light on the surface of the water—a ray which sent a flood into the hearts of the watchers—and from that moment the light began to grow broader and higher, while they suddenly woke to the fact that the boat was moving gently towards the entrance of the cavern, drawn by the falling tide.

After a while there was a tiny archway; then this began to increase as the water sank and rose, but always rose less and less, leaving the sea anemones and the various shell-fish dotted with drops which gathered together, glittering and trembling in the light, and then fell with a musical drip upon the smooth surface.

The little arch increased rapidly after a time, and still the boat drew nearer to the entrance, neither of the boys having the heart to check its progress after their long imprisonment, for the outer world never looked so bright and glorious before.

But they had to pay for their pleasure. As the level sank till there was ample room to thrust the boat out, and they were thinking that to be safe they ought to withdraw a little and wait until they could feel sure that the lugger and her crew were gone—a departure they felt must be some time that evening, when the tide was at a certain stage well known to old Joe—the entrance was suddenly darkened once more by a boat, whose bows came with the stream from the right, and were cleverly directed in, while her occupants began to thrust her along by pressing against the sides, and a couple of lanthorns were held up.

"Aha!" cried the voice the boys had grown to hate, "so ve have found a pair of ze seal sitting in a boat vich zey steal avay. You are right, Joseph, *mon bon ami*. Your boat sall not have gone out of ze pool, and you sall have him back. Aha! Stop you bose, or I fire, and zis time I vill not miss."

"In, in farther, Vince," whispered Mike wildly.

"No: they've seen us, and they could follow us in their boat. It's of no use, Mike; we must give up this time."

"You hear me?" roared the captain fiercely. "I see quite plain vere you sall be. *Venez.* Come out."

"Come and fetch us," said Vince shortly. "You have your men."

The captain gave his orders, the boat was thrust on, and as its bow approached the boys saw the black silhouette of their old companion in many a fishing trip seated on the forward thwart.

This was too much for Vince, who began upon him at once, with bitter irony in his words and tone.

"You there, Joe!" he cried. "Good morning. Don't you feel very proud of this?"

"Dunno 'bout proud, young gen'leman; but I'm precious glad to get my boat back."

"Your boat back!" cried Vince, as one of the smuggler crew made fast a rope to the ring-bolt in their stern.

"Aye. Didn't know as young gen'lemen took to stealing boats altogether."

"You dare to say we stole the boat, and I'll—"

"Well, you took it right away, anyhow. That comes o' beginning with borrying and not asking leave."

"Better than taking to kidnapping people."

Old Joe growled out something, and shuffled himself about in his seat while the boat was drawn out into the sunshine once more, and drifted behind the other rapidly along till she reached the smugglers' cavern.

"Give zem some biscuit and some vater," said the captain. "You, Joseph, take your boat and go on. *Allez!*"

The old fisherman looked at him rather uneasily, then at the boys, and back at the captain.

"You hear vat I sall say?" cried the latter fiercely.

He made a menacing gesture; and the boys took each a deep draught of water, and began to nibble the hard sea biscuit that was their fare.

# Chapter Thirty Four
# The Tightening of the Chains

There was something very grim and suggestive about the captain's behaviour to the two boys later on towards evening, when he came and stood glaring down at them, where they sat in the sand. He had said a few words to one of the men, who went up into the back of the cavern while the other waited; and Vince noted that there was a splashing sound round the corner of the buttress which supported one side of the great arch, so that he was not surprised directly after to see the prow of a boat appear, to be run in and beached upon the sand.

Vince looked up inquiringly when the smuggling captain came and stood before him; but the man did not speak—he only glared down, apparently with the idea that he was frightening the lads horribly. Vince did not shrink, for he did not feel frightened, only troubled about home and the despondency there, as the time went by without news of their fate. For it was evident to him that the time had come for them to be taken on board ready for the lugger to sail.

The second man came back with some fine line in his hand.

"*Vite*—tight!" said the captain laconically.

"You're not going to tie us?" said Vince, flushing.

"Yais, bose togezaire," said the Frenchman, with a grin of satisfaction at seeing the boy moved to indignant protest.

"But if we say we will not try to escape?" cried Vince.

"I vill not believes you. *Non, mon ami*, ve have enough of ze *peine* to *attraper* you again. Two slippery *garçons*. I tie you bose like ze mutton sheep, and zen if von shump to run avays he pull ze ozaire down. *Vous comprenez?*"

"Oh yes, I comprong," cried Vince contemptuously. "Just like a Frenchman. An Englishman would not be afraid of a boy."

"Vat!" cried the captain, showing his teeth, as he raised his hand to strike—when, quick as lightning, the boy threw himself into an attitude of defence; but the men seized him and dragged his arms behind his back.

"That's right, coward!" cried Vince, half mad now with excitement.

At the word coward the captain's face looked black as night, his right-hand was thrust into his breast pocket, and he drew out and cocked a small pistol, while Mike darted to his companion's side, laid his hands across Vince's breast, and faced the captain; but he was seized by one of the men, who passed the line about his wrists after it had been dexterously fastened round those of his fellow-prisoner.

"Never mind, Mike; but I like that, old chap!" cried Vince. "Well done! Let's show him what English boys are like: he daren't shoot us. Do you hear, Jacques? *vous n'oses pas.*"

"Aha! You begin by stumble blunder bad French, you *canaille* boy. I not dare shoot you?"

"No," said Vince defiantly, as the pistol was presented full at his face. "You dare not, you great coward!"

"Aha, *encore*? You call me coward, *une insulte! Mais bah*! It is only a silly boy. Tie zem bose togezaire, my lad, an trow zem in ze boat. Silly boy! Like two shicken *volatile* go to be roace for dinnaire. *Non, arretez*; stop, my lad. Coward! It was *une insulte*. Now you apologise me."

"I won't," said Vince sturdily: "you are a coward to tie up two boys like this."

The black wrath in the Frenchman's face at these words made Mike shiver, and he pressed closer to Vince as the pistol was raised once more.

"Don't—don't," he whispered. "Say something: we are so helpless."

"Aha! I hear vat he say. Yais, you apologise me, sare."

"I won't," said Vince, who, with nerves strung by the agony he felt at his wrists, which were being cut into by the cord, was ready to dare and say anything.

"You vill not?" cried the captain, slowly uncocking the pistol, as his face resumed its ordinary aspect.

"No, I—will—not!" cried Vince. "Put it away. You dare not fire."

"*Non*; it would be a pity. I nevaire like to shoot good stuff. You are a brave boy, and I vill make you a fine man. And you too, *mon garçon*."

He laid his hands on the boys' shoulders, and pressed them hard, smiling as he said,—

"*Non*, I sink I am not a coward, *mon enfant*, but I tie you bose up vis ze hant behint, so you sall not run avay. Aha! Eh? You not run avay vis ze hant, *mais* vis ze foot? *Eh bien: n'importe*: it does not mattaire. You ugly boy," he continued, striking Vince a sharp rap in the chest with the back of the hand, "I like you. *Yais.* You have saucy tongue. You are a bouledogue boy. I vill see you two 'ave a fight some days. Now, my lad, take zem bose into ze boat. Ah, *yah, bête cochon*—big peegue!" he roared, as he examined the way in which the boys' wrists were tied behind their backs. "I tell you to lash zem fast. I did not say, 'Cut off ze hant.' Cast zem off."

The man who had secured Vince sulkily obeyed, and the captain looked on till the line was untied, leaving the boys' wrists with white marks round and blackened swellings on either side.

"Ah, he is a fool," said the captain, taking up first one and then the other hand. "Vy you do not squeak and pipe ze eye?"

Vince frowned, but made no reply.

"Zere, valk down to ze boat vis me. Say you vill not run avay."

"No: I mean to escape," said Vince.

"Bah! It is sillee. You cannot, *mon garçon.* Come, ze *parole d'honneur.* Be a man."

Vince glanced at Mike, who gave him an imploring look, which seemed to say: "Pray give it."

"Yais," said the captain, smiling: "*Parole d'honneur.* If you try to run *il faut* shooter zis time."

"*Parole d'honneur* for to-day," said Vince. "After to-day I shall try to escape."

"It is *bon*—good," said the captain, laughing. "After to-day—yais. Zere, valk you down to ze boat. I like you bose. If you had been cry boy, and go down on your knees, and zay, 'Oh, pray don't,' I kick you. *En avant!*"

He clapped his hand upon Vince's shoulder, and walked with both to the boat, signing to them to enter and go right forward, where they seated themselves in the bows while he took his place in the stern.

"Oh, Cinder!" whispered Mike, with a look of admiration at his friend, "I wish I'd had the heart to speak to him like that."

"What?" whispered back Vince, "why, I never felt so frightened in my life. I thought he was going to shoot."

"I don't believe it," said Mike quietly. "I say, now let's see how they manage to get out of this great whirling pool."

They were not kept waiting long, for the boat was thrust off, sent into the stream, and away they went, skirting the long, low rock which rose in their way; and then, just as it seemed that they were going to be sunk by the tremendous rush of water passing in between two huge masses, the boat was thrust into another sharply marked current, hung in suspense for a few moments, and then glided along the backwater and out at last into the pool. Here the glassy surface streaked with numerous lines told of the rapid currents following their well-marked courses, and the eddies and reflections of the water known to the men and taken advantage of, so that the vessel's side was reached with ease.

As they neared the side the captain, who had been keenly watching the boys and reading their thoughts, came slowly past his men, so quietly that Vince and Mike started on hearing him speak.

"You could manage ze boat now and take him vere you vill? *Non, mes enfans.* It take long time to find ze vay. I sink you bose drown last night, but you have *bonne fortune* and escape. But you get avay till I say go? Nevaire! Shump."

He pointed upward, and the lads climbed aboard, looking wistfully to right and left as they recalled their adventures along the side in the dark, and saw old Daygo's boat hanging by her painter close under the stern.

"Took a lot of trouble for nothing, Cinder," said Mike sadly.

"Yes: can't always win," replied Vince. "Never mind: I'm glad we tried."

Mike had not the heart to say "So am I," though he felt that he ought to have done so; but, catching sight of the old fisherman leaning over the bulwark forward, he said instead,—

"There's that old wretch again! Oh, how I should like to—"

He did not say what, but turned his back upon him in disgust.

"Yes—a beauty!" said Vince, scowling. "I say, Mike, no wonder old Joe was always so well off that he never had to work. Pst! here's the skipper."

"*Non, mon ami*—ze capitaine. *Eh bien*—ah, vell! you are on board again. I sall lock you down upon ze powdaire again and keep you prisonaire? My faith, no! It is vord of honnaire to-day, and to-day last *vingt-quatre heures*— till zis time to-morrow: you understand?"

"Yes," said Vince; and then, frankly, "I beg your pardon, skip—"

"Eh?"

"Captain," said Vince quickly: "I beg your pardon, captain, for calling you a coward."

The Frenchman looked at him searchingly, and then clapped down both hands on the boy's shoulders and held him firmly.

"*Bon!*" he said; "*bon!* Zat is all gone now. I sall not call you out and say vill you have ze pistol or ze arm *blanc*—ze sword. You bose come dine vis me *ce soir*—zis evening, and you not make fool of ze comestible, as ve call him, eh? Now go valk about ze deck. You like to see ze vay out? No; ve leave all zat to my good *ami*, Joseph Daygo. He take ze *Belle-Marie* out to sea vile ve dine. It is ze secret know only to Joseph. I could not do him myselfs."

This only increased Vince's desire to discover by what means the lugger was piloted out from its moorings beneath the towering rocks, where it was completely shut-in, though it seemed that there was a channel behind the rock which spread out in front.

Sunset was drawing near, and it became evident that the time was approaching for a start to be made, for the boat in which they came from the cave had been hoisted up to the davits, and the men were busy preparing for hoisting sails. The hatches were in their places, and the vessel looked wonderfully orderly, being very different in aspect from those of its class. In fact, from stem to stern she was nearly as neat as a king's ship.

Meanwhile Joe Daygo kept close to the bulwark, turning from time to time to note how the men were progressing, and then leaning over the bulwark again to gaze at the perpendicular wall of rock before him, which towered up to a great height and went apparently straight down into the sea. "I know," said Vince at last, in a whisper. "Know what?"

"Joe Daygo is watching that streak of white paint on the rock over yonder."

"I see no streak of white paint," said Mike. "Yes, I do. But what of that?"

"It's his mark," said Vince. "He's going to wait till the tide touches that, and then going to cast off."

"Think so?"

"Sure of it."

But Vince had no opportunity for waiting to see. The glassy current was still a couple of inches below the dimly seen white mark, when there was a peculiar odour which came from a tureen that the cook carried along the deck towards the cabin; and almost at the same moment a hand was laid upon the boy's shoulder.

"Come," said the captain; "it is time for ze dinnaire. You are bose hungry?—yais, I know."

Vince would have liked to decline, so strong was his desire to study the key to the entrance of the secret little port; but to refuse to go down was impossible, and he preceded his host through the cabin-hatch, where a swinging lamp was burning and the deadlights were closed so that not a gleam could escape. The tureen steamed on the table, they were in no danger, and healthy young appetite prevailed, for the soup was good even if the biscuits were flinty and hard.

As for the captain, it seemed absurd to associate him with smuggling or pistols, for he played the host in the most amiable manner when fish succeeded the soup; but as it was being discussed there were hurried sounds on deck. Men were running to and fro; then came the peculiar dull, rasping sound of cables being hauled in through hawser holes, and a slight motion told that they were starting.

Vince ceased eating, and his eyes were involuntarily turned to the side, when the captain said laughingly, —

"It is nozing, my younger *ami*, and ze bulkhead side is not glass: you cannot see nozing. You vant to know? Vell, my sheep is in ze sharge of ze pilot, and ze men cast off. If he take her out quite vell, sank you, ve sall soon be at sea. If he make ze grand error he put my sheep on ze rock, vich make ze hole and you sall hear ze vater run in. You bose can svim? Yais? Good, but you need not try: you stay down here vis me and not take trouble, but go to ze bottom like ze brave *homme*, for ze big tide on'y take you avay and knock you against ze rock. Now eat you feesh."

It was not a pleasant addition to the boys' dinner, but they went on listening in the intervals of the captain's many speeches, and picturing to themselves how the great lugger was being carefully piloted along a sharp current and steered here and there, apparently doubling upon her course more than once. But by the time the boiled fowl was nearly eaten there was a steady heeling over, following the sound of the hoisting of a sail. Then the vessel heeled over a little more, and seemed to dance for a minute in rough water, as if she were passing over some awkward place. The captain smiled.

"My sheep she is lively," he said. "She sink it vas time not to be tied by ze head and tail, so she commence to dance. Zat is a vairy bad place, but Joseph is a grand pilot; he know vat to do, and I am nevaire in his way."

Just then there was a dull thud, as if a mass of water had struck the side, and the vessel heeled over more than ever, righted herself, and then rose and rode over a wave, plunging down and again gliding along upon a level keel. "Eat, eat, *mes amis*," said the captain. "You do not mean that you have *le mal-de-mer*?"

"Oh no," said Vince quickly, as if ashamed to be suspected of such a weakness. "We don't mind the sea; besides, it isn't rough. We're not going over a bar of sand?"

"*Non*: a bar of rocks, vere Joseph can take us safely. Anozaire man? *Non, non.*"

They could not grasp much, as the dinner drew now to an end, and no doubt their imaginations played them false to a great extent; but they thoroughly realised that for a few minutes the great lugger was being slowly navigated through a most intricate channel, where the current ran furiously; after that more sail was made, and the regular motion of the vessel told them that they were getting out into the open sea.

All at once the door was opened, and old Daygo appeared.

"Aha! you are finish, *mon ami*?"

Daygo nodded his head and uttered a low grunt.

"Good. I come on deck."

Old Joe turned and went up the ladder, followed by the captain; and then Mike dashed after them.

"What are you going to do?" cried Vince. But Mike made no reply; and the other followed on deck, anxious to see what was going to take place, for that Mike had some project was very evident.

As Vince reached the deck he saw that Mike was at the leeward side, where a couple of men stood by the rope which held the pilot's boat, while the captain and the old fisherman were walking right forward, talking earnestly. The lugger was sailing gently along half a mile from the shore in the direction of the south point; and Vince's heart leaped and then sank as he faintly made out one of the familiar landmarks on the highest part of the island, but he had no time for indulging in emotion just then, for the captain turned suddenly and old Joe made for his boat.

"Mike isn't going to jump in and try to go with him, is he?" thought Vince; and a pang shot through him at the very thought of such a cowardly desertion. "No," he added to himself; "he wouldn't do that."

Vince was right, for all he did was to rush at Daygo, catch him by the shoulder and whisper something.

The old fisherman turned, stared, and Mike repeated as far as Vince could make out his former question, while the captain stood a little way back and looked on.

Just then Daygo growled out "No!" angrily, and thrust Mike away so roughly that the boy staggered back and nearly fell; but before the old man could reach the bulwark, Mike had recovered himself, leaped at him, and delivered such a kick, that the pilot plunged forward half over the bulwark, and then turned savagely to take revenge upon his assailant. But the captain had advanced, and he said something sharply, which made Daygo hurry over the bulwark and drop down into his boat. One of the men cast off the rope and threw it after him, and the next moment she was astern, with the old man standing upright, his hands to each side of his mouth; and he bellowed out,—

"Yah! Good luck to you both! You'll never see this Crag agen."

Then the darkness began to swallow up his small boat, and the great three-masted lugger glided onward—where?

Mike turned sharply, expecting to be seized by the captain; but the latter had his back to him, and went forward to give orders for another sail to be hoisted, while the boys went involuntarily to the side to gaze at the Crag.

"What was it you asked Joe?" said Vince.

"Not what you thought," replied Mike rather bitterly.

"Why, what did I think?"

"That I was begging him to take me in the boat."

"No, I didn't," said Vince sharply. "I thought at first that you'd run up to jump in, but directly after I said to myself that you wouldn't be such a sneak. What did you say to him?"

"I told him my father would give him a hundred pounds, and that he should never say anything to Joe, if he'd go and tell them directly where we are."

"And he wouldn't. Well, I'm glad you kicked him, for shoving you away like that."

"I should be," replied Mike, "if he wasn't such an old man."

"He isn't an old man," said Vince hotly: "he's an old wretch, without a bit of manliness in him."

"All right, then; I'm glad I kicked him. But never mind Joe Daygo, Vince. It's getting darker, and the old Crag is seeming to die away. Oh, Cinder, old chap, is it all true? Are we being taken away like this?"

Vince could not trust himself to speak, but leaned over the bulwark, resting his chin upon his thumbs, and shading the sides of his face—partly to conceal its workings, which was not necessary in the darkness, partly to shut off the side-light and see the island more easily.

And neither was this necessary, for there were no sidelights, and the Crag was now so dim that had he not known it was there it would have been invisible; but he preserved it all mentally, and thought of the pleasant home, with the saddened faces there, of the happy days he had spent, and now for the first time fully realised what a joyous boyhood he had passed in the rocky wildly picturesque old place, with no greater trouble to disturb his peaceful life than some puzzling problem or a trivial fit of illness. All so bright, so joyous, so happy,—and now gone, perhaps, for ever; and some strange, wild life to come, but what kind of existence he could not grasp.

Naturally enough, Mike's thoughts ran in the same channel, but he gave them utterance; and Vince, as he stood there, heard him saying piteously,—

"Good-bye, dear old home! I never knew before what you really were. Good-bye—good-bye!" And then, passionately—"Oh, Vince, Vince! what have we done to deserve all this? Where are we going now?"

"To bed, *mes amis*," said the captain, slapping them both on the shoulders and rudely interrupting their thoughts. "Come: I take you myself. Not over ze powdaire now. I vill not tempt you to *faire sauter*—make jump ze *chasse-marée*—blow up ze sheep, eh? My faith, no! But you take ze good counsel, *mes* boys. You go to your bunk like ze good shile, and have long sleep. You get out of the deadlight vis ze sheep in full sail. You go ovaire-board bose of you, and I am vair sorry for ze *bonnes* mammas."

"Doesn't seem like it," said Vince stoutly, "taking us off prisoners like this."

"Prisonaires! Faith of a good man! You sink I treat you like prisonaires, and have you to dinnaire and talk to you vis *bonnes conseilles* like ze papa?"

"You are taking us away, and making every one who cares for us think we are dead."

"*C'est dommage*—it is a great pitee, my young friend; but, you see, I have a large propertee at ze caverne. It is vort tousand of pounds, and ze place is vair useful to me and ze *confrère* who come to take it somevere else."

"What, are there more of you?" blurted out Vince.

"Eh? You nevaire mind. But I cannot part vis my store, and I vant ze place to go to ven I bring a cargo."

"But we'll promise you on our words that we will not betray it to any one, if you set us ashore."

"Aha! Not to have anozaire kick at *notre bon* Joseph, eh?"

"No, not even to serve Joe Daygo out," said Vince. "An old wretch! But he deserves it."

"And faith of a gentlemans, on your word of *honneur*, you vould not tell vere ze contraband is kept?"

"On our honour, as gentlemen, we would not: would we, Mike?"

"No," was the eager reply.

"I believe you bose," said the captain. "But you could not keep your vort. It is impossible."

"But we would," said Vince.

"You vould try, *mon garçon*, but you vould be *oblige* to tell. Listen—von vort for all. I have faith in you bose, but no, it cannot be. You cannot go back, so you must act like ze man now."

"Then you are going to take us away?" cried Vince.

"I 'ave take you avay, my boy, and I sall not let you go back till I no longer vant ze cavern store, and ze safe place to hide. Zen you may go back—if you like."

"What do you mean by that?" said Vince quickly.

"Vat I say: if you like. I sink by zat time you bose say to me, 'Non, Monsieur Jacques, ve do not vant to go.' Now I talk no more. Down vis you!"

"Only tell us one thing," said Vince: "where are you going to take us?"

"I tell you ven I can," said the captain.

"What do you mean by that?" cried Mike excitedly.

"Vat I say. I do not know."

He pressed them towards the hatchway, and they descended, feeling that they could do nothing else, while the captain followed and opened a door opposite to that of the cabin.

"Zere," he said. "You can sleep in zose bunk. I keep zat for my friend, and I give zem to mine *ennemi*, you see. I vill not lock ze door, but you listen, bose of you. I am ze capitaine, and I am *le roi*—ze king here. If a man say he vill not, I knock him down. If he get up and pull out ze knife, I take ze pistol and shoot: I am *dangéreux*. If I hear ze strange noise, I shoot. Don't you make ze strange noise in ze night, *mes amis*, but go sleep, as you *Anglais* say, like ze sound of two top hummin. You understand. *Bon soir!* You come to ze *déjeuner*—breakfast in ze morning."

He shut them in, and the two boys were left in the darkness to their thoughts. But they were too weary to think much, and soon felt their way into their bunks, one above the other.

An hour later the door was softly opened, and a lanthorn was thrust in, the captain following to look at each face in turn.

There was no sham this time. Utterly worn out by the excitement of the past hours, Vince and Mike were both off—fast in the heavy, dreamless, restful slumber of sixteen—the sleep in which Nature winds up a boy's mainspring terse and tight, and makes him ready to go on, rested and fresh, for the work of another day.

# Chapter Thirty Five
# How some Folk turn Smugglers

The sea was up before the boys next morning, and in its own special way was making the *chasse-marée* pitch and toss, now rising up one side of a wave, now gliding down the other; for the wind had risen towards morning, and was now blowing so hard that quite half the sail hoisted overnight had had to be taken down, leaving the swift vessel staggering along beneath the rest.

Vince turned out feeling a bit puzzled and confused, for he did not quite grasp his position; but the full swing of thought came, with all its depressing accompaniments, and he roused up Mike to bear his part and help to condole as well.

Mike, on the contrary, turned out of his bunk fully awake to their position, and began to murmur at once bitterly as he went on dressing, till at last Vince turned upon him.

"I say," he said, "it's of no use to make worse of it."

"No one can," cried Mike.

"Oh, can't they? Why, you're doing your part."

"I'm only saying that it's abominable and outrageous, and that I wish the old lugger may be wrecked. Here, I say, what have you been doing with my clothes?"

"Haven't touched 'em."

"But you must have touched them. I folded them up, and put them together, and they're pitched all over the place. Where are my boots?"

"Servant girl's fetched 'em out to clean, perhaps," said Vince quietly.

"Eh? Think so? Well, they did want it. — Get out! I don't see any need for jeering at our position here. Just as if I didn't know better! Here, you must have got them on."

"Not I! Even if I wanted to, one of your great ugly boots would be big enough for both of my feet."

"Do you want to quarrel, Cinder?" said Mike roughly.

"Not here. Isn't room enough. There are your boots, one on each side of the door in the corners of the cabin."

"Then you must have kicked them there, and—"

Mike did not finish, for the lugger gave such a lurch that the boy went in a rush against the opposite bulkhead with a heavy bang.

"Didn't kick you there, at all events," said Vince, who was fastening his last buttons.

"Why, the sea's getting up," said Mike. "Has it been blowing up above?"

"Haven't been on deck, but it has been alarming down here. I had a horrible job to find my things. They were all over the place."

"How horrid! And what a miserable place to dress in!"

"Better than a sandbank in a seal's hole."

"Oh! don't talk about it."

"Why not? It's over. Deal better off than we have been lately, for we have got an invitation to breakfast."

"I wish you wouldn't do that, Cinder," said Mike querulously.

"Do what? I didn't do anything."

"Now you're at it again, trying to cut jokes and making the best of things at a time like this."

"All right: I'm silent, then," said Vince. "Shall I go on deck?"

"Go? what for?"

"Leave you more room to dress."

"It will be very shabby if you do go before I'm dressed. If ever two fellows were bound to stick together it's us now. Oh dear, how awkward everything is! I say, there's no danger, is there?" cried Mike, as the lugger gave a tremendous plunge and then seemed to wallow down among the waves.

"No, I don't see what danger there can be. Seems a beautifully built boat, and I daresay Jacques is a capital sailor."

"A scoundrel!" said Mike bitterly.

"Now, *mes enfans*, get up," cried the skipper's voice; and this was followed by a smart banging at the door, which was opened and a head thrust in.

"If you sall bose be ill you can stay in bed to-day; but you vill be better up. Vell, do you feel vairy seek?"

"No, we're all right," said Vince; and soon after the two boys climbed on deck and had to shelter themselves from the spray, which was flying across the deck in a sharp shower.

It was a black-looking morning, and the gloom of the clouds tinged the surface of the sea, whose foaming waves looked sooty and dingy to a degree, while the boys found now how much more severe the storm was than they had supposed when below. The men were all in their oilskins, very little canvas was spread, and they were right out in a heavy, chopping sea, with no sign of land on any hand.

They had to stagger to the lee bulwarks and hold on, for the lugger every now and then indulged in a kick and plunge, while from time to time a wave came over the bows, deluging the deck from end to end.

But before long the slight feeling of scare which had attacked the boys passed off, as they saw the matter-of-fact, composed manner in which the men stood at their various stations, while the captain was standing now beside the helmsman, and appeared to be giving him fresh directions as to the course he was to steer, with the result that, as the lugger's head paid off a trifle, the motion became less violent, while her speed increased.

"Aha!" shouted the captain, as he found them—"not seek yet? Vait till ve have ze *déjeuner*, and zen ve sall see."

"Oh, we've been to sea before," said Vince rather contemptuously.

"And you like ze sea, *n'est-ce pas*—is it not so?"

"Oh yes; we like the sea," said Vince. "It is good," said the captain, clapping him on the shoulder. "Zen you sall help me. You say no at ze beginning, but bah! a boy—two boy like you brave *garçons*—vill not cry to go home to ze muzzer. It is a fine sing to have a luggar of tree mast like zis, and you sall bose make you fortune ven I have done."

He nodded and turned away, leaving the boys to stand looking at each other aghast, and forgetting all about the state of the sea, till a big wave came over the bows and made them seek for shelter.

They saw but little of the captain that day, except at meal-times, when he was good-humoured and jocose with them in spite of the fact that the weather did not mend in the least. Then the next day passed, and the next, with the wind not so violent, but the sea continued rough, and the constant misty rain kept them for the most part below. The crew were civil enough, and chatted with them when they did not ask questions; but failing to obtain any information from them as to their destination, Vince agreed with Mike that one of them should ask the captain where they were going to first. So that evening, when they were sailing slowly in a north-easterly direction, after being driven here and there by contrary winds, they waited their opportunity, and upon the captain coming up to them Vince began at once with, —

"Where are we going to first, captain?"

"Eh? you vant to know?" he said. "Vell, you sall. In zere." The boys looked sharply in the direction pointed out but could see nothing for the misty rain which drifted slowly across the sea.

"Where's in there?" said Mike.

"You are not good sailore yet, *mon ami*, or you vould have study our course. I vill tell you. You look over ze most left, and you vill see ze land of ze fat, heavy Dutchmans."

"What, Holland?" cried Vince eagerly.

"Yais: you know ze name of ze river and ports?"

"Yes; Amsterdam, Rotterdam," began Vince. "Are we going to one of those places?"

"Aha! ve sall see. You no ask questions. Some day, if you are good boy and can be trust, you vill know everysings. Perhaps ve go into ze Scheldt, perhaps ve make for ze Texel and ze Zuyder Zee, perhaps ve go noveres. Now you know."

He gave them a peculiar look and left them, and as the rain came on in a drifting drizzle the boys made this an excuse for going below.

"Mike," said Vince, as soon as they were alone, "got a pencil?"

"No."

"And there is neither pen nor ink."

"Nor yet paper."

"Then we're floored there," said Vince impatiently.

"What did you want to do?"

"Want to do? Why, write home of course, telling them where we were. We surely could post a letter at the port."

"No: he'll never give us a chance."

"Perhaps not; but we might bribe some one to take the letter."

"What with? I haven't a penny, and I don't believe you have."

Vince doubled his fists and rested his head upon them.

"I tell you what, then: we only gave our word for one day. We must wait till we are in port, and then swim ashore. Some one would help us."

"If we could speak Dutch."

"Oh dear," said Vince, "how hard it is! But never mind, let's get away. We might find an English ship there."

Mike shook his head, and Vince set to work inventing other ways of escaping; but they finally decided that the best way would be to wait till they were in the river or port, and then to try and get off each with an oar to help support them in what might prove to be a longer swim than they could manage.

That evening the weather lifted, and after a couple of hours' sail they found themselves off a dreary, low-lying shore, upon which a cluster or two of houses was visible, and several windmills—one showing up very large and prominent at the mouth of what seemed to be a good-sized river, whose farther shore they could faintly discern in the failing evening light.

"We're going up there," said Vince—"that's certain." But just as it began to grow dark there was a loud rattling, and down went an anchor, the lugger swung round, and the boys were just able to make out that they were about a couple of miles from the big windmill.

"Too many sandbanks to venture in," said Vince.

"No; we're waiting for a pilot."

"I believe," said Vince, "he'll wait for daylight and then sail up the river; and if we don't escape somehow before we're twenty-four hours older my name isn't Burnet."

Mike said nothing, but he did not seem hopeful; and soon after they were summoned to the cabin to dinner, where the captain was very friendly.

"Aha! now you see Holland. It is beautiful, is it not? Flat as ze Dutchman face. Not like your Cormorant Crag, eh? But nevaire mind. It vas time, and soon ve get butter, bread and milk, ze sheecan, ze potate, for you hungry boy have eat so much ve get to ze bottom of ze store."

They asked no questions, for they felt that it did not matter. Any land would do, and if they could escape it would go hard if they did not avoid recapture.

They were too much excited to sleep for some time that night, lying listening for the coming of the pilot or for the hoisting of the anchor; for there was, after all, the possibility of their having anchored till the tide rose sufficiently for them to cross some bar at the mouth of the river. But sleep overcame them at last, and they lay insensible to the fact that about midnight a light was hoisted at the mast-head, which was answered about an hour after by the appearance of another light in the mouth of the river—a light which gradually crept nearer and nearer till about an hour before dawn, when the boys were awakened by a soft bumping against the lugger's side, followed by a dull creaking, and then came the hurrying to and fro of feet on the deck overhead.

"Quick, Mike!" cried Vince—"into your clothes. She's sinking!"

As they hurried on a few things, the passing to and fro of men grew louder; they heard the captain's voice giving orders, evidently for the lowering of a boat, and the boys tried to fling open the door and rush on deck.

Tried—but that was all.

"Mike, we're locked in!" cried Vince frantically; and he began to kick at the door, shouting with Mike for help.

Their appeal was so vigorous that they did not have to wait for long. There was the sound of the captain's heavy boots as he blundered down the ladder, and he gave a tremendous kick at the door.

"Yah!" he roared: "vat for you make zat row?"

"The lugger! She's sinking," cried the boys together.

"I com in and sink you," roared the captain. "Go to sleep, bose of you."

"But the door's locked."

"Yais, I lock him myself. *Silence!*"

Then the lugger was not sinking; but the faint creaking and grinding went on after the captain had gone back on deck, and the boys stood listening to the orders given and the hurrying to and fro of men.

"She must be on a rock, Cinder," said Mike, in a half-stifled voice.

"No rocks here. On a sandbank, and they're trying to get her off."

Then there was a rattling and banging noise, which came through the bulkhead.

"Why, they're taking up the hatches over the hold."

"Yes," said Vince bitterly; "they're thinking more of saving the bales than of us."

"Down vis you, and pass 'em up," cried the captain; and, for what seemed to be quite a couple of hours, they could hear the crew through the bulkhead busy in the hold fetching out and passing up the bales on to the deck in the most orderly way, and without a bit of excitement.

"Can't be much danger," said Vince at last, "or they wouldn't go on so quietly as this."

"I don't know," said Mike bitterly; "it must be bad, and they will forget us at last, and we shall be drowned, shut up here."

"Don't make much difference," said Vince, with a laugh. "Better off here. Fishes won't be able to get at us and eat us afterwards."

"Ugh! how can you talk in that horrid way at a time like this!"

"To keep up our spirits," said Vince. "Perhaps it isn't so bad. She's on a bank, I'm sure, and perhaps—yes, that's it—they're trying to lighten her and make her float."

"They're not," said Mike excitedly. "Why, they're bringing other things down. You listen here."

Vince clapped his ear to the bulkhead and listened, and made out plainly enough that for every bale passed up a box seemed to be handed down, and these were being stacked up against the partition which separated them from the hold.

"I say, what does it mean?" whispered Mike at last.

"I don't know," replied Vince; "but for certain they're bringing in things as well as taking them away. Then we must be in port, and they're landing and loading up again."

"Oh, Cinder! and we can't get ashore and run for it."

"No; he's too artful for us this time. That's why he has locked us up. Never mind; our turn will come. He can't always have his eyes open."

"Is there any way of getting out?"

"Not now," said Vince thoughtfully; "but we might get one of those boards out ready for another time. They're wide enough to let us through."

The soft creaking and grinding sounds went on, but were attributed to the lugger being close up to some pier or wharf, and the boys stood with their ears close to the bulkhead, trying to pick up a word now and then, as the men who were below, stowing the fresh cargo, went on talking together.

But it was weary work, and led to nothing definite. They knew that the loading was going on—nothing more.

"Well, we are clever ones," said Vince at last; and he laid hold of the wooden shutter which let in light and air to the narrow place, but only let his arm fall to his side again, for it was firmly secured.

"Never mind," he added; "we'll make it all straight yet."

Hours had gone by, and from the bright streaks of light which stole in beneath and over the door they knew that it was a fine morning; and, as the dread had all passed away, they finished dressing, and sat in an awkward position against the edge of the bottom bunk, listening to the bustle on deck, till all at once it ceased and the men began to clap on the hatches once again.

Then, as they listened, there came the sound of ropes being cast off, the creaking and grinding ceased, the captain shouted something, and was answered from a distance, and again from a greater distance, just as the lugger heeled over a little, and there came the rattle and clanging of the capstan, with the heave-ho singing of the men.

"We're under way again, Mike," said Vince; "and there's no chance of a run for the shore this time."

He had hardly spoken when the heavy tread of the captain was heard once more, and he stopped at the door to shoot a couple of bolts.

"*Bon jour, mes amis.* You feel youselfs ready for ze brearkfas?"

Vince did not reply, and the captain did not seem to expect it, for he walked into the cabin, while the boys went on deck, to find that the men were hoisting sail, while a three-masted lugger, of about the same build as the one they were on, was a short distance off, making for the mouth of the muddy river astern. They were about in the same place as they were in when anchor was cast overnight, and it became evident to the boys that the noise and grinding they had heard must have been caused by the two vessels having been made fast one to the other while an exchange of cargo took place.

"Where next?" thought Vince, as their sails filled in the light, pleasant breeze of the sunny morning.

He was not long in doubt, for upon walking round by the steersman the compass answered the question—their course was due south.

"Aha! you take a lesson in box ze compais," said a voice behind them. "Good: now come and take one, and eat and drink. It is brearkfas time."

# Chapter Thirty Six
## "To vistle for ze Vind"

Four days passed in the quiet, uneventful way familiar on board a small vessel, with the prisoners sinking into that state of apathy known as accepting the inevitable. They were weary of condoling with one another, and telling themselves that sooner or later their chance for escape would come. They bore their position good-temperedly enough, chatted with the sailors, took a turn or two at steering under the guidance of the man at the helm, and received a nod of approbation from the captain when he saw what they were doing.

"Aha, yais," he said, showing his teeth. "You vill be my first and second officer before long, and zen ve sall all be ze grand contrabandiste."

"Oh, shall we?" said Vince, as soon as they were alone. "We shall see about that."

The captain had been amiable enough to them, and had the boys only felt that those they loved were well and possessing the knowledge that they were safe, the life would have been pleasant enough; but the trouble at home hung like a black cloud over them, and whenever they met each other's eyes they could read the care they expressed, and the feeling of misery deepened for awhile.

They went to bed as usual that fourth night, but towards morning Vince somehow felt uneasy; and at last, being troubled by thirst, he determined to go up on deck and get a pannikin of water from the cask lashed by the mainmast.

He half expected to find the door fastened, but it yielded to a touch; and, after listening at the cabin for a few moments to try and find whether the captain was asleep, he crept up on deck in the cool grey of the coming morning, and, looking back, saw the man at the helm, and forward two more at the look-out.

He had not many steps to go, and there was the pannikin standing ready, and the cover of the cask had only to be moved for him to dip out a tinful of the cool, fresh water, which tasted delicious; and, being refreshed by the draught, he was about to descend, when the beauty of the sea took his attention. The moon was sinking in the west and the dawn was brightening in the east, so that the waves were lit up in a peculiar way. On the side of the moon they glistened as though formed of liquid copper, while on the side facing the east they were of a lovely, pearly, silvery, ever-changing grey. So beautiful were the tints and lights and shades that Vince remained watching the surface of the sea for some minutes, and then the chill wind suggested that he should go down; when, making a sweep round, he felt as if his breath had been taken away, for there, away to the south, and looming up of huge height and size in the morning mist, was unmistakably the Crag, and they were once more close to home.

Here, then, was the answer to the question they had asked one another—Where are we sailing to now?

Yes: there was the Crag, with its familiar outline; and his heart beat fast as he felt that if Mike's father were on the look-out with his glass he would be able to see the lugger's sails.

"No, he must be in bed and asleep," thought Vince. "But I'll fetch Mike up to see. Why, old Jacques must be taking us home. No; he is going to fetch another load!"

"Yais, zat is ze Crag," said a voice behind him, and there stood the captain with a glass under his arm. "Now you vill go down and stop vis ze ozaire boy till I tell you to come up. But zis time you can stay in ze cabin. Mind," he said impressively, "you vill stay. You *comprenez?*"

"Oh yes," said Vince; "but you will let us go as soon as you've got the cargo all on board."

"Aha, you sink so?"

"Yes."

"But you are not so stupede as to sink I can take all away at von trip. *Non, mon ami,* it vill take four or five time more. Now go down, and tell ze ozaire to obey, and not make feel zat I can shoot."

"May I bring him up to see the Crag?" said Vince.

"No," replied the captain abruptly. "He sleep. Let him rest. Better you sleep too."

Vince glanced in at the cabin, to find that the deadlights were up and the place very dimly lit by the tiny skylight. Then, closing the door as he entered the cupboard-like place in which they passed their nights, he found Mike still sleeping; and fearing that he would get into trouble if he tried to watch their approach, he lay down too, and was awakened apparently in a few minutes by Mike shaking him.

"I say, it's awfully late, and we've anchored again." "Dressed?" said Vince in wonder.

"Yes, and I was going on deck, but the skipper pushed me back and banged down the hatch. I say, I haven't the least idea where we are."

"I have," said Vince.

"Well, where?"

"Back at the cavern."

"Nonsense."

"You'll see."

Mike did see, and before long, for half an hour later the captain came down in the cabin, breakfast was eaten, and then the boys were allowed to go on deck, to find themselves in their old berth, with the rocks towering up and shutting them in, while the lugger was safely moored head and stern to the wall-like rock.

Vince involuntarily looked round for the rugged face of old Joe Daygo, and one of the men noticed it.

"Looking for the pilot, youngster?"

"Yes."

"Oh, he came and run us in while you two were asleep, and you don't look as if your eyes were unbuttoned yet."

"It's of no use, Cinder," said Mike, as they turned away: "Jacques don't want us to see how it's all done; but only wait till we get away, and we'll find out somehow."

That was a busy day for every one but the boys; who, quite feeling their helplessness about escaping, quietly settled down to think of their strange position: as the crow flew not above a mile from home, but powerless to make their presence known.

The captain never left the deck, and the boats were going to and fro constantly; but they took nothing ashore, and it was evident that the smuggler meant to clear out the cavern, whose stores were far greater than the boys could have believed. The boats came back loaded down almost to the gunwale; but they were managed with wonderful dexterity, and as soon as they were made fast alongside, the men sprang aboard and their cargoes were rapidly transferred to the hold, which seemed to swallow up an enormous quantity of the contraband goods. So well shaped were the packages and so deftly packed below that they fitted into their places like great bricks in a building, so that by night the lugger was well laden, and it seemed evident that they would sail again when the tide suited.

It was just after dark; all the boats were hanging from the davits, and the tired men busy over a meal the cook had prepared, while the captain was walking thoughtfully up and down the deck, his dark eyes watchful over everything, and the boys, as they leaned over the bulwarks, talking softly together about how well the various little currents were made to work for the smugglers, knew that every motion they made was watched.

"It's of no use, Ladle," Vince said cheerily. "This isn't the place to try and get away. We've tried it, and we know. If it was, I'd say, jump in and swim for it!"

"Pst! a boat," whispered Mike.

Vince turned sharply round, to see that a small boat had suddenly glided out of the darkness, to be borne by the current up against the lugger's side; and the next minute Daygo climbed in, painter in hand, the captain going up to him at once, and then returning to where the boys were standing together.

Dark as it was, they could see a mocking smile upon the man's face, but before he could speak Vince forestalled him.

"All right," he said: "you want us to go below and stay till the lugger is worked out."

"Yais, zat is it," said the captain. "Some day you sall help me, visout ze pilot, eh? Go below, and stop youselfs. Shut ze cabin door. You vill find somesings to eat."

The boys went down without a word, and they had proof that the captain followed them, for a sharp click told that a bolt outside had been shot.

"Eat!" said Vince scornfully; "he thinks that boys are always wanting to eat!"

"Never mind, Cinder," said Mike, sitting down before the table, upon which some fresh provisions stood. "Let him think what he likes; let you and me eat while we have a chance; we may be escaping, and not get an opportunity for hours and hours."

Vince saw the force of the argument, and followed his companion's example, both listening the while and hearing the men hurry on deck.

Soon after they felt the lugger begin to move, and they sat eating and comparing notes as they recalled what they had heard the last time. But they could only build up imaginary ideas about the currents, channels and rocks which the vessel had to thread.

"I give it up," said Vince; "we can't understand it all without eyes."

Just then the captain came down and seated himself to make a hearty supper, and by the time he had done it was evident that they were out to sea once more, for the vessel swayed softly from side to side, but there was little motion otherwise.

"You vill not be sea-seek to-night, *mes amis*," said the captain; "zere is hardly no vind at all. You must go on deck soon and vistle for it to come."

But he did not let them go up till he had himself been there for some time, and when they ascended eagerly, it was to see that the sky was brilliantly studded with stars, a very faint wind blowing from the west, and the Crag looming out of the darkness about a mile away, but Joe Daygo's boat had disappeared.

The lugger was gliding along very gently, on a north-easterly course, with all sail set; and the boys came to the conclusion that the last manoeuvre was to be repeated, but unless the wind sprang up the trip promised to be long and tedious.

But one never knows what is going to happen at sea.

They had been sailing for about a couple of hours, with the captain walking up and down with a long spy-glass under his arm; and from time to time he stopped to rest it on the rail and carefully sweep the offing, as if in search of something, but apparently always in vain, till all at once he closed the glass with a snap, and walking forward, gave a sharp order, whereupon two of the men hurried below, to return directly with a couple of lanthorns, which were rigged on to a chopstick kind of arrangement, which held them level and apart as they were attached to the halliards and sent gliding up to the mast-head.

"Signal," whispered Vince; "but we can't be near the shore."

They searched the soft, transparent darkness for some time, gazing in the direction in which they had seen the captain use his glass, but it was all in vain; till Vince suddenly started, and pressed his companion's arm. Then pointed to where, about a mile away, two dull stars close together seemed to be rising slowly out of the sea to a little distance above the horizon, to stand nearly stationary for a while, and then slowly sink down and disappear.

"Another smuggler," whispered Vince; and then turned to look up at the mast-head of their own vessel, but their signal had been lowered.

"Depend upon it," whispered Mike, "that boat will come up close, like the other did, and they'll make fast together and begin to shift cargo."

"Think so?" said Vince thoughtfully, as it began to dawn upon his mind that possibly Captain Jacques with his fast lugger ran across Channel to various smuggling ports, and brought cargoes over to deposit in the cavern ready for the contraband goods to be fetched by other vessels and landed here and there upon the English coast. He did not know then that he had made a very shrewd guess, and hit the truth of how the captain had for years gone on enriching himself and others by his ingenious way of avoiding the revenue cutters, whose commanders had always looked upon the Crag as a dangerous place, that every one would avoid, but who would have given chase directly had they seen Jacques' long low swift vessel approaching any part of the English coast to land a cargo.

Vince did not ripen his thoughts then—that happened afterwards, for he was interrupted by a hand laid upon his shoulder, Mike feeling another upon his.

"You sink you vill keep ze middle vatch?" said the captain: "*ma foi*, no! Go down and sleep, and grow to big man."

He gave them a gentle push in the direction of the hatch.

"*Bon soir*," he said mockingly, and the boys went down.

"You'll hear the bolts shot directly," said Vince grimly, as he seated himself on the edge of the bunk.

*Click—clack*! came instantaneously, and then they heard an ascending step.

"Don't mean us to see much of what is going on," said Mike.

"Oh, it isn't that," replied Vince. "He fancies we should do something while they're busy—get a boat down, slip on board the other lugger or whatever it is."

"He needn't fancy that," said Mike. "Frying-pan's bad enough; I'm not going to jump into the fire and try that!"

"Nor I either. Well, shall we turn in?"

"May as well: I don't want to stop up and listen to a gang of smugglers loading and unloading their stupid cargo."

"Nor I, Ladle. I say, what a shame it is of old Jacques to be living now, instead of a hundred years ago! Poor old chap, you won't get any plunder after all!"

"I don't see that it's right to be trying to make fun of our trouble," said Mike bitterly; "there's the poor old Crag only a few miles away, and we're shut up here!"

"Don't take any notice," said Vince: "I say all sorts of things I don't mean. No chance of getting away to-night, is there?"

"No—not even to drown ourselves by trying to swim away," said Mike, with a sigh; and they hardly spoke again.

# Chapter Thirty Seven
## The King's Cutter speaks out

"Ladle!"

"Hullo!"

"Wake up!"

"What's the good? We can't go on deck. May as well lie here and rest."

"Nonsense! Get up, or I'll pull you out by one leg!"

"You touch me, and I'll send you flying against the bulkhead."

"Go it!" cried Vince, who was standing on the rough floor, in his trousers; and, quick as thought, he seized Mike's leg and pulled him half out. "Now kick, and I'll let you down bang."

"Oh! I say, Cinder, let go! Don't, there's a good fellow."

"Then will you get up?"

"Yes: all right. Does it rain?"

"No—lovely morning; you can see it is through that bit of skylight."

Mike slipped out and began to dress.

"Wonder what they've been doing in the night?"

"Don't know—don't care," said Vince, yawning. "Oh, how horrid it is to be boxed up here like a rabbit! Can hardly breathe, and perhaps he won't let us out for hours. Here, Jacques, come and unfasten this door," he said in a low, angry growl; and, seizing the handle, he was about to give the door a rough shake, when to the surprise of both it flew open.

"Hurrah!" cried Vince; and they were not long finishing dressing and hurrying on deck, to find that, whatever might have been done, the hatches were in their places, while a good-sized schooner was lying close by with her sails flapping, as were those of the lugger; for the sea was very smooth, save where the currents showed, and during the night they had been carried by one of these well back towards the island, whose north-east point lay about a couple of miles on their port bow.

"That's an English schooner, for certain," said Vince. "What is she?"

"*The Shark*" read Mike from her stern. "Looks as if she could sail better than the *Belle-Marie.*"

"Not she," said Vince, with the tone of authority; "these long three-masted luggers can race through the water."

"Aha! *mes enfans*—my good shildren," said the captain, in his irritating way of giving bad interpretations of his French which annoyed the boys, "I vant you vairy bad. You go and vistle for ze vind, eh? We shall go soon upon ze rock."

"Wind's coming soon," said Vince; "it's on the other side of the island now. Look: you can see the ripple off the point. Looks dark. We don't get it because the Crag shelters us."

"Good boy! I see you sall make a grand sailor some day, and be my first lieutenant; I give you command of a schooner like ze *Shark.*"

He waved his hand towards the vessel, and then looked eagerly in the direction of the rippled water, which indicated the coming wind.

"Is that boat yours?" said Vince.

"Yais! vy you ask? Ah–h–h–ah—ze wind—vill he nevaire com?"

At that moment the schooner hoisted a small flag very rapidly, and, simple as the action was, it completely changed the aspect of affairs. Orders were given sharply; and, to the boys' wonder, they were startled by seeing the men begin rapidly to cast loose the four small long guns, while others were busy fetching up powder and shot from below, passing down the little hatchway which had led to the boys' first place of confinement.

The captain walked sharply here and there, giving his instructions, and in an incredibly short space of time every stitch of sail possible was crowded upon the lugger, while a similar course was pursued by the captain of the schooner.

A thrill of excitement ran through the boys as they saw an arm chest hoisted up from the cabin, placed amidships, and the lid thrown open; but nothing was taken out, and after watching their opportunity, so that the captain should not observe their action, the boys walked by where the chest had been placed, and saw that it was divided longitudinally, and on one side, neatly arranged, were brass-bound pistols, on the other, cutlasses.

They had hardly seen this, when a glance forward showed them the captain superintending the loading of the two bow guns, and as soon as this was done he began to walk aft, while the boys discreetly walked forward along the other side, so as to be out of the fierce-looking fellow's way.

"I say, Ladle," whispered Vince, "this is like what we have often read of. How do you feel? There's going to be a fight. Look! they're loading the guns aft."

"Oh, I feel all right yet,—just a little shivery like. But what makes you say there's going to be a fight?"

"Didn't you see the schooner hoist a flag?"

"Of course I did, but I thought she was a friend. Why are they going to fight? Oh, I know: it's only a sham fight, for practice."

"I don't believe it is sham; the skipper looked too serious. I saw him showing his teeth, and the men all look in earnest. They've been doing something old Jacques don't like, and he's going to bring them to their senses. Here, I say, you're not getting those ready for breakfast?"

They were opposite the galley as Vince spoke, and he had suddenly caught sight of the cook, who was hurrying on his fire, and heating about half a dozen rods of iron between the bars of the stove.

"Oh yes, I am," said the man, with a grin—"for somebody's breakfast. I say, youngsters, I'd go down below if I was you; it may mean warm work if the wind don't come soon."

"What has the wind to do with it?" said Vince.

"To do with it! Everything, my lad. If the wind comes, we shall run, of course. We don't want to fight."

"But why are we going to fight the schooner?"

"The schooner!" said the man, staring. "Nonsense! She belongs to Jarks, and trades to the south coast. Didn't you see her signal?"

"Yes."

"Well, that means one of King Billy's cutters is in sight from there, and she'll be nearing before long."

"But what are those rods for?" said Mike eagerly.

"Don't be such a blockhead, Ladle!" cried Vince excitedly. "Why did we make the poker red-hot when we wanted to fire the old ship gun on your lawn?"

"Look—look!" cried Mike.

There was no need, for Vince had seen the white flying jib of a cutter coming into sight round the end of the Crag, with plenty of wind urging her on, while, by the time she was clear, a faint puff of light air made the schooner's sails shiver, but only for a few moments, then it was calm again, while the cutter, now quite clear of the point, was careening over and gliding rapidly along, with a pleasant breeze astern.

Just then the captain came forward, looking black as thunder, taking no notice of the boys, but giving a few sharp orders to the men to stand by ready to take advantage of the first puff of wind.

"We're not going below, are we?" whispered Mike.

"No; I want to see what's done," said Vince.

"Then you like fighting before breakfast better than I do," said the cook. "Look, there goes her colours, and she'll send a shot across the *Shark's* bows directly. We shall get it next."

He had hardly spoken before there was a white puff of smoke from the cutter, and before the report came echoing from the towering rocks of the Crag the boys saw the water splash up twice from somewhere near the schooner's bows, while within half a minute another shot was fired across the lugger's course, as she glided slowly along with the swift current, which was drawing them nearer the Crag.

"Bad job for us as old Daygo arn't here," said the cook.

"Why?" asked Vince.

The man laughed.

"Why, if he were aboard and the wind came up, he'd run the *Marie* in among the rocks."

"And into the pool?" said Vince eagerly.

"Not likely, my lad. No, he'd manoeuvre her right in, and lead the revenoos after us, till the cutter was stuck on one of the fang rocks, and leave her there, perhaps for good. Bound to say the skipper wishes Master Daygo was here."

Vince looked round, and thought of the fierce currents and sunken rocks, which a sailing boat might pass over in safety, but which would be fatal to a vessel of the cutter's size.

Just then the cook laughed, and the boys looked at him inquiringly.

"They think we are lying to on account o' their guns," said the man; "but only wait till we ketch the wind."

"Do you think they know these vessels are—"

"Smugglers?" said the cook, for Vince had not finished the sentence. "Ay, they know fast enough, and they think they're in luck, and have dropped upon a strong dose of prize money; but they don't know old Jarks."

"Will he fight?" said Mike excitedly. "Is these pokers getting red-hot?" said the man, grinning. "Ay, he'll fight. He's a Frenchy, but he's got the fighting stuff in him. 'Course he'll run. He don't want to fight, but if that cutter makes him, he will. My! I wish the wind would come."

But though the cutter came merrily along, hardly a puff reached the smugglers, and the cutter was now not more than a mile away.

"Look! look!" cried Mike suddenly. "There's old Joe Daygo coming."

"So it is," said Vince. "No mistaking the cut of that sail;" and he gazed excitedly at the little boat, which was coming rapidly on from the other end of the island.

"Ay, that's he sure enough," said the cook. "He's seen the cutter and come to give us warning, but we can see her ourselves now."

Still no wind, and the captain stamped up and down the deck, enraged beyond measure to see two vessels in totally opposite directions sailing merrily on, while the towering crag diverted the breeze and left him and his companion in a complete calm.

Nearer and nearer came the cutter, and the boys' hearts beat hard with excitement as they saw the flash of arms beneath the white sails, and began to feel that before long they would be on board, and that meant freedom.

Mike said something of the kind, but Vince made an allusion to the old proverb about not counting chickens until they were hatched.

"Get out!" cried Mike: "you always make the worst of things. I say, look how beautifully she comes along."

"Yes, and she'll be on one of they rocks if she don't mind," said the cook. "I say, my lads, there'll be no breakfast till all this business is over, but if you step in here I'll give you both some coffee and biscuit."

"Oh, who could eat and drink now?" said Vince. "I can't."

"I can," said the man; "and as my pokers are all hot, I mean to have a snack."

The boys' great dread was that they would be sent below, and consequently they kept out of the captain's way, and saw all that was going on, till the cutter was within a few hundred yards; and then, all at once, the wind failed her, and she lay as motionless as the two smugglers. The same fate had befallen Daygo in his boat, he being a mile away; but they saw that he had put out his oars, and was rowing.

"Going to board us," said the cook, with a sigh. "Now the fun's going to begin."

For two boats dropped from the cutter's sides, and the boys saw an officer in uniform in each, with a couple of red-coated marines, whose pieces glistened in the morning sunshine, as did the arms of the sailors.

But they saw something else as well. At a word from the captain, a dozen of the men went on hands and knees to the arm chest, each sailor in turn taking a cutlass, pistols, and cartridge pouch, and crawling back under the shelter of the bulwarks to load.

Vince drew a deep sigh, and his face was flushed, while Mike looked of a sallow white.

"Then there'll be a fight?" said the latter.

"Ay, there'll be a fight," said the cook. "We're in for it now; but unless it's done with the big guns they won't take the *Marie*."

"Why?" said Vince. "Jacques daren't resist the King's men."

The cook chuckled. "You wait and see," he said. "Look at him."

The boys did look, and saw Jacques standing by the steersman, with a drawn sword in one hand and pistols in his belt, hardly seeming to notice the boats, which had separated, one making for the schooner and the other for the *Belle-Marie*.

"Pilot sees mischief," said the cook. "He's going back. So would I if I could. I say, young 'uns, you'd better go below, hadn't you?"

"No," said Vince sharply. "You won't, will you, Ladle?"

"No: I want to see," replied Mike; and they stood and watched the rapidly approaching boat, with the smartly uniformed officer in the stern sheets, and the sailors making the water sparkle as they sent the trim craft rapidly nearer.

"Ha, ha!" laughed the cook softly; and the boys were about to turn and ask him what he meant, when a movement on the part of the captain caught their attention, while a wave of his hand made his men spring to their feet.

The cutter's boat was still fifty yards away, when a sudden puff of wind struck the lugger, her heavy canvas filled out, and she began instantly to yield to the pressure, gliding softly through the water, and putting fifty yards more between her and the boat.

Then the wind dropped again, and the officer in the boat stood up and shouted to Jacques to lower sail, while his men pulled with all their might, getting nearer and nearer.

"Do you hear?" yelled the officer: "let go everything, you scoundrel!" But Jacques gave no order, and when the boat was within twenty yards he was about to make a sign to his men to seize their arms, when the breeze struck the lugger, and away she went, showing her magnificent sailing qualities, for in a few minutes the boat was far behind, when there was a put from the cutter's side, but not to send a ball across their bows, for before the report reached the boys' ears a peculiar sound came overhead, and there was a hole through the mainsail.

"Now we're in for it," said the cook; and another report rang out, but this shot was at the schooner, which was gliding rapidly away, taking a different course from that of the lugger, but paying no heed to the gun.

Both boats gave up now, for the wind had caught the cutter once more, and she was gliding up to them. There was a short delay as she got both her boats on board, but she was paying attentions to lugger and schooner all the time, sending steadily shot after shot at each, till the schooner tacked out to get round the southern point of the island; and then, as the cutter crowded on all sail, her bow guns were both trimmed to bear upon the lugger, and shot after shot came whistling overhead.

It was nervous work at first, but after the first few shots the excitement took away all sense of fear, and the two boys watched the effect of the balls, as now and then one tore through the rigging.

The schooner was going at a tremendous rate, and her escape seemed certain; so the lieutenant in command of the cutter devoted all his attention to the lugger, which sailed rapidly on, first overtaking Joe Daygo's boat, which lay half a mile away, and rapidly leaving the cutter behind.

Twice over the Frenchman had the after guns turned ready for a shot at his pursuer; but the lugger was going so swiftly that there was no need to use them to try and cripple the cutter's sails, and so make the offence deadly by firing upon His Majesty's ship. Hence the hot irons remained in the fire ready for an emergency, one which was not long in coming, but which proved too great, even for so reckless a man as Jacques.

For, as they sailed steadily along, gliding rapidly by the island, and edging off so that they would soon be leaving it behind, the commander of the cutter, enraged at the apparently certain escape of the expected prize, and disappointed by the trifling damage done by the firing upon the lugger's rigging, suddenly changed his tactics, and a shot struck the starboard bulwark, splintering it for a dozen feet along, and sending the pieces flying.

This roused the captain's wrath, and, giving a sharp order, he went to one of the guns, pointing it himself, while one of the men ran up to the galley where the boys were standing.

"Now, cookie," he cried—"reg'lar hot 'un!" and he whisked a white-hot bar from the stove. "Here, youngsters, skipper says you're to go below."

He ran aft with the bar, scintillating faintly in the sunlight, and handed it to the captain, who bent down once more to take aim, when—*crash!*—a shot struck the stern between wind and water, after ricocheting along the surface. The next instant they saw a brilliant flash, heard a roar as of thunder; and as a dense cloud of smoke arose there was a great gap in the deck on the starboard side close to the cabin-hatch, and the boys grasped the fact instantly that the lugger's little powder magazine had been blown up, while, as they stared aghast at the mischief, and the men making for the boats, the mizen-mast with its heavy sail slowly dropped over the side and lay upon the water, with the effect that it acted like a rudder, and drew the unfortunate vessel round, head to wind.

The disorder among the crew only lasted a few minutes; their discipline was to the front again, Jacques giving his orders and the men obeying promptly.

"She is not going down, my lads," he cried; "ze fire all come upvard. You need not take to ze boats, for ze cutter vould follow and take you. Zere: ze game is up. Ve could fight, but vat good? You see *La Belle-Marie* can do no more. Vat you say? Shall ve fight?"

"If you like, skipper," said the mate quietly; "but if we do the cutter will only stand off a bit and sink us. We couldn't get away."

"*Non*" said Jacques: "luck is against us zis time. I sank you, my brave lads, and I like you too vell to go lose your life for nossing. Ve must strike."

The men gave him a faint cheer, and crowded round to hold out their hands.

"But we will fight if you like, skipper," cried one who made himself spokesman.

"I know, my lad," said Jacques. "Good boys all. Ve nevaire had a coward on board ze *Belle-Marie*."

Meanwhile the cutter was coming up fast, and a few minutes after two boats boarded them full of sailors and marines, when the first thing done was to send a boat-load of prisoners, which included the captain, Vince and Mike, on board the cutter.

# Chapter Thirty Eight
# What the Boys thought

As the boat glided alongside, the master's mate in command ordered the prisoners to go up; but Vince was already half-way over the side, followed by Mike, the lieutenant in command ordering them sternly forward.

"Quick, Mr Johnson!" he cried to the mate, "then back for the rest as smartly as you can. Tell Mr Hudson to make any leakage sound. Carpenter, there: go back with this boat."

"Ay, ay, sir."

"There's no fear of her sinking, sir," said Vince.

"What? How dare—!"

"It's all right, sir," cried Vince. "I know. We were prisoners on board the smuggler."

"You were what?"

"It is right, sare," said Jacques quietly. "I took ze boys avay and kept them as prisonaire."

"Absurd!" said the lieutenant haughtily. "Now then: away with that boat. Smart there, my lads!"

The boat was rowed rapidly back to fetch the rest of the prisoners, and the lieutenant came forward to where his first batch was ranged, to inspect them previous to sending them below.

"You're not going to send us down with them, are you?" said Mike indignantly.

"What?" roared the lieutenant in a rage: "why, you insolent, ruffianly young thief of a smuggler!"

"No, he isn't," cried Vince fiercely; "he's as much a gentleman as you are."

"Indeed!" said the lieutenant sarcastically: "perhaps he's a nobleman, sir?"

"I don't mean that," said Vince sharply; "but he's Sir Francis Ladelle's son."

"What, of the Crag?"

"Yes. We found out the smugglers' cave by accident, and they came and caught us, and have kept us ever since."

"Phew!" whistled the officer, quite changing his manner. "Then pray who are you?"

"I'm Doctor Burnet's son."

"Oh, then of course that alters the case, my lad; but you see you were caught amongst the jackdaws, so you must not wonder that I wanted to wring your neck too."

"Oh, it's all right if you believe me," said Vince; "only, after being prisoners so long, it seemed precious hard to be treated as prisoners when we expected to be free to get home."

"Then this scoundrel took you both, and has brutally ill-used you ever since?"

Vince looked round sharply, found the captain's piercing eyes fixed on his, and hesitated.

"Oh no," he said; "he caught us, and wouldn't let us go for fear we should tell where his stores of smuggled goods are, but he has behaved very well to us ever since."

"Like a gentleman," put in Mike.

"Indeed! Well, then we mustn't be so hard on him. So then, young gentlemen, you two know where the smugglers' depôt is?"

Vince nodded.

"And you could show us the way?"

Vince nodded again.

"Well, then, you'll have the pleasure of being our guide there as soon as we've taken that confounded schooner."

"No, I shall not," said Vince, looking hard at Jacques. "I don't feel as if it would be fair."

"But you'll have to, my lad, in the King's name."

"Yais, you can promise to show zem every sing, *mon ami*" said Jacques, smiling. "My smuggling days are ovaire, and I have been expecting zis every day zese ten years."

"Very well, then," said Vince: "I'll promise to show you by land. I can't by sea, for it's a regular puzzle."

"By land, then. Where is it?"

"Over yonder, on our island."

"What, at the Crag?" cried the lieutenant.

"Yes."

The officer gave vent to a long, low whistle.

"Thank you, my lad," he said; "this is good news indeed! We have been baffled for years, stopped by this hiding-place which no one knew of. Then, when I have taken the schooner I'll land you with a party, and you shall show us the place."

"No," said Vince; "I want to be paid for doing it."

"Indeed!" said the officer, curling his lip: "how much?"

"Oh, I don't mean money. Our fathers and mothers think we're dead, and you must land us to go home at once."

"Impossible, my boy," said the lieutenant, clapping him on the shoulder in a friendly way. "Quite right; but English men—and boys—have to think first of their duty to the King. I must chase that schooner first, and— Ahoy, there! look sharp with that boat.—Look: directly I have taken her I'll land you."

"No, sir; land us now," cried Mike. "You have only to make that little sailing boat come alongside and order him to take us."

"Yes, yes," cried Vince. "He comes from our island."

"What, that fishing boat yonder?" said the lieutenant.

"Well, that is in my way. Yes, I'll do that. Now then, alongside there! Tumble up, you fellows! Marines, take charge, and see them into the hold."

"*Au revoir, mes enfans,*" said Jacques—"*au revoir,* if zey do not hang me. Good boys, bose of you, but von vord. Old Daygo he is a rascaille, an old scamp; but he serve me vairy true, and it vas I tempt him vis *monnaie* to keep my secrete after he show me ze cavern. You vill not tell of him. He is so old, if you send him to ze prisone he soon die."

"Oh, very well; we won't tell tales of him—eh, Mike?"

"I should like to knock his old head off; but you've been so civil to us, Captain Jacques, we will not."

The captain smiled and nodded, and then followed his crew into the hold, where they were shut up with a couple of marines on guard.

By this time the cutter was in full sail, in chase of the schooner, which had reached out for a long distance, to get clear of the long reefs of dangerous rocks, running far away from the northern shore of the island. She was evidently, in fact, obliged, as she had taken that course, to tack at last, and then run straight almost back again; but it would lead her along by the north coast and probably mean escape.

"Schooner captain doesn't know his way through the Narrows, then," said Vince thoughtfully, as they stood watching the now distant schooner.

"I suppose not. Why, he could easily have got round and saved all that."

"I say," cried Vince, "never mind about old Jacques: smugglers are blackguards, and ought to be caught."

"Yes, of course."

"Well, then, let's tell the cutter captain how to get through the narrows and cut the schooner off."

"I couldn't. I should send him on the rocks. Could you?"

"Oh, I could," said Vince. "Here he comes. You'll hail the boat as soon as you're near enough, sir?"

"Eh?—the boat to set you ashore? I'd almost forgotten. Well, I suppose I must. Mr Johnson! Bah, I forgot: he's prize-master aboard the lugger. By the way, you think there's no fear of that craft sinking, my lad?"

"I feel sure, sir. The powder all exploded upward."

"Good. Here, Mr Roberts, hoist a flag for a pilot: that may bring yon fellow."

The little flag was hoisted; old Joe took no heed, however, but went on in his boat, and the lieutenant grew impatient.

"Do you think that man understands the signal?"

"I'm sure of it, sir, for he's the best pilot we have, and knows every rock."

"Then it's obstinacy. By George, I'll sink the scoundrel if he doesn't heave to;" and, giving the order, a shot was sent skipping along just in front of old Daygo's boat, when the sail was lowered directly, hoisted again, and the boat's head turned to run towards the cutter.

"Understands that, my lads," said the lieutenant; "but you must jump down quickly—I am losing a deal of time."

"Never mind, sir," said Vince; "I've been sailing all about here ever since I was quite a little fellow, and I know the rocks too. The schooner must tack round in half an hour's time, and then run east."

"Yes, I know that."

"Well, sir, you can run from here right across, and save miles."

The officer looked at him keenly.

"The passage is called the Narrows, and it's all deep water. You see the big gull rock away yonder—the one with the white top?"

"Well!"

"Make straight for that, and go within half a cable's length. Then tack, keep the south point right over the windmill for your bearings, and sail due east too. Then you can cut the smuggler off."

"Hah! yes; it's down on the chart, but I did not dare to try it. Thank you, my lad; that is grand. Ah! here's the boat."

The boys shrank back, so that old Daygo should not see them, while the lieutenant stepped up to the side and bullied the old man, who protested humbly that he did not understand the signal.

"Well, quick! Here are two passengers to take ashore. Now, my lads—sharp!"

Vince and Mike shook hands with the officer, while a sailor at the gangway held on to the painter of Daygo's boat, which was gliding pretty fast through the water, the course of the cutter not having been quite stopped; then the lads jumped lightly in, the painter was thrown after them, there was a slight touch of the helm, and the cutter heeled over and dashed away, leaving Vince and Mike looking the old man full in the face, while he stared back with his jaw dropped down almost to his chest.

"Then you arn't dead, young gen'lemen?"

"No, we're not dead," said Vince sharply. "Now then, hoist that sail and run us home."

The boys sat there watching the cutter, the lugger and the schooner all sailing rapidly away. Then suddenly it occurred to both the lads that the old man was very slow over the business of hoisting that sail; that he was then the greatest enemy they had, and that it would be very awkward for them if he were to suddenly take it into his head to do them some mischief.

"He's a big, strong man," thought Vince; "he knows that we can ruin him if we like to speak, and— I wonder what Ladle is thinking about?"

"Ladle" was thinking the same.

# Chapter Thirty Nine
# Daygo meets his Match

It seemed to take a long time to hoist that sail, but at last it was well up, the yard creaking against the mast; and standing on their dignity now, and keeping the old man at a distance, the boys made no offer to take the sheet or steer, but let Daygo pass them as they sat amidships, one on each side, and he seated himself, hauled in the sheet, and thrust an oar over the stern to steer.

There was a nice breeze now, they were only about a mile from the shore, and as the boat danced merrily through the little waves a feeling of joy and exultation, to which the boys had long been strangers, filled their breasts. They took long, hungry looks at the shore, and then at the cutter racing along towards the great gull rock, at the schooner careening over as she ran on under all the canvas she could bear; and then back at the lugger, which by comparison seemed to limp along, with a scrub of a spar hoisted as a jury mast, far astern, in place of the fallen mizen, so as to steady her steering.

Then they looked at each other again, those two, as they sat face to face, neither speaking, and carefully avoiding even a glance at Daygo, feeling as they did the awkwardness of their position, and averse to meeting the old scoundrel's eye.

Not that they would have met it, for Daygo was as full of discomfort as they, and with his eyes screwed up face one maze of wrinkles, he stared through between them as if looking at the prow, but really at the big patch of canvas in his sail.

For, as Daygo put it to himself, he was on the awkwardest bit of lee shore that he had ever sailed by in his life.

He had, as was surmised by the cook, caught sight of the Revenue cutter sailing by the north side of the Crag, and hurried down to his boat to warn Jacques or his companion; but, upon finding himself too late, he was making for home again, thinking that, as Jacques was taken and his lugger a prize to the cutter—which looked determined to follow up the schooner, probably to take her too—there would be no owner for the contraband goods still left in the cavern, unless that owner proved to be himself. There were two others, he mused—two who knew of the place and its treasure; but Captain Jacques was, according to the old fisherman's theory, not the kind of man to stick at trifles when such great interests were at stake; and he felt quite satisfied that the two boys would never be seen at Cormorant Crag again. Some accident would happen to them—what accident was no business of his, he argued. They had got themselves into a terrible mess through their poking and prying about, and they must put up with the consequences. They might have fallen off the cliff when getting sea-birds' eggs, or they might have been carried away by one of the currents when bathing, or they might have been capsized and drowned while they stole his boat—he called it "stole"—in any one of which cases, he said to himself, they'd never have come back to the Crag again, and it wouldn't have been any business of his, so he wasn't going to worry his brains. Old Jarks had grabbed 'em, and when he grabbed anything he didn't let it go again.

Joe Daygo was a slow thinker, and all this took him a long time to hammer out; and he had just settled it comfortably, on his way home, when he caught sight of the pilot flag flying, and paid no heed.

"Don't ketch me showing 'em the way through the Narrers to ketch the *Shark*!" he growled; and he kept on his way till the imperative mood present tense was tried, and then he made for the side of the cutter, to receive what was to him a regular knock-down blow, or, as he put it, a wind taking him on a very dangerous lee shore.

So the old fisherman did not look at his passengers, but began thinking hard again. He couldn't take those two home, he said to himself, for, if he did, at their first words he'd be seized by some one or every one, for they all hated him for being so well off, and monopolising so much of the lobster catching, especially Jemmy Carnach. Then Sir Francis Ladelle and the Doctor would come; he'd be locked up, sent by the smack over to England, and be tried, and all his savings perhaps be seized. Just, too, when he had a chance of doubling them by taking the contents of the cave.

He had arrived at this point with great difficulty when the strange silence on board the boat, which had so far only been broken by the lapping of the water and the creaking of the yard, was broken by Vince, who cried excitedly, as he stood up in the boat:

"Look, look, Mike! Nearly everybody's yonder on the cliff. They've heard the firing and the explosion, and they're watching the cutter chase the schooner."

Mike rose too, and with beating hearts the two boys stood trying to make out who was on the look-out; but the distance was too great to distinguish faces. Still they stood, steadying each other by clapping hands on shoulders, quite unconscious of the fact that the old man was now gazing at them with a very peculiar expression of countenance, that foreboded anything but good.

All at once, they both lurched and nearly fell, for Daygo's mind was made up, and he thrust his oar deep down, changing the boat's course suddenly, and making the sail flap.

"Here, what are you doing?" cried Vince, forced by this to speak to the old man at last.

"Think I want to run my boat into that curran' an' get on the rocks? Sit down, will you, and keep outer the way of the sheet."

For answer the boys went forward, quite out of his way, and the boat rushed on again for some ten minutes before they spoke again, though they had been looking about with gathering uneasiness, for they were growing suspicious, but ashamed to speak because the idea seemed to be absurd.

At last Vince said —

"He's making a precious long tack, Mike, and I don't know of any big current here."

Mike was silent, and they saw now that without doubt they were sailing right away from the island, and were in the full race of the tide. Still they felt that the old man must know best how to make for his tiny port, and they sat in silence for fully twenty minutes, waiting for him to make another tack and run back.

But soon the suspicions both felt had grown into a certainty, and Mike said in a whisper, as calmly as he could, —

"Cinder, he has got the conger bat out of the locker. What does he mean?"

"He means that he won't take us ashore," said Vince huskily: "he's going to sail right away with us for fear we should tell about him, and the conger bat's to frighten us and keep us quiet."

There was a strange look of agony in Mike Ladelle's eyes, as he gazed in his companion's, to read there a horror quite as deep. Then neither of them spoke, but sat there listening to the lapping of the water, which spread to right and left in two lines of foam as the little boat sped on.

It was Vince who broke the silence at last, after drawing a deep breath.

"Ladle, old chap," he said, in a low voice, "they're at home yonder, and it means perhaps never seeing them again. What shall we do?"

Mike tried to speak, but his voice was too husky to be heard for a few moments.

"I'll do what you do," he said at last.

"You'll stand by me, whatever comes?"

"Yes."

Vince glanced sidewise, to find that they were pretty well hidden by the sail; so he thrust out his hand, which was gripped fast, and the two boys sat there with throbbing hearts, trying to nerve themselves for anything that might happen now.

Then, without a word, Vince rose, and, steadying himself by the mast, he stepped over the thwart in which it was stepped, and then on to the next, close to where the old man sat steering right astern, and holding the sheet of the well-filled sail as well.

"This is not the way to the Crag," said Vince, with his voice trembling slightly; and the old man grunted.

"Where are you making for?" said Vince, firmly now.

"Didn't I tell yer I didn't want to get run on the rocks?" roared the old man, unnecessarily loudly, after a glance back at the shore, where all was growing distant and dim.

"Yes, you told me so; but it isn't true," said Vince, in a voice he did not know for his own.

"What?" roared Daygo fiercely.

"You heard what I said. Run her up in the wind at once, and go back."

"You go and sit down," growled the old man savagely.

"You change her course," said Vince firmly.

"You go and sit down while you're safe," growled the old man, with his face twitching.

"You had orders from the commander of the cutter to take us ashore. Change the boat's course directly."

"Will you go and sit down, both of you?" cried the old man again, more fiercely, but his voice was lower and deeper.

"No," said Mike; "and if you won't steer for the Crag, I will."

"This here's my boat, and I'll steer how I like, and nobody else shan't touch her."

"Your orders from the King's officer were to take us home. Will you do it?"

"No!" roared the old man. "Go and sit down, 'fore I do you a mischief."

Vince did not even look behind to see if he was going to be supported, for he felt full of that desperate courage which comes to an Anglo-Saxon-descended lad in an emergency like that. He saw the savagely murderous look in the old man's eyes, and that he had quickly seized the conger bat with one hand, after passing the sheet into that which held the oar.

With one spring Vince was upon him, seizing the heavy wooden club, which he strove to tear from his grasp, just as the old man too sprang up, and Mike snatched the sheet from his hand with a jerk which sent the oar, loose now in the old man's grasp, gliding overboard.

Mike made a dash to save it, but was flung down into the bottom of the boat as the old man thrust a foot forward and seized Vince in his tremendous grip.

The boy struggled bravely, but his fresh young muscles were as nothing to the gnarled, time-hardened flesh and sinew of the old savage, who lifted him by main force, after a short struggle which made the boat rock as if it would go over, and Vince realised what was to follow.

"Mike! do something," he cried in his agony to the boy, who was struggling up, half stunned, from where he lay between the thwarts; and in his desperation Mike did do something, for, as Daygo put out all his strength, tore Vince's clinging hands from his jersey, and hurled him right out from the boat, Mike seized the old man fiercely by one leg.

It was not much to do, but it did much, for it threw Daygo off his balance in the rocking boat; and Vince had hardly plunged down into the clear water before his enemy followed, with a tremendous splash, thrusting the boat away, and going head first deeply down.

Vince was the first to rise, shake his head, and begin to swim for the boat. But Daygo rose too directly and looked round, and then he, too, swam for the boat, whose uncurbed sail flapped wildly about; while Mike picked up the other oar to try and steer back to help his companion.

He changed the position of the boat, and that was all. It did this, though,—it gave Vince the chance of making for the side opposite to that for which Daygo aimed, and he swam with all his might to be there first.

But Vince had the greater distance to go, and Mike saw that, unless he helped, Daygo would be too much for them yet.

Quick as thought, he drew in the oar which he had thrust over the stern, turned it in his grasp as he stood up in the rocking boat, and, as the old man came up and stretched out his hands to grasp the gunwale, Mike drove the hand-hold of the oar, lance-fashion, down into his chest.

"I've killed him," groaned the boy, as his enemy fell back and went under again. Then he nearly followed him, for the boat was jerked from the other side, and he turned to find Vince had seized the gunwale and was climbing in.

A sharp drag helped him, and Vince's first act was to seize the conger bat, which lay beneath the after-thwart.

He was only just in time, for, as he turned, Daygo had risen, and swam up again to seize the gunwale with one great gnarled hand.

"Daygo put out all his strength and hurled him from the boat."

Crash came down the heavy club, the hand relaxed, and Daygo went down again.

"Vince! Vince! you've killed him," cried Mike, in horror. "No, no— don't: don't do that!" he shrieked, as Vince thrust his right-hand into his dripping pocket and tore out his big sharp long-bladed knife.

"You take the bat," cried Vince; and, as the boy obeyed trembling, he shouted, so that the old man could hear as he swam after them, "hit him over the hands again if he touches the boat."

It did not seem likely that he would overtake them by swimming, for the wind acted upon the flapping sail and drove them slowly along.

Taking advantage of this, Vince went forward and cut off the long rope from the ring-bolt in the stem, and returned with it to where, wild-eyed and scared, Mike knelt with the conger bat upraised, ready to strike if the old man came near.

"Now," said Vince firmly, "you hold that conger club with both hands, Mike, and if he does anything, or tries to do anything, bring it down on his head with all your might. Do you hear?"

"Yes," said Mike faintly.

"Now, then, you come and take hold of the gunwale with both hands, and let me tie your wrists," cried Vince. "Look out, Mike!"

The old man swam up and put his hands together.

"You arn't going to murder me?" he groaned.

"You wait and see— Ah!" yelled Vince, for the treacherous old ruffian had seized him by the chest and was dragging him out of the boat.

But Mike was ready: the bat came down with tremendous force, and the old man loosened his grasp and sank, remaining beneath the surface so long that the boys gazed at each other aghast.

"Quick! there he is," cried Mike; and Vince seized the oar and sculled to where the old man had come slowly up, feebly moving his hands, and apparently insensible.

"We must haul him in, Mike," said Vince. "He's not likely to hurt us now."

"If he is," said Mike, "we must do it all the same;" and, leaning over, they each got a good grip, and, heaving together, somehow rolled Daygo into the bottom of the boat, where they dragged his head beneath the centre thwart, and then firmly bound him hand and foot, using some strong fishing line as well as the painter and the rope belonging to the little grapnel.

# Chapter Forty
## "Huzza! We're Homeward Bound"

By the time they had done the old man began to revive, but the boat was skimming along over the waves toward Cormorant Crag before he was able to speak coherently.

"Where are you going?" he groaned at last.

"What's that to you? Home!" said Vince sharply.

"Nay, nay; don't take me there, Master Vince—don't! I give in. You two have 'most killed me, but I forgive you; only don't take me there."

"You hold your tongue, you old ruffian," cried Vince, who was steering and holding the sheet too, while Mike kept guard with the conger bat. "Mind, Mike. Don't take your eyes off him for a moment, and if he tries to untie a knot, hit him again."

"Nay, I'm beat," said the old man, with a groan. "My head! my head!"

"Serve you right," cried Mike. "I believe you meant mischief to us."

"Oh!" groaned Daygo; and he turned up his eyes till only the whites, or rather the yellows, could be seen, and then lay perfectly still; while the boat bounded onward now towards the island, as if eager to bear the boys to their home.

Vince looked hard at the big, heavy figure in the bottom of the boat, as he attended to the sailing and steering; and now that the heat of battle was over, and he sat there in his saturated clothes, he began to wonder at their success in winning the day. Then, as Daygo lay quite still, he began to think that they had gone too far, and his opinion was endorsed by his companion, who suddenly leaned back to look at him, with a face full of horror.

"Cinder," he said, "I didn't mean to, but I hit him too hard."

"Put the bat down, and come and take the oar and sheet," whispered back Vince, whose nervous feeling increased as the change was made.

Vince was no doctor, but he had not been about with his father for years, and dipped into his books, without picking up some few scraps of medical and surgical lore. So, bringing these to bear, he leaned over their prisoner and listened to his breathing, studied his countenance a little, and then placed a couple of fingers upon the man's massive wrist and then at his throat and temples.

After this he drew back to where, trembling and ghastly-looking, Mike was watching him, and now whispered, with catching breath,—

"Is he—"

Mike wanted to say "dead," but the word would not come.

"Yes," said Vince, in the same low tone; "he's shamming. Go back and keep guard."

"No, no—you," said Mike; "I'll steer."

Vince nodded, and seated himself on the thwart over the prisoner, with the heavy piece of wood close at hand.

The boat bounded on, and he glanced at the distant vessels, wondering whether the cutter would capture the schooner and the lugger get safely to port. He thought, too, a good deal about the man in the bottom of the boat, and felt more and more sure that he was right in his ideas; for every now and then there was a twitching of the muscles about the corners of his eyes, which at last opened in a natural way, and looked piteously in the boy's face.

"How far are we from the shore?" he said.

"'Bout a mile," said Vince coolly. "Why, Mike Ladelle thought you were dead?"

"So I am nearly," groaned Daygo. "Oh, my head, my head!"

"Yes, you did get a pretty good crack," said Vince; "and you'll get another if you don't lie still."

"But you've tied me so tight, Master Vince: line's a-cutting into my wristies."

"Of course it is," said Vince coolly. "I tied it as tightly as I could. You ought to be pretty well satisfied that we didn't leave you to drown."

"Ah!" groaned Daygo, "don't say that, Master Vince. I've been a good friend to you and him."

"Yes, and we're going to be good friends to you, Joe. You're such a wicked old rascal that it will do you good to be sent to prison."

"No, no; don't do that, my lad. Mebbe they'd hang me."

"What, for a pirate and smuggler? Well, perhaps they will," said Vince coolly.

"But you wouldn't like that, my lad. Untie me, and let me set you ashore, and then I'll sail away and never come near the Crag again."

"Well, but you won't come near the Crag again if I take you ashore. Sir Francis will have you put in prison, of course. Won't he, Mike?"

"There's no doubt about that," replied Mike.

Daygo groaned.

"Oh, Master Vince—don't, don't!" he cried. "I'm an old man now, and it would be so horrible."

"So it was for our poor people at home; and I know you've been pretending you hadn't seen us."

"Ay, I've been a bad 'un—'orrid bad 'un, sir, but I'm a-repenting now, and going to lead a new life."

"In prison, Joe."

"No, no, no, sir," yelled the miserable wretch. "It 'd kill me. Do be a good gen'leman, and forgive me as you ought to, bad as I've been. You untie me and let me run you ashore, and then I raally will sail away."

"What do you say, Mike?"

"Well, I think we might trust him now. He has been pretty well punished."

"Then you'd trust him?" said Vince.

Mike nodded.

"Then I wouldn't. He'd jump up, strong as ever, and pitch us overboard, or take us over to France, or do something. I'm not going to untie a knot."

"Oh, Master Vince," groaned the old fellow; "and after all the fish I've give you, and the things I've done!"

"Including trying to drown me," said Vince.

"Oh, Master Mike, you have got a 'art in yer," groaned Daygo. "You try an' persuade him, sir. Don't take me ashore and give me up."

"Look, Mike," said Vince excitedly, as a white puff of smoke suddenly appeared from the bows of the cutter, followed shortly by another, showing that they had got within range of the schooner, and the firing was kept up steadily as the boat sailed on, fast nearing the shore now, where the cliff was dotted with the people attracted by the engagement.

But the firing did not interest Daygo, who kept on pleading and protesting and begging to be forgiven to one who seemed to have thoroughly hardened his heart.

Then the old man made an effort to wriggle himself into a sitting position, but a light tap with the conger bat sent him down.

"Don't you move again," said Vince sternly; "and don't you say another word, or you'll make your case worse than ever."

Daygo groaned, and Vince watched the shore, which they were fast nearing. Then, springing up, he began to wave his hands frantically.

"Look, Mike! that's my father. Yes; and yours. Ah! they see us, and they're waving their hats. Ahoy! Ashore there! Hurrah! we're all right, father."

Mike sprang up too, forgetting his steering; and the boat would have begun to alter her course, but Vince seized the oar and set her right.

"Now then, jump up," he cried, "and show yourself. They see us. Father's coming nearer down. Mike, we shall be ashore in five minutes."

"Oh—oh—oh!" groaned Daygo. "Marcy, young gents, marcy! I know they'll hang me."

Vince turned upon him fiercely, and took out his long Spanish knife, which he opened and whetted upon the gunwale, while the old man's eyes opened so that he showed a ring around the iris.

"What are you going to do, Cinder?" cried Mike, catching him by the arm.

"I'll show you directly," said Vince firmly.

Just then the Doctor and Sir Francis began shouting to the boys; and the people near, among whom were Jemmy Carnach and the Lobster, took off and waved their caps, and cheered.

"Look here, Ladle," whispered Vince: "will you do as I tell you—I mean, do as I do?"

"Yes; anything."

"I'm soaked. Do you mind being the same?"

"Not a bit," cried Mike excitedly.

"Right, then: follow me. It's only fifty or sixty yards now to the tunnel, and we can wade through. Starboard a little more. That's it."

He pressed the oar his companion held, and the boat glided behind the towering rock, hiding the group on shore from their sight; and now Vince bent forward over their prisoner.

"In with the oar, Mike," he said loudly, "and do as I do."

He bent over the old fisherman, whose eyes, were nearly starting out of his head with horror, and with one clean thrust beneath the cord, divided it and set Daygo's wrists free, and then did the same by his ankles.

Then Vince started up.

"There," he cried; "there's our revenge on you, you old ruffian! You've got your boat: sail away, and never let us see you at the Crag again. Now, Mike, over!"

He set the example; and, as the old man sat up, the two boys dived into the deep clear water together, rose and swam for the tunnel, into which they passed, and were soon able to wade on towards the little dock. A minute later each was clasped in his father's arms.

Wet as he was?

Well, it was only sea water.

Need I write about what took place at the Doctor's cottage and at the old manor? I think not. There is surely no boy who reads this and thinks of his mother's tears who cannot imagine the scene far more vividly than I can describe it. For the long mourned ones had returned, as if by a miracle, and all was happiness once more.

That night it was announced that the cutter had gone east, with the schooner close astern; and three days later she was off the Crag, Vince and Mike being ready to meet the lieutenant when he landed and to act as guides.

The officer of the cutter was for making them show the way into the caverns by sea; but on hearing more he had his men furnished with all the picks and bars that could be provided, and then, with an ample supply of lanthorns, the entrance to the dark passage was sought, Sir Francis and the Doctor being quite as eager to see the place as the sailors.

Half-way through it was found to be blocked; but a pound of powder well placed and provided with a slow match was left to explode, and as soon as the foul air had cleared away the place was found practicable, and the party descended to find enough cargo left to well lade the cutter.

But the men did not hurry themselves, nor the officers neither; for they found the hospitality at the Mount or at the Doctor's very agreeable.

At last, though, the cutter sailed, but not before an attempt had been made to enter the smugglers' dock; only it was given up as being too risky for His Majesty's Revenue cutter.

Previous to going, the lieutenant, who had become a great friend of the boys, said a few words which afterwards bore fruit. They were these:—

"I say, my lads, why don't you two chaps go to sea? You'd make splendid middies."

They did; but it was not till a year after the announcement which came to the Crag that the two boys' names were down as sharers in the prize money distributed to the officers and men of the cutter.

"And it does seem rum, Ladle," said Vince, as they lay on the thyme-scented grass, looking out to sea, and occasionally letting their eyes wander towards the great bluff which hid away the Scraw.

"What seems rum?" said Mike wonderingly.

"That we should get a share in poor old Jacques' treasures after all. I wonder what has become of him."

They heard at last that, by the help of one of his men, who had acted as cook on board the lugger, he had escaped to France; and two years later, when they were growing men, they caught sight of old Daygo in Plymouth town, but the old man managed to avoid them, and, for reasons which the reader can easily understand, neither of the young men felt disposed to hunt him out and ask how he came there. Had they done so, they would have found that Joe Daygo had been saving money for many years, and he was living outside the port, where he could see the sea, as "a retired gentleman."

These are his own words.

And the caverns down by the Scraw?

Sixty years' workings of time and tide have made strange alterations there. Huge masses have fallen in, rocks have been washed away, and pleasant slopes have taken the place of precipice and dangerous rift; but the sea gulls wheel round the rugged cliffs and rear their young in safety, and upon sunny days, when the fierce currents are running strong, the dark olive-green birds may be seen swimming and diving to bring up their silvery prey to gorge, and afterwards fly off to dry their plumage on shelves and slopes of their home—dangerous surf-girt Cormorant Crag.